Also by Samantha Chase

Tangled up in You

SAMANTHA CHASE

sourcebooks
casablanca

Published by Sourcebooks Casablanca, an imprint of Sourcebooks.
P.O. Box 4410, Naperville, Illinois 60567-4410
(630) 961-3900
sourcebooks.com

Printed and bound in Canada.
MBP 10 9 8 7 6 5 4 3 2 1

Prologue

Twenty Years Ago

Sometimes the best opportunities land right in your lap.

"Well, well, well. What have we got here?" Bobby Hannigan took his time sauntering over to where Quinn Shaughnessy was pushing his father's car up the road from the open driver's side door.

Well after curfew.

With a grunt, Quinn kept pushing the car.

Looking at his watch, Bobby noted it was after two in the morning. Yup. Definitely well after curfew.

Growing up next to the Shaughnessys, Bobby was familiar with their comings and goings, and knew the rules of the household. He knew all the family news—such as when one member was grounded and not allowed to take out the car because they had broken curfew.

He grinned. How fortunate that he'd come home late enough to witness this. Strolling casually beside Quinn, he said, "I don't know if you're aware, but…it's kind of late."

Another grunt.

"And I have to wonder why you're pushing your dad's car up the road at this hour." He pretended to ponder that thought. "Did Ian break down someplace and didn't want to call for a tow?" Then he shook his head. "No, no, no—your father's smarter than that."

They still had another five houses to pass before they'd hit the Shaughnessys' driveway.

"Hmm… I imagine it's going to be quite interesting to try and explain a broken-down car to your father." Then he shrugged. "Or maybe you'll let him go outside in the morning and think the car crapped out mysteriously on its own just sitting in the driveway." He made a *tsk*ing sound. "He'll probably freak out and have to miss a day of work—on top of having to pay to get the car fixed."

Still another grunt.

"That's got to be hard on a man who's trying to support six kids," Bobby said solemnly. "I mean, after all he's been through, to add to his stress is just wrong."

And that was the one that finally did it.

Quinn stopped walking and turned to glare at him. He was breathing heavily, hands on his hips, but he didn't say anything.

There were many reasons Bobby found this so amusing. First, he didn't particularly like Quinn. He loved the rest of the Shaughnessy family, but Quinn irked him. Hadn't always, if he was being honest—only in the last several years since his sister, Anna, had developed a crush on the jerk. Second, he'd been looking for an excuse to get Quinn in trouble—something that would prove to his sister that the guy was a waste of her time. And finally, sometimes it was fun to watch someone so smug mess up.

This was that time.

Like an early birthday present.

Facing Quinn, he folded his arms over his chest and waited. "So? What's it gonna be?"

Letting out a long breath, Quinn raked a hand through

his hair. "Okay, fine. There's nothing wrong with the car except a loud exhaust system. Dad's getting it fixed this weekend. But if I drive it down the block and into the driveway, everyone will hear it."

"You know how else no one would hear it?"

"How?"

Leaning in close, Bobby said, "Don't take the damn car out."

The response he got to that was an eye-roll.

"Dude, seriously," Bobby went on, "what is wrong with you? Do you enjoy getting grounded?"

"What do you think?" Quinn asked sarcastically.

"I think you must, because you're constantly doing things to get in trouble. You're sixteen years old, for crying out loud. Grow up a little! Doesn't your dad have enough to deal with without you constantly giving him grief?"

It was only four months ago that the Shaughnessys had lost their matriarch. Lillian Shaughnessy had been like a second mother to Bobby and he felt her loss almost as strongly as her six kids did. And as much as he enjoyed giving Quinn grief, the thought of him adding to Ian's struggles really didn't seem right.

When he looked at Quinn, he saw the regret in his eyes and hated what he had to do.

"C'mon. You keep pushing from there and I'll go around back. We'll get it home quicker."

For a minute, Quinn only stared.

With a huff of annoyance, Bobby said, "Look, it's no secret I don't like you. And right now, I like you even less. If this were any other time, I'd probably go up to your house, ring the damn doorbell, and announce to everyone that you not only stole the car and broke curfew, but snuck out while you're grounded." He paused. "But I'm going to resist the temptation."

Quinn eyed him suspiciously. "Why?"

He shrugged. "I'm not doing it for you, that's for sure."

"So then…why?"

Bobby glanced down the block toward their houses. He sighed before looking back at Quinn. "Because—unlike you—I have respect for your family. No need to give them anything else to worry about." He walked to the back of the old station wagon and got into position. "Ready?"

"Bobby… Um, look. I want you to know—"

Bobby held up a hand to stop Quinn from talking. He wasn't listening. Not really. "I'm feeling kind toward you right now. Don't ruin it. Consider this your one and only favor."

"Yeah, but—"

This time he sighed loudly and walked over to where Quinn was standing. "Look, if it means that much to you, how about this. I do you this one favor, and then you'll owe me one. No questions asked, okay?"

"And no one knows about this? Ever? Not my dad, my brothers, Anna… No one, right?"

"They won't ever hear it from me," Bobby promised.

Quinn hesitated for a minute before saying, "Um, okay. Thanks."

"Just remember, you owe me. Whatever the favor is, you need to do it. No questions asked."

Bobby returned to his position at the back of the car and Quinn shrugged. "No problem. How bad could it be?"

Chapter 1

SEVERAL THINGS HIT BOBBY HANNIGAN AT ONCE.

First, his head was pounding.

Next, this wasn't his bed.

And finally, he was going to smash whatever was making that beeping noise.

Prying his eyes open, he was surprised to find it took a minute to bring everything into focus. His gaze slowly scanned the room—dim lighting, white walls. Then he looked down and noticed the white bedding.

What the...?

The beeping was coming from someplace behind him but he didn't have the energy to move his head to see what it was.

Now panic started to set in.

As things finally came into focus, he groaned, and then he knew—he just knew—he was dead.

He groaned again and slammed his eyes shut.

This isn't happening...this isn't happening...

"Bobby?"

Opening his eyes again, he sighed with resignation. "I'm dead, aren't I?"

A low, deep laugh was the first response. "Hardly. Although, you did scare the crap out of everyone." A pause. "Wait, why would you think you're dead?"

"That's the only explanation for waking up to your ugly face."

Quinn Shaughnessy didn't look offended. Nothing seemed to offend the arrogant SOB.

Stepping closer to the bed, Quinn kept a serene grin on his face. "Yeah, well, I drew the short straw."

"What?" Bobby asked, hating how much effort it took to get the word out.

"It means your parents went back to the hotel to sleep and I volunteered to stay here with you."

"Where's Anna? Shouldn't my sister be here instead of you?" Yeah, he knew he was sounding a bit ungrateful, and Quinn *was* his brother-in-law, but he wished it was Anna—or anyone else—with him instead.

"Dude, she's eight months pregnant and practically on bed rest. There was no way she could have made the drive and stayed up all night. She's pissed off that she's not here, believe me, but between needing to take it easy, and Kaitlyn and Brian—"

"Maybe you should get off my sister and give her a break," Bobby said, but there was no heat behind his words. He didn't have it in him. If anything, he was breathless. "Stop at three, okay?"

Quinn laughed again. "Your sister says the same thing and then—"

"Ugh, stop. Let's just leave it there, okay?"

They were both silent, and as much as Bobby hated asking anything of Quinn, waiting around for answers wasn't an option.

"So, uh…have you talked to any doctors?" he asked warily.

The fact that Quinn looked as uncomfortable as he felt was not encouraging.

"Look, um… Maybe we should wait for him to come in. It's still early and—"

"Damn it, Quinn!" Bobby snapped and winced. Everything hurt, and as much as he wanted to reach out and strangle his former foe, he didn't have the energy.

With a loud sigh, Quinn stepped closer to the bed, raking a hand through his dark blond hair. "Do you remember anything about what happened yesterday?"

The searing pain in his shoulder was a pretty good reminder. "I walked in on an armed robbery," he said slowly, racking his brain to remember what had happened. "I was off duty… I stopped at the convenience store to get gas and went in to grab a soda and…" Then he looked up at Quinn helplessly. "I tried to reason with them, I really did, but…"

"I know, man. I know," Quinn said softly. "You were lucky. This could have been a lot worse."

"I don't see how."

He noticed his brother-in-law was avoiding eye contact.

"Quinn?"

"Bobby, why don't you wait and talk to the doctors? And your parents and the police chief. I'm sure they'll be able to answer all your questions better than I could."

That was the thing: there wasn't a doubt in Bobby's mind that all those people would sit here and explain everything in a very reasonable manner. Right now, however, he wanted someone to just…be honest with him. His parents would try to play down his injuries, a doctor would be way too clinical, and his boss would be more than a little detached. He'd never thought there would come a time when he would want to receive news of any kind from Quinn Shaughnessy, but right now, he did.

Taking a steadying breath, Bobby let it out slowly. "How long have we known each other?"

A mirthless laugh came out before Quinn could stop it. "Too long."

"Dude, we've known each other for almost thirty years. Most of that time, I've wanted to punch you in the face."

"Hey!"

"And each and every one of those times were because you said what was on your mind and didn't care whose feelings you hurt."

"Bobby…"

Doing his best to sit up in the bed, he looked at Quinn pleadingly. "Right now, I need you to pretend you're not married to my sister, we're not family, and that we still pretty much despise one another."

No response.

"You owe me," he said, his tone serious.

"Owe you?"

Nodding, Bobby said, "Remember the car?"

"That was like…what, twenty years ago?"

"Doesn't change the fact that I never called in the favor."

For a minute, Quinn could only stare at him as if he was crazy. "That's not possible. In twenty years, I'm sure I've done you at least one favor."

"I asked you to leave my sister alone, and you didn't."

"Not the same," Quinn argued. "And that wasn't a favor."

"You didn't help me move."

"You didn't ask!" A smile crossed Quinn's face. "I let you stay with us when you come to town to visit, so technically—"

"Still not a favor, dumbass. We're family. That doesn't count."

Quinn muttered a curse.

"I'm serious, Quinn. I need to know what I'm dealing with and I know you aren't going to sugarcoat this. I don't want to be blindsided when the doctor comes in."

Looking over his shoulder toward the door, Quinn let out a long huff of frustration before facing Bobby again. "Okay, look," he began quietly. "You took a bullet to the shoulder."

"That much I assumed."

"Yeah, well…it wasn't exactly a clean shot."

"Meaning what?"

Quinn sighed loudly. "I really think you should wait and hear this from the doctor. Maybe I misunderstood what he said or maybe there are more test results, or—"

"Quinn!" he snapped.

"You lost a lot of blood," Quinn replied reluctantly. "They had to give you, like, three pints of blood in the ER." He paused. "And there's damage. Possibly permanent. They won't know for sure how extensive until the swelling from the surgery goes down. It's your left arm, so I know that has to work in your favor because—"

"Because I'm a righty," Bobby finished, but it did little to comfort him. "What kind of damage are we talking about?"

"Nerve damage," Quinn said grimly. "Some bone was fractured, nicked an artery and the nerves. If nothing else, you've got a long recovery ahead of you."

Bobby let it all sink in. A long recovery meant time off from the force. Permanent damage could mean the end of his career. He couldn't allow himself to think about that yet.

"How many casualties?" he asked quietly.

"Four."

Cursing, he pounded his fist against the mattress.

"I'm sorry, Bobby. I really am," Quinn said after a minute. "You want me to go and find a doctor? A nurse? You want me to call your folks? Their hotel is right across the street."

"No. It's okay. I just… I need to process all of this. There weren't a lot of people in the store, but they were all young and—"

"Don't, okay? Just…don't. Try not to think about it. You need to focus on you right now, and figuring out what happens from here."

"Yeah. Easier said than done."

They both fell silent. Though Bobby wanted more information, his brother-in-law wasn't a doctor and he didn't want to hear it from Quinn. The information he'd relayed already didn't even scratch the surface.

As if sensing he needed time to think, Quinn went and sat down in the lone chair in the room without saying a word. Bobby had no idea what time it was, except that it was early in the morning. Now that he was more awake, he realized how uncomfortable he was—not only his shoulder, which was throbbing, but his whole body hurt. His head was pounding and his throat was dry.

The last thing he wanted—ever—was to have to rely on anyone to help him. He enjoyed being the type of man who could take care of himself. Granted, he'd lived close to his family up until a couple of years ago, but ever since moving away, Bobby found he enjoyed being on his own. Not that he didn't love his family, but he had an independence now that he'd never had before. And on top of that, he didn't like asking for help. He wanted to be the one helping others.

Still, these were extenuating circumstances, right?

Clearing his throat and wincing at how sore it was, he said, "Um... Is there anything to drink? Some water or something?"

"Yeah. Sure." Quinn was instantly on his feet and pouring him some water from the small pitcher on the table. Bobby thanked him and slowly sipped from the cup. His hand was shaking and he felt weaker than he would have thought possible. Quinn helped him, and neither said a word about how awkward it was.

When he was done, Quinn put the cup back on the table and sat down again. Several minutes passed until he couldn't take the silence any longer.

"You know, in that moment, when I knew what was coming, it felt like everything moved in slow motion."

Quinn listened but said nothing.

"I remember thinking there had to be something I could do, something I could say, that would change the outcome. I wanted to stop anyone else from getting hurt." He paused. "But then someone made a break for the door and the guy—the gunman—he just...he freaked."

And just like that, Bobby could hear the shots, the screams. He could hear the glass breaking, the crying... and then the searing pain. Reaching up with his good hand, he carefully touched the bandage and immediately winced.

Not a good sign.

"I've been a cop for almost fifteen years," he went on. "I've been punched, I've been kicked…" He stopped and let out a bitter laugh. "I've even been spat on, but I never thought I'd be here." Then he looked at Quinn and let out another laugh. "Or that you'd be the one with me."

"Yeah, well…"

"I appreciate the fact that you are," he said solemnly. "For real. I think if I had woken up and it had been my folks standing there, they would have freaked me out. My mom would be crying and my dad would be trying to keep her calm."

Quinn stood and came back to the side of the bed.

"And if it were Anna, she would probably punch me in my good shoulder and yell at me for scaring her."

Quinn smiled. "That's my girl."

"So, I guess what I'm trying to say is, I'm…thankful. For you, you know, being here."

Quinn looked as uncomfortable as Bobby felt at the admission. Luckily, they were saved from having to say anything else when a nurse walked in to get his vitals. Window blinds were opened and he had a feeling quiet time was officially over.

After that, everything seemed to move at warp speed. People kept coming into the room to check on him, examine him, change out his IV, replace bandages—there was a steady stream of them until he thought his head would spin. The only problem was that none of them were his doctor. Every time he asked a question, he was told a doctor would be in to see him shortly.

It was maddening.

By the time a doctor came in, all Bobby wanted to do was take a nap.

"Officer Hannigan, I'm Dr. McIntyre," the sixty-something man said as he walked into the room. "How are you feeling?"

"Like I've been shot," Bobby said flatly.

"That's because you were," the doctor replied levelly, studying Bobby's chart. He was quiet for a few moments before he put the chart down and faced Bobby, his expression serious. For the next five minutes he explained in very dry, medical terms all that had happened to Bobby's shoulder and what had been done to repair the damage. He talked in a way that Bobby had a hard time following. Why didn't doctors learn to speak in layman's terms?

"So?" he asked after he took a minute to let it all sink in. "What am I looking at here?"

"A long recovery."

―――∞―――

Later that night, even once Bobby was alone in his room, sleep seemed impossible.

Nerve damage...

Loss of motor function...

Three months of rehabilitation...

None of it sat well with him. According to the doctor and just about everyone else who had come to see him today, it was still too early to tell what the final outcome would look like. Only one thing stood out to him—he wasn't going to be returning to active duty anytime soon.

If ever.

Don't go there, he warned himself. But it was hard not to.

This was the first time today he'd had the chance to really think about the future. After Dr. McIntyre had left, the room had filled with people—friends, family, coworkers. Half of the police department had come to see him, his parents had sat by his side all day, and his phone had rung constantly with well wishes from just about everyone he knew. It had been a great distraction, but now he was left with a whole lot of silence and his own wild imagination.

What if he couldn't use his left arm again? What if he only got partial range back? He wouldn't be able to return to the force. He'd have to retire, and he was too damn young for that. What the hell was he supposed to do if that happened? Being a cop was all he'd ever wanted. He'd worked for that to the exclusion of all else—even avoiding long-term relationships because he didn't want the distraction. So where did it leave him?

Alone.

Completely alone.

He looked up at the bundle of balloons tied to the corner of his bed. His mother had brought them with her this morning as a way of cheering him up. Right. Because a dozen mylar balloons fixed things when you'd been shot and were facing the possibility of your career being over.

Not her fault, he reminded himself. She was doing what she always did—her best to make her family feel better. It wasn't her fault that there wasn't anything she could do. No number of balloons or flowers or freshly baked cookies were going to help.

Although right about now he'd kill for a batch of something sweet.

Grimacing, he did his best to get comfortable. He was a stomach sleeper and having to sleep sitting up wasn't helping at all. That and the pain.

Earlier, a nurse had come in and offered him something to help him sleep. He'd turned that down. She'd offered him a lot of things, all of which he'd declined.

It wasn't anything new. Bobby wasn't arrogant, but he knew women found him attractive. And for some reason, a man in uniform was like catnip to some of them. And now it looked like he could add "injured cop out of uniform" to the list.

Great.

He sighed and shifted a little in the confines of the hospital bed, wishing like hell he could be at home recovering in his own space. It didn't look like that was going to happen anytime soon. He'd be here getting poked and prodded for at least another couple of days, and then what? He wouldn't have to live at a rehab facility, but he was going to need some help since he wouldn't be able to drive or do a whole lot for himself.

Earlier, his folks had offered to come and stay with him until he got settled. He'd turned them down. His condo was a small two-bedroom and he knew it wouldn't take long before the walls started to close in on him. Then they'd offered to have him come and stay with them while they looked into rehab places back home. That one held a little more merit. Not that he was looking to move back in with his parents, but they had a lot more space and a lot more distractions. He wouldn't feel like he was under the microscope all the time.

It was a lot to think about. Maybe he was getting too far ahead of himself.

Or not. After all, what if Dr. McIntyre came in tomorrow and said he could be released to go home? Maybe he'd only need to come in once a week until he was healed and then he'd get a recommendation for rehab. Hell, if that happened, he'd jump at it and pay for his parents to stay at the hotel for a couple more days until he got settled. His mom would protest, but Dad would side with him.

Feeling a little more relaxed, Bobby let out a slow breath and allowed himself to close his eyes. He'd give anything to go back in time and stop all of the things that had happened—not just to him, but to the other victims. Knowing that he couldn't didn't make him feel any better.

Maybe he should have accepted that pill to help him sleep.

Muttering a curse, he reached for the call button and loathed himself for it. He didn't want to be weak. He didn't want to ask for help.

But more than that, he didn't want to be alone with his thoughts anymore.

—◦◦◦—

"This is great, isn't it?"

A shrug was the only response.

"C'mon, admit it. This place is really cool. We're going to have so much fun! We can go to the park, and to the beach, and we have all summer to check everything out!"

Another shrug.

Teagan Shaughnessy looked at her five-year-old son standing in their new front yard and held in a sigh.

Lucas was not thrilled with their cross-country move. He'd made that point abundantly clear all through the long drive. Luckily, her parents had joined them, and the whole group had caravanned from Colorado to the Carolina coast, doing their best to make an adventure of it.

Unfortunately, Lucas wasn't feeling very adventurous.

She knew it was temporary. His moods often were. But just this once, she wished his mood would lighten up sooner rather than later. This move was a big deal for her too. She'd done her fair share of moving all over the country thanks to growing up as an Army brat, and once she'd left home, all she'd wanted was a place to call her own for good. Somewhere she could settle in and call it a day.

But life had made other plans.

"It's hot here," Lucas stated, interrupting her thoughts.

True enough. It was a definite change in climate from Colorado, but she was determined to make him believe it was all for the best.

Even as she felt herself sweating more than she had in a long time.

"Let's go inside where there's air-conditioning and unpack some of your toys. What do you say?"

"I want to go home," he pouted, his little arms crossing over his chest.

As much as she wanted to be angry and demand that he stop being difficult, Teagan did her best to stay calm. It would be great if she had some help—someone other than her parents—but that wasn't going to happen. Lucas's father had been killed in combat before Lucas was born, and it had always been just the two of them. Sometimes—like now—she really resented it.

"Lucas, we promised Meema and Pops we'd meet them for dinner. And that's not going to happen if we don't get some work done around here," she said, calmly but firmly.

"Fine," he said with a loud, dramatic sigh before dragging himself into the house.

They worked together—she used that phrase loosely—for two hours. Lucas had to be coached and directed every step of the way. Teagan knew she'd get much more done alone, but her parents were doing their own share of unpacking and couldn't babysit. For now, she had to do her best to make this a game and try not to cringe at how long it was taking to get even simple things done.

"Can I play one of my games now?" Lucas asked, standing beside her. They finally had his room almost completely set up and normally she wouldn't want him playing video games on a weekday, but these were extenuating circumstances.

"Sure," she said with a smile. "You worked really hard and I'm very proud of you!"

He beamed at her praise. "Does that mean I can have a snack too?"

There wasn't much to choose from, and she glanced toward the kitchen. "Um… I think we have some cookies somewhere…"

"I know where!" he yelled as he took off toward the kitchen.

The house was a small, temporary rental, just a two-bedroom, one-and-a-half-bath bungalow with an open floor plan. Even so, she was truly grateful. The house had been one of the signs that this move was meant to be. Two months ago, her parents had brought her out to visit her uncle and cousins, and they had all fallen in love with the town. It wasn't as if they hadn't been here before, but it had been over a dozen years since their last visit.

Back then, she had often asked why they couldn't live at the beach all the time like her cousins did. But the answer she'd always gotten was that the military was her father's life—like it or not. After a while, she'd stopped asking. So this time, when the opportunity had come to make the trip again, Teagan had been super excited. It had been great to reconnect with everyone, and it was amazing how much the family had grown. Her head was still spinning from trying to remember all the new names. That was something she was going to have to get better at now that she would be seeing them on a regular basis.

The house had come on top of the joy of reconnection, a rental property owned by her cousin Quinn's wife, Anna. Part of her felt a little guilty because of the great deal they'd given her, but she'd graciously accepted their offer and promised to take care of the place as if it were her own. Her parents had found something just as nice a little closer to the beach, thanks to Uncle Ian. Her mother was so excited.

And then there was her job. Back in Colorado, she had been temping as a guidance counselor for elementary schools. There weren't any openings for her to have a permanent position like she wanted, but she filled in where she could. Once she had mentioned what she did for a living to her cousin Aidan's wife, Zoe, she suddenly had a list of people she could contact here in their new school district. Zoe was an interior designer who was very active in the community and seemed to know everyone. Talk about luck—within a week, she had several interviews over the phone and had secured a position!

Everything had fallen into place.

It had all happened so quickly, but Teagan supposed it was better than dragging it out. Her position wouldn't start until the middle of August and it was only the first week of June now, so she had the entire summer ahead of her to settle in and prepare herself. She'd considered getting a part-time job somewhere to help recover the cost of the move but wasn't sure if she should. Not that she wouldn't be able to find one—not with so many Shaughnessys in town with businesses of their own— but because Lucas maybe needed her attention more than they needed the cash right now.

The thought of her cousins made her smile. It had been so long since she'd had more than her parents around. Sure, she had friends and coworkers she adored, but there was something to be said for finally having the kind of big family she'd always longed for. Being an only child and constantly moving wherever the U.S. Army stationed them meant she hadn't had the chance to make and keep friends for long. And while Teagan had sworn she'd never move again, this time would definitely be her last.

Until she had to move out of the rental.

Don't think about that now! she admonished herself.

Looking around, she saw Lucas had indeed found the cookies and was happily settled in front of the television playing one of his favorite games. A small sigh of relief came out before she could stop it. If nothing went wrong, she could have a solid hour to put some work into getting her own room unpacked before meeting her parents for dinner. They'd already received multiple invitations from her uncle and cousins, but until she was settled in, she needed as few distractions as possible.

While reconnecting with her cousins was certainly a perk, she hoped she'd make some friends on her own too. No need to be the clingy relative who'd moved to town.

Unfortunately, no distractions meant having time in her own head for worried thoughts of all that could go wrong with this move.

"Nothing's gone wrong so far," she said to herself. "Stop looking for trouble."

Easier said than done.

While she was used to moving around, Lucas wasn't. Though Teagan knew her son would adjust, there had been a certain comfort for them both in living in Colorado. Probably because it was where he'd been born and she had her own circle of friends she was going to miss.

Ugh, that was a depressing thought for sure.

Pushing her worries aside, she unpacked three boxes of clothes and hung them up before moving on to getting the bathroom unpacked and set up.

"Mom!" Lucas called out. "Is it time to see Meema and Pops? I'm hungry!"

Hungry? Already? But when she looked at the clock, she saw it was definitely close to dinner. Where had the time gone?

"Give me fifteen minutes to freshen up and we'll go, okay?"

"Aww, Mom," he whined, but that was the norm. Lucas hated waiting on anything.

A shower would have been nice, but she'd have to get by with a quick change of clothes and running a brush through her hair.

That was, until she looked in the mirror.

There was no hope. She was sweaty, her makeup—the little she usually wore—was already smeared beyond repair, and her hair was…well, it wasn't pretty.

"No problem. Three-minute showers are fun," she murmured as she turned the water on.

Five minutes later, she felt marginally better.

And clean.

Moving as quickly as possible, she dried off and pulled on clean clothes. With her hair wrapped up turban-style in a towel, she walked out into the living room. "Almost ready!"

Lucas looked over his shoulder at her and groaned. "We're never going to eat dinner."

"Yes, we will," she promised, grabbing her purse from the kitchen island. That was the last place she had stuffed her makeup bag. "We'll be in the car in ten minutes!" As she ran back to the bathroom, she heard her son's cry of disbelief.

And as it turned out, he was right.

It took her fifteen minutes because her hair wasn't cooperating. Though it was a little longer than she normally wore it, even at shoulder length it seemed to take forever to dry. She made a mental note to look for a hair salon. At the very least she was going to need a good cut and style before starting her new job.

When Teagan walked back into the living room,

Lucas had the television off and was waiting by the door. She grabbed her purse, keys, and phone and bent down to give him a loud, smacking kiss on the cheek.

"You took forever."

"I know, bud. Sorry." She ran a hand over his dark hair. "And you will be rewarded for your patience."

His big brown eyes widened. "I will?"

She nodded. "An ice cream cone as big as your head for dessert tonight. How does that sound?"

"Yay!" he yelled as he ran out the door and to their car.

Later that night, after Lucas was finally asleep, Teagan lay in bed staring at the ceiling. Her mind raced.

That had been one heck of a curveball her parents had thrown her at dinner. They were leaving on a two-week cruise next week! At first she had been certain she'd misheard them. After all, they had just moved across the country. Why would they be going on a vacation right away? And worse, how were she and Lucas supposed to settle in without them?

Which is exactly what she'd asked, and as she lay there in the dark, she still couldn't believe the response she'd gotten.

"We thought it best to do this now," her mother said. Catherine Shaughnessy was the best mom a girl could ask for—loving, sweet, and very level-headed.

Right now, she hated that last one the most.

"But…why? We just got here. You can see how hard Lucas is taking the move," Teagan had argued. Fortunately—or maybe it had been planned—her dad had taken her son out on the pier so he hadn't heard any of the conversation.

With a patient smile, her mother responded, "That's why we thought it best, sweetheart. You and Lucas need to settle in together and figure out how to make this move work for the two of you. With your father retiring, we're looking forward to traveling that isn't about work. You understand, right?"

Sadly, she did. It didn't make her feel any better about it, but she understood.

"Why didn't you say anything sooner?"

"There was so much going on and we didn't want to add to your stress. The subject came up when we were here in April. Ian and Martha mentioned they were going on this cruise with some friends and I mentioned that your father and I had never gone on one. Next thing I know, they extended the invitation. Your father was very excited about it." She smiled. "He's worked so hard his whole life, it's nice to see him looking so relaxed."

"I know, I know. And now I feel like a selfish brat because I'm just thinking about myself."

Reaching across the table, Catherine took Teagan's hand in hers. "You're the least selfish person I know. And your concern isn't for yourself, it's about Lucas."

"It's the same thing, Mom."

"No, it's not. You've always put Lucas first, and it's a wonderful quality. And you know how close Lucas and your father are, so you're afraid Lucas is going to be devastated that we're gone."

"I've relied on the two of you too much," she admitted in a low voice. "Lucas isn't a baby anymore. It's time for us to let the two of you have a life."

"The two of you *are* our life." Catherine smiled. "We aren't going on the cruise to get away from you. We're just looking to do a little something for us. Something fun."

"And you deserve it. You really do."

"Plus, it's a chance for us to make some new friends," her mother went on. "You remember Jack and Mary Hannigan, don't you? They're Anna's parents, and they still live next door to Ian and Martha." When Teagan nodded, she said, "They're going as well."

"I'm sure you're all going to have a great time. And after this move, I'm sure you're ready to relax a bit."

"Oh, believe me, we are. But we're not the only ones who need a bit of rest and relaxation. From what I hear, the others are looking to get away just as much."

"What do you mean?"

"Well, Quinn and Anna just had their third baby last month."

Oh, right. She remembered her mom talking about that, but with everything else going on, it hadn't really stuck in her mind. "That's great. What did they have again?"

"A little girl," Catherine said wistfully. "They named her Bailey."

"That's sweet."

"Anyway, Ian and Martha have been helping with Quinn and Anna's two little ones for a while, because Anna was on bed rest for the last month of her pregnancy. And then with the birth of the baby…"

"What about her folks? They're nearby—couldn't they have helped out?"

"Their older son was shot last month. He's a police officer in Myrtle Beach."

"Oh my goodness!" she gasped. "How awful!"

"They say he's doing well, and getting better every day. He was shot in the shoulder and has some nerve damage, but he's recovering."

"Well, that's a good thing."

Catherine nodded and then laughed softly.

"What? What's so funny?"

Her mother waved her off but then said, "They claim he's fussier and more demanding than the new baby!"

"Mom, that's terrible! The man was shot!"

"I know, I know. He's just incredibly grumpy and Mary said he was a lousy patient. So believe me when I say they're looking forward to getting away for a little while."

"Just like you are," Teagan added. "I really am excited for you."

Now as she was looking back, she realized she was both excited and not, all at the same time.

How messed up was that?

The good news was there were plenty of things she and Lucas could do to entertain themselves while her parents were away. Like she'd told him earlier that day, they could go to the beach, the park, and generally explore their new town. There were plenty of cousins for him to play with now and she hoped—in time, maybe once school started—he'd make some friends on his own. They'd scout out the local library and see if there were any kids' programs there, or maybe even some local day camps.

Tons of options.

For Lucas.

It was a lot easier to make friends when you were

five, she thought. Making new friends at twenty-seven? Not quite as easy.

Not that she was shying away from it, but…

Yeah, okay. If she had the choice, she'd avoid it altogether. She was the new kid all over again. You'd think she'd be used to it after so many years of constantly starting over, but the thought of trying now was exhausting.

Ironic, considering how physically exhausted she was right now and yet she couldn't seem to fall asleep.

Kicking off the blankets, Teagan climbed from the bed and went out to the kitchen to grab a glass of water. Standing in the dark, she wondered what she could possibly do to fall asleep.

"Try not thinking about sleep," she murmured. "That should help."

Easier said than done.

A box sat where she'd plunked it on the kitchen table—books and photo albums. She reached in and pulled out the photo album that was on top and took it back to her room, quietly closing the door behind her.

At her bed, she turned on the small lamp and sat down. In the dark it had been hard to tell which album she had grabbed, but once she realized, her heart squeezed hard in her chest.

Lucas's baby book.

Half of it was Lucas's book, anyway. The other half was dedicated to Logan—his father.

With a shaky breath, she leaned back and opened the book to the first page, Logan's official military portrait. Slowly, she reached out and touched it, as though she could still feel his face. He was so young and so handsome in that picture. She hated how that was the way he would be forever. She'd never get to see him grow old. He wouldn't ever grow old with her. He'd never had the chance to meet his son or even know of his existence.

It was six years since he'd died and the pain wasn't nearly as harsh as it had been in the beginning. She still remembered the day her father had come home and broken the news to her. Teagan had never known heartache like that before and she prayed she never would again.

Turning the page, she found several shots of the two of them while they were dating and she couldn't help but smile. They looked like kids and it felt like a lifetime ago. They'd met just after she'd graduated from college, the summer before she'd left to start her master's. They hadn't had much time just to be a couple. She was either away at school or he was deployed. It was kind of a miracle she had even gotten pregnant.

The next several pages held more random shots of the two of them and each one made her smile wider. Pictures of them at a military ball, another at a bonfire, and still another from New Year's Eve. The final picture she had of them was from the day Logan had deployed for the last time. They were hugging and she remembered how tightly he'd held her as he promised to love her forever.

"When I get home," he'd said, "we're going to start planning our future."

Instead, she'd had to help plan his funeral.

With a shuddery breath, she touched that picture and stared at it for a long time until it began to blur. It wasn't a surprise that she was crying—she often did when she thought about that day.

Closing the book, she placed it on her nightstand and shut off the light.

Maybe she would sleep, maybe she wouldn't.

But for right now, she would cry.

―∾∾―

Standing and staring out the front door of his family home, Bobby watched as his parents drove away happily with Ian and Martha Shaughnessy, and another couple who were apparently cousins of Ian's. A cruise. They were leaving him to go on a cruise! He still couldn't wrap his head around the whole thing. It wasn't like his parents didn't deserve a vacation, of course they did. But did they have to take one now? It had only been five weeks since he'd been shot, for crying out loud! His arm was still in a sling and he couldn't drive. What was he supposed to do?

He looked down at the sheet of paper in his hand and frowned. His mother had made him a list of all the people who were willing to come and lend a hand if he needed it—everyone from Quinn and Anna to their pastor.

Great.

Muttering a curse, he stepped away from the door and slammed it shut. Two weeks. He had to fend for himself in an empty house for two weeks. Part of him was thankful finally to have some time alone, while the other was still a bit peeved that his parents couldn't have waited to go on vacation until after he was fully healed.

His thoughts were interrupted by ringing. Dropping his mother's list on the dining room table, he pulled his phone from his pocket and swiped the screen.

"What?" he snapped.

"Wow, I wonder why Mom and Dad were so anxious to go away!" Anna said with amusement. "Still cheery, I see."

Yeah, everyone had been on him about his mood, but what did they know? They hadn't been shot. They weren't in pain. And they weren't living their lives in limbo wondering if they were going to have a career to go back to when it was all over.

"Was there a purpose for this call?" he asked tiredly.

"As a matter of fact, there is. I wanted to invite you over for dinner," Anna replied.

"It's a bit of a walk."

She laughed. "I know that, doofus. Obviously, Quinn will come and pick you up."

"I don't know…"

"Bobby, I don't want you spending all your time alone. It will be good for you to get out for a bit."

"Mom and Dad have been gone all of five minutes, Anna. I haven't been alone in over a month. If anything, I think I'm due for some me time."

She sighed. "I just worry about you."

Of course she did, and he was being kind of a brat right now. "Look, I appreciate the offer, I do. And maybe sometime during the week I'll take you up on it. But for the next couple of days, I'm going to enjoy the peace and quiet. It's nothing personal."

"This is because Bailey spit up on you yesterday, isn't it?"

Bobby knew she was trying to lighten the mood and he couldn't help but laugh. "It's still hard to believe so much came out of that tiny girl." He shuddered. "But no. That has nothing to do with it. If you remember correctly, I was a favorite for Kaitlyn to spit up on and Brian used to pee on me every time I changed his diaper."

Now she was laughing much harder. "That was funny. He didn't do that for anyone else. Only you."

"Yeah, I'm lucky," he deadpanned.

Anna snickered a little more before speaking again. "Okay, I'll give you a couple of days of peace because I know you're right—it's been a while since you've had some time to yourself."

"Thank you."

"Do you have enough food?"

"Mom shopped enough for them to be gone for a month and that's on top of the meals she stuck in the freezer. I only have to heat them up."

"She's good."

And she was, Bobby knew it. Had he remembered to tell her how much he appreciated her help? Probably not. He'd been irritable about everything since the shooting. He made a mental note to remember to thank her—and his father—when they got back.

"Well, I'll let you go enjoy the peace and quiet," Anna said. "But if you need anything, just call, okay?"

"I will. I promise."

When he hung up, he was instantly hit with the silence.

Finally.

Only it wasn't quite as soothing as he thought it would be. For all his complaining about just wanting to be alone, now that he was, it didn't feel as great as he'd hoped.

"Give it more than a minute, you moron," he berated

himself. Bobby walked into the kitchen, grabbed a bag of chips, and reached into the refrigerator for a can of soda. What he really wanted was a beer, but it was only eleven o'clock in the morning. No matter how crappy he was feeling, there was no need to start drinking this early.

Snacks in hand, he made himself comfortable in the living room before turning on the TV. Daytime television had never been his thing, but thankfully his parents had Netflix. He'd been binge-watching many different things lately and it was time to pick something new. If his father were home, he'd suggest something sci-fi. If it was his mom, she'd want something sweet and romantic.

He rolled his eyes at that one.

Scrolling…scrolling…scrolling…kids' movies.

For some reason, he stopped and stared at the screen for a minute. Hell, when was the last time he'd watched something simple and silly? Oh, right. About three months ago when he was visiting Anna, and Kaitlin had convinced him to watch *Frozen* with her.

For the tenth time.

He'd even sung along to all the songs with her.

Of course, it was one thing to sit and watch some cartoon when you were hanging with a bunch of kids, it was another when you were a grown-up home by yourself with no kids of your own.

Still, there was something about a good Disney movie…

Five hours later, he'd watched a short film collection, *Finding Dory*, and *The Incredibles*. Standing, he stretched and realized he'd skipped lunch and was starving. The refrigerator and freezer were loaded with casseroles and soups and all kinds of stuff his mother had made, but he really wanted pizza. And not the store-bought kind, but real pizza that was delivered.

There was plenty of time to eat everything that was already here, so what would be the harm in ordering in for one meal?

Guilt only niggled at him for a moment. Twenty minutes later, Bobby had his next round of movies picked out and a cold beer in his hand while he waited for his dinner to be delivered.

And that became the pattern for the next five days.

By the fifth night, not only did he feel like crap from eating nothing but pizza and chips, but the place was a complete mess. Pizza boxes littered the pantry along with empty beer bottles and soda cans. There was a smell in the air and he couldn't be sure if it was the trash or him.

Closing the pantry door, he realized it was him.

Maybe it was time to take Anna up on her offer to come for dinner.

But first, he had to shower.

Staring at himself in the steamed-up mirror thirty minutes later, he grimaced at the ugly scar on his shoulder. It was healing as it was supposed to, but it certainly wasn't pretty. He was only allowed to have his arm out of the sling to do his physio exercises, and for a few minutes, he slowly stretched it and tried to work out some of the soreness. He couldn't wait to be done with wearing the damn thing. Of course, that didn't mean much of anything—just because the sling came off didn't mean he was healed and good to go. No, all it meant was a little more mobility. Then serious rehab would start.

Something he was, no doubt, going to hate.

Unfortunately, if he wanted to go back to work, he would need to complete the program and get clearance from a team of doctors. And there was no way he was even going to allow himself to think about the possibility of that not happening. He had to work. Needed to work. More than that, he needed it to be the way it was before. There was no way he would go back if he had to rot behind a desk.

"Don't even think about it," he said to his reflection.

Drying off, he walked into his room to get dressed and realized he was out of clean clothes. He cursed and threw on a robe. With no other choice, he straightened up the room, threw all the dirty clothes in his hamper, and slowly dragged it down the hall to the laundry room.

It would easily be two hours before he had anything clean to wear, but hopefully he could still get dressed in time to get a meal at Anna's. As soon as the laundry was going, he went and found his phone.

Which was dead.

"I can't seem to catch a break here," he huffed as he plugged the thing in and looked over at the house phone mounted on the wall. For all the times he mocked his folks for still having a landline, it looked like it was certainly going to come in handy right now.

The cordless phone felt large and awkward in his hand and it made him laugh.

Then he realized he didn't know Anna's number. On his cell phone, he pulled up her name and hit Send. Now what was he supposed to do?

With a huff of annoyance, he hung the phone back up

on the wall. It wouldn't hurt to wait until he could look up his sister's number.

So with no clean clothes and no phone, what was he supposed to do? He breathed in deeply—and then he knew.

Clean the damn house.

It wasn't an easy task to accomplish with one arm, but he did the best he could. He loaded the dishwasher, collected all the trash and put it by the front door—taking it out required more than a bathrobe to cover himself—wiped down the kitchen counter, and even dusted the coffee table where he'd been eating most of his meals. When he was done, it was time to change over the laundry. Stepping back into the living room, he felt good, like he'd accomplished something.

"One more thing," he murmured. He grabbed a can of air freshener from the kitchen and sprayed the entire area for good measure. After the air cleared a bit, he inhaled deeply and let it out with a smile. "Way better."

So the house was picked up, his clothes were drying, and all that was left was to call Anna and see if he could join them for dinner.

"Hey!" she said happily when she answered the phone. "How are you doing?"

He smiled. "I'm doing good. Everything's great. Everything's fine here."

"Uh-huh…"

"How about you? How are you doing? How are the kids?"

She hesitated for a second. "We're all good."

"And Quinn? Is…is he doing okay? Business doing well?"

"Bobby?"

"Hmm?"

"Are you tired of your own company?" she asked and he could hear the amusement in her voice.

"Yes," he admitted with a small laugh. "You have no idea."

"I should make you suffer a little," she said, sounding firm. "Five days and not one phone call. I was worried sick, but I was trying to be respectful. I figured one of us should be."

Her guilt trips always worked. "I know, I know. And I'm sorry. I guess…I don't know. I think I sort of lost track of time. If it makes you feel any better, it's been a rough day because of it."

"Meaning what, exactly?"

He explained about the trash, the house, the smell, his phone, the laundry—and she laughed harder and harder by the minute. "Yeah, well…the place is clean, the trash will go out as soon as I have dry clothes, and I've learned my lesson. Happy?"

"More than you know." She paused. "Have you heard from Mom and Dad at all?"

"They're on a cruise, Anna. I doubt they're even thinking about home."

"Hmm…maybe. I just thought they would have called to check in. Plus, I'm dying to hear about all the fun they're having."

He made a noncommittal sound.

"Although, I guess we'll hear all about it at the big Shaughnessy barbecue when they get back," Anna said.

"What barbecue? When?"

"The Sunday right after they get back. Ian said he wanted everyone to come over since this is the longest he's ever been away on vacation." She laughed. "So everyone will be there. You know, like we always do."

"And that includes me?" he asked with mild disbelief.

"Since when are you not included in family stuff?"

She had a point, and he was smart enough not to argue. "Okay, fine. Big barbecue. Yay, me." That was a meal with more than himself for company ten days from now, but what about tonight?

"Oh, and Bobby?"

"Hmm?"

"Quinn will pick you up on his way home tonight. We're having burgers, corn on the cob, and a big salad for dinner. If you're nice, I'll make brownies for dessert."

His mouth was already watering. "You're a lifesaver, Anna. You know that, right?"

"I do now."

Chapter 2

"Bobby! We're heading over to Ian's! Are you coming?" his mother yelled from the kitchen.

Was he? He still wasn't sure. Even after two weeks of relative solitude, right now the last thing he wanted to do was socialize. His arm was still in a sling after his doctor's appointment the previous Friday, and they weren't impressed with his motor function in his left hand. Bobby had tried to reason that his motor skills would be much better if he was allowed to have his arm out of the sling more.

The doctor disagreed.

He couldn't close his left hand all the way to a fist, and there was more tingling than actual feeling in his arm.

Neither were good signs.

So while he'd welcomed his parents home the day before with a big smile, and listened to all their stories about what a great time they'd had on the cruise, that was about the extent of his ability to put on a happy face. He was angry, disappointed, and basically didn't want to talk to anyone.

"Bobby?" she called up again.

"I'll head over later!" he called back, unwilling even to get up off his bed. Neither parent said anything else. A few minutes later, he heard the front door close and let out a long breath. He knew they were disappointed in him, and to be honest, he was disappointed in himself. Mainly because he wasn't healing fast enough.

Maybe he should go back to his own apartment in Myrtle Beach. Maybe being here, surrounded by his parents and family, was doing more harm than good. He was being coddled and cared for, and it was making him lazy. If he was back at his place, he'd be forced to do more for himself and maybe—just maybe—he'd be able to speed up his recovery.

Mind made up, Bobby looked around the room. It was a mess—that was a given—but with some effort, he could get his laundry done and pack. Then, once his parents were back, he could talk to his father about driving him home in the morning. Yes. That was what he wanted to do. It was time to stop feeling sorry for himself and start being an active participant in his recovery. If he wanted to go back to work full-time in his regular position, he needed to take this seriously.

Rehab? He'd do it. He wasn't afraid of hard work or a challenge, but he had most certainly gotten lazy and it was time for that to end.

Standing, he began collecting clothes and throwing them in the hamper. With the first load going in the laundry room, he straightened up. No doubt his mother would strip his room down after he left and scrub it from top to bottom, so he didn't need to go crazy, but he still needed to put in the effort to clear off the surfaces and throw out any trash.

Moving around the house, he picked up his personal items and organized his packing. Within an hour, he'd made a pretty good dent in it all. Time for a break. He went down to the kitchen and grabbed a beer before stepping outside onto the back deck for a little fresh air.

Off in the distance he could hear laughter. The Shaughnessys' yard was right on the other side of the fence. He could hear the kids chasing each other and squealing with laughter, adult voices calling for them to calm down. He smiled, remembering the days when he was one of those kids. This had been a great place to grow up, lots of great memories. And at any other time in his life, he'd be seriously thrilled to be here. But until he got himself together and healed, this wasn't working for him.

Glancing over at the yard, he saw the smoke billowing from the barbecue and he could smell all the great things they were cooking. Their cookouts were always the same menu—burgers, hot dogs, chicken. On top of that, his mom had made her famous macaroni salad, along with several cakes. No doubt Anna made her potato salad, too. All of his favorites were just a few yards away. Taking a swig of his beer, Bobby had to wonder what harm it would do to just go over and grab something to eat and say hello? He didn't have to stay long, and really, it was the polite thing to do.

His stomach growled just then—manners really had nothing to do with it.

Turning, he walked back into the house, pulled on a pair of sneakers, and made sure he didn't look too disheveled. At closer inspection he noticed the dark circles under his eyes, and wistfully longed for a good night's sleep where he could toss and turn and move around as much as he wanted without setting his shoulder on fire.

"Soon," he said to himself. "Soon."

Grabbing his sunglasses, he put them on and made his way across the front yard to the Shaughnessys'. Stepping into their backyard through the side gate, he saw that just about everyone was there—Aidan and Zoe, Hugh and Aubrey, Quinn and Anna, and Owen and Brooke—along with all their kids. For a moment he stood by the gate and just took it all in.

His parents were talking with Ian and Martha and... some other couple. Who were they? Then he remembered the faces he'd caught through the car window—Ian's cousins. The third couple who'd gone on the cruise.

"Hey! Look who decided to join us!" his sister called out with a smile, making her way over to him. She had Bailey in her arms and he silently prayed she wouldn't ask him to hold her. When she reached him, he bent down and kissed her on the cheek. "We were wondering if you were going to come over."

"Yeah, well...you know. Food."

Anna laughed. "You're sounding a little cavemanish. You need to be among people again." Then she took him by the hand and led him into the yard. Everyone called out a greeting and he smiled and waved.

It was controlled chaos, a dozen different things going on—kids playing, people eating, a game of basketball in the corner of the yard—and right in the middle of it all, his brother-in-law loudly telling a story about one of his latest classic car rehabs.

Typical. When Quinn Shaughnessy had an audience, he loved to brag on himself.

"Go and make yourself a plate," Anna said from beside him. "I'll grab you a beer."

"Thanks." Walking over to the long table covered in food, he made small talk with Hugh Shaughnessy.

"How are you feeling?" Hugh asked.

Bobby shrugged, then winced. "I'm healing at a snail's pace," he responded, while internally cursing how awkward it was to pile food on his carefully balanced plate while making his way down the line one-handed.

Hugh chuckled. "You never were very patient. These things take time, right?"

He nodded, because saying anything would run the risk of him making a snarky comment, and Hugh didn't deserve that. "What about you? What's new with you and the family?"

"We're waiting on a baby," he said, smiling. "If all goes as planned, we should be expecting a call in another six weeks."

Bobby looked up with wide eyes. "Seriously? That's awesome!" He put his plate down and clapped Hugh on the shoulder. "Congratulations! I thought adoptions took much longer."

Hugh shrugged. "The entire process feels that way. Between all the paperwork and waiting for a match, it feels like it's been forever. But now we're in major countdown mode."

"Do you know what you're…you know…having?"

"A girl," he said, his smile growing. "The sonogram showed a girl. Aubrey's thrilled. Hell, I'm thrilled!"

"I'm happy for you, Hugh. Really, that's great news!" Before he could say anything else, Aubrey called out for Hugh to bring another hot dog for their son Connor. Bobby stood there and watched his friend join his family.

With a sigh, he made his way slowly toward the end of the table, taking a little of this and a little of that as he went. The closer he got to the end, the louder Quinn was. He rolled his eyes and reached for a couple of brownies to top off his mountain of food.

"Seriously, is he always like this?" he heard someone ask.

Standing off to the left was a woman he'd never seen before. He studied her for a moment, unsure if she was talking to him or to herself. Then she looked at him and for a second, Bobby couldn't breathe.

Blue eyes so dark they were almost black stared up at him. Her eyes were wide without trying and he was thankful for his sunglasses, because he knew he was staring. She had dark, wavy hair that rested on her bare shoulders. She wasn't petite, but she was certainly shorter than him by about six or seven inches, and she had the perfect amount of curves.

His mouth instantly went dry.

"I mean, he hasn't stopped talking about himself for the last twenty minutes," she said with a conspirator's grin, her voice low and just a little husky with a hint of humor. She looked at Quinn and then back at Bobby. "Someone should really tell him to shut it for a while and give other people a chance to talk."

Unable to help himself, he laughed—an honest to goodness laugh—and it felt great.

"Yeah, well, if you've known Quinn for any amount of time, then you know this is his thing. All the time."

"It's pretty annoying." She crossed her arms over her middle, the action causing her breasts to lift just a bit.

He was going to need a cold shower in a minute.

Not only was this woman beautiful and sassy, she had excellent judgment. Normally he was the only one who made comments about how annoying his brother-in-law was—it was nice to have someone on his side for once. It felt like he had a sexy partner in crime and they were sharing a private joke. It was pretty damn awesome.

Clearing his throat and forcing himself to look away, he said, "Believe me, I know. I've been trying to tell him to shut it for years, but he's yet to listen."

She shook her head. "His wife must have the patience of a saint."

"She does."

Then she smiled at him and he knew he needed to move away before he did something stupid like—

No sooner had the thought entered his mind than he began to lose his grip on his plate. It tilted and the food was going to fall, but he couldn't do anything about it. His left hand wouldn't cooperate, and between that and the sling, he was about to embarrass himself.

"Oh! Let me help you!" she said, instantly reaching out and saving his plate. Holding it for him, she said, "Where are you sitting? I can carry it over for you." She smiled again, and this time he wasn't happy about it at all.

With nothing more than a murmured "excuse me," he turned and walked out of the yard. He knew people were watching, some even called after him, but he didn't care. He cursed under his breath and called himself every kind of name in the book, but it didn't do a thing to make him feel any better. He was so useless, so pathetic, that he couldn't hold on to a paper plate on his own? This was what he'd been reduced to? And on top of that, he had to find that out in front of a beautiful woman? How unfair was that?

He was pulling open the front door of his parents' house when his father caught up to him and held the door so he couldn't move it. Jack Hannigan wasn't a small man—Bobby took after him in height, but his father was built more like a linebacker. "Bobby? You okay?"

Suddenly it was all just too much. He turned and he snapped. "No! No, I'm not all right, Dad! As a matter of fact, I'm the opposite of all right! I'm tired of this!" He motioned to his arm, the sling, his shoulder. "I have hit my limit, okay? I've had enough of not being able to do things for myself!"

He assumed his father would try to calm him down.

He assumed wrong.

"Really? So what are you going to do about it?" his father asked. "All this time you've been recovering, I've been waiting for you to be a little proactive, but instead you've moped around and griped and complained. You're making everyone crazy!"

"*I'm* making…?" he sputtered.

"Yes, *you're* making," his father threw his words back at him. "At first we were all sympathetic, but I have to tell you, Son, you're exhausting us. You're healing exactly as the doctors said you would. There haven't been any surprises. Even Friday's appointment shouldn't have been news to you. You live with yourself every damn day—you can't honestly stand here and say you were surprised when the doctor told you that you didn't have great mobility!"

He had a point.

Bobby was about to argue, just on principle, but his father cut him off.

"I get that you're frustrated, son. I do, and I'm sorry. This is an awful situation and I can't even begin to imagine how disappointed you are—"

"No, you can't."

"But that doesn't give you the right to be rude or disrespectful. You need to go and apologize to Teagan."

For a minute, Bobby could only stare. "Who?"

"Teagan. She was the one you left holding your plate while you stomped off. Seems to me she was just trying to help you—after you made a glutton out of yourself with that mountain of food, I might add—and you rudely left her standing there with it."

"First of all, I wasn't being a glutton, and...wait, who the hell is Teagan?"

"I just told you."

"No, no, I get that, but I mean, who is she? How does she know the Shaughnessys?"

"James and Catherine—Ian's cousin and his wife who went on the cruise with us—she's their daughter. They all just moved here."

"Oh."

"And Teagan's renting Anna's old place."

His stomach sank. "Oh." Not only had he made a complete fool of himself, but chances were that if he stayed here, he was going to see her again.

A lot.

Dammit.

Bobby's head fell back as he let out an irritated breath. "I'm not going back there, Dad. As a matter of fact, I had planned on asking you to drive me home tomorrow so I can just…you know, finish this recovery back in Myrtle Beach."

His father didn't speak for a long moment. "So you're going to run away?"

His eyes went wide. "Excuse me? I don't think going home is running away. Gimme a break!"

"Unfortunately that's what I've *been* doing and look where it's gotten you!" Jack cried.

"Dad! What the hell?" How was this happening? Where was his mild-mannered father?

"I don't think going back to Myrtle Beach is the answer, Bobby. I know right now you think it is, but you're wrong. Now that we're being honest with each other, I think we can finally move forward. We're all here to help you, you know."

Seriously? "There's nothing you or anyone else can do, Dad. This is all on me and no one else. Believe me, I wish there was something you could do—wish there was some way someone else could take away the pain and disappointment, but there isn't. And as long as I stay here, the longer I'm going to sit around and just…I don't know, do nothing."

"Why?" Jack challenged. "Why are you willing to sit here and do nothing, but you think you won't do that back home?"

"Because here I have people around me willing to help. I don't have to put in an effort. I tried it while you were away and lasted all of five days, and then I knew I could run to Anna. I'm getting soft sitting here, and that's no way for me to be. It's not going to get me back on the force!"

His father studied him for a long time.

Then he seemed to admit defeat. With a curt nod, he said, "Fine. If you want to go back to Myrtle Beach, I'll take you. I won't stop you."

Bobby let out a sigh of relief. "Thank you."

"But…"

Great, here it comes.

"You'll have to tell your mother. I'm not doing it for you. And you're going to go back over to the Shaughnessys and not only apologize to Teagan, but you're going to apologize to everyone for making a scene."

"I did not make a scene!"

"Take it or leave it, son. You want a ride back home, this is how you'll get it."

"Dad, come on. Be reasonable."

"I am. Now it's your turn to be an adult." He started to walk away. "I'll see you over at the Shaughnessys," he called over his shoulder, but he kept walking.

For several minutes, he stood on the front porch, still a little stunned by what had just gone down. His father was threatening not to drive him home if he didn't fall in line and go apologize? Seriously? Part of him was incredibly pissed. "What am I, twelve?"

He'd find another way home.

Bobby was about to open the front door when he saw one of the kids sneaking out the Shaughnessys' gate. He stood back and watched to see who was being bold enough to leave the yard. Peeking out, he was surprised that he didn't recognize the kid. Was he a friend of one of the Shaughnessy kids? Moving to the steps, he quietly climbed down and watched as the boy—who couldn't be more than five or six—went and sat under the massive oak tree in Ian's front yard.

He took a closer look and saw the kid looked like he was crying.

Well, damn.

He waited for a minute or two to see if anyone would come looking for the little boy, but when no one did, he walked over. The kid looked up at him with the biggest eyes he'd ever seen on such a small face. They were dark brown and so sad he almost felt himself tearing up.

"Hey, bud," he said casually. "Whatcha doing out here? The party's in the yard."

The kid shook his head. "I wanna go home." He looked down at the grass.

Crouching in front of him, Bobby did his best to keep his voice calm and soothing. Part of his job meant talking to school kids, and he'd even helped his share of lost ones. Smiling, he said, "I know what you mean."

Looking up, the dark eyes went wide. "You do?"

Nodding, Bobby said, "Uh-huh. I was trying to go home, too. But it turns out I need to stay for a little bit longer."

"How come?"

Unable to help himself, he laughed softly. "Because my dad told me to." He thought for sure the kid would be able to relate, only…

"I don't have a dad," he said sadly.

Without a thought, Bobby sat down on the grass beside him. "I'm sorry," he said gently.

Shrugging, the kid stayed silent.

"So how come you're out here when everyone's back there?" he asked, hoping to change the subject.

"Pops is too busy to play with me." Big tears rolled down his chubby cheeks. "I kept asking and he kept saying later, but then I asked again and he still said later! So I said if he wouldn't play with me, I was going to go home." He crossed his little arms defiantly over his chest. "And he didn't even care!"

This was all more than a little confusing. So if the kid didn't have a father, who was Pops? For that matter, he should probably ask his name just so he could call him something other than "kid."

"I'm Bobby, by the way," he said, holding out his hand. "And you are…?"

"Lucas!" someone called out.

A female someone.

Bobby didn't have to turn around to recognize the husky voice. He looked at the kid—Lucas—with more than a hint of shock. This was her kid? Quickly, he came to his feet and faced her.

Teagan.

Studying her approach, he realized the name kind of fit. She gave him only a cursory glance before she dropped to her knees in front of her son.

"You scared me half to death," she said fiercely but lovingly, right before she picked up the boy and wrapped him in her arms. "You know you're not supposed to leave the yard."

It was fascinating to watch. He didn't know either of them and yet he could see how strong their bond was. Lucas rested his head on his mother's shoulder even as he continued to cry. "Pops didn't care when I said I was going home."

Teagan pulled back and cupped her son's face in her hands. "Oh, sweetie, yes he did. We've been looking all over the house for you!"

"But he wouldn't play with me!" he cried.

"Sweetie, he's talking with his friends and he knew there were a lot of kids here for you to play with," she said sweetly. "There are so many of them back there, I can't even remember all of their names."

Lucas straightened and pulled out of her embrace a little. "I know all their names!" he said excitedly.

"You do?" she asked, sounding impressed.

"Uh-huh!" he nodded vigorously. "C'mon, I'll prove it!" Then, taking his mother's hand, he led her toward the yard. Bobby followed quietly.

Teagan noticed, because she looked over her shoulder at him and quietly said, "Thank you."

He smiled and nodded, holding the gate open for them to walk through. When everyone spotted them, he felt beyond foolish. Luckily, everyone was so relieved that Lucas had been found that no one paid much attention to Bobby.

Without a word, his father walked over and handed him a plate of food. "Go sit and I'll grab you a fresh beer."

"Thanks, Dad," he murmured with a sheepish grin.

He was seated and halfway through his burger when Teagan came and sat beside him. Unsure of what to say, he simply finished chewing.

"Thank you," she said.

Bobby offered her a small smile. "I didn't really do anything. I just happened to be at the right place at the right time."

"Not according to Lucas," she said with her own grin.

"What do you mean?"

"Well, according to him you were like a giant who stopped him from running away," she explained. "And you were trying to run away too, but your dad made you stay."

He could feel his cheeks flaming hot with embarrassment.

"He said that was the coolest thing, since he'd never heard of a grown-up getting in trouble. If I hadn't come out, he thought the two of you could have hung out together. Honestly, he was a little annoyed I showed up when I did," she admitted with a nervous laugh.

"I would have brought him to the yard sooner," Bobby said defensively, "but I was trying to figure out who he was and what was wrong. I was just asking him that when you came out."

Teagan reached over and placed her hand on his and gently squeezed. "I wasn't saying you did anything wrong." Her tone was soft, reassuring. "By the way, I'm Teagan. And you're...Bobby, right? Anna's brother?"

Still feeling more than a little embarrassed, he nodded. "It's nice to meet you."

"Same here."

As awkward as it would be, he needed to rectify things. "Listen, about what happened earlier...you know, when I walked away..."

"You don't need to say anything, Bobby. It's not a big deal."

He kind of liked the way she said his name. It probably wasn't the best time to be noticing that.

"No, it is," he countered. "As you can see, I'm recovering and my arm just isn't getting the memo to heal as quickly as I'd like. So when the plate started to slip...I don't know, I just snapped." He paused, hating having to admit any of this. "I don't like needing help. Ask anyone. I've been the worst patient."

Just then, Quinn walked over and grabbed the bottle of ketchup next to Bobby's plate. "True story," he said with a grin before walking away.

Bobby shook his head and laughed. "He really is a pain in the ass."

He was pleased when Teagan laughed with him. "The last time I saw Quinn, I was about twelve, and he was obnoxious then. I just figured he'd grow out of it."

"Yeah, well..." Bobby caught Quinn looking at them and frowned. "He's not so bad. Of course I kind of have to say that, since he's married to my sister, but it's mostly true."

Teagan looked at him as if she didn't believe him before leaning in and whispering, "It's okay if you don't really mean it. It will be our little secret."

And damn if her breath on his face wasn't a turn-on as well.

He'd already walked away from her once, so he had no choice but to sit and suffer in silence right now. The safest thing for him to do was find something to talk about that would keep his mind off of her breath on his skin or how soft her hand felt on his—a hand that was still there.

Interesting.

Slowly, he took his hand away and picked up his burger. "I hear you and Lucas just moved to town. How are you liking things so far?"

"Me? I'm loving it. The beaches are fantastic. I'm renting Anna's old place, as you probably know, and I love it."

"And Lucas?"

Her slim shoulder lifted in a small shrug. "He's not quite on board yet."

"There's a lot of things for kids to do around here. If you ask Anna or any of the Shaughnessys, I'm sure they'll be able to give you some suggestions."

"Oh, they have. Believe me," she said. "Lucas and I have gone to the aquarium and we've gone shell collecting... We're having fun. Once school starts, we'll both be busy, so I'm enjoying this time to settle in."

"Where did you live before?"

"Colorado." She explained about her life growing up with a military father, and how they'd finally settled when her father got stationed at Fort Carson.

He finished eating as she talked and found it fascinating how she'd moved around so much. Bobby had only ever lived on the North Carolina coast before moving an hour south—to the South Carolina coast. He couldn't help feeling a little inferior to her. He'd been perfectly content living and working in his home town for the longest time, then he'd gone and done something stupid and felt the need to immediately move on. Not his greatest moment, but he didn't regret the move. Up until he got shot, it had been really good for him. But where did it leave him now?

What if he didn't get clearance to go back to work? Would he stay in Myrtle Beach or move home?

"Bobby?"

He turned back and realized Teagan was looking at him oddly.

"You okay? You kind of zoned out there for a minute and then your expression got pretty fierce."

"Yeah, um…sorry. My mind wandered and I started thinking of things I'm really trying not to think about." Would he ever be able to not embarrass himself in front of her? "Sorry."

For some reason, her sympathetic smile made him feel better in a way no one else's had.

"You're dealing with a fairly traumatic injury. I'm sure you can't help but be in your head more than you want to be."

He knew he was staring, but…she understood. "Yeah, well. I'm getting kind of tired of it, and so is everyone around me."

Now it was her turn to look fierce. "Tell them they get to have an opinion when they've been shot."

Wow. Just…wow. "You wouldn't mind standing up on the table and saying that to the group, would you?"

He was only partially kidding.

Teagan glanced around the yard, and from the stern look she was giving the crowd, Bobby thought she was seriously considering it.

Now he was truly impressed. Not that he was looking to have her—or anyone—fight his battles, but after the argument he'd just had with his father, it was more tempting to consider it.

She straightened in her chair. "I hate when people try to tell you how you're supposed to think, act, or feel when you've suffered some kind of trauma or loss."

"Speaking from experience?" he asked and immediately regretted it. She opened her mouth to answer and then seemed to think better of it.

Instead, she stood and smiled warmly at him. "Don't let anyone get to you. You're entitled to feel the way you feel." She looked over to where Lucas was playing and waved. "Now if you'll excuse me, I'm going to finish letting my son introduce me to all the kids."

Bobby was enjoying the view as she walked away when someone smacked him on the back of the head. He turned to see Quinn glaring at him.

"Watch where you're looking, dumbass," he said before walking away.

A slow grin crossed Bobby's face. It wasn't the only reason he'd be watching Teagan, but knowing that it annoyed Quinn just made it so much more fun.

––––––––

A week later, Bobby was standing on Anna's doorstep smiling at the shocked expression on her face.

"Bobby? What...? How...? Does this mean...?"

As much as he wanted to shout that everything was perfect, he was completely healed and ready to go back to work, he couldn't. "I only have to wear the sling for a couple of hours a day, and I got cleared to drive."

She launched herself at him for a big hug and it felt good to wrap both arms around her with only mild discomfort. When she pulled back, she was grinning from ear to ear. "And on your first car ride on your own you chose to come and see your favorite sister!"

"Only sister," he corrected and laughed when she stuck her tongue out at him.

Anna stepped aside and motioned for him to come into the house. "So what does this all mean? Are you heading back to your place now or are you going to stay in town?"

"Honestly, I'm not sure. I've been working with the local doctors and I'm already starting physical therapy here, so I thought it would probably be easier to just stay for a little longer. It's not like I can go back to work yet."

The house was way too quiet. Sitting down on the sofa in the family room, he looked around. "Where are the kids?"

"Bailey and Brian are napping, and Kaitlyn's at a playdate with Lucas."

That piqued his curiosity. "As in Teagan's Lucas?"

She nodded and then looked at her phone. "I'm supposed to pick her up in an hour. I didn't expect the kids to nap so long and I'm kind of relishing the silence." She paused and seemed to think for a minute. "I'll call Quinn and ask him to pick her up. No big deal." Then she gave him her full attention. "So? How does it feel to have your arm out of the sling and have a little more freedom to move around?"

He laughed softly. "Right now it's still a little weird. I find myself still holding my arm in that position. But I think I'm going to sleep like a baby tonight."

She nodded. "I imagine sleeping with the sling couldn't have been comfortable."

"It wasn't. Believe me." And as much as he didn't mind talking about it, he couldn't help thinking about Teagan. They'd talked some more at the barbecue last weekend and he found she hadn't been far from his mind all week. She intrigued him, and not just because she was a beautiful woman. She was smart and funny, and pretty insightful. All of that packaged together was damned appealing.

"Although I'm sure you'd be sleeping even better in your own bed," Anna commented.

"Technically, I am," he said with a wink. "It just happens to be my childhood bed."

"Be thankful Mom didn't put the Batman sheets back on them for you."

This time he laughed harder. "A full-size bed is no match for a king, that's for sure. So yeah, ideally I'd like to be sleeping in the one I have at my place."

"Maybe you should be looking for a place here? How long will you be doing therapy?"

"Six weeks minimum. And if it really gets to me, I can commute. It's not like I've got anything else to do." He paused. "If you hadn't rented out your place, I would have loved to stay there."

Anna nodded. "It's a great house and, really, I almost wish you could have."

"How come?"

"The last tenant wasn't the greatest and there's some work that needs to be done to the place. But then Quinn's aunt and uncle came to visit with Teagan and Lucas and…" She shrugged. "As soon as I mentioned the house as an option, they all fell in love with it. Teagan's been great and she said she doesn't mind doing some of the work on the house, like painting and all that, but I still kind of feel bad. If you were living there, I'd give you the whole list to handle."

"Nice. I'm recovering and you're looking for cheap labor," he said with mock offense.

"Free labor," she corrected him. "I wasn't planning on paying you."

"Such a brat," he said with a weary sigh. "So what's wrong with the house?"

"Some of it's just cosmetic. Quinn painted the whole

inside before they moved in and we had a cleaning crew come in, but the bathrooms need some work. I'd love to put a new shower and vanity in the full bath."

He nodded. "That's not a huge job. I'm sure Quinn could do it in a weekend."

"And then there's the roof…"

"What's wrong with the roof?"

"The last hurricane blew off a lot of the shingles and we replaced them, but we had Aidan go over and look at it, and he said the whole roof really needed to be replaced."

"He couldn't give you a deal on that?" Bobby asked. Aidan Shaughnessy was one of the best builders in the business and Quinn's brother. It seemed like a no-brainer.

"He said he'd get the materials for us and help Quinn do the work himself, but we just haven't had the time. And honestly, neither has Aidan. He's got another new development going up and people are buying the homes faster than he can build them!"

"Okay so roof, bathroom… What else is wrong with the house?"

"I don't know, Bobby, it's just a rental, but that doesn't mean I shouldn't want to make improvements."

"Is Teagan complaining?" he asked, even though he was pretty certain she wasn't.

"Of course not, but she's family and I guess I feel a little embarrassed that the place isn't nicer."

"That's all in your head and you know it."

"Some of it, maybe. But Quinn's going over there this weekend to fix a leak under the kitchen sink. I'm afraid once this gets fixed, it will just keep going."

"Why are you looking for trouble?"

"I'm a homeowner, I know how these things work. As soon as one thing breaks, it's like the whole house knows and suddenly wants attention."

"Now you're being dramatic."

Anna yawned and got more comfortable on the opposite couch. "Maybe. I'll look at it when I go pick up Kaitlyn."

"I thought you were going to ask Quinn to do it?"

Another yawn. "Oh, right. Damn. I probably should have napped while the kids were sleeping, huh?"

And that was when inspiration struck.

"Tell you what, why don't you try and get in a short nap now and I'll go pick up Kaitlyn. I've got Mom's car, so there's already a booster seat back there," he said as he stood. "What do you think?"

But his sister was already curling up on the couch. "Don't let the door hit you in the butt on the way out."

He leaned down and kissed the top of her head.

"Thanks, Bobby," she said, her eyes already closed. "You're a real lifesaver."

He wasn't going to argue.

Gardening was probably Teagan's least favorite activity, but Lucas and Kaitlyn were playing in the yard, so it made sense for her to weed out some of the overgrown flower bed to pass the time. She had already filled one giant trash bag, her hands were filthy, and there were two more beds to get to.

Clearly, she should have thought this through before trying to tackle a job so large.

Her mother had offered to come over and help and she

definitely should have accepted the offer. Her mother had a green thumb and a love of all things "plant." Not Teagan. She couldn't seem to find any joy or pleasure in this particular activity, and she wondered if anyone would care if she just stopped now.

"Knock, knock!" someone called from the gate.

Turning, it wasn't hard to see who it was—the white picket fence was short—and she smiled when she saw Bobby standing there. She waved and said, "Hey! Come on back!"

And damn did he look good when he followed her instruction.

He was tall and trim, and in the faded jeans and snug black T-shirt he was wearing, she could tell he was pretty muscular. Then she gasped.

"Your arm! No more sling!"

He smiled and she felt her knees go a little weak. Okay, so her memory hadn't been exaggerating when she'd thought about him. He was truly *that* good-looking. Sandy brown hair that was just a bit shaggy, and a killer smile—he made one very yummy package.

Oh crap! Am I blushing?

Teagan's hands flew to her cheeks just in case.

"Yeah, I got the news today that I only have to wear the sling for a couple of hours a day," he said. His voice was deep and warm and right now, he sounded genuinely happy.

"Good for you!"

"Thanks."

They stood there for a moment before Teagan finally found her voice again. "So, what brings you by?"

"Oh, uh... I was over at Anna's today and she

mentioned Kaitlyn was here. She was exhausted, Bailey and Brian were napping, and since I'm allowed to drive again, I offered to come and pick up Kaitlyn so she could catch a couple of z's."

"That was very sweet of you." And he's a nice guy to boot? She didn't think men like him existed.

Bobby glanced at the flower bed. "You put a good dent in that mess. Do you enjoy gardening?"

She chuckled. "Not even a little bit, but the kids were out here playing, so it seemed like the thing to do." Before she could say anything else, Kaitlyn and Lucas spotted him and came running over.

"Uncle Bobby! What are you doing here!" Kaitlyn said as she jumped into his arms.

Teagan immediately noticed how he turned so Kaitlyn would land more on his right side and she couldn't help but feel for him.

"Your mom needed to take a nap, so I said I'd come and pick up my favorite girl," he said, tapping a finger on his niece's nose. "Maybe you and I can grab some ice cream on the way home."

Kaitlyn's blue eyes went wide. "Really? And I don't have to share with Brian?"

He shook his head. "Nope. It can be a special Kaitlyn-only treat. So what do you say? You up for a date with your old uncle?"

"Yes!" she cried.

"Mom," Lucas said from beside her. "Can we have ice cream too? We have a bunch of it in the freezer. Maybe Bobby and Kaitlyn can stay and we can make sundaes! Can we? Huh? Can we please?"

She crouched down next to her son. "I don't know,

Lucas. It sounds like Bobby has plans with Kaitlyn and—"

"I want to stay and make sundaes here!" Kaitlyn chimed in, squirming out of Bobby's arms. "Can we stay, Uncle Bobby? Please? Pretty please?"

When Teagan looked up at Bobby, he had a lopsided grin on his face that was almost as comical as the look on both the smaller faces. "If it's too much trouble," he said, "we can totally take a raincheck."

Part of her liked the idea of him wanting to come back again. She rose slowly to her feet and looked at the three of them with a smile. "No trouble at all. Although I don't think I have all the makings for sundaes, but we can improvise." She led the way into the house and directed the kids to wash their hands in the bathroom while she did the same at the kitchen sink. When she was done, she pulled open the cabinet doors beneath the sink and groaned.

"Problem?"

She shut the doors and sighed. "Not really. There's a small leak under the sink and I've got a pot under there to catch the water so the cabinets don't get damaged, but it looks like it's getting a little worse."

"May I?" he asked, coming to stand beside her. Stepping back, Teagan watched as Bobby crouched down, opened the cabinet doors, and looked inside. Then she took another step back and found herself admiring how snug his jeans fit across a very fine ass.

The sound of feet running down the hallway had her instantly turning around guiltily. "Okay, let's see what we have to choose from!" she said, knowing she sounded overly enthusiastic.

The next time she looked, the upper half of Bobby was under the sink. He was on his back and now she had to admire how snug his jeans were in the front.

"…and I want chocolate ice cream with a banana and chocolate syrup and nuts and sprinkles and a cherry on top! Mom! Mom!! Did you hear me?"

Teagan looked at her son in mild confusion. "Um… what?"

"My sundae! I just gave you my order for my sundae!" Then he started cracking up. He and Kaitlyn were sitting at the kitchen island on the two stools she kept there. "It's like we're at an ice cream shop and you're working behind the counter, right, Kaitlyn?"

The little girl giggled and nodded her head.

"Okay, so you wanted plain vanilla ice cream, right?" Teagan teased and when both kids started laughing all over again, she couldn't help but join in.

"Mom."

"Oh, no—wait, it was…strawberry ice cream with… raisins!"

"Yuck! No way!" Lucas said between laughing fits.

"Wait…wait…now I remember," she said, touching a finger to her chin. "You wanted some peanut butter and pickles instead!"

"Ew, gross, Mom!"

She sighed dramatically. "Then I guess you'll have to remind me because I have no clue what you wanted."

"Me and Kaitlyn both want chocolate ice cream with a banana—"

"Like a banana split!" Kaitlyn said.

"—with chocolate syrup and nuts and sprinkles, with a cherry on top!"

"Hmm… That sounds like a really big sundae," Teagan said thoughtfully. "You sure you're going to be able to eat it all?"

Both kids nodded.

"Okay, two chocolate banana splits coming up!" When she turned to walk to the freezer, she glanced over at Bobby, who was still under the sink. Rather than bother him with silly questions and distractions, she'd wait until he was done.

The kids were chattering as she pulled the ice cream from the freezer. Bowls, toppings, spoons—she began making the kids' sundaes first. Just as she was placing their bowls in front of them, Bobby stood up and washed his hands in the sink—watching the water continue to drip into the pot below.

"Well? What do you think?" she asked, handing him a towel to dry his hands.

"I'm no plumber, but it all looks bad. I can see some spots that look loose, so I'd say we should start by replacing some of the fittings."

"Fittings?"

He nodded. "It's not a big job. I can run to the hardware store and grab everything I'd need."

"Oh," she said, somewhat flustered. "Quinn said he'd come by this weekend and do it."

But he waved her off. "It's not really a big deal. Why wait? Besides, I know how busy Quinn is and I'm sure Anna would appreciate him being home with her and the kids."

It made sense, but she felt bad putting him to work.

"Besides," he went on, as if sensing her hesitation, "I used to live here too. When Anna bought the place,

I lived here with her for a year to help out with some of the work and the bills. I'm familiar with the plumbing here."

"Are you sure? I feel really bad asking you to do this. Your first day of sling freedom and you want to work on my home repairs?" she asked with a nervous laugh.

He chuckled and shrugged. "It will feel good to be productive after sitting around for so long."

Again, it made sense, so maybe she should just say thank you and move on.

Bobby leaned on the island, looking at the kids. "So neither of you is willing to share, is that what you're saying?" he teased. "Just one bite?"

Lucas was laughing and Kaitlyn—begrudgingly—scooped a tiny bit of her sundae onto her spoon and held it out to him. "Just one," she said firmly.

For a minute, Teagan thought he'd tell his niece no or to forget about it, but instead he took the spoon and ate the small amount there while making silly lip-smacking noises that delighted both kids.

"You're funny, Uncle Bobby!"

"I know, I know," he said, straightening. When he turned to Teagan, he said, "If you don't mind Kaitlyn hanging out here for a bit longer, I can run to the store now."

"I don't mind at all, but what about your ice cream?" she asked and suddenly felt very lame.

He smiled and it was lethal. "I'll save it for when I'm done." With a wink, he was on the move. At the front door he turned back. "Would you mind calling Anna and letting her know I'll have Kaitlyn home a little bit later?"

"Um, sure. No problem."

And then he was gone. Teagan stared at the door for a solid minute before Lucas got her attention.

"Mom, I think the ice cream's melting on the counter!"

That spurred her into action and in minutes the ice cream was cleaned up, all the sundae makings put away, and both kids were covered in chocolate.

"Go wash up and then you can play," she told them.

"Can we watch a movie?" Lucas asked and Teagan agreed.

"I'll pull up Netflix while you two get cleaned up, okay?"

"Yay!"

Ten minutes later, the kids were sitting quietly on the couch watching *The Secret Life of Pets*. Once she saw they were settled, she called Anna and told her what was going on.

"That's so weird," Anna said.

"How come?"

"Because Bobby and I were just talking about all that and he knew Quinn was going to take care of it this weekend. Why would he offer instead?"

"I don't know, but it seemed like he was excited about having something to do. I mean, I didn't ask him for help," she quickly explained. "He just happened to be in the kitchen when I checked the pot under the sink."

"It's okay, Teagan."

"I don't want you to think I was complaining or I was being ungrateful or anything."

"That wasn't what I meant at all, but—"

"And then he was gone before he could even have his ice cream, and I'm sure it's not going to take long and—"

"Wait, ice cream? What ice cream?"

After a brief explanation about how they came about making sundaes, she heard Anna laugh. "What's so funny?"

"My brother has the biggest sweet tooth of anyone I've ever met. He must really be desperate for something to do if he was willing to wait to have a sundae." She sounded amused. "I never thought I'd see the day Bobby would put off dessert. Miracles never cease, huh?"

"Kaitlyn gave him a small taste of hers."

"And knowing my daughter, it was a *very* small taste. She takes right after him, the little stinker. She never even lets *me* have a bite of her dessert."

"She made him work for it, believe me," Teagan said, laughing as she remembered how silly he'd been.

"Oh, he doesn't mind that. He's great with the kids. I know Kaitlyn, Brian, and Bailey are his biological nieces and nephew, but he treats all the Shaughnessy kids the same. He's the fun uncle and they all go wild when he's around. I'm glad he's finally coming out of his funk, because the kids were all getting a little freaked out."

"Well, I'm sure it hasn't been easy for him. Especially being the fun uncle and not being able to play with the kids like they're all used to." She thought of how he'd shifted to pick up Kaitlyn and knew the last two months had probably been even harder to explain.

"It was rough. Every time we saw him, I had to remind the kids to be gentle. One day, Brian jumped on him and I swear I thought Bobby was going to cry. I saw it on his face. Brian didn't mean to hurt him, but he's little and doesn't really pay attention to the rules sometimes."

"One time, when Lucas was about three, my dad

had thrown his back out. He was miserable and in so much pain. We went over to visit, and as much as I warned him not to jump on Pop, he ran in the door and did just that. It was the first time I ever saw tears in my father's eyes."

"Oh man. That had to be hard."

"Big time."

Anna sighed. "So Bobby's going to fix the sink, and you're sure you don't mind Kaitlyn hanging out longer?"

"She's been great. No trouble at all."

"I hate taking advantage."

"You're not," Teagan said lightly. "She and Lucas are watching a movie, and by the time it's over, Bobby should be done with the repairs. I promise to call when they're leaving here so you'll know when to expect them."

"Thanks, Teagan. And next time the kids can play here so you can have some time to yourself."

"I don't even know what I'd do with myself!"

"There's a great salon in town about a block over from the pub. They do hair and nails, and it's the perfect spot for a little pampering. If you're interested, I'll text you their number and whenever you want to go, Lucas can stay and hang out here with us, okay?"

It sounded glorious.

It wasn't as though she never got time for herself, because her folks were usually willing to babysit when she needed them. But after all the work with the move, it seemed like maybe she was a little more desperate than usual to have some time just for her.

"I'm definitely going to take you up on that. Text me their number and I'll make the appointment and get back to you."

"Good girl."

They hung up and Teagan went back to work. When Bobby knocked on her door twenty minutes later, she'd cleared out under the sink, put a couple of towels down by the open cabinet, and made sure the water to the house was shut off. And he was carrying a lot more material than she was expecting.

"What's all this?" she asked as he walked in.

"If I'm going to replace the pipes underneath, it just makes sense to replace the faucet too. It's kind of old and the sink was looking a bit rough, and they had them on sale, so…"

"Bobby," she began, walking behind him through the house, "it's too much! It was just a small leak. You don't need to do all of his!"

He looked at her and grinned. "Don't worry. I'm billing Quinn for all of it." Then he winked and set himself up in front of the sink. As he lowered himself to the floor and slid under the sink, he called out, "And I'll skip the banana on my sundae, but lots of chocolate ice cream, chocolate syrup, whipped cream, and sprinkles, please!"

Laughing, she walked out of the kitchen to check on the kids—she could easily see them from the kitchen but figured Bobby might appreciate it if she wasn't hovering while he worked.

Lucas and Kaitlyn were thoroughly engrossed in their movie and after a few minutes, Teagan knew she needed to find something to do with herself. She started picking up the toys the kids had scattered across the house. Off in the distance she heard several muttered curses coming from under the sink and cringed each time. She was always careful to watch her language in front of her son and she was sure Quinn and Anna were the same way, but she hated the idea of going out there and scolding Bobby, however gently. Especially when he was doing something to help her.

The next sound she heard was filled with pain, and that was when she went running.

"Bobby? Are you okay?" He was holding his shoulder and grimacing in pain. He hissed out a breath and she knew he must have strained himself too hard. Dropping to her knees beside him, she gently said, "Come on, come out of there and sit up."

He was already on the move, but he glared at her. When he was sitting up, he was still holding his shoulder. "I'm fine."

If he hadn't been gritting his teeth, she might have believed him.

"What can I do?" she asked, more than a little concerned. "Ibuprofen? Ice?"

Bobby blinked at her and seemed to take a moment to compose himself. Then he let out a long breath and lowered his hand. "I'm sorry," he said gruffly. "I twisted when I shouldn't have. I wasn't thinking. Then I lost the grip on the wrench and—" he hissed out a curse and Teagan instantly looked over her shoulder to make sure the kids didn't hear him. When he realized what she was doing, he hung his head. "Sorry."

"It's okay. They didn't hear you," she said softly. Unable to help herself, she reached out and placed a hand on his forearm. "I'm serious, Bobby, what can I get you?"

He scanned her face. His eyes were a gorgeous shade of gray, and his look was intense, and Teagan felt it like a caress. It was wrong, but she felt a strong pull to lean into him. It was something she hadn't experienced in a long time, for years, and she started to freak.

"I just need a minute. I may have bitten off more than I could chew on this project," he admitted sheepishly. "If it's okay with you, I'm going to finish with the pipes and I'll come back tomorrow to replace the sink and faucet."

"You really don't have to," she told him. "I'm sure Quinn can come and finish it for you."

It was clearly the wrong thing to say. The look on his face turned fierce and she knew she had offended him. "What I mean is—"

He held up a hand to stop her. "It's fine. I get it. You don't think I can handle it." Carefully, he lay back down and slid under the sink. "I'll be out of your way as soon as possible."

"Bobby," she pleaded, but he wasn't listening. "That's not what I meant."

She watched him finish changing out the pipe with impressive efficiency, especially since he was in pain. In that moment, Teagan knew she had two choices. She could sit here and wait him out and try to explain herself again, or she could be a woman of action.

Climbing to her feet, she stepped away and grabbed her phone, dialing Anna's number.

"Hey! Are they on their way?" Anna asked when she answered the phone.

"No, not yet. The kids are finishing a movie and your brother's not quite done."

"Oh, okay."

"Listen, the reason I'm calling is because Bobby

bought some extra stuff for the job—new faucet, new sink, the whole nine yards."

"Oh no."

"No, no, no. It's not a problem, but I just wanted you to let Quinn know it's all under control. You guys should plan to do something fun as a family this weekend. We've got this all under control here."

For a minute, Anna didn't seem able to form a response. Then she cleared her throat. "Well then…okay. Wow. Thanks. Tell my brother I said—you know what? I'll tell him myself when he brings Kaitlyn home. I'm sorry it turned into a bigger job for you. Is it a mess?"

"Not even a little bit," Teagan replied, noticing Bobby coming to his feet and looking at her curiously. "So yeah, tell Quinn to take you and the kids someplace this weekend and enjoy yourselves. There's nothing for him to do here."

When she hung up a minute later, she gave Bobby a very satisfied grin. And before he could say a word, she strode over to the freezer and pulled out the ice cream. Looking at him over her shoulder, she said, "Chocolate ice cream, no bananas, chocolate syrup, whipped cream, and sprinkles, right?"

He nodded.

"And since you worked so hard, I'll even let you have a cherry on top," she said saucily and was extremely pleased when he burst out laughing.

Chapter 3

Two days later, Quinn knocked on Teagan's door.

"Oh—hey!" she said, somewhat confused. "What are you doing here?" She noted the toolbox in his hands and sighed.

Bobby wasn't coming back.

Smiling, she stepped aside and motioned for her cousin to come in. "There really wasn't any rush on this."

Quinn waved her off as he walked over to the kitchen. "It's not a big deal. This will be quick, especially since Bobby already bought everything. I just need to switch it all out. I'll be here an hour, tops."

The curiosity was killing her. Why had Quinn come over instead of Bobby? When he had left the other day, he told her he'd be back and had sworn his shoulder felt fine. Had he lied? Was he embarrassed or upset because she'd seen how badly he was still hurting?

She glanced over and saw Quinn was already setting up and getting started. Would it seem odd that she was asking?

Only one way to find out.

"So, um… I thought your brother-in-law was coming back to do this? That's what he said, anyway," she continued, hoping she sounded casual and not overly curious.

With a shrug, Quinn began cutting the caulk around the sink. "He went back home yesterday."

"Back?"

"Yeah, he lives in Myrtle Beach now. Since he got his clearance to drive, it seemed crazy for him to stay. My in-laws drove him home."

She shouldn't be disappointed, but she was. Bobby Hannigan was the first guy in a long time that Teagan had enjoyed hanging out with. The fact that he was also incredibly handsome was just a perk.

She hadn't even considered dating after Logan had died. Going back to school to get her master's degree and raising Lucas had kept her extremely busy, and she didn't even miss dating.

Until now.

And now she was missing it more than she thought she would.

It wasn't as if Bobby had asked her out. He hadn't even given a hint that he wanted to. But if he did, he would be the first man Teagan even considered saying yes to.

You know, should he ask.

And now he was gone.

With a small sigh, she turned toward the refrigerator. "Can I get you something to drink?"

"Nah, I'm good." He was crouching down to get under the sink. "Where's Lucas at?"

"Oh, my folks took him to Wilmington today. They were going to tour the USS *North Carolina*. He was very excited about it."

Quinn chuckled from under the sink. "I want to take Brian there when he gets a little bit older. I mentioned it to Kaitlyn once and she looked at me like I was crazy. She wasn't the least bit interested."

"It's probably more of a boy thing," she replied. "Plus Lucas has grown up near the army base, and he loves anything military related."

"I bet." He paused. "So how are you settling in?"

He couldn't see her, so she didn't even try to hide her mild disappointment. She was settling in all right overall, but at that moment she was restless and didn't know why.

"It's all going okay," she said. "We've had fun exploring and I'm enjoying having the beach so close by."

"It is definitely a perk."

"I hadn't been to one since the last time we came to visit your family when we were kids," she said with a small laugh. "I had forgotten how great it felt to have the sand between my toes."

"You know what's weird? I think we take it for granted since we live here. I mean, we go to the beach, but not nearly as often as you'd imagine. We have the pool in the yard and we tend to hang out there more."

"That must be nice."

"You and Lucas need to come over and swim. I think it's great that he and Kaitlyn have hit it off, and Anna can't stop talking about how much she likes you."

"I like her too," she said, leaning on the counter to watch him.

He crawled out from under the cabinet and stood to lift the old sink out. "I'll be right back." He took the sink and the old faucet out to the trash and came back a minute later. "Come over tomorrow, bring Lucas. We'll barbecue and swim and it will just be us—no big family hoopla, you know?"

"Sounds great. But shouldn't you run it by Anna first?"

He grinned. "Probably, but she's not going to mind. So let's plan on it, okay?"

Just then her dryer beeped, letting her know the cycle was done. Teagan excused herself and left Quinn to finish installing the sink while she folded laundry. And that's really when it hit her—she led a very boring life.

When her parents had offered to take Lucas for the day, she'd thought Bobby was coming over to finish with the sink. So she'd put a little extra care into her appearance and cleaned the house until it sparkled, and what did she have to show for it?

She was standing alone in her hallway folding towels. *Awesome.*

When she was done, she put the laundry away and made herself busy doing…nothing. There was nothing to do but walk in aimless circles.

Whole lot of good that did me.

Back in the kitchen, she saw Quinn tightening the new faucet. "Wow, it looks great!"

"Yeah, Bobby has good taste when he's spending my money," he replied with a deep laugh. "But it's definitely an improvement."

"There wasn't anything wrong with the old one, Quinn. It was really just the leak under the sink. I hate that you had to do all this."

He shrugged. "Anna and I have been talking about doing work on the house for a while. If you hadn't rented it, we probably would have let the place stay vacant for a while so we could get it all done. I know she feels bad that things aren't in better shape for you."

"Please, I grew up in military housing. This is way

better than some of the places we've lived. And I have to admit, the fact that it's just me and Lucas living here makes it even better."

He studied her for a minute. "You lived with your folks all this time?"

She nodded. "Except when I was away at college for undergrad. I did my master's closer to home, since I'd just had Lucas. It was easier to live with them so they could help with him."

Quinn leaned against the counter, his arms folded over his chest. "Damn, Teagan. I had no idea."

It wasn't as if her life was a secret or that she was ashamed. If things had been different—if Logan had lived—maybe people wouldn't feel so sorry for her. And after all this time, she had gotten used to the pity and knew how to handle it graciously.

"I'm lucky my folks were so willing to take us on. It had been a long time since they'd had a newborn in the house and they really spent more time with him than the average grandparent would have. But they were amazing, and with the way it all happened…well. I'm just very thankful for them."

"I always thought your folks were great," he said, picking up the trash from the installation as he talked. "And I think it's awesome how they've been there for you." He paused. "I guess that's why you all decided to make this move together, huh? It would have been hard to live so far apart."

"Honestly I didn't realize how serious they were about moving here. They mentioned it a time or two, but after we came to visit, it was like they couldn't leave Colorado fast enough!" She laughed at the memory. "I think Lucas and I could have stayed behind and been okay, but I felt like I was ready for a change. Plus, the job opportunity here was better than anything I was finding back home."

He nodded. "I get that. You have to go where the work is."

Even though she didn't say anything, her mind immediately went to Bobby. He had to go back to Myrtle Beach because that's where his home and his job were. Part of her wished he worked locally. Maybe then she'd get to see him again.

"I thought for a while there that you were sort of working all over the country." She changed the subject. "What made you settle here?"

Quinn picked up the last of the trash and placed it in a bag. "I always knew I'd open a shop here, but originally I figured I'd set it up and work here for a while and then move on and leave a crew in charge." He shrugged. "But once everything was underway it seemed like everyone else was moving back home and settling down." He grinned. "And then things got started between me and Anna, and I knew I couldn't leave."

It wasn't hard to tell how much the man loved his wife. "You two were friends forever as kids. It's amazing how you transitioned."

"Ask anyone and they'll tell you how blind I was to the fact that the perfect woman was right there in front of me and I didn't realize it."

With a knowing glance, she asked, "Do people remind you of it?"

He seemed amused. "All the time. Particularly her brother."

Well…if Quinn was the one to bring him up, then she guessed it was okay. "Really? He didn't approve?"

"That's putting it mildly," Quinn said, grimacing. "Although we've come a long way in the last several years. For the longest time—particularly when Anna and I started dating—Bobby was not happy about it at all."

"But you won him over?"

He chuckled. "I don't know if I'd go that far, but… we understand each other better now."

"I'm sure it makes things easier since you're family." There were dozens of questions swirling in her head that she wanted to ask, but she wasn't sure how. "You two seem like you have a…I don't know, respect for one another."

Shrugging, he said, "I know he was just looking out for his sister and I can respect that. I know I was harsh on guys Darcy dated when she was younger, and believe me when I say we all gave her husband hell when he first came around."

That sounded about right, she thought.

"Anyway, having Bobby living further away has certainly helped, but he comes back and visits often enough. He's even stayed with us a couple of times rather than at his parents' place, so I guess that's progress."

"Did he always work in Myrtle Beach?"

This time Quinn looked at her funny and she braced herself for him to catch on that she was fishing for information, but luckily, he didn't push the question. "Nah. He moved down there a few years ago. He'd been on the local police force here in town. There were some changes, he got a new partner—a woman—and…well, it didn't go well."

"He was against working with a woman?"

Now her cousin looked uncomfortable. "Not exactly."

"Then what?"

Rolling his eyes, Quinn picked up the bag of trash. "Let's just say he liked working with her a little…too much. Lines got blurred and he decided it would be best if he moved away."

"Wow. That's a bit drastic."

"That's Bobby. It's all black or white with him. There's no middle ground." Then he chuckled. "Plus, I think it was time for a change."

"How come?"

"He's dated every woman in town and never got serious with any of them. I think he was ready to move on to something new. New dating pool, new conquests, whatever. Either way, it was a good move for him." Without another word, Quinn walked out with the last of the trash. Two minutes later he was back. He turned the water on, tested the faucet, and checked under the sink to make sure everything was working properly. When he was satisfied, he faced Teagan. "All done!"

"Thanks again, Quinn. I appreciate you coming over to finish up."

"No problem. If I didn't know any better, I'd swear Bobby did this just to mess with me—letting me believe I'd have a day off and then taking it away from me." It was said lightly, like he was joking, but suddenly Teagan had to wonder if that had truly been Bobby's motive.

And that thought annoyed her. The last thing she wanted was to be some sort of pawn in a childish game.

"You sure I can't get you something to drink?"

"Nah, I'm gonna head home. We're taking the kids to

the aquarium this afternoon." He leaned over and kissed her on the cheek. "And don't forget about tomorrow. Come on over around two and we'll swim and barbecue and hang out. Sound good?"

Smiling, she nodded. "Sounds great. Thanks, Quinn."

After he left, Teagan wasn't quite sure what to do with herself. It was too late to make an appointment to get her hair or nails done, there was nothing to do around the house, and she was seriously bored. She picked up her purse and decided that maybe a little retail therapy would help.

Three hours later, all she had to show for her efforts were a pack of super hero underwear for Lucas and a tube of toothpaste.

As she walked back into her house, she put the lone bag down on the counter and sighed. "You're a real rebel, Teagan. Way to be wild on a Saturday."

Since shopping didn't do it for her, there was only one other option.

Ice cream.

Lots and lots of ice cream.

And the brain freeze was totally worth it.

A week later, Teagan was bouncing on her toes, watching the clock. She had finally made the appointment at the salon and all she had to do was drop Lucas off at Anna's. Then the rest of the afternoon would be filled with pampering and relaxation.

She couldn't wait!

Last weekend, when she and Lucas had gone over to Quinn and Anna's to swim, they had made the plans. All week long, she had been looking around for something new and exciting to do with her hair. She had some ideas now, and hoped her stylist would be able to make them work.

Fifty-five minutes.

It was like the clock didn't want to move!

Lucas was in his room packing up a bag of toys to bring to Kaitlyn's place. She'd limited him to three, and he'd been trying to decide on which three for over an hour.

The sound of her phone ringing practically had her jumping out of her skin. She saw her mother's name on the screen and smiled. "Hey, Mom! What's up?"

"Are you all set for your spa day?"

Sitting on the couch, Teagan felt her smile grow. "You have no idea. Just thinking about the mani-pedi I'm going to get has me giddy!"

"Good for you! You deserve it."

"Thanks, Mom. What are you up to today?"

"Your father and I decided to take an impromptu trip up to Virginia this weekend. We're so excited!"

"Really? What brought that on?"

"After touring the battleship last week with Lucas, your dad started doing some research and found there were more to see up in Virginia. There's the USS *Wisconsin* and the Mariners' Museum. So we're going."

"Good for you! I'm sure you'll have a great time."

Her mother made a noncommittal sound.

"Don't you want to go?"

"It's not that I don't want to go…"

"But…?"

"But it would be nice if we could do something

that isn't military related. Maybe something I'm interested in."

"Have you mentioned that to Dad?"

"All the time. It's like he conveniently forgets that I say anything and then he makes these plans for both of us."

"Dang. Sorry."

"I'm sure there's plenty of other things to see and we'll explore beyond the battleship. And at the end of the day I'll make him take me out for a nice dinner."

"There you go!" Teagan said, chuckling. "It's a bit of a silver lining." She was about to say more when her phone beeped with an incoming call. She glanced at the screen and saw it was Anna.

"Mom? I need to go. Anna's calling."

"Have a good afternoon, and we'll be back on Wednesday."

"Have fun!" She quickly hung up and switched lines. "Hey! I'm counting down the minutes until we can head over to you!"

"Oh, um…"

"Do you need me to pick up anything?"

Anna sighed loudly. "Okay, please don't hate me…"

"What's going on?"

"We're sick."

"What?"

"Sick. Brian and Kaitlyn are both sick," she said miserably. "It's a stomach thing and it's ugly. Save yourself."

Teagan's heart sank.

"I am so sorry. It all just started this morning and I hate canceling on you like this, but there's no way I want to expose Lucas—or you—to this. Can your folks watch him for you?"

"Unfortunately, no. My mom just called to say they're on their way to Virginia to look at battleships."

"Oh, Teagan. I'm so sorry. Maybe you can call Zoe or—wait, hang on," Anna murmured to someone on the other end of the line, but it was muffled and she had no idea who was Anna was talking to. Probably Quinn.

What was she going to do? She hated to look for a babysitter at the last minute, especially in a new town. What rotten timing!

"Okay, phew! Crisis averted!" Anna said happily. "I've both ruined your plans and saved them all in the same call."

Teagan couldn't help but laugh. "What are you talking about?"

"Like I said, I don't want to expose you or Lucas to this mess, but Bobby was just at the door and Quinn wouldn't let him in because we're self-quarantined."

"And…?"

"And we asked if he would mind hanging out with Lucas so you could go and have your spa day. You don't mind, do you?"

Before she could answer, Anna was talking again.

"He's great with kids and I know Lucas likes him, and it's only for a few hours, so…what do you say?"

Don't sound giddy, don't sound giddy…

"Are you sure he won't mind? I mean, I'm sure he has better things to do than babysit. And it's not like he really even knows us."

"Oh, stop. My brother is like a big kid himself," Anna assured her. "He likes finding excuses to watch

Disney movies and play video games. I'm thinking he and Lucas are going to be best friends by the time you get home."

That had Teagan second-guessing everything.

Other than her father, no other man had really interacted with her son more than casually. Since she didn't date, it had never been an issue. Of course, now that they were living close to so many relatives, Lucas was getting more and more comfortable having men other than his grandfather around, but would he get attached to Bobby? Maybe too attached? Wasn't she at risk for the same thing?

"Um, Anna, maybe I should just reschedule. It's not a big deal. Really. I can just—"

"No! Absolutely not. I refuse to let you do that. You never make time for yourself, and I'm here to make sure you at least take today—this one afternoon—and make it all about you. I swear you don't have to worry about Bobby. He's great with kids. I would never recommend him if he weren't."

Her mind was racing and before she could second- or even third-guess herself, she said, "Okay. You're right. It will be fine. I'm sure the two of them are going to have a great time."

——∿——

"Whoa! I beat you again! Yes!" Lucas shouted, jumping to his feet and fist-bumping the air.

Bobby was on the floor, and he leaned back against the sofa and shook his head. Beaten. Again. By a five-year-old. Clearly, he was losing his touch. He laughed softly as the kid did a victory dance of sorts around the coffee table. As much as he hated to admit it, Lucas had some serious video game skills. Maybe they needed to move on to another activity.

"What do you say we put the game away and go outside and toss a ball around?"

Lucas instantly stilled and eyed him warily. "Why? This is so much fun!"

Because you're the one winning, Bobby wanted to say. But he held his tongue. No need to get snarky with a kid. "It is fun, but it's also a great day out and we should be out there enjoying it!" He stood up and made the adult decision that video game time was over. Lucas whined—which was to be expected—but didn't argue.

Much.

"So what's your favorite sport? Basketball? Baseball? Football? Soccer?" Bobby asked as they made their way out to the backyard.

Lucas shrugged and looked down at the ground.

When they were in the middle of the yard, Bobby turned to him. "No favorites?"

Another shrug.

Then something occurred to him. Crouching down so he was eye level with Lucas, he softly asked, "Have you ever played any ball games?"

Lucas shook his head but wouldn't look at him.

That would mean there weren't any balls or equipment out here for them to play with.

Damn.

Straightening, he said, "How would you like to go for a ride with me?"

The boy looked up at him suspiciously. "Where?"

"Just to the store. You know… Walmart. Nothing major."

"Did my mom say we could?"

Bobby hadn't thought of that and wasn't sure he'd be able to get an answer from her. He didn't want to call and interrupt her spa time. His sister had been adamant that Teagan have the afternoon to herself.

"Tell you what, I'll text her and let her know, because she's getting her hair and nails done and might not be able to talk on the phone."

"I'm not supposed to go anywhere unless my mom knows," he said solemnly. "Not even with people I know."

He stared down at the boy and pulled his phone out of his pocket and quickly typed out a text to Teagan asking if she was available to talk. Less than a minute later his phone rang.

"Is everything okay?" she asked nervously rather than greeting him.

He laughed softly even as he shook his head. "First of all, calm down. Everything's fine."

"Oh…okay." Bobby could hear the relief in her voice.

"I wanted to take Lucas to the store with me and he said we couldn't go unless you said it was okay."

"Why are you going to the store?"

"We came outside to play after your son annihilated me at video games, and he doesn't have any kind of outdoor sports stuff. I thought we'd go to Walmart and pick some things up. You know, if it's okay with you."

"Um…"

"It's no big deal, Teagan," he quickly said because he had a sense she felt like he was accusing her of something. "I thought it would be fun to kick a soccer ball around or toss a Frisbee or even get a kite and go down to the beach with it."

"What does Lucas think?"

He looked down at the kid who was watching him like a hawk. "Why don't you ask him?" He handed the phone to Lucas.

"Hey, Mom!" He paused. "Uh-huh…yeah…I guess so." He looked up at Bobby for a minute as he listened to whatever his mother was saying. "Okay. Thanks, Mom! Bye!" Then he handed the phone back to Bobby.

"Everything all right?" he asked.

Teagan laughed, and it was husky and sexy as hell. Not something he should be thinking about with her son standing right in front of him.

"It's fine. We've sort of never done a lot of outdoor sports. Normally it's the swings at the park or the jungle gym or we go to museums and stuff. So I don't think he knows what to expect."

"Ah, okay. No problem. If it's okay with you, I'd still like to take him to the store and when we get there, I'll let him decide."

"You really don't have to do that. There's plenty of stuff for him to do at home to keep him busy."

"Does he play cards? Because he's such a whiz at games I have a feeling he'd be great at poker too," he teased. He could hear someone talking to Teagan and realized he needed to let her get back to her appointment.

"Listen, go and enjoy your afternoon," he said before she could say anything. "We'll see you when you get home, and don't worry, we'll be fine."

"Bobby…"

"Tell your mom bye," he said to Lucas and held the phone out to him.

"Bye, Mom!"

Bobby hung up, and when he looked down at Lucas, he smiled. This so wasn't the plan he'd had for himself today. He hadn't planned on coming back to town at all quite so soon. After being home for only a week, he felt like he'd done all that he could—settled back into his apartment, checked in with his regular doctor, even had a meeting with his captain about his recovery. But when he'd gotten up this morning, he'd felt a little lost about what to do with himself.

He missed his family. Plus, he felt bad about dumping the rest of the work in Teagan's kitchen on Quinn—no matter how much he claimed otherwise.

When he'd shown up at his sister's earlier and found out the kids were sick, Bobby figured he'd come over here and finish the sink project, but Quinn had already taken care of that as well.

That's when Anna had suggested helping Teagan out in another way. He'd never thought he'd be thankful that his niece and nephew were sick, but right now, he kind of was. How twisted was that?

To her credit, Teagan didn't look at him any other way than she always had—welcoming him into her home and thanking him profusely for coming to her rescue. He had been riddled with guilt the entire drive over because he was certain she was going to call him out for his disappearing act. And he was prepared for it. But…she didn't say a word. If anything, she was overly chatty about where everything was, what Lucas was allowed and not allowed to do, and how he should help himself to anything he wanted to eat. Then she'd given him her number, kissed Lucas goodbye, and was out the door with a wave.

Part of him wished she would have at least tried to sound disappointed. He was used to women flirting with him or playing coy, but Teagan wasn't like the women he usually dated. She didn't flirt or pretend to be helpless, she was just herself. Something as simple as having ice cream with her last weekend had been better than the last several dates he'd gone on before getting shot. And clearly she wasn't looking to play any games with him, so he wasn't quite sure what to make of her.

It was oddly unsettling.

"Bobby? Are we gonna go to the store now?"

A quick shake of his head to clear it and he was smiling down at Lucas. "Absolutely! You ready to go?"

Lucas nodded, and together they locked up the house and headed out.

Teagan had left him well prepared, so he had a key to the house and Lucas's booster seat. Once they were in the car, he began quizzing the boy on what kind of ball game he thought he'd like best.

"I don't know," he replied after a minute. "What's your favorite?"

"Hmm... I played baseball and football in high school. And now I'm on a softball team with the police department."

"You're a policeman?" he asked with awe.

Bobby nodded. "I sure am."

"Wow! That is so cool!"

Apparently now everything he said was way more interesting and Lucas—who wasn't particularly shy to begin with—became even more animated and talkative.

Almost a little too talkative.

Bobby would have sworn the kid hadn't taken a breath for a solid ten minutes, because he kept asking questions but never waited for an answer. The entire time they were in the store, he clung to every word Bobby said about the different types of ball games and outdoor gear they could buy.

"You played baseball, so I think I want to play base-ball," Lucas said. But as soon as he began picking out bats and balls, the kid changed his mind. "Or football! You said you played that one too! Can you teach me how to throw a football?"

"Yeah, sure." Bobby returned the gear to the shelf and walked down the aisle a little further to find a selection of footballs.

"Wait, what's softball? Is it like baseball? Can I join your team with the other policemen?"

While it was hard to get a word in, Bobby had to admit it was more fun shopping with Lucas than when he'd last taken Kaitlyn to the toy store. They'd spent an hour in the Barbie aisle. An entire hour. He'd never seen so much pink in his entire life. Now, as Lucas continued to chatter, he decided to just get a T-ball set and start from there.

They checked out, drove back to the house, went to the backyard to set up, and Lucas was still talking.

How did Teagan stand it? And where was the boy's father? Was he back in Colorado? He must not have been much of a father if Lucas didn't even know how to hit a ball.

There was no way he'd ask Lucas about his dad, and he wasn't even sure he should ask Teagan, but he could ask Anna. Maybe she had some idea.

Then he remembered Lucas saying he didn't have a dad.

Was that literally or figuratively?

Something to think about later, because right now Lucas was jumping up and down impatiently.

"Can I hit it? Can I hit it? Is this how I hold the bat? Are you gonna catch the ball?"

He was exhausted before they even began, but the kid's enthusiasm was infectious. For the next few minutes, Bobby patiently explained the proper way to hold the bat, how to stand, and how to swing. The first few attempts weren't pretty, and the ball didn't move, but Lucas was determined to do it. Bobby wasn't sure who was more surprised at the sound of the bat hitting the ball for the first time. They looked at each other in wide-eyed wonder and neither cared where the ball went. Scooping Lucas up in his arms, he cheered and high-fived him.

"Way to go, Bud! That was awesome!"

"I did it! I really did it! Can we do it again? Will you catch it this time?"

"You know it!" Bobby replied, setting Lucas down. He jogged across the yard and found the ball and set it back up. After giving Lucas a few more pointers, he moved back about ten feet and waited.

Lucas's face was one of total concentration. His tongue stuck out slightly to the left, his dark little brows furrowed. Then he swung and the ball flew directly toward Bobby. He caught it easily and watched as the boy did a victory dance similar to the one he'd done after beating Bobby at video games.

That was their pattern for the next hour. Occasionally Bobby would hit the ball and let Lucas try to catch it, but after each ball Lucas would ask if he could be the batter again. Rather than push, he figured it wasn't a big deal to let him get comfortable with one skill at a time. Maybe next time they'd work on playing catch.

Next time? Was he seriously standing here thinking of when he could hang out and play ball again? Sure, he wasn't opposed to it and he really was having a great time, plus he really wanted to get to know Teagan better...

No, he wasn't going to use Lucas in an attempt to win over his mother. It was wrong on so many levels. What he really wanted was to find a way to see her again in a bit of a different setting—one that didn't involve a big family gathering or babysitting. That shouldn't be too hard, right? Maybe if he could just—

Whack!

The next thing he knew, something hit him hard, his eye was stinging like it was on fire, and he was stumbling back.

"Oh my God!"

"I'm sorry! I'm sorry! I'm sorry!"

Eyes squeezed shut, Bobby bent at the waist as he hissed out a breath. It didn't take long to realize Lucas was on one side of him and Teagan on the other.

When had she gotten back?

His eye stung like a...well, he wanted to let loose a string of curses, but was mindful of the five-year-old beside him. No doubt if Bobby could get it together, he'd see Lucas's big brown eyes looking scared.

Pull it together, Hannigan, he chided himself. *You were shot, for crying out loud. This was a plastic ball to the eye! Man up!*

Slowly, he straightened and let out a long breath,

forcing himself to open his eye—which was now tearing up wildly.

Awesome.

Teagan stepped in front of him and cupped his cheek in her hand while she looked at his eye. "We're going to have to put ice on that. Come on." She took him gently by the hand and led him back to the house. Lucas grabbed his other hand and Bobby had to fight the urge to pull away from them both because they were treating him like an invalid.

Or maybe he was just acting like one.

They stepped through the back door and into the kitchen. Bobby sat down on one of the bar stools while Teagan prepared an ice pack. Between the pain and the tearing, his vision was slightly blurred, but not enough that he couldn't tell that the woman fussing over him had received a bit of a makeover. She had different makeup on, her nails were painted a bold, bright pink, and her hair was full of curls that looked like they had been kissed by the sun. He knew enough about women to know how to compliment a good haircut and highlights, but this was the first time he'd been stunned speechless by the sight of them.

She looked younger and more carefree than he'd seen her before.

Except now she was frowning at him.

"Here," she said softly, lifting the ice pack over his eye. "Hold this on there for a few minutes. Can I get you something for the pain?"

"No. I'm fine, really. It looks worse than it feels."

Even though it felt pretty painful, he had to remember that he'd been hit by a plastic ball, not another bullet.

"It's my fault, Mom," Lucas said, his small voice coming from the stool beside him. "I hit the ball before he asked if I was ready." Bobby could hear the tremor in his voice and had a feeling the kid was going to start crying any minute.

Resting one arm on the counter, Bobby turned and mussed up Lucas's hair. "It wasn't your fault, Lucas. I wasn't paying attention. You've got nothing to be upset about, okay?"

Lucas's eyes went wide. "But—but you got hurt and—"

"And that's what happens when you don't pay attention," Bobby said firmly but gently. "It's an important lesson to remember when you're playing sports. You always need to be paying attention or you could get hurt." Then he pointed to his eye and gave a lopsided grin. "Just like this."

Lucas studied him and then looked at his mother before turning his attention back to Bobby. "So…you're not mad at me?"

Bobby shook his head. "Nope."

"And maybe you still want to play ball with me?"

"Any time," he said with a nod.

"Like right now?"

"Lucas," Teagan quickly interrupted. "I think Bobby needs to rest for a little while. Why don't you go and read for a bit, okay?"

"But Mom—"

Before Teagan could respond, Bobby leaned close to Lucas and whispered, loud enough for her to hear, "This is another important lesson to remember—don't argue with your mom."

"Oooh," Lucas said, dragging out the word. "Okay." Then he hopped down and ran to his room.

When they were alone, Bobby found Teagan looking at him. For the life of him, he wasn't sure what he was supposed to say. Should he apologize for interrupting her when she was talking to her son? Or maybe apologize for teaching the kid how to hit a ball? Her expression was mild and a little unreadable, and it made him feel sort of uncomfortable.

"Teagan, listen. I know I should have—"

She held up a hand to stop him. "Can I just say something first?" she asked gently, glancing over her shoulder at the door to Lucas's room.

He nodded.

"You handled that very well and I appreciate it. And while I hate that you ended up getting hurt, I'm very thankful you didn't take it out on Lucas."

Placing the ice pack on the counter, he looked at her like she was crazy. Had someone else done that to the kid? Had his father been abusive? Was that why they were willing to move so far away from him? Then another thought hit him—had this unknown, unnamed man been abusive to Teagan, as well?

Swallowing the rage he was feeling, Bobby took a minute to gather his thoughts. "First of all, I meant what I said. I was the one at fault, not Lucas. And yeah, it stung like son of a—" He stopped when he saw that Lucas's bedroom door was open. "Anyway, it hurt. But there was no reason to get mad at anyone except myself."

Teagan laughed and gently touched the skin right under his eye. "I don't think there's any permanent damage, but you'll probably have at least a bit of a bruise there. Sorry."

Unable to help himself, Bobby captured her wrist to keep her hand on his cheek. He heard her soft gasp, saw the surprised look on her face.

He had so many questions that he was dying to ask—about her life, about Lucas's father—but he couldn't make himself form the words. Now wasn't the time. His gaze lingered on her face. "Your spa day agreed with you. You look beautiful." And even that felt awkward coming out of his mouth. Normally, he could sweet-talk his way around any girl. He was good at it. But right now with Teagan, he felt like a teenager around his first crush.

She blushed. "Thank you."

He swallowed. "It's true. Not that you didn't look beautiful before," he quickly corrected. "But right now, you just look…amazing."

He almost groaned at how lame he sounded.

Slowly, she pulled her hand from his and took a step back. "You, um, you should really keep the ice on your eye for a little longer." She turned and walked over to the refrigerator. "Can I get you something to drink? Some soda? Water?"

She was nervous, and Bobby found it cute as hell. This was something else that was new—a woman who wasn't afraid to be herself. Most of the women he'd dated since—well, forever—were very practiced and calculated in how they responded to him. But everything about Teagan was honest and sweet, and it made him feel totally out of his element.

"I'm good," he said, but it was a lie. He wasn't good.

Right now he was feeling things he wasn't used to feeling, and suddenly he wasn't particularly sure of himself.

When she faced him, she cocked her head to one side and she looked as if she could see right through him. "How's your shoulder?"

"Uh…it's good. You know, healing."

She nodded. "And how's physical therapy going?"

That one he wasn't really interested in talking about. "It's going."

Another nod.

They stayed like that until it started to feel awkward. It was too quiet, her expression was too knowing. He stood and walked over to put the ice pack in the sink.

The sink he should have installed.

"He did a good job," Teagan said, interrupting his thoughts. She walked closer and stood beside him. "It was pretty quick, too."

There wasn't anything he could say.

"I hope they reimbursed you for the materials," she added. "And maybe you charged for the labor."

He knew she was teasing, but he couldn't make himself laugh.

Turning his head, he looked down at her. Her expression still hadn't changed. "I'm sorry."

One perfectly shaped brow arched at him.

"I was embarrassed," he admitted in a low voice, and saying it out loud nearly killed him. "I overdid it that day and it annoyed the hell out of me because I'm so damn tired of being in this recovery mode. I'm ready to move on and get my life back, and something as simple as holding a pipe had me in pain." He paused and let out a long breath. "I've never had to deal with anything like this before, and every time I think I'm good to go—that everything's going to be all right—I'm not."

She didn't say anything. Didn't offer him empty words or even sympathy.

Shifting slightly, he went on. "This whole recovery has been rough. I had to come home and live with my parents—had to ask them to do pretty much everything for me—and I hate it. I hated every minute of it. I've always been independent. I started my own business when I was Lucas's age because I wanted to have my own money to buy important things like ice cream and candy."

Teagan laughed. "What was the business?"

"I raked leaves and helped people move their trash cans to the street and back on garbage pickup days."

"Really?" She was smiling and definitely looked amused.

"Scout's honor," he replied. "It's just the way I am. I don't like having to rely on anyone for anything. I don't know why, it's just always been my thing. And up until this injury, I've never had to rely on anyone."

"You've never gotten hurt on the job? How is that possible?"

"Don't get me wrong, I've gotten injured, just not to the point of being incapacitated." He sighed with frustration. "And now all I want is to get cleared to go back to work, but it's not happening."

"It hasn't happened *yet*," she corrected. "That doesn't mean it's never going to happen, Bobby. You have to be patient."

"That's what I'm saying!" he shouted and instantly regretted it. The shock on her face wasn't necessary to prove he was out of line. "Sorry. I'm just…this whole thing is making me crazy."

"Maybe you need to talk to someone. Like a professional," she said warily, and Bobby was sure his expression was horrified.

"Uh, no," he said adamantly. "Not gonna happen." Then he looked over his shoulder toward the clock on the microwave. "You know what? I should go. I didn't realize how late it was. So I'll, um… I guess I'll see you around." He started to walk toward the front door. "Tell Lucas to keep practicing with that T-ball set. He's really getting the hang of it."

He was only five feet from the door when Teagan stepped in front of him. Bobby stopped short so he wouldn't slam into her.

"Oh no. You are not doing this again."

"Excuse me?"

With her arms crossed over her chest, she nodded. "This running away crap? I'm done with that."

He still wasn't sure he understood what she was getting at, and she must have figured that out.

"First time we met? You walked away after a plate almost slipped out of your hands."

"Teagan…"

"Then you pretty much sprinted out of here last week after you hurt your shoulder."

"I had ice cream first."

She gave him a sour look. "And you didn't come back like you said you would." She stepped in close to him. "I prefer it when people honor their word."

Now he was getting a little annoyed.

"I think if Anna hadn't asked you to come today,

I'd probably never have seen you again. I mean, sure, maybe at some Shaughnessy family event years from now, but other than that, you would have done whatever you could to avoid me. Except thanks to Anna, you did come back, and you've played with Lucas and by now he's got some sort of hero-worship thing going on with you. So if you think I'm going to just let you pull another disappearing act, you're crazy!"

She was doing her best to keep her voice down, but there was no mistaking how angry she was. Now what was he supposed to do? Or say?

Teagan must have taken his silence for something else because she let out a huff of annoyance and stepped aside, motioning toward the door. "Fine. Whatever. Just go."

He heard her annoyance, but he *saw* her disappointment. And that got to him more than anything else.

Instead of walking out the door, he advanced on her. Her eyes went wide and she took a step back, even as he took another toward her.

"You're wrong," he said, his voice low and gruff. "I did want to see you again. Since the day we met, I've wanted to see you again. Even after I stormed off like a jackass, all I could think about was how good it would be to see you again."

Teagan took two steps back and hit the wall. Bobby moved in until they were toe-to-toe. "I don't like asking anyone for help or needing help, but the fact that I kept embarrassing myself in front of you? It was almost more than I could stand."

"Bobby, you had nothing to be embarrassed about. I totally understand what you're dealing with," she argued.

But he shook his head. "You don't. You can't," he countered. "I'm just a man, Teagan, and I can't help but have a little pride. I don't like looking weak. I don't like *being* weak. If we had met at any other time—"

"But we didn't," she whispered.

Yeah, it was crazy to wish for something he couldn't have. In a perfect world, he wouldn't have gotten shot. In a perfect world, he would have been confident enough to ask her out. And in a perfect world, he'd have every right to close the distance between them and kiss her.

She swallowed hard, her big blue eyes never blinking, and watched him as if waiting for…something.

"What is it you want from me, Teagan? You want me to apologize for walking away? For not coming back? What? Tell me what it is you'd like me to do."

He hoped and prayed she wanted the same thing he did.

"I want you to stop running. You have nothing to fear from me," she said, brutal in her frankness. "I don't care that you're still recovering. I don't care that you may need help from time to time. But I expect honesty from my friends, Bobby. Always."

Friends.

The kiss of death.

Dammit.

So many retorts were on the tip of his tongue, yet he couldn't speak. Friends? So the attraction he'd been feeling was all one-sided? For a man who never had to put much effort into getting a woman, this was like being hit in the face with the ball all over again.

"Friends," he finally said.

She nodded. "It's all I can offer you." Apparently, he

was that transparent. "My main priority is Lucas, and I'm not looking to get involved with anyone. Especially someone who…" She paused and looked down at the floor.

"Someone who what?" he prompted, feeling more than a little annoyed now.

After a moment, she looked back up at him. "Someone with a history of being a serial dater," she said defiantly. "If I were single, no kids, it would be one thing, but I have my son to worry about. I don't get involved in casual relationships. I can't. As it is, I was scared even to let you come and watch him today, because other than my dad, Lucas hasn't had any other male role models. Now that I see how quickly he bonded with you, I regret my selfishness."

"How the hell were you selfish?"

"I was desperate to have a day to myself!" she cried. "To get my nails done and my hair cut and do all the things I haven't had the time to do in forever. And now I'm going to be hearing all about you for who knows how long!"

Now he was thoroughly confused.

"So now I'm not good enough even to have around as a friend?" he asked incredulously.

"That's not what I'm saying, Bobby. I'm saying… I don't want to confuse Lucas. I don't want him getting attached to someone who has no interest in sticking around."

Again the questions about Lucas's father came to mind, but he was too wrapped up in all the ways Teagan was insulting him right now to ask.

He leaned in close. "You don't know anything about me." He meant to sound menacing, and he felt like he pulled it off.

"I know enough. People talk," she replied confidently.

"People? What people?"

"Quinn," she said with a smug smile. "He told me all about you."

If he thought he was angry before, it was nothing compared to how he felt right now. How dare his brother-in-law say anything derogatory about him! That crap was supposed to be all ancient history.

"You know my history with your cousin," he countered. "Of course he was going to talk trash about me. And why would you even ask him? Why not just come to me if you wanted to know something?"

"Because you were usually walking away. When was I supposed to ask you anything?"

Okay. She had a point. But still...

This wasn't getting them anywhere. He wasn't doing himself any favors with the way he was acting right now, and thanks to Quinn, she already had a bad opinion of him, one that he would have to fight. Stepping away from her, he raked a hand through his hair and let out a weary sigh. Maybe it was time to just let this go. His life was total crap right now, and she wasn't looking to get involved with anyone, so why was he fighting this?

When he faced her again, he had his answer.

Because she was beautiful.

Because she challenged him.

Because she had the potential to break his heart.

In a perfect world, all the obstacles would be removed. But this wasn't a perfect world and he was an imperfect man. And because he had nothing left to lose, he leaned in and kissed her.

Chapter 4

BOBBY HANNIGAN WAS KISSING HER.

At first, Teagan had no idea what to do. The kiss was so unexpected and it had been so incredibly long since a man had kissed her. First it felt foreign.

And then it felt oh-so-right.

Slowly, she stepped in close to him and reveled in the feel of his arms going around her as he deepened the kiss. It was slow and sexy and felt more intimate than anything she had ever experienced before.

The man had serious skills.

As if of their own accord, her hands smoothed up over his chest—mindful of his shoulder—and carefully wound around him as she pressed up against his body.

Oh, how she had forgotten how good it felt for a man to hold her. So long. It had been so long since she had felt like this—had wanted to feel like this—and Bobby was pure male perfection. Even as she let the sensations wrap around her, there was a little voice inside of her reminding her how out of her league this man was. He was so big and sexy and virile and—at least according to her cousin—could have any woman he wanted. So what was he doing here with her?

"Mom! Can I stop reading now?"

It was like a bucket of cold water being dumped on her.

Teagan almost jumped out of Bobby's arms and quickly turned away. She needed a minute to compose herself, so she stepped around him and replied to her son. "Five more minutes, okay?"

Lucas mumbled his agreement, and for once, she wished he would have argued. Just so she would have an excuse for a little more time before having to look at the man who'd effectively turned her world upside down in a matter of seconds.

"Teagan."

That was it. Just her name, yet it was as soft as a caress. She turned around and prayed she didn't look as nervous as she felt.

His expression was filled with heat. If Lucas hadn't called out to her, she had no doubt Bobby would still be kissing her right now.

She glanced down at the floor before looking at him again and was surprised to see how close he was standing. He reached out and caressed her cheek.

"I'm not sorry for kissing you," he said, his voice so low she almost couldn't hear him. Then he moved in closer and rested his forehead against hers. "And I hope you're not sorry you kissed me."

Right now, she couldn't be sure.

The kiss had been amazing, awakening a part of her she'd thought was long gone. But there was no way she was going to admit that to him.

Unfortunately, he was staring at her, waiting for a response.

She let out a long, low breath. "I don't know how to respond to that."

The smile he gave her almost had her melting right

there at his feet. "The truth would be a good place to start," he prompted.

He was right. She didn't believe in playing games or lying—no matter how uncomfortable or embarrassing the truth was. "I'm not sorry either," she admitted softly. "But—"

Bobby immediately placed a finger over her lips. "No buts," he said. "Not right now. Not yet."

Cautiously, she grasped his wrist, pulling his hand away. "It won't change how I feel, Bobby. I meant what I said earlier. I'm not looking to get involved with anyone. I can't."

"I think you're wrong."

That was a little surprising. From everything she had heard about him from Quinn and what she'd observed on her own, he should be thankful she was giving him an out. Couldn't he see how complicated her life was? Why would he want to yoke himself to a woman with a child? He wouldn't be the center of her world. Someone else would always get most of her attention.

She looked up at him, into those amazingly clear blue eyes, and did her best to pull off a patient smile. "I think right now we'll have to agree to disagree." She paused. "We both have a lot of baggage that isn't...conducive to any kind of relationship."

"Even friendship?" he asked, but his tone was way more serious than it had been a minute ago.

"Considering what just happened here, I don't see how we could possibly have even that. There would be temptation—lines would get blurred—and that's not really fair to either of us."

Now his expression turned fierce. "So what are you

saying? That this is it? I'm just supposed to leave and, what? Never see you or Lucas again? What happened to the things you said earlier, about how walking away wasn't fair to your son? One kiss and now I'm just supposed to disappear?"

Okay, he had a completely valid point there. She was throwing out mixed signals, but it was only because she was so confused! Teagan wanted to believe she was the kind of person who could be friends with a man she was completely attracted to. But after that kiss? Every time she saw him, it would be all she could think about.

"Look, I—I wasn't expecting this. You," she corrected. "It's been a long time since I even had to think about this kind of situation." Then she stopped and shook her head. "That's not true. This is the first time I've *ever* had to deal with this kind of situation."

She saw the confusion on his face and knew she had to finish what she started.

"Give me one minute." Before he could respond, Teagan walked over to Lucas's room—but he was asleep on his bed, his book still in his hand. She closed the door most of the way and walked back to the living room, motioning for Bobby to sit down.

"I haven't dated anyone since Logan died," she said quietly.

He sat opposite her, his elbows resting on his knees as he studied her. "Logan?"

"My fiancé. Lucas's father," she replied. "We dated for three years and were planning on getting married. He was in the army and had gotten deployed to Afghanistan." She took a steadying breath before continuing. "He never came home. Never knew I was pregnant."

Bobby hung his head and she heard him mutter a curse.

"He's been gone for six years, and during that entire time, all I could focus on was my son. Every day was a struggle, and dating wasn't even on my radar."

He looked up at her with nothing but sadness and compassion. "I'm so sorry, Teagan. I had no idea."

She remembered her cousin saying the same thing to her when he was here. "It's not something I like to talk about."

He nodded.

"Most of the time, I'm okay. Lucas keeps me busy and our life is very good. My folks helped me out so much—they still do. I was able to continue my education and get my master's, and now I'm finally starting the job that I have been working toward for years." She looked at him sadly. "I'm only human, Bobby. My time and energy has to go to my son first, and then to this new job. This—this thing between us, I don't know what to make of it. Except that I…I *can't* make anything of it. Not now. Please tell me you understand."

The look on his face told her he didn't.

But he didn't argue.

"Bobby? Say something. Please."

He leaned back against the sofa. "As much as I'd like to believe being around me would be too much of a temptation to you, I don't think that's the case. I think you're an incredibly strong-willed woman who wouldn't allow that to happen."

He paused and seemed to consider his next words. "Here's the thing. I like spending time with you. I like hanging out with Lucas. He's a great kid. And as much as you may not believe this, we're bound to keep running into each other because of our families. My parents are best friends with Ian and Martha Shaughnessy. Your parents are starting to hang out with all of them too. My sister is married to your cousin, and we have a tendency to get together for big family meals all the time. So…if this is where you're going to be living, and if you'll be spending time with your cousins, we'll see each other. Wouldn't it be better if it wasn't awkward or if we weren't trying to avoid one another?"

Damn. She hadn't thought about that. "I guess it makes sense," she said. "But—"

"No," he cut her off. "No buts. This isn't something that can be settled right now or wrapped up in a neat little bow. I can't help the way I feel, Teagan. Maybe you can. Maybe you've had to out of necessity, I don't know. But for now, all I can do is promise to take things as they come. I can't predict how either of us is going to think or act or feel—tomorrow, next week, next year."

And dammit, even *that* made sense! Normally, she was the voice of reason and it felt weird for someone else to do that for her.

"I just don't want you to expect anything of me," she admitted after a minute. "You don't live around here, and while I know your family does, I'm going to notice if you start showing up all the time. I need space, and I don't want to feel pressured."

He nodded. "Have I done anything here today to pressure you?"

"You kissed me," she blurted out and wanted to be offended when he laughed.

"Sweetheart, you kissed me right back."

She had.

"When you pulled away," he went on, "I didn't stop you. When you wanted to talk, I sat down."

He was right. He had.

"I don't know what happens from here."

Then he smiled—nothing more, nothing less. "From here, I thank you for getting me an ice pack for my eye. Then I tell Lucas goodbye and encourage him to keep practicing while promising we'll do it again sometime, and then...I leave." His gaze bored into hers. "And we both know we're going to see each other again. Maybe not tomorrow or two days from now, but soon."

She was so entranced by his words and the confidence behind them that she almost asked him "when." When would they see each other again.

But she didn't. She couldn't. It wasn't who she was.

At least, she didn't think it was who she was.

Right now, she almost didn't recognize herself.

He stood and looked toward her son's room.

"He's asleep," she said, coming to her feet. "You must have exhausted him."

Bobby nodded and looked back at her. "Then please relay my message to him. I think he did great today. He'll be ready to try it without the stand in no time."

"I will."

They stood like that—facing one another silently, hungrily—until he looked away and took a step toward the front door. "Thanks for the ice pack. It helped."

He'd said he would say that to her.

"You're welcome."

Opening the front door, he paused. "So... I guess I'll see you around."

She nodded.

And then he was gone.

It was what had to happen. So why did the door closing behind him suddenly make her feel so alone?

Pulling away from Teagan's house was harder than Bobby had imagined. He could stay—but he wasn't. He was going back to Myrtle Beach. Why? Because he needed time alone to think about everything that had just happened. Between the kiss and learning about Lucas's father…it was a lot to take in.

And he felt a little guilty about making her discuss something that was clearly still painful for her.

If he could, he would take all her pain away—he'd do what he could to make her happy. He wanted to see her smile, to never see that sadness in her eyes again.

And that's when fear grabbed him by the throat.

What was happening to him? And why now? Of all the women he'd ever known, what was it about this one that had him so freaking head over heels so fast?

She was right—they both had a lot of baggage. That more than anything else should have been enough to scare him off. Or at the very least, been enough to make him realize he was lucky they hadn't taken things any further. But rather than making him feel better, he felt worse. He was discovering that he didn't mind her baggage. He was already crazy about Lucas. Bobby had always enjoyed being an uncle, and not just to Quinn and Anna's kids. Somewhere in the back of his mind, he'd always assumed that one day he'd get married and have kids of his own.

Only…it had started feeling more and more like an elusive dream. He hadn't met anyone he'd felt the kind of connection with for thoughts of marriage and a future.

Wait, wait, wait—was that what he was thinking about now? Already?

"No," he said adamantly as he pulled onto the interstate. "No way. You like Teagan, you're attracted to Teagan, but that's it. You just want her because you can't have her."

Yeah. That had to be it. Once he realized that the only reason he felt like this was because she wasn't fawning all over him like women usually did, he could move on and they could just be friends.

Simple, right?

What he needed to do was stop thinking about Teagan and put his focus back where it belonged—on recovering and getting back to work. If he could just get that all worked out, no doubt he wouldn't have time to be thinking about her. They'd see each other occasionally at some family function and it would be no big deal.

So that's what he did.

Once he got home, he called his physical therapist and told him he wanted to try to up his therapy. There wasn't much he could do at home except for some light strength training. But it was a start.

Once that was done, he contacted his captain and asked about what he could do to get back to work. He still needed medical clearance to return to active street duty, but the captain was open to the idea of having Bobby in a desk position.

He hated the idea, but he could at least try it out.

That lasted a day.

His captain pulled him aside by the end of the afternoon and told him—point-blank—that he needed to focus on healing because he wasn't ready to be back to work in any capacity. And Bobby had no one to blame but himself. He'd snapped at everyone who made any kind of comment about him sitting behind a desk, and twice he'd tried to go out on a call that came in for assistance.

Captain Seaton was always fair, and Bobby had never disagreed with his personnel decisions. And he still didn't. If he said Bobby wasn't ready, then he had no choice but to accept it.

That left him back at home with way too much time on his hands. He stared at the ceiling and thought about how much he wished things in his life were different. Which led to thoughts of Teagan. It had been less than a week since he'd seen her—since he'd kissed her—and it felt like much longer.

Was she thinking about him? Was she second-guessing her decision to let him walk away? And was it wrong that he hoped she was?

There was still one aspect of their situation that hadn't been dealt with.

Quinn.

If it hadn't been for the fact that Kaitlyn and Brian had been sick that day, Bobby would have driven over there after he'd left Teagan's and given his brother-in-law a piece of his mind. How dare Quinn warn Teagan away from him! After all the years of antagonism and animosity, he'd thought they were over it. And yet the first chance he had to maybe say something nice, Quinn had gone and put him down.

Part of him understood. After all, how many years

had Bobby said and done everything possible to warn his sister off of Quinn? But it had all worked out in the end. Why did the guy have to make such a douchebag move?

He huffed with irritation as he sat on his couch. He had half a mind to call Quinn up and confront him, but right now he was a little too annoyed to do it. The way he felt now, it would turn into a childish game of trading insults, which wouldn't get him anywhere. And then Quinn would find a way to tell Teagan he'd behaved badly again.

And that wouldn't help his cause in any way, shape, or form.

So where did it leave him? What was he supposed to do to fill his time? He'd proved that working a desk job wasn't going to happen, and even if he went for physical therapy every day, all day, it still wouldn't help. His body was going to heal at its own pace no matter how much he wanted it to happen faster.

Grabbing the remote, he flipped on the TV and channel surfed for a little while. Nothing caught his attention, and he eventually settled on watching sitcom reruns. It was mindless entertainment, and right now, pretty much exactly what he needed.

Three episodes later, his phone rang. He smiled when he saw his mother's face on the cell screen.

"Hey, Mom," he said. "How are you?"

"That was going to be my first question to you," she said with a small laugh. "Anna mentioned you were in town on Saturday, but I never saw you. Is everything okay?"

"Oh yeah," he said, hesitating just a little. "I was

bored and thought I'd hang out with her and the kids, but they were sick."

"She told me. Poor little things," Mary said sympathetically. "They're finally on the mend, and they were just lucky that little Bailey didn't get it. But I'm afraid Anna's going to come down with it next. I've got plenty of hand sanitizer in the house and I'm prepared to head over to help out if it happens."

No doubt his mother would. She was the ultimate mom and grandmother.

"Hopefully you won't have to," he said. "Then you'll risk getting it."

"I've got a great immune system. It takes a lot to get me sick these days."

"Let's not test that theory," he said with a laugh of his own. "So what else is going on? Anything exciting?"

"Why don't you tell me?" she said cryptically.

"What do you mean?"

"Well, I heard that after you got booted from your sister's house, you went and babysat for Teagan."

He groaned and his head lolled back onto the sofa cushions. Why did his sister have to share *that* information?

"Um…yeah. I did. Anna was supposed to watch Lucas, and Teagan had plans. I was already in town and her parents weren't, so she didn't have anyone to help her out. I had nothing to do, so it wasn't a big deal."

"Hmm…"

"What? What was that sound about?"

"I just find it interesting you'd volunteer for babysitting duty. You barely know Teagan and Lucas. I mean, I know you met them at Ian's, but your behavior that day was…a little less than friendly."

He didn't hold in the groan this time. "Yeah, well, I felt bad about that. I figured I should do something about it and try and show Teagan I wasn't a complete jerk."

"Any particular reason you want her to know that?" *So. Not. The. Conversation. To have. With. Your. Mom.*

"Just trying to be nice to family, Mom." Maybe by emphasizing the family connection, she'd back off.

"Teagan's not your family."

Okay, clearly he underestimated his mother's intuition.

"She basically is. She's Quinn's cousin. Quinn's married to my sister. Therefore, family."

Mary sighed patiently. "You know what I mean, Bobby."

"Look, can we stop tiptoeing around this? Just say what you're trying to say."

She was silent for a moment before she said, "Fine. I think Teagan is a beautiful young woman. She's very smart and funny, and I think maybe you're a little attracted to her. Personally, I think she'd be very lucky to date—and maybe marry—you. She'd be good for you."

Now he wanted to bang his head against the wall. Marry? His mother had gone there? Already?

"Mom…"

"What? What did I say?"

"I think you've got a wild imagination," he said. "And you're way off base here. Trust me."

"I don't think so."

"Mom," he warned gently.

"Robert Hannigan, let me tell you something…"

Gone was his sweet mother and in her place was the firm voice of a disciplinarian who was comfortable making her children squirm.

No matter how old they were.

"You aren't getting any younger, and neither am I. Now, I sat back and watched as every girl in town chased after you. Personally, you're too good-looking for your own good," she chided. "But the fact remains that you're getting too old for that kind of behavior. You need to start thinking about settling down."

"I really don't think—"

"I'm not finished talking," she interrupted, and Bobby's mouth instantly snapped shut.

"Believe it or not, I think you getting shot was a good thing."

"Mom!" he cried. "What the hell?"

"Oh, hush and let me finish," she said patiently. "The recovery time has forced you to slow down. Now, I had hoped you would start to…maybe reevaluate your life. Unfortunately, you spent most of your time being surly and uncooperative and even downright bratty."

"Aren't I a little too old to be called bratty?"

"Aren't you a little too old to be acting bratty?" she countered.

Touché.

"All I'm trying to say is that maybe now is a good time to think about your future. You've still got some time left before you return to work—"

"If I return to work."

She sighed. "Bobby, you know how proud of you we all are. You've chosen a very noble and honorable career, and you put your life on the line every single day. I know what happened in that convenience store was horrible and I hate that it happened, but you've been given the opportunity to have some time to focus on you and nothing else. Have you given any thought to your future? About what will happen if you…can't go back to being a police officer?"

It was all he'd been able to think about. The only problem was, he didn't have any answers. And for all his stress about the possibility, he hadn't given any thought to what he'd do if it became a reality.

"I'm not saying any of this to upset you," Mary went on, "but for weeks we've all tried to be very careful about what we said around you and not to upset you. I don't think that was such a good idea."

"Why not?"

"Because your father and I pride ourselves on being honest. We've never candy-coated anything for you or Anna."

He snorted with annoyance.

"Do you know how many times we begged your sister to move on from Quinn?"

Okay, this was new information. "Really?"

"We did. But some things are inevitable. They needed to take that bumpy road to get to where they are now. We always supported her, even when we didn't always agree with her choices." She paused and let that sink in. "That's why I feel it's important for us to talk right now, Bobby. We're worried about you. Not just about your arm, but about all of you."

"What does any of this have to do with Teagan?" He instantly wished he could take the question back, because he wasn't thrilled with the interrogation he was already getting.

Although talking about his mental health wasn't much of an alternative.

"Hearing you went to help out Teagan gave me hope that you were snapping out of your funk. It meant you were engaging in life again, at least a little. I've never known you not to chase after a beautiful woman, so it seemed like we were getting a glimpse of your old self."

That last statement bothered him.

A lot.

Okay, so he did chase after women. That wasn't wrong, or new information. But now it was clear that it was how everyone else saw him too.

And not just Quinn.

Dammit.

"I was really just trying to do something nice to make up for acting like such a jerk to her at the barbecue."

"And when you started to fix the kitchen sink," she added.

"How the hell do you know about that?" he cried with frustration. Seriously, was nothing off-limits?

"Please, your sister tells me everything. This can't be news to you."

Unfortunately, it was. He'd never given much thought to how much people—and his family—talked about him. Now he knew. A lot!

"So I suppose everyone thinks I'm a jerk, right? Everyone including the Shaughnessys are talking about how awful I was to Teagan?"

"Well, Riley and Savannah weren't in town…"

"Not funny, Mom!" he snapped. "So now what? Am I going to have some sort of angry mob chasing after me? Are her parents going to get an earful and warn her and Lucas to stay away from me?"

"Do you want them to be warned to stay away from you?"

Oh, she was good. His mother was crafty, and why had he never realized how devious she could be? Hell, she could probably get a job on the police force with these interview techniques!

"Can't I just do something nice and have everyone leave it at that?" he asked wearily. "I realized I was wrong and I tried to make it right. That's it. End of story."

Mary sighed loudly. "Fine," she said primly. "End of story."

"Thank you."

"But let me just say this..."

He knew she'd given in too easily.

"Teagan and Lucas have already dealt with enough in their lives. That poor child will never know his father, and Teagan carries a lot of responsibility for someone so young. Her parents are lovely people and they help her out in every way they can, but...it's not the same as having someone special there for her."

Yeah, he knew exactly what she meant, because he felt the same way. From the moment he'd first seen her, he'd felt protective. That feeling only grew stronger every time he was around her.

Which wasn't often enough.

"Teagan and Lucas are a tight little family unit, and I don't think she's looking for someone to save her. She seems fiercely independent."

"She is. She needs to be. But it doesn't mean at the end of the day she doesn't wish there was someone there beside her to share some of the responsibilities."

"You can't know that, Mom."

"And yet I do."

For some reason his heart began to race. He needed to know, but didn't want his mother to realize how important that information was to him.

"I spent two weeks with her parents, Bobby. Martha and I talked a lot during the cruise, so I probably know more than I should about Teagan and her life."

"Like—like what?" he asked, the words feeling wrong even as he spoke them.

"It's not my story to tell," Mary said softly. "But Teagan's strong because she has to be. Having a military dad meant she didn't really get to be overly dependent. Don't get me wrong, they're great parents, but her father was a little more…structured than he was nurturing. And those were Catherine's words, not mine," she quickly amended.

He thought he understood what she was trying to say. Teagan couldn't—or wouldn't—show weakness or talk about how much she was struggling because that wasn't how she'd been raised. Maybe her father expected her to be strong, to roll with the proverbial punches, and now it was just what she did. But if things could be different, what would she do?

"Believe it or not, the two of you are very much alike," she said, interrupting his thoughts.

"What do you mean?"

"You're both too independent. You hate asking for help."

"You just said her parents help her all the time."

Mary laughed softly. "They do that because they love her and Lucas. She doesn't really have to ask, they've all just settled into a routine. But when she really needs help, she's a little more hesitant to ask. Almost downright stubborn. Like someone else I know."

"It doesn't make us bad people, Mom. There's nothing wrong with wanting to take care of ourselves."

"There is when there are people who can help."

Why? Why were they still talking about this? Why couldn't she accept that this was who he was? "I let you and Dad help me after I got shot."

"Only because you didn't have a choice," she reminded him. "If there had been a way for you to handle everything on your own, or if you'd had a partner by your side, you would have."

"Well, yeah," he said, not seeing her point. "But I wouldn't have liked it, either. It wouldn't matter if it was you or Dad or Anna or...or a girlfriend or wife, I couldn't ever be happy with needing someone to do everything for me."

"You need to get over that."

He laughed. Hard. "Easier said than done, Mom. Sorry."

"I just worry about you. It's a mother's right," she stated.

"I know, and I love you for it."

"Aww, and I never tire of hearing you say that."

He smiled even though she couldn't see him.

"And I hope you think about what I said. You really do need to start thinking about what you're going to do, Bobby. Nothing is guaranteed—not our jobs, and not our tomorrows. What are you going to do if you can't go back on active duty?"

"I know it's a possibility, Mom, but I can't bring myself to think beyond that. It's just...it's too hard."

"Fine. I won't push."

"Thank you."

The conversation finally turned to more mundane topics like the weather and how she and his father were already planning their next vacation. He loved how they were nearing retirement and were finally getting to enjoy their lives a little more.

"So I hope we'll see you next weekend?"

"Why? What's going on next weekend?"

"It's Brian's birthday, silly," she said, chuckling. "I can't believe you didn't remember."

Neither could he.

"Oh, okay. Great. Of course I'll be there. I'll drive up Friday and shop and "

"Not this weekend, Bobby, next weekend—as in a week and a half from now."

"Oh. Right." Where was his calendar? Oh yeah, on his phone, which was currently pressed to his face. "Okay. I'll still plan on coming in on Friday, if that's all right."

"Of course! You could even come in on Thursday after your last physio appointment for the week, if you don't have anything to do. Assuming you're still on the same schedule, you could leave right after and make it a four-day weekend."

It was scary how much she knew about his life—even at this age.

"Sounds good, Mom. I'll see you then."

By the time he hung up, he was mentally exhausted.

And almost an hour had gone by.

It was late in the day, and he supposed he could grab something for dinner. As much as he'd tried to convince himself to do a full grocery-shopping trip and restock his pantry and refrigerator, he'd yet to get to it. The only options he had on hand were cereal, rice, or grilled cheese—minus the cheese.

So...toast.

"None of that's going to work," he said, forcing himself to stand up and stretch. Walking into his bedroom, he looked at himself in the mirror and grimaced. He barely recognized himself. He seriously needed a haircut and he hadn't shaved since coming back from Teagan's. His stomach growled loudly, but he convinced himself a shower and shave would go a long way toward making himself feel better first. And no doubt the public would appreciate it if he put a bit of effort into his appearance before leaving the house.

Another hour had gone by before he walked out his front door. The drive into the heart of town felt good. It was busy and there were people everywhere since it was the summer season, but he enjoyed the chaos it provided—as long as it was orderly chaos.

For the first time since the shooting, he drove past the convenience store where *it* happened. He tensed, and it was almost as if his shoulder knew where they were and began to throb. It wasn't possible, but it sure felt that way. There was no reason to stop, no reason even to slow down, but that's just what he did.

Pulling into the parking lot, he noted how new the glass on the front windows looked. His mind flashed back to the glass breaking in the hail of gunfire. Now he was fighting a panic attack as his heart raced and memories washed over him.

Just drive away. You don't have to be here.

He couldn't move. He was momentarily paralyzed, staring straight ahead until everything began to blur. Time stopped, and he didn't even realize that people were coming and going—life had gone on. It wasn't until someone knocked on his window that he was able to turn away.

Standing beside his car was Nick Moceri—one of his brothers on the Myrtle Beach police force. Forcing himself to take a few deep breaths, Bobby stepped out of the car.

"Bobby! Hey, it's great to see you!" Nick said, clapping him on his good shoulder. "How are you doing?" He was in uniform and on duty, and Bobby couldn't help but feel a little envious.

"Getting better every day," he said, hoping he sounded confident. "How about you? How are things?"

They made small talk and Nick caught him up on the precinct gossip, mostly centering around unusual arrests and colorful suspects. It was conversation he normally loved to hear, but right now it just left him feeling…empty.

"So any word on when you'll be back?" Nick asked. It was a completely normal and obvious question, and yet it had him tensing. Something he knew he needed to stop doing.

"I wish," he said honestly. "My arm and shoulder are getting stronger, but they're not one hundred percent yet."

Nodding, Nick said, "Well, it was great to see you, but I have to run. Hopefully we'll be seeing you back on duty soon. We all miss you."

"Thanks, man. I appreciate it." And then he was

standing there alone. Rather than go into the store and risk having another panic attack in the middle of a public place, Bobby quickly got in his car and drove home.

Completely forgetting about getting anything to eat.

———ᴡᴡ———

"Thank you so much for the help," Anna said, placing a tray of cupcakes down on her dining room table. "I think it really does take a village to set up a children's birthday party."

Teagan laughed. She couldn't really agree or disagree—back in Colorado they'd had fairly small birthday parties for Lucas, with only a few friends, so this was all brand-new territory for her. But considering how large the Shaughnessy family was, and how many kids they all had, it was no wonder it took so many people to set up.

Besides Teagan, Mary and Jack Hannigan were here helping Ian and Martha, and Quinn was outside hanging up streamers. Her own parents were on their way too. Hard to believe this much went into a child's birthday party.

"I hope we have enough food," Anna said distractedly.

"We've got about twenty pounds of hamburgers and hot dogs alone," Jack Hannigan said as he walked through the dining room. "And that's on top of all the chips, dip, fruit, salads, and cakes. If we don't have enough food, something's definitely wrong."

Laughing, Teagan finished setting up all the paper goods for the dessert table and then asked where else she was needed. Lucas was running around outside with Kaitlyn and Brian, but it didn't stop Teagan from

walking over to the sliding glass doors and looking outside. There was a pool out there and her son wasn't a
great swimmer. There was a child-safety fence around
it and Quinn was out there, along with most of the other
adults, but she was still nervous he might get curious
and get too close to the water.

"You need to stop worrying," Anna said, coming up
behind her. "He's fine outside, and there's an alarm on
the gate if someone tries to get in without a security
code." She smiled. "At first I thought it was overkill, but
the first time Kaitlyn tried to scale the fence, we knew it
was a great investment."

"I'll bet."

Anna looked around the room and then faced Teagan
again. "Is it possible we're done? We really got it all set
up with time to spare?"

"It looks that way," she replied, smiling.

"So I meant to call before you came over, but the
morning sort of got away from me," Anna said.

"What's up?"

"Tonight, Connor—Hugh and Aubrey's son?—he's
sleeping over along with Aidan and Zoe's daughter Lily.
We were wondering if maybe Lucas wanted to sleep
over too."

Her eyes went wide. A sleepover? Other than staying
with his grandparents, Lucas had never had one of those
before. "Um…"

"It's okay if you say no. I completely get it. I mean,
you know us, but you don't really know us," Anna quickly
explained. "We just thought it would be fun. We adore
Lucas and he and Kaitlyn pal around a lot, so we figured
a sleepover with all of the older cousins could be fun."

It did sound fun and she had a feeling Lucas would love it.

"Just think about it, okay?"

She nodded and stepped outside, and couldn't help but smile as she heard her son laughing off in the distance. The backyard was huge, with a massive jungle gym in the corner and a large grassy area for the kids to run around in. It was like a children's nirvana. As she continued to look around, her uncle came up beside her, kissing her on the temple.

"How are you today? Have we exhausted you yet?" he teased.

"Not yet, but I have a feeling it won't be long."

He laughed. Ian Shaughnessy was an extremely mild-mannered man—so much the opposite of her father—and she had missed him all these years they'd lived so far apart. "You've got quite the large family, Uncle Ian. How do you keep up with all of them?"

Smiling, Ian said, "It certainly isn't easy. Luckily, we're not together all the time, so I have some time to get to know each of the grandkids one-on-one. Even so, I still get them mixed up sometimes, and they all laugh at me. And I don't mind one bit."

She hugged him. "You're a very lucky man."

"Well, I don't know about luck, but I know I'm blessed." He paused and looked out at the yard and watched as Lucas, Kaitlyn, and Brian ran by. "Boundless energy. I wish we could bottle some of it and keep it for when we're older, like me."

"That would be nice."

"So what about you, sweet girl? How are you doing? Have you settled in?"

She nodded. "I have. The house is wonderful and I think we've finally unpacked and managed to get everything just the way we want it."

"Good for you!"

"I'm feeling a little restless though. Summer vacation tends to do that to me. Part of me wishes I had a small part-time job or something to keep busy, but I think this particular summer it's important for me to be home with Lucas. This move was a big thing for both of us and we'll both be starting school soon, so...I'm trying to make the most out of our last bits of free time."

"That's smart. But remember to take some time for yourself too." He pointed to where the kids were playing on the jungle gym. "Sometimes it's okay for kids to play without having their parents right on top of them."

She nodded, because she understood exactly what he was saying, and thought about Anna's offer for a sleepover. It would be nice to have the night to herself. She could go home and take a nice hot shower, enjoy a glass of wine out on the back deck, and look up at the stars. Of course, in a perfect world she'd have a giant, spa-like tub to relax in and then someone to curl up in bed with who would—

Stop it! Where the hell had *that* thought even come from? Teagan had long ago given up on that kind of romantic fantasy. It wasn't going to happen for her for a very long time, if ever. She'd had her chance, it had been taken away from her, and now this was her life. She was a single mother and there was no room for romance in her life right now. She didn't even read romances, so why was she suddenly imagining a night with a man beside her?

Out of the corner of her eye she spotted the exact reason why.

Bobby Hannigan.

He strolled into the backyard and all the kids ran over to him—including hers. He scooped them up one by one as he placed a giant blue gift bag down on the ground. She felt herself holding her breath as she watched Lucas talking to him, gesturing wildly. He was no doubt telling Bobby about how much he'd been practicing his T-ball skills. Bobby's face lit up as he listened, and she knew she was in deep. A ridiculously attractive man who was good with kids? He was practically catnip.

Her uncle gently cleared this throat. "I'll go see what else my son needs help with. No doubt everyone's going to start arriving soon." He kissed her cheek and walked away but Teagan barely noticed.

As if he sensed her stare, Bobby turned to her and smiled. Her stomach felt like it was full of butterflies, and she knew she was blushing because he'd caught her.

And man, did she want to be caught.

Stop it! She had to stop herself from rolling her eyes. This was crazy. So what if he was good-looking? She'd met plenty of good-looking men before, a lot of them since Logan had died. Why was this particular man causing her to act like a hormone-crazed teenager?

Because never mind sex, you haven't even felt a man's touch in six years.

Oh, right. That.

"Mom! Mom! Did you hear? Did you hear?" Lucas cried as he ran toward her. She pulled her gaze from Bobby's and smiled down at her son.

"Hear what, baby?"

"Everyone's sleeping over tonight! Like, everyone! And Kaitlyn said I could too!"

Nodding, she forced herself to keep smiling. "I was just talking to Anna about that a few minutes ago. We'd have to go home and get you some pajamas and a change of clothes. I'm sure we could—"

"Can't you do it?" he begged. "I don't want to leave the party! And can you bring back my T-ball stand? I want to show Bobby how good I've gotten and how I always wait for you to tell me it's okay to hit the ball when we're playing together. And how I haven't hit you or anyone in the face ever again! Can you? Please?"

He was breathless by the time he finished his entire speech, and she simply nodded.

"Thanks, Mom! You're the best!" Then he gave her quick and powerful hug before saying, "I love you!" and running away.

And it was those little phrases that made it all worth it. She'd sneak out at some point to go pick up his stuff and bring it back. Then she'd plan on what she was going to do with all of her alone time tonight.

"Hey," Bobby said as he approached her.

So many images flashed in her mind of how she'd like to spend her alone time with him, but she kept them to herself.

Painful though it was.

"Hey," she replied, hoping she sounded casual and not at all breathless.

"So, Lucas says he's been practicing hitting the ball while not hitting anyone in the face." He was grinning and Teagan couldn't help but laugh.

"It's true. If anything, he's overly cautious and asks me at least three times if I'm ready and watching the ball."

He chuckled with her. "I'm glad he's taking it all so seriously."

"Believe me, he is. He's going to sleep over here tonight with all the kids and asked if I could bring his T-ball stand back with me so he can show you all the progress he's made." She said it lightly, conversationally, but she noticed his expression change. Heated. She swallowed and tried not to think too much about why. "So, um…yeah. You can expect a full presentation sometime later. Be prepared."

Nodding, he took a step closer. "I think Quinn may already have a T-ball stand here. You should ask him."

Her heart was beating like mad and she had to fight the urge to move in closer and touch him. "Thanks. I—I will." She paused. "But I still need to run home and get him pajamas and a change of clothes."

They stood like that, and even though Teagan knew people were arriving and there were suddenly more voices in the yard than there'd been just a minute ago, she couldn't make herself move.

It wasn't until Anna came up behind her and said hello to her brother that the spell was broken. Embarrassed and more than a little self-conscious, she excused herself and went to see if her parents had arrived.

Fortunately, they had, and it was the perfect armor to keep around her to keep from gravitating back toward wherever Bobby was. Not that she wasn't aware of his every move. It was like she was suddenly hypersensitive to his presence. After a little while, however, sitting and talking to her cousins, it was easier to get distracted and not think about him.

Her rock star cousin Riley was here, and she found herself sitting with him and his lovely wife, Savannah. He introduced her to his two kids, who immediately took off to go play with their cousins, before he spent time catching up, telling her about the tour he was on right now with his band, Shaughnessy. The only reason he was able to come to the birthday party was because the band had a week off.

"We're going to be in Myrtle Beach in a couple of weeks, if you want to come to the show," Riley said.

"You really should try to make it," Savannah chimed in. "It's an amazing venue and the band has never sounded better." She smiled at her husband and Teagan almost felt like she was interrupting a private moment.

"Um, that would be great, but I think Lucas is a little young for me to take to a concert. Since it's out of town, I'm not sure what I'd do with him for the night."

Riley grinned. "There's never a shortage of babysitters in this family, and trust me, I'm old news to them. They don't come to my local shows anymore."

"Really? I find that hard to believe," she commented.

"It's true. They all came to our show in Raleigh at the beginning of the tour. We had a team of babysitters at the hotel for all the kids. But this time, I don't think anyone's planning on coming, so you'd have your pick of cousins to take Lucas for the night. Or maybe your parents wouldn't mind."

Teagan wondered if her parents would be interested in seeing their nephew perform in concert and thought they might enjoy it. Not that she'd ever known them to go to rock concerts, but you never knew. Maybe they'd make an exception this time.

"So what do you say, Teagan? Can I put you on the list?"

"What list?"

She looked up and saw it was Bobby asking the question. So much for her radar knowing where he was at all times. He stood right behind her chair and she could feel the heat of his body. She wanted to rest her head back on him or maybe have him put his hand on her shoulder. Something, anything to have some contact.

She was losing her mind. It was the only explanation.

"I was inviting Teagan to the show next month in Myrtle Beach," Riley said and then his eyes lit up. "Hey, you're coming to the show, aren't you?" he asked Bobby.

"I'd planned on it. I mean, as long as I can get some VIP seats."

Riley laughed. "Dude, anytime. I've told you that a million times. But what I was getting at was maybe you could bring Teagan with you. I was just telling her how I'm old news to everyone here and no one's planning on going to the show. So maybe you could bring her with you so she isn't going alone."

"Oh, Riley, that's not necessary," Teagan quickly said. "I'm sure—"

"Not a problem," Bobby interrupted. "I would love to take Teagan to her first Shaughnessy concert."

She glanced up at him and saw him grinning. Shifting awkwardly in her chair, she forced herself to smile at her cousin. "Actually, I was going to see if my parents were interested, since they've never seen you in concert either."

Bobby's hand rested on the back of her chair and she could feel his knuckles grazing her shoulder.

"Not a problem," Riley said, oblivious to her inner turmoil. "I'm sure Bobby would totally be a tour guide to the whole family, right?"

"Absolutely," he agreed and after that, Teagan had no idea how to get out of the entire situation. She'd talk to Bobby about it when the time got closer, but she didn't want him to feel obliged to take her anywhere.

Liar.

After that, the party got into full swing, and everyone was eating, talking, and chasing after kids. It was a madhouse, but it was more fun than she could remember having at a kid's party. There was enough food to feed them all twice, and once all the leftovers were put away, she decided it was the perfect time to run home.

Finding Anna in a sea of Shaughnessys, she tapped her on the shoulder. "If your offer still stands, Lucas would love to sleep over tonight."

"Oh yay!" Anna cried, hugging her. "I'm so glad!"

"Since we just finished eating and it's going to be a while before we have cake, I figured now was a good time to sneak out and get his things. Is that all right?"

"Absolutely! And just bring a pillow for him. We have a ton of sleeping bags for him to choose from."

"Awesome. Thanks!" And with a wave, Teagan made her way through the yard to let Lucas know she'd be back soon, stopping and saying a quick word to everyone before finding her parents so they could keep an eye on Lucas while she was gone.

By the time she reached the gate, she was relieved to finally have some peace and quiet. She couldn't remember the last time she'd talked so much. Taking a moment to just breathe, Teagan made a mental list of everything she needed to pack for her son—pajamas, a change of clothes, underwear, socks, his pillow, toothbrush and toothpaste, and his T-ball stand. Yeah, that one might not make it back. There was no way they needed to add more activity to the backyard today.

Feeling confident that she had a plan, she walked around to the front of the house and frowned.

Her car was blocked by three other cars.

Cursing herself for not parking on the street earlier, she wondered where her parents were parked. Maybe she could just go grab their keys and take their car. After scanning the driveway and the block, she didn't see it. And then she realized why—they lived only a couple of blocks away. No doubt they'd just walked over. Still, she could get their keys, walk to their house and…

This was getting way more complicated by the minute. "Problem?"

Turning, she saw Bobby coming around the side of the house toward her. "Uh…" She shook her head and couldn't hold back a small laugh. "I need to run home and get Lucas's stuff, but my car's blocked. Then I figured I'd just take my parents' car, but they walked. After that, I was thinking I'd walk to their house and get *their* car but…"

"Seems like a bit much," he said, laughing with her. "C'mon. I'm parked right over there. We won't have to bother anyone and we can get back faster than if you walked to you parents' place."

While she knew he was right, she wasn't sure this was a better solution.

Before she could voice her concerns, Bobby was already across the yard and walking to his truck. The last thing she wanted was to seem ungrateful, and she certainly didn't want to be gone too long and miss singing happy birthday to Brian, so…

"Teagan? You coming?"

Nodding, she made her way over to him. "I guess I am," she murmured, more to herself than anyone else, and prayed things didn't get awkward.

Chapter 5

ALL DAY. ALL DAY HE'D BEEN WATCHING HER MOVE around the yard talking to people, smiling at everyone, and he'd nearly gone out of his mind. When he'd found her talking with Riley and Savannah, just standing behind her had been torture. Something had to give—and soon—because he felt like he was slowly going insane.

They were halfway to Teagan's house when she finally spoke. "I really appreciate you doing this. I feel bad for taking you away from your nephew's birthday party."

He shrugged. "It's not a big deal. There are so many people there, I'm sure Brian won't even notice I'm gone. He has four other uncles there to distract him, if need be."

"It's so weird to me."

"What is?" he asked, looking over at her. God, she was beautiful. She was wearing a pair of white capris and a teal-blue halter top, and with all that skin showing, she was beyond tempting.

"Having so many relatives so close by," she said, staring out the window. "I always knew I had all these cousins, but because we were always moving and traveling, I barely remembered what it was like to be around all of them."

"What about on your mom's side of the family? Do you have a lot of relatives there?"

She shook her head. "Not really. My mom has one

sister who has two sons and we haven't seen them in years. They live up in Michigan and don't like to travel."

"Well, that sucks."

"It does." Then she turned and looked at him. "But they were never as fun as the Shaughnessy side of the family. Every time we got together with that crowd, we had the best time. We went on several vacations with them to Myrtle Beach and to me it was more fun than going to Disneyland."

He chuckled, because he knew what she meant. For as long as he'd known the Shaughnessys, they just had a way of making even the most mundane things entertaining. It was a gift that he realized he'd never really appreciated the way he should have.

"Have you ever gone to Disneyland?" he asked.

"No. I always wanted to and I think it's something I'd like to do with Lucas when he's just a little older." She smiled at him. "I have to plan it so I have time to recuperate afterward before going back to work. I hear a Disney vacation isn't particularly relaxing."

"I've heard that. I think Quinn and Anna have been trying to plan something too, and I don't know, maybe all of the Shaughnessys would go, but you should ask her about it. It's more fun when you go with the group. Of course, they're going to the Florida Disney and not the California one."

"I don't think I'd mind which one we went to, as long as Lucas had fun."

"How could he not, right?"

It was a perfectly normal conversation. Nothing that should have his mind wandering to anything sexy, yet all he had to do was look at her and his mind went there.

Maybe offering to drive her home hadn't been the smartest idea.

A little too late to come to that realization, dummy, he chided himself.

Two minutes later they pulled into her driveway and climbed out of the truck. He thought about offering to just wait outside but realized he was being a little overdramatic. Surely they could handle being alone in her house together without him pouncing.

Maybe.

Teagan unlocked the door and Bobby followed her into the house. "Just give me five minutes and we'll be good to go," she called out as she walked to Lucas's room.

While she was gone, he took a minute to look around the space. He'd been in her house twice before but never really noticed the details. She had a ton of framed photos on display, mostly of her and Lucas, and they made him smile. His sister had done the same thing when she lived here. Walking over to the built-in bookshelves, he examined some of the photographs more closely. There was one of Teagan holding a newborn Lucas. She looked so young, and so happy. Unable to help himself, he reached out and touched the picture as if he could actually feel them.

He moved over to the next picture, when Lucas was maybe a year old and Teagan was blowing bubbles. Next was a birthday picture where the boy had cake all over his face. The more Bobby looked, the more he realized it was like watching Lucas grow up right before his eyes. In every picture, Teagan smiled so beautifully, so happily, that it wasn't hard to see how much she loved being a mother.

The last picture was of her wearing a cap and gown and holding Lucas. It didn't appear to be from that long ago. He remembered her telling him about getting her master's and figured that's what the photo had to be from. It was hard to imagine taking on as much as Teagan had. Bobby imagined some people would abandon their dream of finishing their education if they were in her shoes. But she had done it and now she was getting ready to tackle a new job in a new state, and… damn. Did she ever just want to give up? Throw in the towel because it was too hard? How did she find the strength to keep going?

Here he was facing one obstacle and he was ready throw in the towel.

"It wasn't easy balancing the cap and tassel on my head with a four-year-old who thought it was some sort of pull toy," she said softly from right next to him. "Luckily, my mom is quick with a camera and got the shot before he pulled the cap off my head completely." She was smiling as she looked at the picture.

"You've got some great memories here," he said, his voice a little gruff. He cleared his throat. "You've done an amazing job with Lucas. He's a great kid. You can see how happy he is just by looking at these pictures."

"Or maybe we're just good at capturing him at the right moment," she teased. "I told you my mom is good with a camera."

He knew she was trying to make light of the compliment, but he wouldn't have it. Facing her, he reached out and caressed her cheek. It was impossible not to. "It's not a trick of the camera or just getting him at the right moment. It's you, Teagan. You did all this.

You're raising an amazing kid because you're an amazing mom." He paused and moved just a little bit closer. "But that's not all there is to you, you know. You're an incredibly beautiful, talented, and sexy woman."

"Bobby," she said, but it was barely a whisper.

Taking it as a good sign that she wasn't nearly as unaffected as she'd like him to believe, he moved in closer still. Her big, beautiful eyes gazed up at him and he saw the same desire there that he knew mirrored his own.

It was too much. Being this close to her tested him beyond his self-control. Bending slightly, he lowered his head until their lips were nothing but a breath apart. "Tell me to stop."

But she didn't. Instead, she shook her head and surprised him by saying, "I can't."

He said a quick prayer of thanks just before his lips touched hers. For as much as he thought his self-control was gone, the moment Teagan leaned into him, it was back. Where he thought he wanted to plunder, all he could do was slowly sip at her, taste her, until they both sank into the kiss. Bobby's hands cupped her face as his tongue teased at her lips. He was content to keep doing this, to do this and never stop, but then her hands grazed up his chest, over his shoulder, and up into his hair. Her nails raked along his scalp and that's when he knew he was wrong.

He wanted more.

Much more.

Her lips opened to his, their tongues touched, and all hints of slow and sweet were gone. Now he wanted to devour. His hands got in on the action as they moved from the soft skin of her face down over her throat and around to her bare back. All afternoon he'd been dying to touch her there. Her skin was hot and smooth, and he knew she'd feel like that all over. His hands fairly twitched with the need to explore and find out.

Standing in the middle of the living room wasn't working for him. He needed to lay her down on a soft surface and feel her under him, over him. Slowly, he maneuvered them until they were next to her couch, and then he guided her down. Teagan went willingly, and as he lay down beside her, she simply wrapped herself around him.

He was a goner.

Never had the simple act of kissing a woman aroused him so much. Never had he felt so consumed to touch and savor being touched. This? Right here, right now with Teagan? Was beyond anything he'd ever experienced. It would only get better. It had to.

He moved his lips to kiss her cheek, her shoulder, and then up to the sensitive spot right below her ear. She tasted even better than she felt. He could feast on her for hours, and with the way she was moving against him, he knew she wouldn't mind. Bobby kissed, licked, and touched everywhere he could reach. He murmured her name against her skin and loved the way she trembled in his arms.

For her part, Teagan was still holding his head, tugging his hair, and it was sexy as hell. He wanted to keep moving his way down her body but wasn't sure he could be so bold with her. Not yet. But then she was guiding him and moving so his lips hovered over her breasts. In that moment, he felt like the universe must really love him, because he was being rewarded for something in ways he hadn't dared imagine.

Through the thin fabric of her top, he kissed her, savored her. Then he settled in against her breast and they both sighed at the contact. Flicking his tongue against her nipple felt wildly erotic. Teagan's back arched as she cried out his name.

That was like hitting the launch button.

Need for her threatened to overwhelm him. There was so much more he wanted to do to her, *with* her. As much as he was enjoying making her squirm, the need to hear her cry out his name again and again took over.

Quickly, he moved back up and captured her lips, kissing her until they were both breathless. He settled over her, between her legs, and the contact as he nestled between her thighs was like finding heaven. Suddenly, he was sixteen again and ready to make his big move right there on a living room sofa, and he didn't even care. It wasn't until he rocked his hips, rubbed against her, that Teagan broke the kiss. She was breathless, her lips red and wet, and he was ready to dive in for another taste before she stopped him.

She looked up at him, her eyes a little dazed. "Bobby," she began, taking a minute to catch her breath, "we have to... I mean, we can't... I'm not ready for this. I'm sorry."

Those last two words did it. He quickly moved off her—off the couch entirely—and sat heavily on the one opposite it. He raked a hand through his hair and did his best to catch his breath before looking at her. Once he did, she was sitting up, looking completely tousled and sexy, and he practically had to sit on his own hands to keep from reaching for her again.

And he actually groaned when she licked her lips.

"Okay, look," he said, hoping he sounded calm and reasonable, "please don't freak out on me. Please. I feel like we keep taking one step forward and then, like, ten back." He paused because she wasn't looking at him. She was looking at her hands, tightly clasped in her lap. "Teagan?"

He could tell she was nervous. She smoothed her hair and fidgeted in her seat for a moment. "I—I don't even know what to say," she said, her voice barely above a whisper. "That was all…unexpected."

"No, it wasn't," he said with a little more heat than was necessary. He was seriously frustrated, and he wasn't going to let her shut him out again. "You and I both know why it happened, and that it will probably happen again." He jumped to his feet. "So why keep denying it?"

Now it was her turn to stand. "Because I have to! I've already explained my position to you, and I can't keep saying it over and over. You have to accept my feelings!"

It was a crock of bull and they both knew it.

Taking the two steps to face her, he countered, "For someone who keeps saying she's not looking to get involved, you certainly didn't do anything to stop what just happened! I asked you to tell me to stop and you said you couldn't. There is no way I'm taking all the blame for this. That's not fair."

She covered her face with her hands, and he felt awful for losing his temper. Taking a steadying breath, they sat down beside each other.

"I'm sorry," he said. "That was uncalled for."

Lowering her hands, she looked at him. "You don't have to apologize, Bobby—I do. You're right. I knew exactly what I was doing, and what I wanted, and it was wrong of me to try and put the blame on you."

Her apology made him feel only marginally better. "I don't think we need to be assigning blame. What we need to do is talk about this, because—let's face it—it's not going away. We can both acknowledge we're attracted to one another, and after what just happened here, I think we can also agree we both want more than to be friends."

And then he held his breath, because he seriously thought she'd deny it.

She didn't.

Looking back down at her hands, she said, "I don't know how to do that. My life is…it's complicated. There's no way I can enter into some casual affair. Not even for you."

She was ripping his heart in two and didn't even realize it.

"Who says it has to be casual?" The question surprised him, even as he was speaking it.

The look on her face showed she was equally stunned.

"I'm serious," he said, reaching for her hands. "I know all about you, Teagan. I'm aware that you're a mother first, and nothing is more important than that. I'm just asking for a chance to be a part of your life."

She was about to answer—he saw it in her eyes— but her phone rang, ruining the moment. Reaching for her purse, she grabbed the phone and answered. From what he could overhear, it was one of her parents asking where she was and when she'd be back. Apparently, they were getting ready to serve the cake.

So this…*whatever* it was would have to wait.

Again.

Once she hung up, she turned toward him, her expression sad. "We, um, we need to get back."

Desperate times called for desperate measures. "We're not done with this."

"I know, I know," she said wearily. "But now's not the time."

"Let me come back with you tonight," he said, hating the desperation in his voice. "Lucas won't be here, there won't be any interruptions. Please."

Her eyes went wide. "I don't think it's a good idea."

"Why?"

"Because... I, um..."

Bobby walked over to her and just as he had earlier, cupped her face in his hands. "You've accused me of walking away whenever things got uncomfortable, and I'll admit that it's a bad habit of mine. But now it's you who's running. All I'm asking for is you to please sit and talk with me. That's it. Just talk."

She frowned and it was cute as hell. "I think we both know that's a lie. We may say it now, but later on..."

Yeah. He knew it too and was glad he wasn't the only one thinking that way. "I'm not willing to let this go, Teagan. I can't."

Her shoulders sagged with defeat. "You're right."

He'd give everything he had to know what she was thinking right now. Was she even aware of just how much he wanted her, how much he wanted simply to be alone with her for any amount of time she was willing to give him?

He nodded. "Okay, then. We'll come back here after the party and...talk."

With a nod of her own, she moved away from him

to pick up Lucas's bag. Neither spoke as they left or for the entirety of the ride back to the party. As soon as he parked the truck, he let her walk into the yard alone while he sat and watched.

How was he going to survive the rest of the day knowing tonight he'd finally have her all to himself?

The party was winding down, only a handful of people left. Teagan was sitting around one of the patio tables along with her cousins—and Bobby. While she loved having this time with her family, it was hard to focus on anything anyone was saying. She could feel his eyes on her, just as she had felt his hands on her earlier.

God, what had she been thinking? If the phone hadn't rung when it did, she believed she would have begged Bobby to make love to her. She'd been so far gone, so overcome with need for him, that it was all she'd wanted.

And if she were honest, it was still what she wanted.

No doubt all she had to do was say the word and he'd give her exactly that. And no doubt she'd enjoy every single second of it. Then why did she feel so... bad about it all? Why was she second- and even third-guessing herself? She'd been celibate for six years, for crying out loud! Wasn't she entitled to have one night of fun for herself?

Really, no matter what Bobby said, she knew he wasn't interested in more than that. His reputation spoke for itself. Right now she was a novelty. Something he wanted but couldn't have. Once he had her, he'd be more than okay with moving on.

But would she?

It wasn't as if she'd have a choice. She was an adult, and surely she could handle having one night with a man she found to be incredibly sexy and attractive and… She sighed.

Everything.

Bobby Hannigan was really the total package. So why not take that one night? If her heart broke afterward, it would be all right. It had been broken before and she'd survived. Barely, but she'd survived. The only difference was this time, no one would know. Any grief and disappointment she felt would be hers and hers alone.

And if she had to avoid certain family gatherings for a while just so there weren't any awkward encounters, then…so be it. It wasn't the end of the world, right?

Feeling confident that she could not only do this, but do it with few to no regrets, Teagan finally felt like she could breathe. All around her people were talking and laughing, and when Aidan asked her about her new job as the guidance counselor at the local elementary school, she was excited to reply.

Soon the sun was setting and the kids clamored to get their sleeping bags ready. Quinn promised to order pizzas, which made them even more excited to head inside.

"So what are you going to do with yourself tonight?" Anna asked. "You'll have the house all to yourself!"

Smiling, Teagan replied, "I don't really have anything planned, but I think there's a glass of wine and a good book in my future."

"Ooo, that does sound good," Zoe chimed in. "I can't remember the last time I had the entire place to myself."

Aidan looked at his wife and frowned. "I haven't had the place to myself either, you know."

Before they could go any further, Riley spoke up. "It's not a competition, kids," he teased and then looked over at Bobby. "What about you, Hannigan? Now that you're free of your sling, I bet you're out on the prowl again."

Teagan shifted uncomfortably in her chair.

"Nah," Bobby said with a small laugh.

"Oh, come on," Aidan said with a laugh of his own. "You're in town for the weekend, it's like seven o'clock on a Saturday night, and you're telling us you have no plans to go down to the pub and find a hookup?"

For his part, Bobby didn't look at all put out by the questions. "That's what I'm sayin'."

Quinn snorted as he stood up. "Right. Because you enjoy sitting in your parents' living room watching reruns of *Law & Order*. Come on, dude. Fess up! We all know it's what you're gonna do. It's what you always do. Why deny it?"

Before Bobby could respond, Teagan rose. "I think I'm going to go kiss Lucas good night and head out. That peace and quiet is definitely calling my name!"

She kissed her cousins goodbye before heading into the house to do the same with her son.

"Be good for Anna and Quinn, okay?" she said as she hugged him close.

"I will, Mom, I promise," he said before he scrambled out of her arms and ran to join his cousins.

For a minute, she stood and stared after him. It wasn't until Anna came up next to her and put her arm around Teagan that she turned her head. "He's going to have a great time, don't worry about a thing. Why don't you pick him up tomorrow after lunch—say around two? Will that work?"

"Are you kidding?" she laughed. "I don't know what I'm going to do with all that free time!"

Anna hugged her close. "I'm living vicariously through you, so sleep late, eat doughnuts in bed, and watch a good chick flick without any interruptions."

"Wow. You've really put some thought into this, huh?"

"You have no idea." Then she turned Teagan toward the front door and gave her a gentle nudge. "Go. Have a good night and we'll see you tomorrow."

"Thanks again," she said as she made her way to the door.

Out in the driveway, she was relieved to find that her car was no longer blocked in. She held her breath as she waited to see if Bobby was going to come out of the yard and pounce. In the distance, she heard a round of laughter and could detect his voice among the others. She let out her breath and shook her head. Maybe this really wasn't meant to be. Hearing her cousins all egging him on about one-night stands made her sick to her stomach. If she did this—if she allowed him to come home with her and spend the night—she was no better than the faceless women everyone was just talking about.

And that definitely wasn't who she wanted to be.

That answered that. She'd text him and tell him she'd changed her mind and would see him around.

Climbing into her car, she quickly typed out the text before turning her phone on silent for the drive home. Better to do it sooner rather than later. She was out of the driveway and about to put the car in drive when Bobby jogged up to her. There was no way to pretend she didn't see him, so she stopped.

He held up his phone to her. "What the hell?"

Don't cave, she warned herself. *Stand firm.* "I changed my mind," she said, but couldn't make herself look him in the eye.

"Bullshit," he said, bending down so they were face to face. "What's going on, Teagan?"

She let out a huff of annoyance. "Seriously?"

He nodded.

"Let's just say I was on the fence about this to begin with. And after listening to that whole conversation back there, I realized I didn't feel like being one of your hookups. After hearing the way everyone talked about it, I realized I couldn't. It's not what I want, and I certainly wouldn't ever want anyone talking about me that way."

His expression was hard and she could tell he was angry, and she tried to tell herself she didn't care.

But she did.

More than anything, she wanted to be carefree and not let the gossip bother her. But she was a practical and responsible woman, and that was hard to just push aside and forget—no matter how badly she wanted to. Casual wasn't her thing, no matter how much she tried to tell herself otherwise.

"I still think we should talk," he finally said.

Shaking her head, she replied, "It won't change anything. I'm not someone who fits in your world, Bobby. And honestly, I'm not ready for this."

"Okay, maybe not now," he said, his voice calm, gentle.

But she shook her head again and looked at him sadly. "I don't know if I'll ever be." Glancing toward the house, she saw Aidan and Zoe coming around from the side gate. "I should go."

He nodded, straightened, and took a step back. And didn't say a word.

Before she could change her mind, she pulled away. A glance in the rearview mirror showed him still standing in the middle of the street. She wondered what Aidan and Zoe would say when they saw him there and then realized she was better off not knowing.

The drive home was short, and once she was inside, she kicked off her sandals and collapsed on the sofa. Bad idea. Images of what she and Bobby had done earlier surrounded her.

"Nope. Not going there," she muttered, jumping to her feet. Walking into the kitchen, she went to pour herself a glass of wine but found she didn't have any in the house. Ready to bang her head on the wall, she said, "I just cannot catch a break tonight."

It was early enough that she could run to the store to get a bottle, but that required more of an effort than she was willing to put in right now.

"Maybe I should just crawl into bed and try to forget this day ever happened." Easier said than done. "But first I should have ice cream. Lots and lots of ice cream."

Reaching into the freezer, she pulled out a container of chocolate ice cream, one of cookies and cream, and one of butter pecan, followed by raiding the cupboards for all of her favorite toppings—chocolate syrup, sprinkles, and whipped cream—and made herself one massive sundae. Once everything was put away, she looked at the bowl and tried to make herself feel bad about it, but she couldn't.

"Tonight's special is the pity-party sundae. Enough ice cream for three people, but only served to one."

Dipping her spoon in, Teagan took a giant bite and instantly regretted it. "Brain freeze! Dammit!"

Tossing the spoon down, she held her head and gave herself a minute to let the pain pass. Then she let out a long breath, picked up her bowl, and walked into her bedroom. If she wasn't going to get any pleasure from a man in bed tonight, she'd have to settle for getting it from food.

"Crappy substitute," she mumbled, crawling onto her bed and reaching for the TV remote. Channel surfing was the only thing that accomplished, nothing catching her eye. If anything, it was as if every show had been specifically chosen to annoy her. "I should have gotten the wine. And maybe a hotel room on the beach with a big bathtub."

She was three bites in when there was a loud knock on her door.

It didn't take a genius to figure out who it was.

"Seriously cannot catch a break," she sighed, putting the ice cream down on the kitchen island as she walked by. Nervously, she smoothed her hair and her top before she even attempted to open the door. And when she did, all the air rushed out of her lungs.

Bobby was standing with both hands braced on the doorframe. His hair was a mess and there was a fire in his eyes that she was coming to recognize was there whenever he looked at her. She whispered his name, but she barely heard herself.

"Did it ever occur to you that the way people perceive me isn't who I really am?" he asked instead of greeting her. "I can't change the way people think, or what they think they know. Did I date a lot when I lived here? Yes.

I was young and a little wild and a whole lot stupid. But I haven't been that guy in years and no one seems to realize it. I moved away because I wanted to change. I needed to change. And my reasons were… Well, they're not important right now."

"Bobby—"

He held up a hand to stop her. "I'm not going to lie to you, I never had to work hard before to win over a woman, but I was always respectful. And the fact that you're different—not blatantly throwing yourself at me—is something I've never experienced before."

"So maybe that's all this is to you," she said, feeling a little defensive. "I'm a challenge. But what happens if you get me, Bobby? You'll walk away once the challenge is gone. And you know what? I don't want to play that game. It's insulting to us both."

He hadn't moved from his position bracketing the doorway. "You're right. It would be insulting. And it's not why I'm here. It's not why I'm attracted to you, Teagan."

"Please don't," she said. "Don't stand here and make excuses. We're adults and we should at least be honest with each other."

"That's what I'm trying to be! Dammit, you still don't get it, do you?" He didn't wait for an answer. "You know what first attracted me to you?"

She shook her head.

"The fact that Quinn annoyed you. I had never met anyone who seemed as genuinely annoyed by him as I was."

"That's not—"

"It is and it was," he countered. "Then it was the way you talked to me at the barbecue. I was pissed off at the world and everyone was trying to coddle me and tell me

I shouldn't be upset or I shouldn't feel the way I was feeling. You were the first person—the *only* person—who seemed to understand how I felt."

She remembered the look on his face when she'd told him that.

"Don't let anyone get to you. You're entitled to feel the way you feel."

"I watched you with Lucas, I listened to the things you said, and more than anything, I thought 'this is a woman I want to get to know.' This isn't about looking for a hookup or a way to pass the time, I genuinely like you," he explained. "I like your honesty, and the way you don't mince words. I'm in awe of your parenting skills and the way you love your son. But even more than that, I look at you and I just…I feel better. You're like this incredible breath of fresh air in my life."

Wow. She hadn't expected that.

"All of your cousins? They're married and settling down and sickeningly happy—one of them to my sister! I look at them and I see everything I want. And as much as everyone talks about me playing the field, what no one realizes is…it's mostly because no one wanted anything more from me. It wasn't only me who didn't do commitments. None of the women I dated wanted one from me."

Then he hung his head and muttered a curse. "Probably should have left that part out. Not the best endorsement when I'm trying to convince you to take a chance on me." He dropped his arms and he took a step back. When he looked at her, his expression was bleak. Defeated. "I'm sorry. I—I should go."

It took her a minute to understand he was really leaving. She called out to him and stepped onto the front porch. "Wait!" she cried when he didn't turn around. The only option was to chase after him.

Barefoot, she caught up to him on the driveway. When he finally looked at her, Teagan had no idea what to say. Staring at him, she wished she could convey what she was feeling.

Reaching up, she cupped her hand around the nape of his neck and pulled him down until her lips touched his. She kissed him and poured everything—every thought, every feeling, all that she had—into it. It took less than a second for Bobby to wrap his arms around her and pull her close, effectively taking control of the kiss.

Control she gladly gave to him.

It was madness. They were standing in her driveway where anyone could see them, and she didn't care. All that mattered was getting closer to him, touching him, loving him.

Bobby was the first to break the kiss. His breath was ragged and his eyes tortured. "Teagan," he said quietly, "I can't do this again. I can't start this and have you send me away one more time." Slowly, he took a step back. "So it's… I mean, I should go."

Was he serious? Panic had her by the throat. Could she really let him walk away? Who knew relationships could be this much of an emotional roller coaster? When Bobby turned to open the truck door, she frantically reached for his hand.

"No!" she cried and almost smiled at the shocked look on his face. "Don't go."

"We've been here before, and it was wrong for me to push." His look was borderline pitiful. "I never should have done it."

"You didn't push me—"

"But when you're ready, I'll be waiting, okay? I want you to know that. You mean that much to me. I think about you all the time and—and I think we could have something special." He paused and let out a long breath. "That's why I can wait. Because I know we'll be worth it."

She studied him for a moment. "And when I'm ready, you'll be waiting?"

He nodded.

"And…what would I have to do—or say—to let you know I'm ready?"

One hand rose to caress her cheek, but he lowered it before he could actually touch her. "You just have to call and tell me you need me," he said, his voice a gruff whisper. "And I'll be there. Wherever you want me."

Nodding, she cocked her head to the side. "Wait, did you hear something?"

He looked at her oddly. "Hear what?"

"I think it's my phone," she said, looking toward the house and then back to him. "Can you just give me a minute? It could be about Lucas."

"Go," he said quickly. "I'll wait here."

She ran into the house, pulled her phone out of her purse, and smiled. It never rang, she hadn't heard a thing. She pulled up Bobby's number and hit Send. As it rang, she was practically bouncing on her toes.

"Hello?" he asked hesitantly.

"I need you," she said softly and—hopefully—seductively.

She heard him chuckle. The sound was deep and rich and husky and made her tingle from head to toe.

Then he was standing in her entryway looking both

vulnerable and sexy, and everything she could ask for in a man.

"Where do you want me?" he asked.

Confidence sparked up in Teagan, more than she had ever felt in her entire life. Walking toward him, she reached around him, shut the front door, and locked it. Then she looked up at him and gave him the sexiest smile she could.

"Everywhere, Bobby. I want you everywhere."

—✺—

Mind. Blown.

That was the only way to describe the feeling that coursed through him at Teagan's words. There wasn't a doubt in his mind that he should have left after admitting everything he had. Never in a million years would he have predicted that she would turn the tables on him like this.

But damn. He was glad she did.

There were so many things he wanted to say, but the thought of waiting any longer to touch her was too much.

Later, he told himself. There'd be plenty of time to talk later.

Right now, all he wanted to do was move them from the entryway to—well, anyplace else. His hands ran up and down her back before settling on her bottom and gently squeezing. She hummed her approval and pressed closer.

"Wrap your legs around me," he growled against her lips as he lifted her. She did as he asked, mouth hot against his jaw as he walked them toward the couch. When she realized where he was going, Teagan shook her head.

"Bedroom," she said breathlessly. "Please."

This girl, he thought with a grin.

Taking the few extra steps to get them to her bedroom, he gently set her down on the bed. As much as he hated to break the contact, he just needed to look at her for a minute. Her dark hair fanned out against the soft, dove-gray comforter that covered the queen-size bed. For a moment, he pictured her sprawled out on his bed back home. The king bed was larger, his decor a lot more masculine, but the image of her there was so vivid he knew he'd find a way to make it a reality.

Part of him was ready to go for it, but the rational part of him, the one that had showed up earlier and was prepared to leave, held him back.

"This isn't right," he said, hating how heavily his conscience was weighing on him.

Teagan propped herself up on her elbows and looked at him with confusion. "What do you mean?"

"I should have asked you out on a proper date," he said, shaking his head. "We could have gone to dinner or…or a movie. But what do I do instead? I come here and carry you to bed. Don't you see how wrong that is?"

Tilting her head, she stared at him for a solid minute. He had no idea what she was thinking. Was she going to ask him to leave? Suggest they go somewhere and talk? Although…she had been the one to invite him in, and she was the one who'd pulled *him* in for one hell of a kiss. Why was he overthinking this so damn much? And why now? He was so close to having everything he wanted. Why would he open his mouth and ruin it?

Okay, *ruin* wasn't the right word. He'd only spoken

the truth. He should have taken her out on a date. Several dates. And instead he'd skipped the whole getting-to-know-you phase of a relationship and jumped to the physical.

I loathe myself.

"So, you're saying you don't want to do this," Teagan said, as if trying to get a better grasp on the situation. "And you'd rather take me out on a date."

He nodded.

"Can I ask you something?"

He nodded again.

"Would going out for breakfast count as a date?"

When he met her gaze, he saw the sassy grin on her face and the twinkle in her eyes. He might just be the luckiest man alive. Trying to hide his amusement, he responded, "I believe it would."

"Hmm…" she hummed, rising to her knees on the bed. Then she reached for him. "How about we try that tomorrow. You know, after we both wake up?"

Bobby almost sagged with relief. Banding an arm around her waist, he pulled her flush against him. "Sweetheart, I'll buy you the biggest breakfast we can find. That's a promise."

"I'm going to hold you to it," she said against his lips. And then she kissed him.

He pulled back to look at her face, taking in her impish smile and the way her eyes were practically dancing. "As long as I get to hold you all night, then I'm good."

Then they were done talking.

Guiding them both gently back down to the mattress, he claimed her lips with his. Teagan's silky limbs slowly wrapped back around him as he settled between her thighs. This was so much better than how it had been earlier in the day. Now he knew why—they were done running. They were both in this together, and after tonight, everything was going to be different.

Better.

More.

They kissed each other like they were each other's lifeline. As much as he loved the way her lips felt, the way her tongue danced against his, he wanted more. He wanted to feel her skin beneath his hands, wanted to kiss every inch of her. And after that... His thoughts immediately veered in X-rated directions.

Rising up, he broke their kiss and disentangled Teagan to work at gently sliding her capris down her legs. He laughed as she kicked them away instead. He slid his hands under her top and pushed it over her head before tossing it away over his shoulder.

She was a living, breathing fantasy, dressed in nothing but simple white cotton panties.

Bobby swore he'd never seen anything sexier. She must have taken his silence for displeasure, because she started to squirm.

"Had I known where this night was going, I would have invested in something a little sexier."

The uncertainty in her voice only made her more attractive to him. He'd always thought her honesty was one of his biggest turn-ons, and this proved it. Placing a hand over her stomach, he took a moment to revel in the warmth of her skin. Then he looked up at her face, saw her biting her lip, and said, "There is nothing you could have worn that was sexier than this."

She rolled her eyes and let out a nervous laugh. "Bobby, come on…"

"I'm serious. The way you look right now is better—sexier—than I even imagined." He paused and gave her a lecherous grin. "And believe me, I've imagined plenty where you're concerned."

As she swatted at him playfully, he leaned forward and captured her wrists, pinning them above her head. Her eyes went wide and she licked her lips.

Did she have any idea how sexy she was? How turned on he was?

"I think one of us is overdressed," she said, feigning a struggle to get out of his grip. All it did was cause her breasts to sway seductively.

He instantly released her and whipped off the rest of his clothes. When he was down to his briefs, he joined her back on the bed. "I believe this makes us even."

But rather than being pleased, she pouted.

"What? What's wrong?"

"I was kind of hoping…well…" She went back to biting her lip, and a blush covered her cheeks.

It wasn't hard to figure out what she was trying to say.

Without breaking eye contact, he slowly took off his briefs. Teagan's gaze held his, although he did catch her glancing down once. When he was naked, he rolled toward her and pulled her in close, holding her skin to skin. They both sighed at the contact.

"Bobby?"

"Hmm?"

"Make love to me."

Reaching up, he caressed her cheek. "Sweetest words I've ever heard."

—∼—

It was well after midnight and the house was completely dark. Teagan stared up at the ceiling and tried to will herself into calm. Her heart was racing, her stomach was roiling, and if she didn't know any better, she'd swear she was having a panic attack.

Then the tears started.

Bobby was sound asleep beside her, and the last thing she wanted to do was have him wake up and hear her crying. She wiped furiously at her eyes, doing her best to stop the tears from falling, but she couldn't. There were too many, falling too fast to stop anytime soon.

Carefully, she rose from the bed, grabbed her robe from the hook on the bathroom door, and tiptoed out to the living room, closing the bedroom door behind her. She sank down on the couch, pulling her knees to her chest as she cried.

She felt like the world's biggest fraud. She was an emotional wreck, and why? She'd just spent hours making love with an amazing man who'd both let her set the pace and somehow knew exactly what she needed. It had nothing to do with him—he was perfect. It was her.

Logan had been the only man she'd ever slept with, the only man she'd ever loved. Sleeping with Bobby tonight had been like finally taking that last step to move on. And for the life of her, she didn't know if she was crying because she was happy or because she was sad.

Having the courage to take that step tonight was something Teagan hadn't believed she'd ever have. But there was something about Bobby that made her want to be brave. And everything about these last hours had been wonderful. For all that she'd loved Logan and how special their relationship had been, they had been so young. No more than kids, really. The man in her bed right now was…well. He was more than she expected. He'd made her feel things she'd never felt before, and made her want to do things she'd never done before.

It was sexy and exciting and…terrifying. Yes, terrifying. As much as she didn't want to think about how much experience Bobby had, or how much he'd dated, it was obvious that in the bedroom, he was way out of her league. She only hoped he wasn't disappointed in her.

Lifting her head, she wiped her tears away and took several steadying breaths.

"If he wasn't disappointed in you before, he certainly would be now," she murmured.

Someone's hand descended on her shoulder and she screamed.

Bobby walked around and sat down in front of her on the couch. It was dark, the moonlight was offering a mere sliver of illumination in the room, but she could see him and the concerned look on his face.

She went to speak but he placed a finger over her lips.

"I didn't mean to eavesdrop. But when I woke up and you weren't in bed, I came looking for you. I wasn't expecting to find you out here crying." She heard the pain in his voice and knew she had to put his mind at ease.

"It's not what you think—"

"You don't have to tell me," he quickly interrupted. "I was just wondering where you went. And when I opened the door, I heard you crying."

"Bobby…"

He stroked one finger down her cheek. "I don't know why you would think that I'm disappointed, but I'm not. Everything about tonight has been amazing. You're amazing," he clarified. "If anything, I was worried I had hurt you."

She stared at him as if he were crazy. "Why would you think that?"

"What am I supposed to think when I find you out here in the dark?" he asked softly. "Teagan, I'm not stupid. We've talked enough. I know it's been a long time for you since, well, you know."

She nodded.

"And I know I was a little…aggressive."

She smiled. "I kind of liked that. Actually, I liked it a lot," she said shyly.

"Really?"

"Really. And I wasn't crying because of anything you did. It was me. I got too deep into my own head and… tonight was just—it was—" She huffed with annoyance because she couldn't seem to find the right words.

"I get it," he said, saving her from having to scramble. "It's the same for me."

"What?"

Now it was his turn to nod. "What we have? What we started here tonight? It's like a new chapter for the both of us."

Her shoulders sagged and she scrambled to climb into his lap to hug him. "That's it exactly." As he held her tight, she rested her head on his shoulder. "Can I ask you something?"

"Anything."

"Can we work on this chapter a little more tonight?" She was thankful for the darkness hiding her blush, because she couldn't believe how bold she was being.

Carefully, he stood with her in his arms and walked back to the bedroom, kicking the door closed behind them as he passed. "We can work on this chapter over and over until we get it right," he promised.

And in that moment, she fell a little in love with him.

Chapter 6

"YOU KNOW THIS WASN'T QUITE WHAT I HAD IN MIND, right?"

Teagan took a bite of her pancake and grinned. "Have I ever told you how much I hate going food shopping?"

Laughing, Bobby reached for his coffee cup and took a sip. "So your idea of a date is sending me to the grocery store, is that what you're saying?"

She shrugged and took another bite. After a minute, she said, "Maybe. But then I made the food for you, so it kind of balanced out." Then she smiled at him and he couldn't help but smile back. Teagan Shaughnessy was not what he'd expected. If nothing else, he was enjoying the way she kept him on his toes.

"I was all ready to take you out to the diner and let someone else do all the work," he explained. "The last thing I want is for you to feel like you have to cook for me."

Another shrug. "Believe it or not, there is a reason why I chose to go this route."

He looked at her expectantly.

First she took a sip of her coffee, then she looked at him sweetly. "In this scenario, we don't have to talk to anyone else, we don't have to feel rushed, and I get to stay in my pajamas for a whole lot longer."

Reaching across the table, he gently ran a finger

over her robe. "You're not wearing any pajamas," he said huskily.

"Hmm... You do seem to have a point there," she replied, giving him a sassy grin. "I guess that means we have less to deal with when we head back to bed."

Bobby knew his eyes were widening almost comically. He thought for sure she would be looking for excuses to send him on his way now, say that she needed to go and pick up Lucas. But...

Standing, she reached for the tie on her robe and pulled it loose. Just the sight of her naked body under the basic flannel was enough to make him hard. Walking over to him, she opened the robe even more and surprised him further by straddling his lap.

"I—uh... I thought you'd need to go pick up Lucas," he said lamely, fighting to hold on to his self-control.

"I don't have to be over to Anna's until around two." Glancing over her shoulder at the wall clock, she turned back to him. "And it's only nine." Her arms draped over his shoulders. "So unless you have anywhere to be..."

Even if he did, he would cancel it.

He cursed his shorts and the fact that there were plates covered in syrup on the table, because the thought of laying her out right here as part of his breakfast was too good to bear. Swallowing hard, he let his gaze linger over her exposed breasts, up her throat to her lips, where it paused for a moment before coming to rest on her eyes. They were a little dazed, a little heated. Her breath came out in little pants, and he knew it would take very little to give her exactly what she wanted, bring her over the edge.

"Tell me what you need, Teagan," he said, his voice dark, low, a near-growl.

"Touch me," she whispered.

His hands came to rest beneath her robe at her waist. "Like this?"

She shook her head, but her head fell back slightly as his thumbs gently stroked her skin.

Slowly, he moved his hands up until they cupped her breasts. "This?"

Her hips moved against him in a way that left no doubt what she wanted. Clasping her hard around the waist, Bobby lifted her as he stood, and it only took two steps to set her on the kitchen island. She gasped with surprise, but he didn't wait to hear if she'd say anything else before claiming her lips with his.

If he could, he'd be touching her everywhere at once. As it was, his movements were frantic and not at all smooth. One hand yanked her robe off her shoulders while the other went to unfasten his shorts. He was about to take what he wanted—what they both wanted—when he paused and cursed.

Teagan straightened and looked at him oddly. "What? What's the matter?"

Rather than answer, he ran into the bedroom, grabbed a condom, and quickly sheathed himself.

And then it was purely, simply heaven.

It was everything he'd ever dreamed of—*she* was everything he'd ever dreamed of.

They moved together perfectly, wild and untamed, and it was over way too fast, but that didn't matter.

Carefully, he lifted her and carried her back to bed where they curled around one another breathlessly.

"Wow," she said, her head on his shoulder, her hand on his chest. "That was—wow."

Smiling, he kissed the top of her head. "Yeah. My words exactly."

Looking up at him, she asked, "Really?"

After their brief conversation last night in the living room, he knew she was more than a little insecure. Tucking a finger under her chin, he said, "Really. You completely blew me away. I wanted to swipe all the dishes off the table and have you right there."

Her eyes went wide with wonder. "Wow."

"Yeah, wow," he said with a small laugh. "Teagan Shaughnessy, you are the sexiest woman I've ever met."

Wonder turned to disbelief. "You don't have to say that, Bobby. I know who and what I am."

He held her face so she couldn't look away. "Clearly, you don't if you think I'm lying. You know what I thought last night when I stripped you down?"

"That I wore plain underwear and had stretch marks?"

While her tone was light, her eyes told him she was serious. He shook his head. "No. I thought you were a living, breathing fantasy."

When she tried to move away, he held her firm, and she looked up at him skeptically. "How is that possible? I have mirrors, Bobby. I know I'm in decent shape, but...I've had a baby. There are stretch marks on my belly and even a few on my breasts. I live for plain cotton underwear. You can't tell me any of that is sexy. I'm sure the women you've slept with wore thongs and all kinds of lacy crap."

Many of them had, but for some reason, he couldn't picture a single one of them right now.

"Teagan, it doesn't matter what you're wearing.

It's not the underwear making you sexy, it's just you. Everything about you is a complete turn-on to me."

"Come on…"

"Look, I don't expect you to take my word for it right here, right now. But someday, you're going to realize I'm telling the truth."

He released her chin and relaxed against the pillows before instantly tensing up when Teagan kissed his shoulder—more specifically, the raised red scar from the gunshot wound.

"What are you doing?"

She looked up at him in confusion as she shifted to lie on her stomach beside him. "The lights have kind of been dimmed since you took your shirt off last night, and when we were in the kitchen you had most of your clothes on. This is the first time I've seen your shoulder with the light on."

Self-consciousness flooded him. Although, now that he thought about it, he was thankful his left arm and hand had cooperated all night and not given him any issues. How embarrassing would that have been?

Her fingers gently traced the ugly scar. The only people to ever look at it that closely had been medical professionals. This was a new, exposed feeling and oddly unsettling. He stilled her hand.

"Don't, okay? Just—it's pretty gruesome to look at still."

"Not to me," she said quietly.

"Teagan…"

"The way you feel about this scar?" she said, her voice firm but gentle. "That's the way I feel about my stretch marks. I know they're not the same, but… You look at me and say you see a sexy woman, even though I know I've got things wrong with me. Why is it so hard to believe I can look at you and see your scar and not be bothered by it?"

Okay, she had a point, but some faint stretch marks were nothing compared to that one hideous patch of scarred and puckered skin.

Not that he was going to argue with her about it right now.

"Can I say something without you freaking out?" she asked.

He nodded.

"Last night—and even all day yesterday at the party—your arm didn't seem to be causing you any issues. Have you talked to your doctor about maybe going back to work?"

It was funny—for weeks he'd been seriously anxious to get his medical clearance. And now all he could think about was how going back to work would mean he'd be two hours away from her. From Lucas.

What the…?

He gently cleared his throat. "Um. I have physical therapy tomorrow and a follow-up appointment with my doctor on Thursday, so…"

She smiled and he knew she was genuinely pleased for him. Didn't she realize what it would mean if he got approved to go back on duty? Didn't she care?

"You know if I go back to work I won't be around much, right?" he said, a little too defensively.

"O-kay…"

"I'm serious, Teagan. I work twelve-hour shifts, and my shifts aren't always the same. Before I got shot, I only came home to visit something like once a month. Doesn't that bother you? I mean, here we are in bed together, talking about starting this new chapter in life and...and...what? Now we're just okay with me not ever coming around?"

Twisting, she sat up and pulled the sheet to cover herself before looking at him.

Patiently.

Like he was an overacting idiot.

Which—he kind of was.

"Bobby, I don't expect you not to go back to work because we slept together."

And man, was that the wrong thing to say.

Jumping up from the bed, he reached for his boxers and put them on. "Seriously? That's what you're focusing on? Us sleeping together?"

Her sigh was definitely laced with annoyance, as was her expression. "Let me rephrase that. I don't expect you not to go back to work because we're *dating*. Happy, now?"

Honestly? No.

"If you hadn't gotten shot and we happened to meet at Uncle Ian's barbecue anyway, would we be here right now? I don't know," she said thoughtfully. "I'd like to think we would have."

"We would," he confirmed adamantly.

"We were attracted to each other, Bobby. And if the feelings we've been talking about are real, then we should be able to handle your work schedule no matter what it is. And let's not forget that in about a month I'm going back to work, Lucas is starting school, and my schedule's going to get complicated."

"You'll have weekends off. I might not."

"Okay, and we'll deal with that when the time comes," she said calmly. Soothingly. "Why look for trouble?"

Why, indeed?

Maybe because shit just got real. This was the first time he'd had to think about someone else where his life, his job, and his schedule were concerned. He didn't want to be away from her—or Lucas—for weeks on end. How were they ever going to really get to know each other and have time to settle into a relationship if he was never around?

"We don't have to have all the answers right now," she said, reaching for his hand and holding it. "And I don't want to spend our few precious hours alone arguing. Tomorrow, you'll go and do your physiotherapy and we'll talk. Then you'll go to the doctor and we'll talk again. But for now, can we just enjoy the time we do have?"

He knew she was right and he didn't want to waste their morning fighting. Between Lucas's schedule and Bobby living so far away, chances were it could be a very long time before they had an opportunity for an entire night to themselves again.

Bobby stripped off his boxers and joined her under the sheets, and spent the rest of the morning focusing on the here, and now, and her.

Dating was a lot more difficult than Teagan remembered it.

For starters, they lived two hours apart. So even if they wanted to see each other, logistics simply weren't on their side. They talked on the phone every day and she told herself it was enough. Bobby was doing his physical therapy and had met with his primary physician before being referred to a specialist for further testing on the nerve damage in his arm. It had been a lot of back-to-back medical appointments, with very few answers. She knew he was frustrated and she really felt for him.

Then there was Lucas.

When she had picked him up from his sleepover that afternoon, he had been so excited about his adventure. And when Bobby came over to their place later that afternoon and played ball with him again, it had made him hyperexcited, so he'd been a nightmare to deal with. Getting him to bed that night had been a herculean task. Luckily, Bobby hadn't been there to see it, because she wasn't proud of being a little short-tempered with her son. Between his behavior and her lack of sleep the night before, it had been a rough evening.

And every day since, Lucas had asked when Bobby was coming back to play.

Something she wondered too.

And to cap it all off, there was her cousin. Somehow Quinn had gotten a whiff of the tension between her and Bobby at the party and was doing his best to warn her away again. While she tried to distance herself from the images of the town playboy Quinn was painting, it was hard.

Okay, it was impossible. Every word Quinn said had her feeling a little sick to her stomach, and so self-conscious.

So how did she handle it?

She lied.

Teagan prided herself on her honesty, but in order to make Quinn stop, she didn't have a choice. "You're way off base here, Quinn," she'd said. "Whatever you think you saw, you're wrong. Bobby is a friend and I'm not looking to get involved with anyone. I appreciate your concern, but believe me, I'm good."

He seemed to believe her, but she felt awful about it anyway.

So here she was two weeks later, wondering if maybe…it wasn't a lie. Bobby hadn't come back to town. Maybe she had over-romanticized what had happened and they were going to end up being just friends.

Just friends who had a lot of wild sex, one night only.

Ugh…she was a cliché.

Ouch.

It was late Friday afternoon and she was contemplating getting pizza for dinner when there was a knock on her front door. Her mother was supposed to stop by with some clothes she had picked up for Lucas, so she called out a distracted "Come in!" while she searched for the takeout menu.

She heard the front door open and close as she rummaged through her junk drawer.

Strong hands clasped her waist. "You know, it's dangerous to leave your door unlocked."

Holding in a scream, she turned to find Bobby staring down at her with a big smile on his face. She launched herself up into his arms and was relieved when he kissed her—long and deep and wet, just the way she liked it.

Slowly, he lowered her to her feet as he broke the kiss. "I'm serious, Teagan. You shouldn't leave your door unlocked, or invite people in without knowing who's knocking."

She swatted him away playfully. "I was expecting my mom. That's the only reason why I did that."

He looked at her skeptically but stepped back when she made a move toward the door. "Where's Lucas?"

"He's out back playing with a soccer ball."

"Soccer?"

She nodded. "He wanted to try something new and soccer's easy to play on his own without hurting anyone. Or himself," she added playfully.

There was another knock and she was about to call out, but one look at him and she walked over to the door instead, confirming it was her mother before opening it. "Hey, Mom!" she said, giving her a quick hug and kiss on the cheek.

"Hey, sweetheart," Catherine said, holding up a large shopping bag. "I know, I know. I went overboard. It's just—" She stopped the instant she spotted Bobby standing in the kitchen.

He walked over and held out his hand in greeting. "Hey, Mrs. Shaughnessy. How are you?"

Teagan had to cover her mouth to keep from laughing. Her mother looked positively stunned.

"Oh, um… Bobby, hi," she said, shaking his hand. "It's good to see you." Then she glanced at her daughter briefly before returning her attention to him. "I didn't realize you were back in town."

He nodded. "Just for the weekend."

For a minute Teagan had to wonder at what her mother was thinking. No doubt she was wondering why Bobby was there, but how close was she to figuring it out?

"So let's see what you bought," Teagan said, choosing to ignore the awkwardness in the room. Placing the bag on the sofa, she reached in and pulled out several T-shirts, two pairs of shorts, and a red baseball cap. "These are great, Mom. They're going to be perfect for when he starts school."

"Yes, that's what I thought too," her mother said before looking at him again. "So what brings you over, Bobby?"

Panic gripped Teagan. She hadn't mentioned her relationship with Bobby to anyone.

As if sensing her thoughts, he replied, "I…um, I just wanted to stop in and say hello. And see how Lucas was coming along with his T-ball practice."

"Oh."

If Teagan wasn't mistaken, her mother sounded mildly disappointed, and that seemed to encourage Bobby.

"But I was hoping to take them both out for some pizza." He smiled at Teagan. "That is, if you don't have any plans."

She was blushing and could feel her cheeks heating, as well as her mother's stare. "Uh, sure." Teagan cleared her throat. "That would be great. I was just looking for the takeout menu to order pizza for us."

He nodded and slid his hands into the back pockets of his jeans. He looked utterly and boyishly adorable. If her mother wasn't standing right there, she would have walked over and kissed him.

Nibbling on her bottom lip, she said, "I should go and tell Lucas. He'll be excited that you're here."

She'd made it all of two steps before her mother interrupted. "You know, we were hoping to have Lucas tonight for a sleepover. Your father wants to go see that new Pixar movie and has been talking about it all week. I thought I'd mentioned it to you."

Shooting her mother a look that said *Really?*, Teagan had to keep herself from snorting with disbelief. For starters, there had never been any mention of a sleepover. If there had, she would have instantly tried to make plans with Bobby. And on top of that, her father hated going to the movies to see anything, let alone a children's movie. She knew exactly what her mother was doing and was…well, she was thankful.

Exceedingly thankful.

"Oh, I guess I forgot," Teagan said awkwardly. "Um… Give me a few minutes to pack a bag for him." As she walked away, she could hear her mother talking to Bobby.

"I hope you don't mind me taking Lucas."

"No. No, not at all. I'm going to be in town for the whole weekend so, um. I'll catch up with him and his T-ball skills at some point."

Peeking out at the living room, Teagan watched her mother eyeing Bobby. "You know, I bet Teagan wouldn't mind going out and grabbing something to eat. Something that isn't quite so kid-friendly."

Oh, dear Lord! Was her mother trying to set her up on a date?

"Kid-friendly?" he repeated.

"Yes. Eating with Lucas means she's stuck choosing the places he prefers—burgers, pizza, that sort of thing. I'm sure she would love to go someplace for a sit-down dinner where you don't draw on the placemat, if you know what I mean."

Yup. That's exactly what her mother was doing.

Teagan groaned and stepped away. She quickly packed a bag for her son before going out to tell him about this recent change of plans.

"Hey, buddy," she said, stepping into the backyard. "How goes the soccer?"

"It's kind of boring with just one person," he said with a pout. "Of course I can get a goal every time. There's no one to stop me."

"Hmm... I see your point. Maybe you can get Pops to practice with you tonight," she suggested.

"He's here?" he asked excitedly.

"No, but Meema's here and she wants you to sleep over tonight and go to the movies! Won't that be fun?"

He jumped up and down. "Yeah!" Then he stopped. "But if we go to the movies, when will Pops play soccer with me?"

"Maybe before the movie? Or after, since it doesn't get dark until late. Or maybe even tomorrow before I come and pick you up. How does that sound?"

"It's the best!" he cried, running into the house.

She knew the minute he spotted Bobby.

"Bobby! Are you here to play ball with me? Do you want to come to the movies with me and Meema and Pops? Then we can all play!" He turned when Teagan walked into the room. "We can have a whole soccer team, Mom! It's gonna be so cool!"

Thankfully, her mother stepped in before Lucas could plan any further. "Tell you what, let's get home to Pops and make our plans for pizza and the movie, and then tomorrow your mom and Bobby can come over for lunch and we'll all play ball in the yard. How about that?"

Teagan hung her head. Her mother wasn't even trying to play it cool with any of this. What if Bobby didn't want to have a family day with them? It was totally presumptuous of her, and the last thing she wanted was for him to feel pressured.

"That sounds great, Mrs. Shaughnessy," Bobby said happily. "How about Teagan and I pick up some sandwiches and salads and bring them over around noon?"

Her mother grinned sweetly. Only Teagan noticed the hint of smugness. "That would be lovely, Bobby. Thank you." Then she looked down at Lucas and reached for his hand. "Sandwiches and soccer! What a perfect way to spend a Saturday!"

Her son readily agreed so Teagan picked up his bag and walked with them out to her mother's car. Lucas gave her a quick kiss before climbing into his booster seat. Once he was settled, she closed the door and faced her mother.

"Smooth, Mom," she said quietly. "Could you have been any more obvious in there?" Crossing her arms over her chest, she thought she sounded pretty put out.

Clearly not, because her mother laughed softly. "Please, the two of you have been dancing around one another for weeks. I don't believe for one minute that Bobby came here to play T-ball, and if that's what you think, then you need to have your head examined."

"Mom…"

"Go out and have some fun, Teagan. You're allowed to! You're a young, beautiful woman and it's time you put a little effort into your personal life."

Where the hell had this all come from? "It's not that easy. I have Lucas to think about."

"Lucas is fine," her mother countered. "And it's time for you to worry a little more about yourself. Bobby's a wonderful man and he's obviously smitten with you."

Teagan rolled her eyes. "Nobody says *smitten*, Mom."

"I believe I just did," she said with a wink, turning to open the driver's side door. "And we'll see you at noon tomorrow." She climbed in and waved.

Stepping back, she waved and watched them drive away. When she turned back toward the house, Bobby was standing in the doorway.

Was it wrong that she didn't care if they didn't eat dinner at all?

From the look in his eyes as she got closer, he was thinking the same thing.

When she was standing right in front of him, she looked up. "Why didn't you tell me you were coming to town?"

He reached for her hand, tugging her through the doorway and shutting the door behind her. "Because I wanted to surprise you."

"Consider me surprised," she said sassily. "How long are you here for?"

"That depends," he said cryptically.

"On what?"

"On you. Well, you and Lucas."

She looked at him with confusion.

"Next week is the Fourth of July and there's a lot of great stuff to do around here—there's a big fireworks show down by the pier, a parade, and a carnival that I know Lucas would love." He paused, kissing her softly on the tip of her nose. "Only I didn't know if you'd already made plans or if maybe I could spend the holiday with you."

"Wow, that sounds like a lot of fun. Anna had mentioned all that, and Aidan and Zoe are hosting a barbecue at their place. So I was kind of on the fence about where we were going."

Now he wrapped his arms around her waist. "My original plan was to invite the two of you to Myrtle Beach to spend the holiday with me there."

"Oh?" In that instant she realized she liked the sound of that way more than any of the local activities.

"But then, Riley's show is only two weeks away and I thought we'd save the Myrtle Beach trip for that. Except... I was hoping it would just be you coming for that one."

She really liked *that* plan even more.

"I hate to admit it, but I hadn't given it much thought." She grimaced at how bad that sounded. "But I guess I can talk to my folks about babysitting. I mean, it's just one night."

Bobby shook his head. "I was really hoping you'd come for the weekend. You know, drive down on Friday morning and not leave until late Sunday afternoon."

Thoughtfully, she stepped out of his embrace. "Oh wow. I don't know. I've never been away from Lucas for that long before. It's a lot to ask of my parents. And— and I don't know if I'm ready for something like that."

She expected him to tell her she was wrong or that she was overreacting, but he didn't. Instead he took her by the hand and led her to the sofa. "It's okay, Teagan. It was just a thought. We can mention it to your parents tomorrow and see if they're even available to watch

Lucas the night of the concert or…you know, if they want to come to the show too. I'm sure Riley wouldn't mind adding two more people to the list. Three, if we bring Lucas."

"I think he's a little too young for it," she said, resting her head on his shoulder. "And if they really want to go, then I'll see if maybe Anna wouldn't mind another kid in the house for a night."

"Or two," he added lightly and she didn't try to correct him.

"New topic," she said cheerily. "What should we do tonight? This is all new to me, so…"

"So I guess we try that date thing we talked about way back when," he teased. "You know—dinner, a movie, maybe a walk on the beach. What do you say?"

"I think all those options sound great." She straightened and looked at him. He was dressed casually— jeans, T-shirt, sneakers—so anything fancy was out of the question. "There's this seafood place down on the pier everyone talks about. I'm sure you've eaten there hundreds of times, but I haven't been yet. Could we maybe go there?"

"Wherever you want, that's where we'll go," he said easily, and she found she was getting excited. A real date, like a leaving-the-house-and-going-out-in-front-of-other-people kind of date. It was exciting and nerve-wracking and—if she didn't stop now, she'd probably start hyperventilating.

"Sorry that my mom sort of pressured you into this."

He laughed and hugged her close. "I wouldn't say pressured. More like strongly suggested."

"Either way, I can't believe she did that. I'm mortified."

"Well, don't be. At least that's one Shaughnessy we don't have to worry about."

When she turned and looked at him, she saw the frown. "You too, huh?"

That surprised him. "Why? Who's been saying something to you?" He cursed under his breath. "Quinn, right?"

"Well…"

"I swear I want to go over there and just beat the crap out of him. I'm regretting all the years I didn't do it because Anna asked me not to."

She'd been aware of the hostility, of course, but didn't realize quite how deep it ran. "He's just being protective. No different than how you were when it was Anna, right?"

"It's different, Teagan. My sister had been crushing on him for years and he treated her like crap. He never gave her feelings any consideration. He's just warning you off of me because he's a jerk."

While she didn't necessarily agree with the way her cousin was handling things, she knew Quinn's heart was in the right place. "I can't help that my family is a little overprotective." She shrugged and tried to make light of it. "All they know is that I'm a single mom who hasn't exactly had it easy. And, to be fair, you do have a bit of a reputation."

A growl of frustration was his first response. "I already explained to you—"

"I know, I know," she said, quickly cutting him off. "But you can't expect anyone to think differently if you don't give them a reason to."

"I shouldn't have to prove anything to him. Or anyone,

for that matter," he said emphatically. "The way I live my life isn't anyone's business, and nothing I ever did hurt any of them. So why am I being punished for it?"

Okay, things were starting to get just a wee bit out of control, and the last thing she wanted was for their night to be ruined before it even started.

In the blink of an eye, she was straddling his lap and kissing him soundly on the lips. When she raised her head a minute later, she rested her forehead against his. "Let's not think of any of that tonight. Tonight, let's go and have something to eat, maybe take a walk on the beach, and then come back here and enjoy having the place to ourselves. I missed you."

That seemed to do the trick. She could feel him relax and it made her smile. "We do still have one problem," she said with a small sigh.

"What's that?"

"It's still early. Too early to go to dinner." She hummed and leaned in just a little, pressing her breasts against his chest. "What are we going to do until then?" She pretended to think about it. "Maybe we can walk around town, do a little shopping, or maybe go to that sweet art gallery on Main. What do you think?"

Getting in touch with my inner vixen is way too much fun.

"How do you feel about dessert before dinner?" he asked.

She purred and then smiled as she felt him harden beneath her. "That seems awfully...naughty."

One hand came up and cupped her nape. "I think you enjoy being naughty, Teagan," he growled against her lips. "And you're very good at it. Believe me."

"How about I prove it? You know, just in case," she said, a little breathless with anticipation.

Rather than answer, he stood and carried her to the bedroom.

———

It wasn't like Bobby was prone to paranoia, but it seemed like he was experiencing more than his fair share of bad luck on a night that had started off so well.

When they'd left Teagan's house, he felt like the luckiest man in the world. They had made love, showered together, and then made love again. They were both ravenous for something to eat and she was so excited about going to this seafood place that he had forgotten he'd briefly dated the hostess.

"Hey, Bobby," Victoria had all but purred when she saw him. She'd completely ignored Teagan and run her hand over his bicep. "It's been way too long. Are you in town for the weekend?"

He'd practically tripped over his own tongue as he tried to deflect her while apologizing to Teagan.

Victoria finally took the hint but gave him a wink as she led them to their table and wished them a good night.

That's when Kate—another ex from a brief fling— showed up to take their order. She wasn't quite as bold as Victoria, but brazen nonetheless.

And all the while, Teagan kept a smile on her face.

Once they finished eating and he paid the check, he all but dragged her from the restaurant and breathed a sigh of relief. They walked down to the beach and he felt like he could finally relax. Taking Teagan's hand, he was all set to ask her about how she was enjoying living by the ocean when someone called out his name.

You have got to be kidding me.

When he turned, he spotted Bree Tanner. His former partner. He held in the curse he was dying to let out and forced a smile onto his face. Bree was one of the reasons he had moved away. After getting assigned to work together, he'd found himself attracted to her, and he'd acted on it.

And things had gotten awkward fast.

Bree really wasn't into him at all, had told him so right to his face, and even though he knew it, working with her became a major distraction. His biggest blunder of all had been losing his focus so badly that he'd gone to protect her when they were in the middle of an arrest. There had been a very real chance he was going to get hurt, or worse, hurt someone else because he wasn't paying attention.

The next day he'd put out feelers and started the process of changing jobs, changing cities, and changing his entire life.

Now as she walked closer, he wondered what he'd ever seen in her. She was tall, blond, and very curvy, with a take-charge attitude. Bobby glanced at Teagan, who was observing all of this—again—with mild amusement. The two women were as different as night and day, just like Teagan had been different from Victoria and Kate in the restaurant, and he seriously had to wonder what the hell he had ever been thinking. The woman standing beside him was so much more of a match for him than anyone he'd ever met, and if they ever got a few minutes alone, he was going to tell her so.

"Hey, Bobby! I thought that was you," Bree said, walking up to them. She was in a black one-piece bathing suit that really showcased her physique, but it did nothing for him. "How are you? I heard you got shot. Everything okay?"

As much as he hated talking about it, it had gotten easier the more time had passed. So he recounted the story of what had gone down in the convenience store and how his recovery was going.

"Basically, things are healing the way they should, but slowly," he said. "Thankfully, I've got a great support network around me, including this girl here." He squeezed Teagan's hand and then introduced her to Bree. "We used to work together."

Teagan didn't react and her smile never wavered. "It's nice to meet you, Bree."

"Same," Bree said, smiling. "You've got one of the good guys. Seriously, we all miss him around here."

"Somehow I doubt that," Bobby said, feeling mildly uncomfortable. "You've got a great squad and I heard the guy who replaced me was awesome."

Bree shook her head. "He left about three months ago. Took a position up in Raleigh because he got bored. Thought we were too much of a small town."

"Really?" That was interesting. Maybe he'd look into coming back.

"In case you're interested," Bree went on, "the position is still open. I know Captain Holt would love to talk to you."

Now probably wasn't the time to be thinking about it, but he couldn't help it. This was the first bit of good news he'd had since he and Teagan had walked out of her house that evening. If he could get his doctor to sign off, he'd be completely open to reapplying here and moving back. And not just because of Teagan but… yeah, who was he kidding. She was his main motivation.

"Want me to put in the word to Holt? Maybe you can give him a call while you're in town," Bree suggested.

"I'm still waiting on clearance," he explained. "Maybe once that happens I'll reach out to him. But thanks."

Off in the distance, someone called Bree's name. She turned and waved before facing them again. "It was great to see you, Bobby, and it was nice meeting you, Teagan. You guys have a great night!" Then she jogged off in the opposite direction.

He cautiously glanced at Teagan and couldn't even imagine what must be going on in her mind. Their first date had been a total disaster, and he wasn't sure there was a way to recover from it.

"So," he began, "what should we—"

Pulling her hand from his, she stepped in front of him. "Before we go any further, is this how it's always going to be? We go out and everywhere we go, we run into a woman you dated?"

"Um…"

"Because I have to tell you, this was not particularly fun for me tonight."

He hung his head. "I know, I know, and I'm sorry." Then he looked at her and grabbed both of her hands. "I swear to you this has never happened before. I'm just as upset as you are!"

"Somehow I doubt that," she murmured.

When she went to pull away, he gently pulled her back. "I get it, okay? I get that you're pissed. To be

honest, I am too. And now I can see why people think
the way they do about me. But, dammit…" He dropped
her hands and raked his fingers through his hair in frustration. Taking a couple of steps away and then back
again, he tried to collect his thoughts.

"You want to know what I was thinking tonight?"
he asked.

"That you probably should have stayed in Myrtle
Beach?"

"Fine, be snarky," he snapped, but there wasn't much
heat behind his words. "All night I kept asking myself
what I was thinking. All the years I've been messing
around and thought I was a big deal because I was with
all these beautiful women."

"You're seriously not helping yourself right now—"

"But," he interrupted, "I realized how wrong I was.
Teagan, I look at you and see so much more than I
ever saw in any of them. Ever. There is so much more
to you, so much more that I want to know about you.
You've got substance! You're smart and caring and—
and I know I'm messing this up and you're probably
thinking of ways you can just walk away right now and
leave me here."

This time he did mutter a curse and put some space
between them. "Come on. I'll drive you home and…
and I'll go."

When she didn't argue, he knew he was in trouble.
Rather than have a romantic walk on the beach, they
were walking in silence back to his truck.

Rather than saying sexy, flirty things about what they
were going to do when they got home, they weren't even
looking at one another.

And rather than having some hope at redemption, he had to face the fact that his past was just too big of an obstacle for them to overcome.

Dammit.

The drive back to the house was short and Teagan was opening the door even before he came to a complete stop in her driveway. Part of him knew he should just let her go, let her have some time to think things through. But that was the coward's way out. He was many things, but a coward wasn't one of them.

Slamming the car into park, he yanked the keys out of the ignition and went after her. He caught up to her at the front door.

"You said you'd go," she reminded him as she unlocked the door.

"Yeah, well. I think we need to talk about this, don't you?"

She stepped into the house and sighed loudly. "I honestly don't know, Bobby. That was the worst date ever. And while I know it wasn't directly your fault, it still… kind of was."

"You have no idea how sorry I am," he said bleakly. "I don't have an excuse and I can't promise it's never going to happen again."

Tossing her purse on the sofa, she turned and looked at him. "I don't think I'm cut out for this. I don't want to have to be on alert every time we go out. I want to know we can go out and women won't be throwing themselves at you. Do you understand that?"

He nodded. "I know I'd hate it if guys were hitting on you while we were out."

Her expression turned sad and it just about gutted

him. "I'm not willing to let this end, Teagan. You mean too much to me." When she stayed silent, his mind began to wander. Was she trying to come up with the right words to break up with him? He couldn't let that happen. "Tell me what you want me to do. Do you want me to look up every girl I ever dated and tell her I'm off limits? I'll do it!"

"That's ridiculous," she said with a hint of disgust.

"Should I take out an ad in the paper? Make a post on social media telling everyone I'm in a serious, committed relationship and to back off?"

"If you're not going to take this seriously—"

"But I am!" he argued. "I have no idea how to fix this and I'm grasping at straws here! Don't you get it? You mean everything to me and it sucks that you're just so willing to walk away from me. From us! Hasn't this meant anything to you?"

And then he remembered something he'd learned a long time ago: never ask a question you didn't want the answer to.

Right now, seeing how upset she was, he wasn't so sure he wanted this answer.

"These last few weeks have meant a lot to me," she said calmly—almost too calmly. "But I'm a fairly private person, Bobby. I'm not…I mean, there just doesn't seem to be a solution to this. At least, not a reasonable one." Her shoulders sagged and she looked at him sadly. "This is for the best."

"No. No, it's not. And I get it, my reputation's apparently never been worse. But…I thought that maybe you could see beyond all that. I thought we'd moved past it. We've had the discussion before, Teagan."

"I know we did, and when we were talking about it, it seemed fine. But the reality was very different. You can't expect me to deal with that every time we go out. Or worse, if we're out with Lucas. I won't subject him to that."

Damn. He hadn't thought of that.

So this was it. Over before it even had a chance to begin.

He'd never been in a situation like this. He hadn't broken up with anyone because he'd never really been *with* anyone. And now that he was here, it hurt like hell. It hurt more than he ever thought possible and he hated it, wanted to scream at the unfairness of it.

How was it that they had just been talking about spending the Fourth of July together and her coming to Myrtle Beach for a weekend, and now they were done? Weren't they supposed to have lunch with her parents tomorrow? He was supposed to play ball with Lucas, and missing out on that hurt almost as much as the thought of walking out the door.

"You should go," she said quietly.

One step toward the door and he stopped. Facing her, he said, "No."

"Excuse me?" Her eyes went wide and her tone was incredulous.

It was bold and would possibly backfire on him, but he really didn't have anything else to lose.

"You know what I see when I look at you?" he asked.

"We've had this conversation already," she replied wearily, but he wasn't listening.

"I see a fighter. I see a woman who suffered a great loss and somehow managed to keep going. You had to fight to accomplish what you wanted to. You were pregnant, you lost the man you loved, and you had to finish your education."

"Bobby…"

"Then you had a child and you're raising him on your own, and he's amazing." He wasn't above obvious flattery at this point. "But even that wasn't enough. You went on to get your master's degree while raising a toddler. Those aren't the actions of someone who just gives up, Teagan."

"It's not the same."

Feeling bold, he walked right up to her and gently grasped her shoulders. "You overcame obstacles that would have crippled some people. You've got the most challenging job there is—you're a single mom who is practically a superhero, and you're telling me that you can't get over a couple of forward women acting badly?"

The look she gave him showed how unimpressed she was with his speech.

"You're thinking a little highly of yourself, Hannigan," she stated. "If you think this relationship is on the same level of losing someone to death or to the challenges of being a single parent, then you're delusional."

Yeah, okay. Maybe he'd misjudged his own importance. Maybe he should just concede defeat.

"However," she said, interrupting his thoughts, "you do have a point. I am better than those other women. Anyone who would hit on someone with their girlfriend right there isn't worth my time."

He wasn't sure if he should agree or keep his mouth shut.

Ultimately, he shut up.

She eyed him warily. "I want you to know, if anything like that happens in front of my son, we're through." When he tried to speak, she held up a hand to stop him. "I know you have no control over how someone else behaves, but you need to know the rules going in. If we're going to continue with this relationship, you need to know where my limits are. And that's one of them."

He nodded. "Understood."

"Know this, Bobby Hannigan. You need me way more than I need you. I've been on my own for a long time and I know I can do it again. I care about you a lot, and I'm not saying that it wouldn't hurt if this ended, but it wouldn't destroy me. Do you understand?"

He swallowed hard and wasn't sure if he was seriously impressed or totally put in his place. *Both*, he told himself. He'd always known she was a fighter, but her words just proved it. "So," he began hesitantly. "Can I stay?"

Her first response was another wary glance.

Opting for a different approach, he stepped in close. "I was thinking of sundaes in bed," he said softly, seductively. "Followed by hours of making you feel good. And when that's done, holding you in my arms while we sleep. Then tomorrow morning, we get up and make breakfast together, make love, make our plans for the fourth, and then go have lunch with your folks and Lucas."

Boldly, he wrapped his arms around her waist. He had to hide his smile when she only mildly resisted, then leaned against him.

"I'm still disappointed, Bobby."

He nodded. "I know."

They stood like that in silence for several moments.

"I'd stand in the middle of Main Street and yell out to

anyone who'd listen that I'm sorry and I never meant to hurt you. I'd shout from the rooftops that no one better hurt the woman I love."

They both startled at his admission.

"Bobby," she sputtered. "We're not... I mean, you can't be—"

Placing a finger over her lips, he stopped her words. "I can be," he said slowly. "But I get that it's too soon to say it. It doesn't change how I feel, though."

This time when she went to speak, he silenced her the only way he knew how—he kissed her. He kissed her with all the love, need, and frustration that he felt, and was relieved when she responded in kind.

It wasn't perfect—but hey, neither was he.

There would be other obstacles, other arguments, but for tonight, he wanted to make it up to her in any way he possibly could. And he began the only way he knew how.

Kissing his way across her cheek, down to her shoulder, and down to her breasts, he waited until she was trembling in his arms. Once her head fell back and he had her panting for more, he led her to the bedroom and lavished her body with every exquisite pleasure he could. He loved her until they were both weak and exhausted. He touched her until she was crying out his name.

And he held her until the sun came up.

Chapter 7

"Mom! Mom! We're gonna be late! We have to go!"

Teagan put her hair up in a ponytail and checked her reflection in the mirror for the tenth time—and it was barely nine in the morning. Today was the Fourth of July, and that meant a day full of family-friendly activities.

And she was in the mood for zero of them.

Bobby was due to pick them up in a few minutes, and she knew if she could just get her head in the game, she'd be fine. But right now her stomach was in knots, and if she had her way, she'd crawl back under the blankets and cancel the whole thing.

Lunch with her parents a few days ago had been fine. Even great. They both seemed genuinely thrilled that she and Bobby were dating and had offered to keep Lucas for the entire weekend of Riley's concert.

Something Bobby had smiled about like a kid on Christmas morning.

Seeing her parents at the parade wasn't going to be a big deal. It was the rest of the family she was dreading.

After they had gotten home from her parents' place, they had decided the cat was officially out of the bag. They were a couple and they weren't going to hide it. Which meant that today's festivities would be spent with just about every Shaughnessy family member she knew. Including her less than thrilled and most vocal cousin, Quinn.

"Why couldn't it have rained today?" she murmured, smoothing a hand over her hair one more time.

Dressed casually in a pair of denim shorts and white tank top, Teagan's addition of a red hair band made her feel at least a little festive and patriotic. When she walked into the living room, she was glad to see Lucas wearing the clothes she'd put out for him, including the T-shirt with the American flag. He was running around talking about all the things he wanted to do while they were out: see the parade, eat hot dogs, swim in somebody's pool, and watch a really cool fireworks show.

His words, not hers.

It wasn't as if this was the first time they were celebrating the Fourth. They'd lived near the army base his entire life, so there was always a big celebration. For some reason, though, this year was big for him, so she tried to hide her own nerves and foul mood and pasted a smile on her face.

The knock at the door startled them both and Lucas beat her to answering it.

"It's Bobby! It's Bobby! It's Bobby!" he cried, running to pull the door open.

"Hey, buddy," Bobby said, walking in and high-fiving her son. "You ready for an awesome day?"

"Uh-huh!" Lucas cried, jumping up and down.

And he hasn't even had any sugar yet, she thought, already feeling exhausted.

While she patiently waited for her turn to say hello, Teagan studied Bobby. Khaki shorts, white T-shirt that hugged him like a second skin, and his hair askew as usual—it all had her itching to just walk over and wrap herself around him.

She wouldn't, but she wanted to.

Lucas had seen her and Bobby kiss goodbye and he questioned her on it, something she hadn't been completely prepared for. But after explaining how she and Bobby liked one another and would be going out on dates, he'd simply said, "Oh, okay," and that was the end of it. But then again, how much did a five-year-old really understand about dating?

"Hey, beautiful."

Teagan was ready to melt into an impossible puddle at the nickname.

"Hey, yourself," she said, leaning in for the kiss he was ready to give her. It was short and sweet and left her groaning softly.

"I know," he replied, for her ears only. When he stepped back, he clapped his hands together and looked over at Lucas. "Okay, is the cooler packed?"

"Yup!"

"Lots of bottles of water?"

"Yup!"

"Fruit?"

"Yup!"

"Good job!" Then he looked around and said, "You got a hat to wear to help keep the sun out of your eyes?"

"I got the new one Meema got me!" he said excitedly, running into his room to get it.

Once he was out of sight, Bobby turned to her and smiled. "So he's a little excited."

She laughed. "Just a wee bit. I don't know why this is such a big deal to him, but it is. And as exhausting as it is, I'm glad he's looking forward to it."

"It's going to be great. My folks have already got our

spot blocked off in front of Anna's pub and there's plenty of room for all of us. Which is close to thirty people, so…"

"I have to tell you, it still feels weird to be going places with such a large group. It's been just me and my parents for so long, and then Lucas. It's overwhelming to wrap my brain around thirty people going from point A to point B together all day."

Leaning in, he kissed her on the head. "You'll get used to it." Looking toward the kitchen, he asked, "Is the cooler really all packed?"

She nodded. "And I have a tote bag filled with some other stuff—sunscreen, some granola bars, a hat for me, and a change of clothes for Lucas, including a bathing suit."

"You're not bringing one for yourself?" he asked, and there was a glint in his eyes that told her he was really hoping she was.

"I hadn't planned on it," she said, going to grab the bag. In her bedroom, she let out a small shriek when Bobby grabbed her waist. She spun in his arms. "What in the world?" But she was laughing too.

"Bring a bathing suit. Preferably a bikini," he said, his voice low and sexy. When he talked to her like that, it made her tingle all over.

"Sadly, I don't even own a bikini."

"We need to do something about that."

Swatting him away playfully, she picked up the bag, which he immediately took from her hands. "I got it. And I'll go grab the cooler and put it in the truck."

"Wait, I thought we were taking my car? We need Lucas's booster seat." She saw the instant he remembered that. "My keys are on the entryway table."

"Okay," he called over his shoulder as he walked out of the room. He was smiling, but she knew he would have preferred to drive his truck around today rather than her practical little Camry.

Teagan was taking a last look around the room to make sure she hadn't forgotten anything when something crashed to the ground in the hall. Running out of her room, she heard Bobby curse and saw the contents of the cooler spilled all over the kitchen floor. Lucas appeared from his room, staring. Considering the tension she could practically feel emanating off of Bobby, she thought it best to distract her son.

"Lucas, do Mommy a favor and go grab your soccer ball from the yard. We'll bring it with us so you can play later, okay?" He readily agreed. That would take him several minutes, because he'd play with the ball on his way back.

Cautiously, she walked over to Bobby and crouched down to help him pick up the ice, food, and drinks.

"Just—don't, okay?" he snapped. "I got it."

"It's not a big deal. I'm only—"

"I said I got it!"

It was on the tip of her tongue to try to comfort him, but she knew her words wouldn't do much good right now. He was angry and embarrassed, and as much as she hoped it was simply a case of the lid not being on tight, it wasn't that kind of cooler. The handle was still attached, and nothing looked broken. So that only left one thing—he'd lost his grip. He hadn't seemed to have any issues with his arm in a while, but maybe he just wasn't telling her about it.

Standing, she walked over to the freezer and grabbed

the ice tray. Luckily, there was enough so she could replenish most of what was now all over the kitchen floor. Next she grabbed some towels and a mop and cleaned up the water. They silently worked side by side until the cooler was repacked and the floor was dry. Bobby walked out without saying a word, and luckily Lucas walked in after everything was put away.

"You ready?" she asked, forcing a smile.

He nodded, but she could tell he sensed something was wrong. Together they walked to the door. Bobby had the car started and was sitting in the driver's seat looking seriously uncomfortable. She was almost afraid to approach him. The last thing she wanted today was for things to be tense between the two of them. She was already on edge about hanging out with everyone and facing Quinn's judgment. And who knew what other surprises were waiting for them on Main Street in the form of Bobby's former fan club.

Lucas ran outside and climbed into the car, and she smiled when Bobby turned and talked to him. Good. At least he wasn't taking his bad mood out on Lucas.

Grabbing her purse, she locked the door and walked out to join them.

Neither spoke while they were on the road, though at one point Teagan startled when Bobby reached over and took her hand. He was watching the road, and she took a moment to simply enjoy watching him in return.

Maybe today wouldn't be so bad. Granted, it wasn't off to the best start, but it could get better. Right? Rather than obsessing on it, she sat back and relaxed and decided she was ready to face whatever else came their way.

—∞—

What the hell else could go wrong?

Seriously. Bobby scanned the crowd and wondered why he'd thought any of this would be a good idea. If it weren't for Teagan and Lucas, he would be heading straight back to Myrtle Beach right now. Damn hand.

Even now, as they were walking down the street, he could barely feel Teagan's hand in his and that was freaking him out. But he kept his game-face on. No one was going to know there was a problem, and he wasn't going to ruin anyone's day.

Even though his day completely sucked right now.

At the pub, their tables were already almost completely filled. Besides his parents, Anna and Quinn were there with the kids, as well as Ian and Martha Shaughnessy. Teagan's parents were sitting beside Ian, and as he got closer he spotted Aidan, Zoe, and their kids.

"Hey! You made it!" his mother called out when she spotted them walking up. She hugged him and then Teagan and Lucas in turn.

He knew he smiled and shook hands with everyone, but it was all kind of a blur. The feeling in his hand wasn't coming back as quickly as it normally did. Without being obvious about it, he tried flexing his fingers and making a fist—without much success. "Excuse me," he murmured to no one in particular as he turned and walked into the pub.

"Bobby?"

He was almost to the men's room when he heard his father call his name. Hanging his head, he stopped and waited.

"Everything okay?"

What could he possibly say? This wasn't the time or place for some kind of heated, frustrated discussion, but how could he lie?

Looking up, Bobby simply shook his head.

As if sensing his son's pain, Jack led Bobby back to Anna's office and closed the door behind them. "Okay, what's going on?"

Bobby held up his arm and shook his head again, words failing him.

His father understood. "Are you in pain?"

"No."

"Well, that's something, I suppose. What happened?"

Bobby relayed the story about the cooler dropping out of his hands and how he still didn't have much feeling back. "Normally, if I flex my hand a couple of times, it gets better, but his time it's not."

"And you're freaking out."

He nodded.

"What do you need to do? Call your doctor? Your physical therapist?"

"I don't even know. It's never happened like this before, and on top of that, it's a holiday." He growled with frustration as he raked his good hand through his hair. "This is so not what I needed today!"

"What do you mean?"

"This is the first time Teagan and I are out together with everyone, and I already feel like all eyes are on us. We had a disastrous first date Friday night. We ran into *three* different women I used to date—including Bree— and it was awful. So now I'm on my guard, in case anyone else approaches me in hopes of…well, you know."

His father smirked.

"And on top of that, I have to wonder when Quinn is gonna pounce. I can't focus on shit because all I can think about is my hand. I swear, I can't catch a damn break! All I wanted was to make this a great day for Lucas and Teagan and—as usual—I've messed it up."

Rather than offer sympathy, his father laughed softly.

"Seriously? I'm practically pouring out my heart here and you're laughing?"

His father instantly sobered. "You're right. That wasn't very nice of me."

"No, it wasn't." Hell, he was on the verge of pouting.

"I apologize," Jack said as he leaned on the corner of his daughter's desk, sighing. "Tell me what you need."

"That's just it, Dad. I don't know."

"Can I make a suggestion?"

"Of course."

"Go back out there, sit with your beautiful girlfriend and her adorable son, and enjoy the parade."

"Dad, that's really not going to help anything."

Jack shrugged. "I disagree."

Rolling his eyes, Bobby glanced toward the office door. He should go back out there. Teagan was probably looking for him and wondering where he'd snuck off to.

"And might I say that I think you're finally doing the right thing."

His head snapped around as he looked at his father in confusion. "Excuse me?"

Jack explained, "For years your mother and I used to say you were too good-looking for your own good. You've had girls chasing after you since you were five and you never even had to try. You always got the girl."

While Bobby had no idea where this was going, he had to admit, he was curious.

"You never got serious with any of them, and you seemed content to play the field. To be honest, there was part of me that was impressed." He chuckled. "Your mother, on the other hand, couldn't wait for you to calm down. Maybe think about settling down."

Ah, now he was getting it.

"I know this relationship with Teagan is new, but I hope you realize how different she is. How special. We don't really know her that well, but we know enough," he went on. "So if I'm wrong and you're just killing time, then don't lead her on. But if you're serious, and you plan on turning this into something meaningful, then don't hide from her. If you're struggling, you need to tell her. If you're hurting, tell her. Nothing kills a relationship faster than lack of communication. Don't make that mistake."

"I don't want to ruin her day," he admitted quietly.

"Believe it or not, you're well on your way to doing that by simply being in here while she's out there."

Dammit, he was right.

Pushing off of the desk, Jack clapped a hand on Bobby's shoulder and offered him a small smile. "C'mon. No one's expecting you to be perfect, but we are expecting you to put on a smile and have a good time today. Okay?"

Unable to help himself, he smiled in return. "Okay, Dad. Thanks."

They walked back outside together and rejoined their group. Bobby immediately went over to where Teagan was talking to his sister. Both women looked at him quizzically, although Teagan's face showed a little more sympathy. His sister had a very knowing—and disapproving—expression.

"Sorry," he said, mostly to Teagan. "My hand still isn't cooperating and...I kind of freaked out. I didn't mean to take my mood out on anyone."

She surprised him by taking his hand in hers, tugging him close, and kissing him right there in front of everyone. He knew it wasn't likely, but it felt as though everyone around them had stopped talking. Or maybe it was just that he was focusing so fully on the woman who had turned his world upside down. When he lifted his head, he smiled at her. "I hope that means I'm forgiven."

She moved in close and hugged him. "Nothing to forgive. But thank you for sharing with me."

When she looked up at him that way, he wanted to promise he'd share everything with her. She had a way of making everything feel better. Making it all feel right. He caressed her cheek and was already trying to come up with a way to have some time alone with her when his sister cleared her throat. Loudly.

They both turned and looked at her.

"So I'm just supposed to stand here and watch this while no one explains what's going on, is that it?" Anna said defensively.

But he knew his sister. She was all bark and no bite, and more than likely was playing at being outraged when she was really pleased.

With his arm around Teagan's waist, he said, "Yup. That's exactly what we're saying. Mainly because it's none of your business."

Teagan laughed, Anna gasped, and he had to fight to keep a straight face.

"Oh…um, okay. Sure. I mean I just thought…" Anna stammered. Bobby put her out of her misery and gave her a playful punch on the arm.

"Just kidding." Laughing, he went on, "I met Teagan at Ian's house after everyone got back from the cruise and—"

"Oh my gosh! It's been going on since then and no one told me?" she cried, which only made Bobby and Teagan laugh harder.

"Not quite," Teagan replied after a minute. "Let's just say we were both interested after that meeting. But it wasn't until after the sink incident that we started talking about…possibilities." She smiled up at him. "It was the night of Brian's birthday party that we finally decided to give this a try."

Anna squealed with delight. "This makes me so happy!" She hugged them both. "Oh! We can double date! And—and whenever you need us to keep Lucas so you can have a date night, all you have to do is ask. This is so exciting!"

"What's so exciting?" Quinn asked as he walked over, holding Brian.

"Bobby and Teagan are dating!" Anna exclaimed. "Isn't that awesome?"

The scowl that his brother-in-law was famous for was Quinn's only response before he turned and walked away.

"Uh-oh," Teagan said softly.

Anna frowned after her husband. "Don't mind him. He's not big on change of any kind. You should have

seen him when his father first started dating Martha."
She shuddered. "It wasn't pretty."

"Yeah, well, what he did there was just rude," Bobby
said, glaring at Quinn's retreating back.

"I agree, Bobby, but don't make a scene here, okay?
I'll talk to him when he calms down a bit."

Right now, he wanted to argue. He wanted to storm
through the crowd and tell Quinn that he was wrong.
But he also knew his sister was right. It wasn't the
time and really, hadn't he already caused enough
problems today?

"Fine. But I'm not happy about this, Anna," he
stated firmly.

"I know. I'm not either, but need I remind you how
there was a time when you behaved the exact same
way toward him?"

"It was different. My issue was because he treated
you badly for years. He's making assumptions right now
that he has no right to make." While he hoped that he
sounded firm but in control, the fact that his teeth were
clenched certainly didn't help.

Off in the distance, he heard the whistle of the drum
major kicking off the parade. So for now, he was going
to find a seat with his girl and enjoy the festivities.

Lucas came over and grabbed his mother's hand so
they could sit together. Looking around, Bobby found the
chairs his parents brought for them and motioned for
the two of them to sit. As they settled in, Lucas in his
lap, he realized how good this felt. His father was right.
He was doing something good here. Something positive.
There was something to be said about having a casual
day with your family to put things into perspective.

Was his hand feeling better? A little. But as he looked over at Teagan, who was watching Lucas, he knew there was no place else he'd rather be. He bounced Lucas on his knee and loved how the kid giggled with pure glee. This was what life was all about. Maybe he should take a page from the boy and look at today through his eyes. Kids had a way of finding the wonder in it all. He should forget about the pain and the ugliness of life, push all the negative thoughts and feelings aside and take some joy from the simple things. Like a parade.

"Here they come!" Lucas cried. "The band is coming! Can I get a drum? Please?"

One thing Bobby was learning about Lucas was that he wanted to try something new on a daily basis: different sports, different hobbies, and apparently now, an instrument.

"We'll see, buddy," Teagan replied, turning her attention back to the band that was still half a block away.

Lucas leaned forward as far as he could, but Bobby had his arm loosely draped around Lucas's waist in case the kid tried to make a run for it. He looked to the left and then to the right in quick succession, then back again, probably trying not to miss anything. He leaned back against Bobby's chest and clapped his hands.

"You're excited for the parade, huh?" he asked, but Lucas shook his head.

O-kay…

"I thought you were looking forward to it?"

If anything, the kid relaxed against him even more.

Bobby glanced at Teagan, who looked at her son and shrugged. Maybe she wasn't concerned or curious, but he sure as hell was. Bouncing his knee under Lucas, he gave him a playful shake. "C'mon, out with it. What were you just looking at?" he asked lightly.

Straightening, Lucas turned to him with the biggest, purest expression of happiness that Bobby had ever seen in his life.

"I was looking at all the people, because this is the first time I'm just like them," the boy explained and again, Bobby and Teagan looked at each other quizzically.

"What do you mean, sweetheart?" Teagan asked.

"We're a family," Lucas said simply. "This is the first time I'm here and have a mom and a dad with me and that made me happy."

Teagan's heart stopped at her son's statement.

A family. That's what he felt like this was, and she could see how his young mind had made those connections. Right now, though, she wasn't sure if she should correct him or just let the statement go. And if she was freaking out this much, she had to wonder what was going on in Bobby's mind.

She knew he understood there was more to a relationship with her than just the two of them. He understood there would be obstacles where her son was concerned, but this was all too new for them to have talked about how Lucas would view him. And she certainly never imagined her son would put Bobby in the position of a father quite so soon.

Bobby's hand reached out and squeezed hers, and when she looked at him, he whispered, "It's all right. We'll talk with him later, okay?"

She knew he was right. This wasn't the time, or the place.

Hell, it seemed like there were quite a few conversations needed today, yet none of them could happen.

Stupid parade, she thought miserably.

For the next hour, they sat and cheered, watched the floats go by, and listened to the assorted bands play. Once the last of the parade floats rode by, though, no one in their group moved. They stayed put while all the people around them gathered their things. She looked at Bobby to ask if they were going.

"We tend to hang back for a few minutes," he explained. "It's chaos to try and get out of here for at least another thirty minutes."

Behind them, Anna announced that the pub was open for anyone in the family who needed to get out of the sun. One by one, everyone started moving, gathering their belongings before heading inside.

"Mom? I need to go pee," Lucas said. Before she could answer, Bobby offered to take him inside. She waved to them and went back to picking up their bags.

"Let me help you with that," Quinn said, coming up beside her.

At first she thought it was nice, then she straightened and glared at him.

"What? What's the matter?" he asked.

Crossing her arms over her chest and striking her most intimidating pose, Teagan studied him long and hard, until he was all but squirming. "While I appreciate you stopping to help, I figured I'd just stand here until you start listing your reasons for not approving of my relationship with Bobby." Pausing, she waved him on. "Come on, let's hear them."

"Teagan, c'mon. It's not like that."

"It's exactly like that. You've been warning me off him even before anything started. And now you're going to stand here and pretend that you don't have an issue?"

He sighed loudly, lolling his head back. He seemed to be either trying to control himself, or seriously organizing his thoughts.

When he straightened and looked at her, she was ready for whatever he threw her way.

"Bobby Hannigan is not the right man for you. Okay?"

"As a matter of fact, no," she said, holding her ground.

"You don't know him like I do," Quinn explained. "I've known the guy for most of my life, and trust me, I know him way better than you do. He's not someone you should be involved with."

Because she was a rational person, she let those comments sink in and process before she responded. "Quinn, before I moved here, when was the last time we saw one another? Or spoke?"

"I don't know—ten years?"

"More like fourteen," she countered. "I think it's safe to say that you don't know me all that well."

"That's not the point," he said wearily. "Bobby is… well, he's kind of a player. I've never known him to date someone for more than a week. He'd sleep with them, no strings attached, and as soon as he got bored, he moved on. And the women he dated were…let's just say they're different than you."

Yeah, she'd figured that out Friday night. The

women from Bobby's past that she'd met had all been tall, blond, and definitely curvier and sexier than she'd ever been.

"You deserve a guy who isn't like that," he went on. "Honestly, I never understood why the women of this town went so crazy for him. It was like he had his own fan club when he lived here."

Yup, she'd gotten that impression too.

"You and Lucas don't need that kind of heartache. Trust me, I'm just trying to look out for you."

The logical part of her brain completely kicked in. "Can I ask you something?"

"Sure."

"Did *you* ever date Bobby?"

That made her cousin sputter and almost choke. "What? No! Why would you even ask?"

She shrugged. "It just seems like you're trying a little too hard to warn me away. I figured I needed clarification on that front."

"That's your psychology training kicking in," he said blandly. "You just moved here, Teagan. You haven't really had a chance to meet anyone else. Why are you rushing into something with him?"

"I don't consider it rushing, and really, Quinn, what if I was? I'm a grown woman who deserves to have a life!" she cried. "And I'm not looking for your approval, I'm looking for some respect. I don't have a problem with Bobby, okay? And if you do, then you need to work on that, not me."

"You don't know him like I do," he repeated.

"Okay, I get it. He was overprotective of Anna. That's fine. That's what big brothers are supposed to do. But it doesn't mean he isn't a good man, Quinn. You need to get over whatever it is that you have against him and move on."

He was pacing now and part of her felt bad for bringing all this up. He stopped right in front of her. "What are you going to do when this thing ends, huh? How are you going to pick up the pieces? Especially when you have a child to take care of and a new job? Don't you think that's too risky?"

Before he could go any further, she had a question for him. "Quinn, other than your mom, have you ever lost someone you loved?"

He thought for a moment and then shook his head. "No. No, I haven't. I lost a good friend while I was on the racing circuit, but…"

"I have," she said sadly. "I lost the man who was the love of my life. I lost him before we ever got to have our future." She paused. "None of us is promised tomorrow, so what am I waiting for?"

Placing a hand over her thundering heart, she went on. "You know what? Bobby may very well break my heart. He may call me tomorrow and break things off and give me the ol' 'it's not you it's me' speech. And you know what? I'll be okay. I've suffered greater losses and I'm still here to talk about them."

"Teagan…"

"No, you got to have your say, I'm having mine," she reminded him.

He nodded and stood in silence.

"Ever since Logan died, I've been overly cautious and careful to the point of not living. Yes, I have my son and he's everything to me, but I'm ready for more!

I'm ready to have more in my life, even if it's only for a short time."

"Yeah, but—"

"Unh-unh," she said, cutting off anything else he was about to say. "Bobby's been nothing but honest with me about his past and about his faults. Everyone is entitled to a second chance, Quinn. You can't stand here and tell me Anna didn't give you one, or that you've always been an upstanding guy with no faults or flaws, because I wouldn't believe you."

"That's not what I'm saying—"

"Tell me something good about Bobby," she demanded quickly.

"Um, what?"

"You heard me. Right now. I want you to think of one positive thing to say about him."

"I'm not going to do that," he said stubbornly.

"Fine. Don't. I'll just go inside and ask everyone in there, one by one. I can handle that."

She saw her cousin pale slightly and was happy he was as uncomfortable in this conversation as she was.

When she turned to reach for the pub's door handle, he stopped her. "Okay, okay, okay," he said with a huff. "Geez, you're tenacious."

That made her smile.

He huffed again, raked a hand through his hair, his annoyance palpable. "Something good about Bobby," he murmured. After several minutes he said, "He's... he's good with the kids. There, happy?"

"Kind of an obvious thing to point out, but I guess it will have to do."

"What? It's not obvious, it's true! When Kaitlyn

was a baby, he was one of the only people who could get her to go to sleep. I used to rock her until my arms were ready to break, and if Bobby was there, he would just hold her for, like, less than five minutes, and she'd be asleep."

"Wow," Teagan commented, still smiling. "That's kind of sweet."

"And…when Anna first bought the house and was struggling with doing renovations and paying the bills, Bobby moved in and paid for half of everything so she wouldn't have it so hard."

Teagan figured she'd just let him talk. He seemed to be on a roll now.

"When we were moving into our house, he was there every weekend to help with painting and all the work we wanted to put in." He stopped and chuckled. "He completely demo'd our downstairs bathroom all on his own and then refinished it himself, too."

So he was good with kids, good with his hands, and willing to help out family, she thought to herself. Did her cousin realize just how much he was proving her case?

He must have, because he looked at her and she would almost say he was contrite. "You know what? He's the bravest guy I know." He frowned slightly. "I was there when he woke up after getting shot. Most people would have been freaking out, but… It was just the two of us in the room and he wanted me to tell him what happened so he could wrap his head around it all. I think he didn't want to freak out in front of his folks, you know?" Quinn paused again. "I didn't know a whole lot about the specifics of his injury and I felt like crap, because all he wanted was a little reassurance that he was going to be okay."

She nodded with understanding even as her heart broke just thinking about Bobby in that situation.

"When the doctor came in and explained the injury and how this could mean he wouldn't return to the force?" He shook his head. "He just sat there and took it calmly. I would have been ranting and raving and demanding a second opinion if it were me."

"Did he get a second opinion?"

Quinn laughed softly. "I think he got a second, third, and fourth."

"Oh."

Then he looked at her with a small smile. "Look, during his recovery, he was a major pain in the ass. He was surly and mean, and we were all counting the days until he could go home and be on his own again. But as I'm standing here talking with you, I realize he's been different in the last few weeks." He shrugged. "I don't know, maybe he's just trying to get on my good side so I don't go and kick his ass for messing with my cousin."

"Quinn…" she warned.

"Okay, fine," he said wearily. "You can't be mad at me for looking out for you, Teagan. I just want you to be happy."

"I get it and I even appreciate it, but maybe just tone down the attitude a bit. Trust me when I tell you that the whole going-caveman thing? It doesn't work. It doesn't make me feel cared for, it annoys the crap out of me. So stop it."

Then he laughed and pulled her in for a hug. "You

know, I don't remember you being so mouthy when we were kids."

She hugged him back. "Yeah, well, unfortunately, I do remember you being a big pain in the ass. I had hoped you would have grown out of it." She squeezed him a little tighter. "But I love you and I know your heart is in the right place."

He pulled back and gave her a lopsided grin. "It really is. I swear."

"Your delivery could use some work," she teased and moved to grab her tote bag. Reaching for his hand, she said, "C'mon. Let's get inside and see what everyone's up to next."

When they entered the pub, she looked around until she spotted Lucas and Bobby. They were sitting at a long table with everyone and when they both saw her and smiled, her heart felt like it would burst.

So this is what it could be like, she thought. A family.

She had given up that fantasy long ago. She'd thought that if she couldn't have a family with Logan, then she wouldn't have one at all. But standing here and looking at not only the two of them, but the room as a whole, Teagan felt a longing like she'd never known before.

She wanted more of this. And not just for a holiday or for random weekends. She wanted it all the time.

Was Quinn right, though? Was it too soon? Was she rushing things? Was this all simply because this was the first time since Logan that she'd ever allowed herself to be in this kind of a situation?

She shook her head. No. This wasn't about convenience or proximity. What she felt for Bobby was much deeper than that. And as much as she hated to admit it, it was even more than what she had felt for Logan. Guilt made her cringe. She hated to think less of the man who hadn't had a chance to live his life. She had no idea if they would have grown together into a deeper relationship, and as much as it pained her, she would never know. She would never get those answers.

What she did know was that she had been given a second chance. It was too soon to say "at love," but she had a second chance to see if something could be it. She was learning to open her heart again. As much as it scared her, she knew it was worth it.

Bobby was worth it.

And to hell with what anyone else thought.

It was almost midnight when they walked through Teagan's front door. Bobby was carrying Lucas, who was sound asleep.

Quietly, he followed her to the kid's room and put him gently down on the bed. Teagan placed a finger over her lips to keep him from saying anything and then motioned that she was going to get her son changed into his pajamas. Giving her a thumbs-up, he walked out of the room and went back out to the car to get the rest of their things.

Fifteen minutes later, they were sitting on the couch with her head on his shoulder. More than anything, he wanted to stay the night. It wasn't right, and they already had a lot to talk about, but it didn't stop him from wanting to sleep beside Teagan. Living two hours apart already meant they didn't get to see each other very often. Add to that the fact that when he did come to town, they couldn't rely on asking people to keep Lucas for the night. Bobby was an adult and he understood it, but that didn't stop the desire for the things he couldn't have.

Tonight he had almost asked his sister if Lucas could stay at her house, but Anna and Quinn both looked ready to drop by the time they were leaving the fireworks show. It hadn't stopped them from inviting everyone back to their place for dessert, but asking them for anything more at that point would have been incredibly selfish.

"I asked my mom if Lucas could stay with her tonight," Teagan said, interrupting his thoughts. "I think she knew I was asking because we wanted to have some time alone." She paused. "She even apologized for being too tired."

At least it was something, he told himself. It didn't help him right now, but at least that was an option to look forward to.

Placing a kiss on the top of her head, he said, "I know it was a long day for everyone."

Lifting her head, she looked at him. "This probably isn't what you bargained for when you asked me out, huh?"

"Are you kidding me?" he asked, mildly offended. "Look, I'm not going to lie to you, I would love to stay the night. I miss you and I miss holding you and making love with you, but it's not like I don't understand. Lucas is part of this relationship and I wouldn't trade that for anything."

He could tell he had surprised her.

"Bobby…"

"I'm not a kid, Teagan. I can control myself. I may

not want to, but I can do it." With a wink, he leaned in and kissed the tip of her nose.

"I wish things could be different," she whispered, resting her head back on his shoulder.

"What do you mean?"

"I don't know," she said, then yawned. "I want to have my cake and eat it too, I suppose. Like, if I could be the kind of mom who was more comfortable with having you stay the night without worrying that I was traumatizing my son."

Shaking his head, he held her close. "I don't want you to be that kind of mom. You're perfect the way you are."

They sat in silence for several minutes in the dim space, only the light from the kitchen illuminating the room.

"When are you going home?"

"You mean to my parents, or back to Myrtle Beach?"

"The beach."

"Tomorrow," he said solemnly. "I have therapy in the afternoon and a doctor's appointment on Thursday, so..."

She nodded. "How's your hand? We didn't talk about it after the parade. You didn't seem to have any problems the rest of the day."

He had, but he'd kept it to himself. Even now he still hadn't regained full sensation and it was freaking him out when he thought about it. Then he remembered his conversation with his father earlier.

"I—it's still not great," he said slowly. "Since it's my left hand, unless I'm trying to balance or carry stuff, I can maneuver around just fine." He shrugged. "Everything I did the rest of the day—"

"You did with your right hand," she finished for him.

"Bobby, maybe you need to change doctors or find a new therapist. Perhaps there's something—"

He shook his head and carefully considered his next words. "It's not getting better," he said flatly. "And it doesn't matter if I go see new specialists or try a new therapy. I've already consulted with more medical professionals than I ever wanted to and the prognosis is the same."

"Which is?"

"Time. It's the only answer, and it's not a guarantee. That's why I stayed away for a couple of weeks. I was in one appointment after another and...I was angry. Really angry."

"And now?"

"I still am."

She shifted beside him and then stood, holding out her hand. He looked up at her quizzically.

"We can set the alarm for around five. Lucas won't be up before seven. That will give you time to get up and sneak out before he comes out of his room."

"Teagan..."

As much as he wanted to argue, he was on his feet and letting her lead him to the bedroom. Then he let her take the lead in making him feel good.

It was the first time in a long time that he didn't mind the help.

Chapter 8

PULLING INTO THE PARKING LOT OF BOBBY'S CONDO complex the following Friday, Teagan felt herself sag with relief. She'd made it.

Getting out the door that morning had been quite chaotic. Lucas wasn't cooperating, because he wanted to go with her rather than stay with his grandparents. He'd never argued with her about sleepovers before, but because she'd admitted that she was going to see Bobby, he automatically felt he should have been included in those plans. As a compromise, she'd promised that the next time she came to visit, he could come with her.

Once at her parents' house, they'd started grilling her about how serious the relationship was getting and what she and Bobby were planning, considering the current logistics. And it didn't matter how much she tried to put them off by saying they hadn't really talked about it yet—and they hadn't—her parents were fairly persistent in giving *their* opinions.

She felt like she'd barely escaped with her life at that point.

While she was packing before leaving, she'd realized she didn't have anything sexy to bring, or even anything trendy enough to wear to a concert. That had necessitated a one-hour side trip to do some shopping on her way down.

So to be parking her car and seeing Bobby come

out the front door to greet her felt like a major accomplishment.

Climbing from the car, she stretched and was instantly swept up into Bobby's arms. He kissed her soundly before putting her down on her feet. "I'm so glad you're here," he said, and she could see the truth of that written all over his face. Without asking, he pulled her suitcase from the back seat before taking her hand and leading her into his house.

Stepping inside, Teagan was pleasantly surprised. It was beautifully decorated, if a little masculine for her taste, and was impeccably tidy. Bobby turned to look at her and laughed softly.

"Don't be too impressed. I hired a cleaning company to come in yesterday and scour the place from top to bottom," he admitted.

"You didn't have to do that," she said, unable to hide her amusement. "But it is greatly appreciated."

Putting her suitcase down outside his bedroom door, he gave her a quick tour of the place. "Living room, dining room, kitchen," he said, indicating each area that was part of a fairly open floor plan. "Master bedroom and bath are to the right. There's a half bath by the front door, and upstairs is a guest bedroom, full bath, and a loft."

"Wow," she said, seriously impressed. "This is great. And how long have you been here?"

"A couple of years." He led her to the back of the room and opened the sliding glass doors. "You can't hear the ocean from here, but we're only a couple of blocks from the beach. The nice thing about this unit is that it's at the back of the complex so there's nothing behind me except that wall of trees that separate us from the houses behind us. It's a little private, and I have a deck so I can grill if I want to."

"It's a wonderful space," she agreed and then looked up at him, smiling. "Will we be grilling tonight?"

Pulling her in close and wrapping his arms around her waist, he shook his head. "Nope. This weekend I'm taking you out and spoiling you rotten."

Her eyes widened. "Bobby, you don't have to do that. There's something to be said for having a cozy and private dinner in."

"That's what breakfast and lunch are for," he said with a sexy grin. "I've got our weekend all planned. I talked to Riley yesterday and he invited us to have a late dinner with him and Savannah after the show tomorrow night. I hope you don't mind, but I said yes."

"Are you kidding? That's awesome!" She gasped and pulled out of his arms. "Does this mean we'll get to go backstage?" Another gasp. "Oh my gosh. I don't know if my outfit is good enough to meet the band and go out with Riley and Savannah!"

"Teagan…"

"I stopped and went shopping on my way here and now I'm second-guessing everything and I'm probably going to look like a total dork in front of everyone and Riley's going to wish he never invited me—" She stopped and groaned, collapsing on his massive sofa in despair.

Bobby joined her, laughing.

"What? What's so funny?" she demanded. "I'm having a crisis here!"

"That's what's so funny." Taking one of her hands in his, he explained. "You're usually the most level-headed person I know, and to stand here and watch you freak out over your outfit just is a little…well. It's so out of character for you that it's funny."

"Easy for you to say," she murmured, "all you have to do is put on a pair of jeans and a T-shirt and you're good to go."

"Hardly."

She glared at him because she knew she was right, and he was just trying to placate her.

"Either way, I'm freaking out."

"Wait, you said you shopped on the way here?"

She nodded.

"Are the bags in your suitcase?"

"No, they're out in the trunk. I didn't think to grab them."

"Are your keys in your purse?"

She nodded. "Why?"

"I'll go get them. And I think you need to show me what you bought so I can calm you down."

"Bobby…"

But he wasn't listening, already walking out the front door. Except maybe that was a good thing. She could model some of her new purchases for him—including the ridiculous amount of lingerie she'd purchased from Victoria's Secret. Never had she felt so giddy about parading around in her underwear!

When he walked back in two minutes later, it was the pink shopping bag that he was dangling in front of her with a wicked grin on his face. "Whatever you have in here, I can guarantee it will not make you look like a dork."

With that, she laughed and came to her feet, taking

the bag from his hands. "The contents of this bag are the least of my worries."

"Why don't you let me be the judge of that." Taking her by the hand, he led her to the bedroom and sat down on the bed. "You can change in the bathroom— or right here," he added. "That is, if you don't mind an audience."

Decisions, decisions.

"You wait here," she said saucily as she turned and walked into the en suite, shutting the door behind her. Glancing at her reflection, Teagan almost didn't recognize the face looking back at her. She was flushed with excitement, her hair in mild disarray, and her heart was beating rapidly.

She'd never been happier or felt so carefree.

Stripping quickly, she reached into the bag and pulled out the first bra and panty set, a deep crimson set that was primarily lace. Once she'd put the garments on and looked at herself in the mirror, she had to admit she looked sexier than she'd ever thought possible. For the first time in forever, she wasn't going to obsess about her stretch marks or the fact that her stomach wasn't completely flat. Right now she felt like some sort of sexy pinup girl, and she was loving it.

And when she opened the bathroom door and caught Bobby's reaction, she loved it even more. Striking a sexy pose against the door frame, she asked, "Do you like it?"

Slowly, he came to his feet and simply stared. "How many of these did you buy today?"

She had to hide her smile. "All together? Six sets."

Nodding, he said, "I promise to buy you six more."

"Oh, really? And why would you need to do that?" she asked, her voice becoming more and more breathless with anticipation as he moved toward her.

"Because I know I'm not only going to be ripping these off of you any minute, but if the others are anything like them, they'll be gone too."

"Hmm. Makes me think I should have stuck to my white cotton."

"It wouldn't matter," he said when they were toe-to-toe. "I enjoy ripping those off of you too."

She was practically panting now with the need for him to do just that.

So what if she'd just spent a ridiculous amount of money on lingerie that was barely going to get worn before getting destroyed.

Stepping away from the door, Teagan leaned into Bobby and let out a sexy little moan. "Then what are you waiting for?"

After that it was purely, simply, madness.

His hands were everywhere. She was airborne in the blink of an eye, landing on the bed with a quick bounce. In an instant he was right there beside her.

"Maybe we'll just order in tonight," he said, nipping at the swell of her breast.

"It's barely lunchtime," she replied breathlessly. "I think there's still time to go out."

He shook his head and used his teeth to move the lacy cup aside. "I don't think that's going to be a possibility. Not after seeing how good you look in red lace. Now I want to know what other colors are in the bag."

It was on the tip of her tongue to argue—she didn't want to ruin all of them in one afternoon—but then his mouth began traveling and doing some absolutely sinful things to her body and she gave up the fight.

Best money ever spent.

———~~~———

The setting sun found them walking on the beach hand in hand.

As much as he was reluctant to let her out of the house knowing what she was wearing under her clothes, Bobby figured he should stick to his original plan of spoiling her and taking her out on some proper kid-free dates.

Although he kind of missed Lucas.

Not that he was going to bring that up right now. Teagan had called her son before they left the house and was a little teary-eyed by the time she hung up, so he didn't want to do or say anything to make her feel worse.

"We're walking to the restaurant?" she asked.

Nodding, he said, "It's not too far and I thought it was a great night to do this. When was the last time you've been to Myrtle Beach?"

"Oh, my goodness. I was maybe twelve or thirteen," she said, smiling at the memory. "We used to meet Uncle Ian and everyone here. We used to do it a lot more when I was really young, before Aunt Lily passed away."

Sometimes he forgot they had so much history in common.

"She was an amazing woman," Bobby said. "My mom was her best friend and I always considered her to be my second mom. I think I cried as much as her kids did when she died."

They walked in silence for a few minutes. "My folks

were devastated that we couldn't fly in for her funeral. My dad was deployed and we just couldn't afford it. That's something that's always bothered them." She paused and looked at him. "Do you realize if we had come, you and I would have met back then?"

He hadn't thought of that. "We would have been kids."

"Well, I would have," she reasoned. "You're older than me." Then she elbowed him playfully. "You wouldn't even have noticed me."

Sadly, she was right. There was a bit of an age difference and right now it wasn't a big deal, but back then? Uh, yeah. It would have been weird.

Talking about Mrs. Shaughnessy always made him melancholy, and no doubt Teagan was feeling it too. He'd gone from avoiding conversation about Lucas so that she wouldn't be sad to talking about her dead aunt and making them both sad.

Man, he seriously sucked at this conversation thing.

"Okay, so…surf and turf," he said, quickly changing the subject. "This place has some of the best steaks in town, and the lobster is even better."

"Ooo, two of my favorites!"

And just like that, the mood shifted. They walked and talked about everything and nothing, and by the time they were walking up to the restaurant, Bobby felt like he'd redeemed himself a little.

"That was a glorious walk," she commented as they climbed the steps up to the front door. "Although I have a feeling that I'll be cursing that same gorgeous view later on when I'm way too full from a delicious dinner."

Damn, he hadn't thought of that either.

"I can run back and get the car for you if you want. You know, after dinner," he quickly amended.

"Bobby, I was only kidding. I'm going to enjoy dinner and the walk back. I really love living on the coast, and I don't take advantage of it nearly enough. So thank you for making this a part of our night out. It's perfect."

And…redeeming himself again. It was like a damn roller coaster. Maybe this was why he'd avoided seriously dating anyone for so long—it was exhausting.

An hour later, however, he decided the exhaustion was worth it. The food had been delicious, the atmosphere was romantic, and the look on Teagan's face showed how much she was enjoying herself, which had been his goal all along.

After they ate, they danced out on the deck under the stars, the sounds of the waves crashing on the shore behind them.

"Mmm," Teagan hummed as she swayed in his arms. "I must say, Mr. Hannigan, you certainly do know how to spoil a girl."

That made him laugh softly. "You think so, huh?"

"Absolutely. This is the most perfect night to be outside." She gently pulled one hand from his and tried to smooth her hair, strands blowing in the breeze. "Although I'm pretty sure I'm a bit of a mess. Between the walk here and now the wind coming off the water, my hair is all over the place."

Shaking his head, Bobby reached up and gently combed her hair behind one ear. "You're beautiful. Right now. Tonight. Always."

And then he kissed her.

It wasn't rushed, it wasn't heated, it bordered on chaste. Yet it felt like one of the greatest kisses ever.

After that, they danced some more, talked a lot, and when the small band announced they were going to take a break, Bobby suggested they start heading back to the car. She readily agreed but they strolled at a leisurely pace, simply enjoying the night and the fact that there was no rush. They didn't have to watch the clock. Tonight they had all the time in the world.

Tomorrow he planned on making her breakfast in bed, maybe doing a little sightseeing and lunch out, before coming back to get ready for the concert. Riley had sent him the tickets and VIP passes so they could get in early and hang out before the show. He hadn't gotten to tell Teagan about that part before she'd started freaking out over her wardrobe, which still made him laugh.

So he'd surprise her and they'd get to the arena early. Bobby had met the guys in the band several times already and he didn't look at them as celebrities anymore. They were just a cool bunch of guys who happened to work with a good friend. He had been off-duty the last several times the band had played locally so he'd been able to get in as backstage security. It was always great to hang out with them, and he hoped she would relax enough to enjoy it.

Maybe having Savannah there would help.

Either way, it was going to be a great night. Shaughnessy always put on a powerful, high-energy show, and to see that and then go for dinner with Riley and Savannah was going to make for a pretty spectacular night. Then he'd be two for two.

Beside him, Teagan let out small sigh.

"You okay?"

She nodded. "It's been a long time since I've done anything like this. Knowing that I have no responsibilities, taking a night for myself… It feels a little weird. And I feel guilty that I'm enjoying myself so much."

"I don't think you need to feel guilty. It's only natural that you feel something, I guess, but that's only because you don't take enough time for yourself."

"It's not like I have a choice, Bobby. That's what being a parent means, especially a single parent. My son comes first."

He nodded. "I know, and I didn't mean to make it sound like you shouldn't feel that way. I'm just glad you're here with me now."

He was walking with her on his left side when he started to feel a tingling in his hand and wanted to curse. Why? Why was it acting up now? Carefully, he flexed his hand and hoped she didn't notice.

"Ooo, look at the size of this shell!" Teagan exclaimed, releasing his hand to crouch down in the sand. The moon was pretty full but it was still dark and hard to see. How the hell had she noticed the shell? When she straightened, she held it up. "Lucas and I—whenever we go to the beach—we always challenge each other to see who can find the biggest shell. I can't wait to show this to him." She slipped the shell into her purse and rejoined him, ending up on his right side.

He wanted to be mad, or deny that anything was wrong, but right now he was more than a little relieved they could walk in the dark and he could flex and stretch his hand without drawing too much attention to it.

Even though he knew she was aware of what he was doing, for now he could pretend that she didn't.

For the rest of their walk, Teagan chatted about her son's reactions to seeing the beach for the first time, and some of the activities they've done on each visit. By the time they reached the car, he felt a little less rage at the tingling in his hand and resigned himself to the fact that the feeling would fade whenever it wanted. He wasn't going to let it ruin their night.

Back at the house, it felt marginally better, but not great. Not that he let it stop him.

Nothing was going to ruin the fact that he had Teagan in his home, in his bed, where she was going to sleep in his arms all night long.

"Oh my God! That was amazing!!"

Smiling, Bobby nodded as Shaughnessy took their final bow and walked off the stage. They had to wait a little while before going backstage, per Riley's instructions, and considering they were in the second row of the arena, it would be a while before they were moving anyway.

"So you enjoyed it, huh?" he asked.

Nodding enthusiastically and with a broad smile on her face, she said, "Absolutely! It still blows my mind that I'm related to him! He's so talented!"

Yeah, it was crazy to look up on stage and see the scrawny kid he'd grown up with, singing to tens of thousands of people and looking every inch a rock star. "Riley's voice has always been amazing, and I swear he just keeps getting better."

Their row had emptied out, but the two of them stayed sitting.

"I can't even remember the last time I was at a concert," she said. "Any concert. Well, unless you count *Sesame Street Live*."

Laughing, he leaned back in his seat, stretching his legs out in front of him. "I'm sure this was much louder."

"Way louder. I think I'm going to be shouting later and embarrassing myself." Then she looked at him sternly. "Don't let me do that."

He promised.

"This has been an amazing day, Bobby. Thank you."

It hadn't been just amazing, it had been damn-near perfect. Waking up this morning, he'd snuck out of the bedroom and made them breakfast before serving it in bed. After they ate, they'd made love twice before taking a shower together.

He really loved that part.

Then they'd gone into town for some miniature golf, thanks to some comments she'd made about how much she'd enjoyed doing that as a kid. They'd played a round in the spirit of good fun, and he had to admit, he'd had a good time. Lunch had been on the boardwalk where it was loud and crowded, but the open-air atmosphere was great. They'd run into several friends of his and he'd enjoyed introducing her to everyone, amused by the looks of surprise they gave him when he called Teagan his girlfriend.

Another big first for him.

She'd insisted on buying souvenirs for Lucas and they'd gone to lots of the little shops on the boardwalk so she could pick out T-shirts and hats and even a Frisbee to take back. By the time they were done, Bobby'd taken her back to his place to get ready for the show, which they'd almost been late for anyway.

And the thought of the ways they had spent those few hours before the early arrival were enough to make him hard just sitting there in the emptying arena.

"Do you know where we're going for dinner?" she asked. "Neither Riley nor Savannah mentioned it." She looked down at herself. "Do you think I'm dressed appropriately? Do we have time to run home so I can change?"

She always seemed to be worrying about how she looked, and each time it sounded more and more endearing. It didn't matter that her cousin and his wife had been dressed casually when they saw them earlier, she still questioned her choice of clothing. Meeting Matt, Dylan, and Julian—the guys in the band—had her blushing adorably. And for a minute there, he found himself feeling mildly jealous as she gushed over each of them. Those guys were all happily married to incredible women, so he wasn't jealous of them hitting on Teagan, it was her reaction to them that was bothering him.

But he got a grip and remembered that she was going home with him and only him.

And it felt great.

A burly security guard walked over to them. "Mr. Hannigan? Ms. Shaughnessy?"

They nodded.

"You can follow me," he said with a nod toward the side of the stage.

Walking along the halls backstage, Bobby noticed a lot of activity—even several cops and security team members running in the same direction. He motioned to the guard who was escorting them. "Any idea what that's all about?"

He shook his head, but Bobby had a feeling the guy knew exactly what was going on and just wouldn't say. Part of him twitched with the need to run down the hall, catch up to some of the guys he recognized and be part of the action. Teagan grabbed his hand, reminding him of why he couldn't. Before he knew it, they were being greeted by Savannah and ushered into the dressing room.

"So? What did you guys think of the show?" she asked excitedly.

Teagan immediately answered for them both, which was fine with him because he was still mildly distracted by what was going on outside.

Riley walked over and clapped him on his good shoulder, motioning for Bobby to join him on the other side of the room.

"What's up?"

"Don't freak out," Riley said, his voice barely above a whisper.

Bobby immediately tensed.

"We have to hang out here for a little while because there was a shooting near one of the parking exits. Our security team is here with us, but the local force is going out to check out the situation."

Dammit. "I should go and see."

He didn't have the chance to move before Riley stopped him. "You can't go out there, Bobby. Beside the fact that you're on leave, you're a guest of mine and you're on the list of people who need to stay back here where it's safe."

Rolling his eyes, he let out a loud sigh. "It's not dangerous out in the arena, for crying out loud. If this happened in the parking lot, then it's possible it has nothing to do with anything in here."

But Riley shook his head. "Sorry, man. Not gonna happen. You're not leaving."

"Riley—"

His words were cut off by a commotion near the dressing room door. Looking over, he saw the rest of the band coming in with their wives. Everyone was laughing and smiling like it was no big deal that something was going down outside—or how badly it was freaking him out to have to stay in.

"It's all going to be okay, all right?" Riley said, casually leading Bobby toward the rest of the group. "We're just going to hang out for a while and then head back to the hotel for a late dinner."

"Yeah, but—"

"I don't think you should freak out Teagan," Riley said casually. "She seems to be having a great time and I would really hate for her to get upset. So for no other reason, do it for her."

And that was the kicker. Riley knew the exact thing to say to calm him down.

At least outwardly.

With no other choice, Bobby walked over and greeted the guys again, smiling as Teagan began talking to Julian's wife. Charlotte was a social worker, and given Teagan's job as a guidance counselor, the two instantly seemed to bond over career talk. All he could do was stand back and marvel at how Teagan glowed when she talked because she was passionate about her job.

So was he, but for some reason he never looked quite like she did. And people didn't always respond in kind.

"You're frowning," Riley sang as he walked by.

Fine. He was, and he hated it. Rather than try to deny it, he went for distraction, striking up a conversation with Matt, the guitarist. They had grown up not far from one another, so it was easy to slip into talk about people they knew.

"So you and Riley's cousin, huh?" Matt said with a grin. "How's that going?"

He shrugged but couldn't fight a grin. "It's great. She's great," he clarified.

"How do the other Shaughnessys feel about it? I mean, you're family to them already but…"

Laughing, he told Matt about Quinn giving him grief. "But that's just Quinn. It seems like it's his life's ambition to annoy people."

"You talking about my brother?" Riley asked, coming up behind them. But he was grinning, so Bobby knew he wasn't offended.

"You know anyone else who likes to annoy people?" Bobby asked.

That just made Riley laugh. "I happen to know quite a few people like that. But I also happen to know that if you're the one talking about it, the answer's going to be Quinn." He shook his head, still chuckling. "When are the two of you just gonna hug it out and move on? Everything's good, everyone's happy, why is there still so much animosity?"

Bobby shrugged. "You'll have to ask him. All I know is that Teagan and I are good even though your

TANGLED UP IN YOU

brother trash-talked me to her. This one time, I'm completely blameless."

"Which means there were times when you weren't," Matt stated, clearly amused.

Another shrug. "Let just say there were a lot of years I needed to punish him for."

"But for the record," Riley said diplomatically, "he and Anna are totally happy and in love and that's the most important thing, right?"

It was and Bobby knew it, but…old habits died hard. "Someone should tell your brother that. He really freaked Teagan out for a little while there."

"Yeah, but I heard she put him in his place," Riley said.

And she had.

Still made him want to punch Quinn in his stupid face, but he'd refrained.

"So," Matt said, "is this serious?"

"Yes," Bobby said confidently. "It is. I'm crazy about her. She's amazing and sweet, funny and kind, and—I don't know, man, just everything about her is just… It's everything I ever wanted."

"She's got a son, right?"

He nodded. "Lucas. He's five and he's really a great kid."

"Still," Riley interrupted, "it's got to be hard, right? I mean, Teagan's my cousin and I love her, so no disrespect there. But what about you? Isn't it hard to take on raising someone else's kid?"

"Maybe for some people," he explained, "but so far we haven't really had any issues. I've hung out with Lucas a lot—even babysat for him, so it was just the two of us—and we got along fine. No problems."

"What about his father?" Matt asked. "I would imagine it's got to be hard to share the parenting responsibilities and know where your boundaries are."

"Uh… Lucas's father died before he was born. He was in the military and was killed…you know."

"Damn," Matt murmured. Beside him, Riley nodded sadly.

"If things were different," Bobby said solemnly, "I don't know if this would even be an issue. No doubt Teagan and Logan would be married and raising Lucas together."

And how much of an ass did it make him that he hated even to think about it?

No one spoke for a moment and Bobby felt like the conversation had definitely taken a turn to the depressing. Clearing his throat, he said, "So where to next? Where's your next stop?"

That brought the conversation back around to music and the tour, where it stayed for a while. Julian and Dylan joined the conversation, while their wives stayed talking with Teagan.

"Is it just me or does this feel like one of those middle school dances where the guys all stand on one side of the room and the girls on the other?" Dylan joked.

"Slightly," Julian agreed. "Perhaps we should do something about that."

"I wish we knew when we could leave," Matt said. "I'm starving and Vivienne and I were planning on—" He stopped and grinned. "Never mind. Let's just say we were looking forward to going back to the hotel tonight."

"Smooth, dude. I'm sure none of us can crack that cryptic message." Dylan rolled his eyes. "But I get it. Daniel's been a little fussy and we were hoping to get back before the midnight bottle and give the nanny a break."

The conversation immediately switched gears to parenting and as much as Bobby wanted to contribute something, he couldn't. Other than hanging out with Lucas a few times, he had nothing. And that's when it hit him hard.

He wanted to contribute. He wanted to be able to talk about his kids.

His gaze instantly went to Teagan, who was laughing at something. She was smiling, her eyes were full of pure joy, and he knew—he just *knew*—he wanted the kids he talked about to be theirs.

His and Teagan's.

It was fast. Too fast. Not that he doubted how he felt about her. That was never in doubt. But he had to wonder if this was…normal. For some reason he started to sweat. Looking around the room, it felt like the walls were starting to close in on him. Panic attacks weren't something he was prone to, but right now, it sure as hell seemed like what he was feeling.

"Dude, you okay?" Riley asked.

"Is it too soon to be in love and wanting a family with Teagan?" he blurted out before he could even stop himself.

Four pairs of eyes looked back at him with everything from shock to amusement. And as if the guys were of one mind, they all moved a little farther away from the women.

"First of all, breathe," Riley said.

"And second," Matt added, "remember that's his cousin you're talking about."

Dylan and Julian laughed.

Riley frowned at them all before putting his focus back on Bobby. "You and me? We're cool. You've always been like family to me, and on top of that, I know you're a good guy. So the fact that you're dating my cousin isn't a big deal to me."

"I'm sensing there's a *but* coming," Julian murmured.

"*But*," Riley began with emphasis, "I've never known you to get serious with anyone. And it makes me a little skeptical that what you're feeling right now is really love."

"Yeah, but—"

"And don't even get me started on the having a family part," he finished.

Now Bobby felt completely deflated. He'd thought he had an ally in Riley, but apparently he was wrong.

Holding up a hand, Dylan spoke. "For starters? Wow," he said, glaring at Riley. "So basically what you're saying is that because Bobby's never been in a serious relationship before, he can't possibly want one now?"

"That's not what I meant," Riley argued.

"But it's kind of how it came off," Matt interjected.

"Fine, then let me clarify," Riley said, sounding mildly defensive. "Bobby, we've known each other for most of my life. I respect you. However, this is all new for you, so maybe it's just not…you know, *love* yet. And what's the rush? You two have been dating for, like, what, a month? Two?"

Rather than speak, Bobby nodded.

"It's just a little fast. That's all I'm saying."

"Wait," Matt said. "How long were you with Savannah before you knew you were in love?"

"That's not the point."

"Yes, it is," Dylan said. "And for the record, it was under three months for me and Paige."

"It wasn't even a month for me and Viv," Matt responded.

"If anyone should have been avoiding a serious relationship, it was me," Julian added. "But when I met Charlotte, I just knew. You can't set your watch by it. You know when you know."

For the first time in several minutes, Bobby felt himself begin to breathe and relax. "So I'm not crazy?"

Three out of four of them shook their heads before they looked over at Riley, who immediately rolled his eyes. "Okay, fine. I guess it's possible that it's not too soon."

Bobby chuckled softly. "I hate to break it to you, but I really wasn't looking for your approval."

"Oh!" Dylan laughed. "I did *not* see that coming!"

It would have been easy to joke and make light of the whole thing, but Bobby didn't particularly feel like making jokes right now. He held his ground. "Here's the thing. While it would be nice if everyone was happy for us, ultimately, it doesn't really matter. The only opinion I'm worried about is Teagan's."

Riley studied him hard for a moment. "You know you have a lot to overcome, right?"

"Not you too," Bobby muttered with frustration. "I've heard it all already from Quinn."

"I'm not talking about your history, I'm talking about hers." Motioning over his shoulder toward Teagan, Riley continued. "She's had to work like a hundred times harder than most. Being a single mom and losing the man she thought she was going to marry?

That would crush most people. I know my aunt and uncle have always been there for her, but that may not be a good thing. You're going to have to deal with them on some level too. You have to try to find your way in their family dynamics."

He hadn't really thought of that.

"And on top of that, you've got the kid. You're not just dating Teagan, you're dating Lucas too."

"I know. They're a package deal and I don't have a problem with that."

"And right now, he probably doesn't either. But as this relationship progresses and you want to have Teagan's attention, you have to know that any attention you get is being taken away from her son. And he's a kid who's only known this one way of life. Are you prepared to deal with that?"

Bobby nodded confidently. "I am. I can't say it's going to be easy or that I'm prepared for everything, but I know I'm going to try my best to make sure they're both happy. And really, isn't that all any of us can do?"

He was saved from the possibility of hearing any negative comments when a knock sounded at the dressing room door. It was Mick, the band's manager.

"Okay, we've got clearance to start heading out," Mick said. When he spotted Bobby, he walked over and shook his hand. "Good to see you, Bobby. It's a real shame what happened out there. Glad to know you're in here and safe."

"What are you talking about?"

Pointing over his shoulder, Mick said, "The shooting outside. It was a traffic stop. Officer got shot." He shook his head. "So senseless. From what I'm told, the parking lot is still pretty much at a standstill, but we're clear to go out the back way with a police escort." He looked around the room. "We'll meet out in the hall in ten minutes!" And then he was walking back out of the room.

Bobby felt like he was going to be sick. How many of these shows had he worked? How many times had he pulled someone over on the way out due to reckless driving or speeding? Before he knew it, he was being led over to a sofa and nudged to sit down.

"What's going on?"

Looking up, he saw Teagan walking toward him, worry written all over her face. She was instantly at his side, taking his hand in hers.

"We just… I mean, Mick told us…"

"An officer was shot outside," Riley said quietly. "That's all we know. It's why we had to stay back here."

She didn't say anything, didn't offer any commentary on the situation, and he wasn't sure if he was angry or relieved.

"Okay, let's all get out of here," Julian called out to the room. Leaning over, he shook Bobby's hand. "Always good to see you, man. Take care of yourself." Then he smiled at Teagan. "It was nice to meet you, Teagan."

"Thanks," she said. "You too."

Bobby watched as Teagan hugged Charlotte, Paige, and Vivienne goodbye in turn. Slowly, he came to his feet and shook both Matt and Dylan's hands and waved to their wives. When it was down to just Riley and Savannah in the room with them, Bobby fought the urge to bail on their plans for dinner. But that wouldn't help anything. He was back to the distraction method instead of running, something that was beginning to majorly annoy him. But for tonight, it was his only option.

"You can ride to the hotel with us and we'll have someone bring your car when the lot clears out," Riley said. "That is, if you're okay with it."

Teagan readily agreed and Bobby simply nodded. It wasn't ideal, but considering the circumstances, what choice did he have?

Within minutes, they were being herded out of the building flanked by security guards. Each of the guys had their own car, even though they were all going to the same place. The only thing keeping him somewhat sane was hearing Teagan giggle as she climbed into the limo.

"I didn't think you'd have an actual limo," she said as she settled into her seat. "I figured it would be some kind of town car or SUV—nothing this fancy."

Riley laughed as he sat next to his wife. "Sometimes we do, sometimes we don't. I don't know if you noticed, but the other guys have the big SUVs today. I guess Mick figured we might want a little more space this time."

Bobby watched as a security guard shut the door, wondering if they were going to drive by the crime scene. Would he be able to see anything? Would he recognize anyone? Slipping his phone from his pocket, he didn't think twice about doing a quick online search of the local news to see if there was any information out there.

Nothing yet.

Putting his phone away, he reached for Teagan's hand and did his best to join the conversation. She was still gushing about the concert and he could tell how much Riley was loving it. Savannah glanced his way as if to prompt him to participate.

"You guys really did sound great, Ry," he said when there was a lull. "I think the time apart really did wonders for all of you. You're sounding better than ever."

"Thanks," Riley said, grinning happily. "So listen, we wanted to share something with you guys that we haven't shared with the rest of the family yet."

"Really?" Teagan squealed happily.

Savannah smiled and took Riley's hand in hers. "We're going to be back home for Labor Day, but we're just dying to tell someone!"

Bobby didn't even have to guess. "You're having a baby," he said, a smile of pure happiness on his face.

They both nodded. "I did tell Owen," Riley explained, "but that's a given."

"Of course you did," Teagan said. "He's your twin. I would have thought you were crazy if you told us before him."

"Well, we tend to try and make these announcements in person and to be honest, we didn't think we were going to be making this one again."

"Total surprise pregnancy," Savannah said, but it was easy to tell that she wasn't disappointed at all about it. She placed a hand over her belly. "We're barely at eight weeks and we're thankful the tour is winding down. As much as I love traveling with the band, I kind of want to be back home and have some down time with the kids for a while."

"Plus," Riley said, a little more subdued, "we need to put the house on the market." He shook his head.

"We've tried to think of ways to make it work, but it was never made to be a house for a big family."

"I'm really going to miss those views," Savannah said wistfully. Resting her head on her husband's shoulder, she added, "That's really what made me fall in love with Riley."

"Hey!"

They all laughed, and within minutes they were pulling up to the hotel.

"Are any of the guys joining us for dinner?" Teagan asked.

"We can totally ask them if you want," Riley replied, "but I thought it would be nice for just the four of us to hang out. I know we've seen more of each other in the last few months than we have in the last ten years, but there's always so many people around. I was hoping to have a little quiet time to catch up."

Which is exactly what they did. Dinner was waiting for them up in their suite, and after checking in on Riley and Savannah's sleeping kids, they all sat down to eat.

Conversation flowed easily, and even though Bobby was always up-to-date with the Shaughnessys, he enjoyed hearing Teagan talk about her life. There was so much he still didn't know about her, and he loved listening to it all. Every time she shared a story about something in her life before she'd moved, he got to know her a little bit better.

He already knew her strength, her intelligence, and her incredible selflessness and determination. But what he was learning about more and more was how she had a great sense of humor, loved romantic comedies and eighties rock, and she wasn't afraid to make fun of herself.

Basically, she was perfect.

Perfect for him, perfect in every way. And everything about her just made him want her more.

What the hell time was it? Was his car here yet? Could he take her home now? Hadn't they visited long enough?

As if on cue, Riley's phone beeped with an incoming text. He looked at the screen and nodded before looking at Bobby. "Your car's here and the keys are at the front desk."

"Thank you so much for doing that for us, Riley," Teagan said. "I can't imagine how long everyone must have been stuck in the parking lot."

"Yeah, it's a shame something like that had to happen."

"Bobby," Savannah started, "you've worked a lot of these shows, right?"

He nodded.

"Thank goodness you weren't the one working tonight," she said. "It's scary when it hits so close to home. And with what you've already gone through, I for one am thankful you didn't have to be a part of that."

He knew what she was saying and yet…it still irked him a little.

"I think Bobby's done playing superhero, right?" Riley asked.

"What do you mean?" he asked, mildly defensive.

"I would think after what happened to you, you'd be a little more cautious about wanting to go back to work. You've been on the force for over fifteen years, Bobby. Maybe it's time to look at other job options that don't put you in harm's way," Riley replied.

"What happened to me didn't happen on the job,

Riley," he countered. "I was on my way home, I wasn't even in uniform."

"But still," Savannah chimed in. "It has to make you think a bit. I mean, look what happened tonight. Wouldn't you prefer to be doing something...safer? Something that wasn't about putting your life on the line? Especially...well, now?" She glanced at Teagan and Bobby knew exactly what she was getting at. He braced himself for Teagan's response.

But she didn't say anything. She didn't even look at him. She simply pushed the last of her dessert around on her plate.

"When are you heading back to work?" Riley asked.

"I'm not sure. Getting medical clearance is...complicated. I have a meeting on Monday, so I'll know more then."

The conversation felt stilted after that.

At least for him.

"So, a new baby?" Teagan said after a long, awkward moment. "Do you think you'll get the twins this time? It seems Owen's gotten the bulk of those genes, huh?"

No matter how annoyed he was, Bobby couldn't help but laugh along with everyone else. Riley's twin brother was the quietest kid he'd ever met, and he'd grown up to be one of the quietest and smartest adults he'd ever known. No one ever thought Owen would be the one to end up with two sets of twins—and yet.

"We've thought about that," Savannah said with a nervous laugh. "That whole thing normally skips a generation, but—as usual—Owen proved that theory wrong. I'm seriously hoping that in our case it skips a generation. I'm not sure I could handle twins."

"You'd be surprised what you can handle," Teagan said softly. Bobby knew exactly where her mind had gone, and his heart ached for her. "When it comes down to it, you do what you have to do. Sometimes you find it's the greatest joy you can ever imagine."

There was a knock on the door and Riley got up to answer it. Several members of the hotel staff appeared to clean up the dishes and take them from the room. When Riley asked if anyone wanted anything else, they all declined.

Bobby saw this as their cue to leave. It was late, and no doubt his friend was exhausted after putting on one hell of a concert.

"We should probably go," he said. "Thank you so much for dinner and for the tickets to the show. It was amazing, as always."

Riley smiled and shook his hand. "Glad you could come. We'll see you for Labor Day, right?"

After that it was a flurry of goodbyes and well wishes and by the time it was just the two of them in the elevator, Bobby was exhausted.

Neither spoke on the way down or after they picked up the car keys from the front desk. They had an hour's drive back to his place, and other than idle talk about the show, the music, and an overall recap of that part of the night, they didn't say much.

He fought the urge to turn on the radio and wait for the news, but it didn't mean he wasn't thinking about it.

When they pulled up in front of his condo, he looked over and saw that Teagan was asleep, her head resting against the window. She looked so peaceful, but he knew she couldn't be comfortable. He whispered her name and gently shook her to wake her up. Her eyes fluttered open before she turned to look at him in confusion.

"We're home," he said. "Wait there." Climbing from the truck, he walked around to the passenger side and lifted her out.

"You don't have to," she said around a loud yawn.

He laughed quietly and kissed her forehead. "I think I did," he teased. Once they were inside, he carried her straight through to the bedroom and lay her down on the bed. She put up some token resistance when he pulled off her sandals, but then she seemed to relax when his hands went to the waistband of her jeans and began to pull them down. It had been a long day, a bit of an emotionally draining night—and yet looking at her in a white thong, the white beaded halter top, and nothing else had him hard and aching.

"I'm suddenly not so sleepy," she whispered, sensing his thoughts.

It was all the encouragement he needed. One knee on the bed, he quickly pulled his shirt off before lowering down on top of her. Teagan wrapped her limbs around him and when he kissed her, there was nothing else in the world he could think about.

Right now, that was exactly what he needed.

He wanted to go slow, wanted to be gentle because she was still midway between sleepy and fully awake, but his need for her was too great. So maybe he was a little rough when he whipped her shirt off. And when he tore off her thong and she cried out, he might have felt even more turned on. But when her hands seemed just as frantic to open his jeans and push them off, he knew they were on the same page.

The same wild and sexy page.

And he said a prayer of thanks for it.

They battled for control, but Bobby ultimately won. With Teagan beneath him, her hands pinned above her head, and her breath coming out in short pants, he had her exactly where he wanted her.

And he kept her there for a very long time.

Chapter 9

"ARE YOU SURE YOU CAN'T STAY ANOTHER NIGHT?"

They were eating breakfast out on Bobby's back deck when he asked her that question—for the fifth time. Part of her really wanted to say yes, but besides missing Lucas like crazy, she knew Bobby was distracted. He might not realize it yet, but he needed her gone.

Last night they had made love in a way that was overwhelming. It was all wild need and heat, and more passionate than anything they'd ever done before. Afterward, she was sure she had blacked out. The next time she opened her eyes, she was alone in the bed. Quietly, she had tiptoed out of the room and found him sitting on the couch in the living room, speaking on the phone with someone in the police department, with his laptop open to the local news.

"I really need to get back," she said before taking another bite of the pancakes Bobby had made. "This is the longest I've ever been away from Lucas, and I'm afraid I'm going to get a speeding ticket on my way home."

"I understand," he said with a small pout. "I just hate the thought of saying goodbye."

And wasn't that just incredibly sweet? "Me too."

They ate in silence for a few minutes before she decided to broach some sensitive subjects. Mainly because she didn't believe in avoiding them. "So what did you find out about the shooting last night?"

He sighed and slid his plate away. "It was a traffic stop. The driver exited the wrong way out of the arena parking lot—drove over cones, cut people off, nearly ran over one of the cops directing traffic. When they pulled him over a block away, he got out and opened fire."

She gasped. "Oh, my gosh! That's…that just seems so random!"

He nodded. "And senseless." Raking a hand through his hair, he continued. "I know him. The officer who was shot. He's a rookie, a good kid. His injuries are serious but not life threatening and…I don't know, it just makes me so damn angry that shit like this happens."

Suddenly her appetite was gone. "Is this really what you face every day?"

He nodded.

"I mean, I'm not stupid. I realize law enforcement is a dangerous career, but I guess I'm just naive. I thought it was only dangerous if you went into dangerous situations. This was a traffic stop. He pulled over someone who'd gotten fed up with sitting in a traffic jam. That officer had no idea what he was up against."

"None of us do," Bobby said grimly. "It goes with the job, unfortunately."

Teagan thought about the conversation last night, about Savannah's questions.

Wouldn't you prefer to be doing something safer? Something that wasn't about putting your life on the line?

And how Bobby had never really answered. He'd just deflected to talk about his medical clearance. Which meant he *wouldn't* rather be doing something safer. He was clearly okay with putting himself in harm's way no matter what the cost.

Just like Logan.

Her heart squeezed hard in her chest. By moving forward with this relationship, she would be facing this sort of thing on a daily basis. With Logan, she'd lived with it when he was deployed, but then he'd come home and she knew everything was okay. He was safe. Bobby would never be safe. Every time he walked out the door she would know this fear, this blinding panic, that he might not come home.

Swallowing hard, Teagan knew she had to leave. She needed time to think. She couldn't just blurt this out to him, not right now. And the longer she stayed, the greater the chance that she would.

As casually as she could, she stood and gathered their breakfast plates and carried them into the kitchen. Bobby followed and they cleaned up together. After a few minutes, he gently wrapped his arms around her waist and forced her to look at him.

"Hey," he said softly. "You okay? You got real quiet."

"Just thinking about all I need to do this week. We're not used to this year-round school thing and going back to work soon has me feeling a little frazzled. I guess I sort of zoned out there. Sorry."

Liar. Hadn't she just been thinking about how she didn't like to avoid the tough issues? So why was she doing it now?

She moved out of his arms and put some distance between them. "I'm lying," she said ruefully. "I was thinking about your job and the dangers that come with it, and comparing it to…"

"Logan," he said quietly.

Why deny it? "Yes. I hated when he got deployed. It

only happened twice, mind you, and the second time he didn't come back."

"Teagan—"

She didn't let him finish. "All I can think of is how I worried each and every day that he was gone. The first time, he was gone for seven months, I was sick to my stomach every day for seven months, and you know what? For most of it, he didn't see any combat. There was no threat to him." She let out a long breath. "And when he came back, I was so damn relieved. Because he was safe, and he was home, and everything was just better."

"It's not the same."

Shaking her head, she said, "No. What you do is worse because it's every day, all the time. There isn't a time limit, there isn't a date to mark on the calendar when you won't be in danger anymore."

"What happened to me had nothing to do with my job," he said, his voice low and gruff and a little shaky. "I was just an innocent bystander. It can happen to anyone at any time. There are no guarantees."

Her eyes stung with unshed tears but she knew she had to be honest—had to tell him the truth even as it was just coming to her.

"While I know that's true, Bobby, I don't think I can willingly be in a relationship where fear is going to be present every day. I know there are things we can't control. Accidents happen all the time, I get it. But Lucas and I have already lost so much. I can't do that again."

The panic on his face almost made her take her words back.

"What—what are you saying?" His words were barely audible.

"I need to think. I need time," she said, her heart breaking with every word.

"You knew this is what I do," he said carefully. "You knew my career when we met."

"I know," she said sadly. "But we've been living in this sort of limbo where I knew about it, but it wasn't real. That could all change this week and, like I said, it all just…hit me."

He slid his hands into his pockets and took a step back. "So, um. I don't…I don't know what I'm supposed to say here. Are you telling me I have to quit my job? That if we're going to be together I have to find another career?"

It was on the tip of her tongue to say yes, but she knew it wasn't right. It wasn't fair.

"I'm not—" She stopped and tried to collect her thoughts. "I just need some time to think, Bobby."

Expecting an argument, she was surprised when he didn't say anything. What he did do was walk out of the kitchen and into the bedroom. She followed a minute later and was surprised to see him making the bed and straightening up the room. Part of her wanted to talk even though she knew it would turn into an argument. Crazy as it was, she almost wanted that. Instead, she finished packing up her bag. Once she was done, she found him back in the kitchen wiping down the countertops.

"I guess I should go," she said slowly, bracing herself for…something.

Nodding, he tossed the sponge into the sink and walked over to pick up her bag. "I got this."

Silently, Teagan followed him to the car. She stood back and watched him place the bag in her back seat.

When he shut the door and faced her, his expression was completely closed. It wasn't hard to understand why, but that didn't mean it didn't hurt.

"Text me when you get home so I know you made it okay," he said flatly.

All she could do was nod.

When she reached for the driver's side door, Bobby grabbed her and spun her around. She gasped as he planted a searing kiss on her lips before quickly releasing her.

Then he stepped back and waited for her to get in the car and drive away.

Which she did.

Quickly.

And less than a mile away, she pulled over to the side of the road and let herself cry.

～～～

It was dark and Bobby wasn't sure how long it had been that way. Was it hours, or was it days? Between Teagan's words on Sunday and his disappointing appointment on Monday, he'd stopped paying attention to the time. He'd come home, shut the door, shut the blinds, and simply…sat.

His doctor's words echoed in his ears.

"I'm sorry, Bobby, but there's no way I can sign off on you going back to work. Not in the same capacity you were in before. The nerves are still healing and there's no way of knowing how long that will take. I will send in my report recommending that you return to work in an office position at the precinct. I know it's not what you wanted to hear, but at least we're moving in the right direction."

Thinking back, Bobby wasn't sure how he had even gotten home. He'd been so angry he was nearly blind with it. He clearly had made it home in one piece, but the trip would always be a blur.

His phone was on the coffee table in front of him, his notification light flashing. There'd be texts and phone calls waiting for him, but he ignored them all. No doubt none of them were from Teagan. Not after the way things had gone down on Sunday. She'd texted, but just one word—*home*. Yeah, she was pissed, but so was he. She was giving him an ultimatum. As much as she might not want to admit it, that's essentially what it was.

Look, he understood where she was coming from. He did. Not everyone was cut out to be involved with or married to a cop.

That didn't make it any easier on him.

He loved what he did. His whole life, he'd only ever wanted to be a cop. Now he was going to lose that job. Either to his injury, or to Teagan.

How was that fair?

It wasn't, not any of it, and in that moment he felt dead inside. It would have been better if the damn bullet had killed him, because this wasn't the life he wanted to live. He was alone, his career gone and…he groaned, his head rolling back on the sofa. This—this *despair*—was all so foreign to him. At any other time in his life, he would go home to his folks and that would be enough to make him feel better.

Then again, he'd never dealt with this kind of life-crushing news.

The thought of going home now was supremely unappealing. No one would understand what he was feeling.

Everyone he knew was happily married with a houseful of kids or happily married with an empty nest after years of family life. And what did he have? Nothing.

Why would he want to surround himself with the kind of people he only wished he could be?

Wished he could, and probably never would.

Great, could he possibly come up with any more depressing thoughts on his life?

"This isn't good," he murmured.

Not that it changed anything. He was still sitting alone in the dark with no idea what day it was. He couldn't remember the last time he'd had anything to eat. His stomach growled loudly, right on cue, but the last thing he wanted to do was cook. Reaching for his phone, he called in a pizza order for delivery and then took the time to scroll through his notifications.

Four calls from his parents.

Two calls from his captain.

Two calls from his sister.

Followed by six texts, also from her.

His heart racing, he kept scrolling, kept searching, hoping for one from Teagan. Nothing. And that had him spiraling right back down into the dark. Which is where he stayed until the doorbell rang with his pizza delivery.

Once he had his order, Bobby finally turned on some lights. When he sat back down on the sofa, he looked at his phone a little more closely.

Wednesday.

Shit.

He'd been sitting here for almost three days just… existing. Breathing in and out and nothing else.

For the moment, it was all he could do. That and eat

some pizza. Maybe drink a beer or two. It was all too overwhelming. Eventually, he'd call his family, then he'd probably call his captain. Beyond that, he couldn't say. Life was going to be a one step at a time sort of thing.

Halfway through the pizza, his phone beeped with an incoming text. This time he did look at the screen and saw his sister's name.

And then another notification followed by four more.

Tossing his slice down, he picked up the phone and read the messages.

Anna: WTH?

Anna: If you don't answer me soon, I'm coming down there.

Anna: I'm not kidding. Mom's keeping the kids because she's worried too.

Anna: This is your last warning.

If nothing else, his sister was tenacious. Not that he was scared of her. Maybe Anna coming here was exactly what he needed to get out of this funk.

The phone beeped again.

Anna: Quinn's volunteered to drive down now to check on you.

Oh, hell no. There was no way he could handle Quinn right now. Wasn't Bobby dealing with enough already? Didn't anyone get that?

With a sigh of resignation, he decided to make the call. No more, just this one.

Anna answered immediately. "What the hell, Bobby?

We've all been trying to reach you for days! Do you have any idea how freaked out everyone is?"

"Yeah, uh…sorry."

Liar.

She was silent for a minute and he knew she was waiting for him to elaborate. Instead of talking, he picked up his half-eaten slice of pizza and took a bite.

Anna's loud huff of annoyance almost made him laugh.

"Fine. This is how you want to play this? Let me guess. The appointment on Monday didn't go as planned."

He didn't respond.

"So, what now? You're just going to hole up in your condo and not talk to anyone ever again? Is that your plan?"

Again, he didn't respond.

This time when she sighed, he could tell she wasn't quite as angry as she had been a minute ago. "Bobby," she began wearily, "come on. I know you're disappointed, but you can't hide out. Come home. Come visit. I know Teagan couldn't possibly want you sitting there by yourself."

"I wouldn't be so sure about that." Damn. He hated how his voice just about cracked as he admitted it.

"What do you mean?"

"We're not…I mean, she's kind of not speaking to me at the moment."

"Oh, dear Lord. What did you do?"

"How do you know it was something I did?"

"Seriously? You're seriously asking me that? You're my brother, Bobby. I know you." The huff of frustration was back. "I can't believe you messed it up with Teagan."

Yeah. Neither could he.

Mainly because he still couldn't understand how his job was suddenly an issue now when she'd known about it all along.

"Are you going to tell me what happened?" she demanded.

"No."

"Fine. I'll just go and talk to Teagan. She'll tell me the whole truth."

There was no way he was taking the bait. He knew exactly what she was doing—goading him into giving his side of the story—and she'd be going to talk to Teagan no matter what.

"Problem solved," he said miserably, tossing the crust of his pizza back into the box. Suddenly he wasn't feeling so good. Maybe after not eating for almost two days, an entire pizza hadn't been the best choice.

"You're really not going to talk to me about this?"

"Nope." He paused. "Look, I gotta go. Tell Mom you talked to me and I'm alive. I'll call her this weekend, okay?"

"No, it's not okay, Bobby! You need to talk to someone about this! It's not healthy for you to hide out. Please. Come home and just—just be around people who care about you."

It was tempting. He'd done just that in situations less devastating than this, and it had helped. But right now, he didn't want to be helped. He couldn't be helped. All he wanted was to sit in his misery and be left alone.

"I gotta go, kiddo. I'll talk to you soon." He hung

up before Anna could say anything else and tossed the phone on the other end of the couch.

It was better this way.

Maybe if he just stayed where he was, he'd know that Teagan and Lucas could be happy. They'd suffered enough. Even though the thought pissed him off, because he'd really seen a future with her, her happiness and peace of mind meant more to him than anything else.

Who knew, maybe one day they could be friends. There wasn't a doubt in his mind that, thanks to their family connections, they'd be seeing one another at family functions for the rest of their lives. For now, he'd keep his distance and make things easier for her.

As for himself…he had no idea what he was going to do. A desk job was akin to being tortured. There was no way he could sit in the station all day and watch other guys go out on calls—or even just out to do their patrol. It would kill him.

"And we're back to square one," he muttered, rising from the couch. He stretched and picked up the pizza box, tossing it on the kitchen counter on his way to the bedroom. His limbs felt heavy and his stomach was in knots, but he was starting to smell. That made him drag his ass to the master bathroom to take a shower.

Standing and waiting for the water to get hot had him remembering being in here with Teagan. How she had cried out his name over and over, how he'd lathered her body up from head to toe…and how much he'd loved loving her there.

"Great. Now there's an image that's going to stay with me."

Stripping, he stepped under the hot spray. It stung his skin and he hissed out a breath, letting the water beat down on him for a few minutes. Unfortunately, the longer he stood there, the more images of Teagan played in his head. Cursing, he grabbed the shampoo and soap, doing a half-assed job of washing himself. Turning off the water, he stepped out and realized he hadn't remembered to grab a towel. The words flying out of his mouth would have made a truck driver blush. He pulled a towel out of the linen closet and hastily dried himself off before tossing the towel on the floor and stalking into his bedroom.

The room was already dark, the bed unmade, and Bobby crawled between the sheets. He closed his eyes and tried to block out the knowledge that he could still smell her perfume—and how it was all he was going to have left of her.

—⁓—

"Thank you so much for having me over," Teagan said, setting a tray of brownies down on the counter. "Lucas was so excited to come and hang out with Kaitlyn."

Smiling, Anna put out a tray of lemonade and glasses for them. "Oh, I know. It's all she's been talking about today. I'm just glad you were free!"

As if Teagan had anything else to do.

Okay, that wasn't completely true. Her get-ready-for-school list had been long, but she was organized, and it hadn't turned out to be that hard to do.

Fine, she was totally ahead of schedule and was now bored out of her mind. So the invitation to dinner at Quinn and Anna's had been a godsend.

"Hope you're hungry!" Quinn said with a big smile when he walked into the kitchen, kissing Teagan on the cheek. "We've got burgers, corn on the cob, potato salad, and mac and cheese."

"Mac and cheese?" Anna asked. "Since when?"

"Since Brian and I decided we wanted some," he said with a wink. "Hey, is Bobby joining us?"

At the sound of his name, Teagan's heart squeezed. Since getting back from Myrtle Beach five days ago, she hadn't told anyone about what had happened between them. She couldn't. And not a day—hour, or even a minute—had gone by where she wasn't thinking about it.

Or obsessing about it, whatever.

"Uh…no," she answered. "He's not in town."

"Oh," Quinn said with a shrug before turning and heading toward the sliding glass doors. "I'll light the grill and stay with the kids out back."

"And I guess I'm making mac and cheese," Anna murmured.

"Anything I can do to help?"

Handing Teagan a glass of lemonade, Anna replied, "Nah. Just sit and talk to me. I've been home all week with the kids because Brian's been upset whenever I leave to go to the pub. I had to hire another server to help cover my hours."

"Oh, that's too bad. You've said how much you enjoyed getting out of the house for a few hours a week."

She nodded. "I really do, but he's got some separation anxiety. The pediatrician said it's normal and it's partly because I'm leaving and partly because of Bailey." Anna shrugged.

"Really?"

She explained, "He's not the baby anymore, so he's already getting a little less attention. Add to that the fact that I would leave before he went to bed and he wasn't sure when I'd be back, so…Quinn and I talked about it. For now, we're just going to deal with me being a stay-at-home mom."

"Wow. And you're okay with it?"

"At first I wasn't, but that lasted for all of three minutes." She smiled. "I love my kids and they mean the world to me. So if they need me here with them a little more, then that's what I'll do."

Teagan knew exactly what she meant. There wasn't anything she wouldn't do for Lucas.

"Anyway, enough about me," Anna said. "Talk to me about you. Are you ready for school? Is Lucas?"

"He is so excited. I know I am going to cry like a baby that first day."

"You'll be right there with him. Literally. You're working in his school! You can see him anytime you want."

"I know, I know. But it's just the fact that he's not a baby anymore," Teagan said with a sad smile. "This is only the beginning, and it's been just the two of us for so long. I kind of hate to think about him not needing me as much."

"He's always going to need you, that's never going to change." Anna placed a pot of water on the stove and turned it on. "Although there will come a day when it will be my baby going—and by baby I mean Bailey, because she's it for us—and I'm sure I'll feel the same way."

"You're not nervous about Kaitlyn going to school?"

Anna shook her head and grinned. "Are you kidding?

I'm thrilled! I had no idea how much the dynamic would change when we went from two kids to three. I'm looking forward to having only two kids at a time again, for at least part of the day."

Teagan felt a pang of envy she hadn't felt in a long time. After having grown up as an only child, she had always thought she would have more of her own. That she wouldn't do that to any child of hers. What would it be like if Lucas had a younger brother or sister? Or both? She gave herself a snort of disapproval.

Hard to consider having more kids when you don't get involved with anyone.

Then she wanted to shout back at her inner voice and remind herself how she *had* gotten involved with someone—someone she'd really thought she had a future with, but it didn't work out.

"Damn, whatever it is you're thinking about has made your face go all scrunchy," Anna said, sitting down beside her. "Want to talk about it?"

Did she?

"Okay, I promised myself I wasn't going to bring this up, but…who am I kidding? I have to," Anna said with a small laugh. "What happened with my brother?"

Her eyes went wide. "What do you mean?"

The look Anna gave her told her she wasn't fooled.

So Teagan completely unloaded, sharing everything that had happened over the weekend. Everything from the great time they'd had, to the concert, the shooting—and finally the realization that Bobby's job wasn't something she could handle.

"I know it doesn't make me a very nice person," she said after a minute. "As he pointed out to me, I knew exactly what he did for a living when we met. It just wasn't until after the shooting Saturday night that it really hit me and…I panicked."

"And now? Are you still panicked?"

She shrugged. "Yes. No." She sighed loudly. "Honestly, I don't know. The only thing I do know is that I can't go there again. Not even for Bobby."

"Teagan—"

"No, Anna. It's true. I…can't. Lucas never met his father, and he never will. But he knows Bobby and adores him. How can I possibly expose Lucas to a life where he would have to know that fear? Or worse, find out how painful it is to lose someone he loves?"

Anna studied her for a moment. "Okay, I get it. Believe me, we all feel that way about his job, and for the most part, it hasn't been an issue. But there are risks every single day for all of us. When Quinn used to race cars, do you have any idea how many accidents he was in? I swear I think I aged a hundred years every time I would watch him race!"

"But he stopped before he got hurt, Anna," she argued. "Quinn didn't get hurt and then go back to it."

"Okay, okay. I get what you're saying," Anna began carefully, "but what about Lillian?"

"Aunt Lily?"

She nodded. "Do you think for one minute anyone expected her to die like that? It was an accident! An awful, horrible accident. And you know what? We can't live our lives in fear of what may or may not happen, because that's not living."

All Teagan could do was nod. Her throat was clogged with emotion and she knew what Anna was saying was right, but it didn't make things any easier. Her head could agree but her heart couldn't.

Then, to her embarrassment, she started to tear up.

"Dammit," Anna muttered before hugging her. "I'm sorry. I'm so sorry. The last thing I wanted to do was make you cry."

"The grill's—" Quinn stopped short when he spotted them. "What's going on?" He was instantly next to them. He took one look at Teagan and crouched down beside her. "Hey, you okay?"

"She and Bobby broke up," Anna said. "And then I wouldn't let it go and now—"

He was instantly on his feet and storming out of the room.

"That can't be good," Teagan said, wiping away her tears. "Maybe I should go talk to him."

Before either of them could do anything, Quinn stormed back into the kitchen with his car keys in his hands. "The grill is ready. I'll be back later."

"Quinn! Stop!" Anna cried before he could leave the room. "Where do you think you're going?"

"To talk to your brother," he said heatedly. "Someone needs to set him straight!"

"There's nothing for you to straighten out, Quinn," Teagan said, coming to her feet. "I'm the one who broke things off with him. Bobby didn't do anything wrong. I swear."

Some of the fight seemed to leave him. "Well, shit." Quinn tossed his keys on the counter and let out a long breath. "Are you sure you're okay?"

She nodded. "I'm not great, but...I'm tougher than I look."

He stared at her for a minute and grimaced. "I still want to go and kick his ass."

"And I appreciate that," she said with a small smile, "but it's completely unnecessary."

"Well, I need to do something!" he exclaimed. She really did appreciate how he was hurting for her.

"How about this—grill me a big, fat burger, and don't judge me when I have seconds on everything and eat at least two brownies. Deal?"

He laughed and hugged her. "Deal."

Two nights later, Teagan wasn't feeling much better. If anything, her nerves were more than a little frayed. Lucas had begun asking about Bobby. "When is Bobby coming over?" and "Why can't we go visit Bobby?" which was usually followed by "It's not fair that you got to go to Bobby's house, and I didn't." She was exhausted and could feel her patience coming to an end.

She was just about to start making dinner when her doorbell rang.

"Please be pizza, please be pizza," she murmured as she walked to the door. Pulling it open, she stared in stunned silence for a moment. "Mom? What are you doing here?"

Catherine Shaughnessy smiled and kissed her daughter on the cheek before walking in with an armload of grocery bags. Teagan was about to repeat herself when her father walked in.

"How's my girl today?" he asked, kissing her on the other cheek before following his wife.

"Um…did we have plans tonight?"

"We sure didn't," her mom said. "But your father and I were talking earlier and he mentioned how it's been a while since he and Lucas had a boys' night out. He thought tonight would be the perfect night for it." She began unloading the bags. "So I figured it could be fun for us to have a girls' night!"

Fun wasn't quite the word Teagan would have used.

"I think Lucas and I are going to go bowling and have some pizza," her father said on his way to the yard, where her son was playing. "Then we'll go home, put on pj's, eat too much ice cream and candy, and watch one of those Pixar movies until we both fall asleep on the couch."

"Dad!" she called after him, but he wasn't listening. Turning to her mother, she said, "I don't think that's a good idea at all."

"Oh, stop. I think it's sweet he wants to do this. He misses us having Lucas over. Between our traveling and your relationship with Bobby, well... We had a great time with Lucas last weekend and realized it had been a while since he did anything with just the two of them."

"But you just said you had him over last weekend," Teagan reminded her. "He didn't have to rush over again so soon. I'm perfectly capable of taking care of my son, you know!"

She didn't even need to look at her mother's face to know she was sounding a little defensive and crazy. "Sorry."

Rather than say anything, her mother continued to unpack bags and start pulling out pots and pans.

"Mom! Mom! Did you hear? Pops is gonna take me bowling! We're having a boys' night!" Lucas cried as he ran into the house and straight to his room. Her father followed a minute later.

"I don't think he needs to pack anything. We have clothes and pajamas for him at the house. I think he's just grabbing his soccer ball. He wants to practice for the next time Bobby's here."

Don't snap at anyone, she told herself.

Forcing a smile to her face, she said, "That's great. Between bowling and soccer, he'll be asleep before the opening credits of any movie," she said lightly.

Within minutes, her father and Lucas were gone and her mother was pounding some boneless chicken breasts. Curious, Teagan walked over to inspect the other ingredients on the counter.

Bread crumbs, eggs, spaghetti, parmesan cheese, mozzarella cheese, olive oil, a container of homemade sauce, and a bottle of wine.

"We're making chicken parm?" she asked.

Nodding, Catherine continued to work. "I was craving it and your father wasn't. How I married a man who doesn't love Italian food is beyond me."

Teagan laughed. It had been a long-running joke in their family because her mother was Italian and her father was Irish. For her entire life, the only Italian food her father ever wanted was pizza.

"His loss," she said and then walked over to wash her hands. "What can I do to help?"

"Get the sauce into a pan and let's get it simmering. I made it yesterday and you know it always tastes better—"

"The second day," Teagan finished for her. They laughed and began working side by side to make their meal. Soon the chicken was frying, the sauce was simmering, and the whole place smelled wonderful. After washing her hands again, she pulled two wineglasses down from her cabinet and poured them both a glass of wine.

"To girls' night," her mother said.

"To girls' night."

They each sipped before Catherine removed the chicken from the pan and began to prep it to go in the oven. Teagan put on the pot of water for their spaghetti and set the timer before they both sat down at the table.

"Okay, now that dinner's cooking, why don't you tell me what's really up," Teagan said. "We've never done a girls' night, and Dad hates watching kids' movies. So spill it."

With a mild huff, her mother put her glass down. "I had lunch with Mary Hannigan yesterday."

Doing her best not to react, Teagan nodded and waited.

"Bobby didn't get clearance to go back to work on patrol, only in a desk position," Catherine said, "and he's devastated. Mary thought I knew all that, since the two of you have been dating. But when I said it was the first I was hearing of it, we got a little suspicious."

It was on the tip of Teagan's tongue to ask for more information, but she refrained.

"Anyway, we were talking and then Anna called, so Mary asked her if she knew anything and she said the two of you broke up!" She shook her head. "How could you keep something like that to yourself, Teagan?"

"Because I'm still trying to come to grips with it myself," she said with just a hint of defiance. "And all I said to Bobby was that I needed time to think."

"But...?"

"But the more I thought about it, the more I realized

it didn't matter how long I thought about it. It wasn't going to change anything."

"Oh, sweetheart. I had no idea you were struggling with this!" Reaching over, she took one of Teagan's hands and squeezed. "I'm glad I came over tonight."

That sounded both sweet and ominous.

Before she could comment, her mother was up and adding spaghetti to the pot of boiling water and checking the tray of chicken in the oven. Without being asked, Teagan grabbed dishes to set the table while they made small talk that had nothing at all to do with either Bobby or the breakup.

That all started up again after they each took their first bite of dinner ten minutes later.

"So what do you need to think about?" her mother asked casually.

"Where do I even begin?" It was pointless to try to avoid the topic or play dumb. She was going to have to get used to talking about it, no matter how much it hurt.

"I would imagine at the beginning."

"Not helping, Mom."

Placing her fork down, Catherine reached for her wineglass but didn't drink. "Do you remember how much we moved around when you were younger?"

Weird change of topic, but okay…

Teagan nodded.

"Do you remember what you used to say to me every time we had to pick up and move?"

"I hated it," she said. "I always told you how much I hated moving away and leaving my friends."

"And what else?"

Oh. That. "That I would never do that to my kids."

She paused. "Which I haven't, so I don't know where you're going with this."

"It wasn't just the moving, Teagan. You hated military life. Those last few times your father deployed—we would talk about it, remember?"

She did.

"You were so passionate about it," her mother went on. "That's why I never understood why you started dating Logan."

"We lived in a military town, Mom. Any guy there was either already in the military or on his way in. What choice did I have?"

Catherine laughed. "Sweetie, you went away to college and met plenty of nonmilitary men. Of that I am sure."

"Yeah, well, it didn't matter. I fell in love with Logan. End of story."

"Well, not really."

Teagan's fork clanked down onto her plate. "What is it you're getting at?"

"I'm going to say something, Teagan, and I want you to listen and not react."

"I can't guarantee that."

"Try," Catherine said firmly. Then, after a steadying breath, she fixed her serious gaze on her daughter. "I don't doubt that you fell in love with Logan. He was a very nice young man, handsome, and he treated you very well." She paused. "But I don't think he was the great love of your life."

Denial was right there waiting to be spewed, but she held it in and mentally counted to ten. Clearing her throat, she asked, "Why would you say that?"

Catherine sipped her wine before responding. "For

starters, you both seemed more like good friends than lovers."

"Mom!"

"What? It's true! You were never overly concerned about the relationship while you were away at school, you always seemed fairly casual—almost blasé—when you talked about any plans the two of you made for when you were both home." She shrugged. "I think if Logan had lived, you would have married him and it would have been comfortable. But it wouldn't have been a great love story."

"I hate to break it to you, Mom, but most people don't have great love stories."

"I disagree."

"Of course you do," she muttered.

"Don't get snippy, Teagan Marie," Catherine warned. "I met your father when I was twelve years old."

Here we go.

"And he was sixteen. I had such a crush on him, but he was way too old for me. We were in the same youth group at church, and I used to spend way more time looking at him than I did looking at my Bible."

"Mom, please—"

"When he graduated high school and announced to our group that he was enlisting in the army, I was heartbroken." She sighed. "He came back four years later to speak at our church, and when he smiled at me, I knew he was the man I was going to marry."

"Okay, then…"

"I learned pretty fast that I hated being a military wife."

Wait, this was new.

"Oh, I can't tell you how many nights I laid in bed and cried myself to sleep because I thought I'd made the biggest mistake of my life!"

Taking a sip of her wine, Teagan asked, "So what changed?"

"For a long time, nothing. I was miserable, we kept moving around, and each move took me farther and farther away from my family." She sighed. "I never told you this, but...I filed for divorce."

"What? How...? When...?"

"It was the worst month of my life. And I did it all while your father was deployed," she said with a sad smile. "He came home and was so happy to be there, and I served him with divorce papers."

"Oh my gosh!"

"Talk about bad timing."

"So—what happened? How did he change your mind?"

"He let me go. He gave me space." She took a bite of her dinner before continuing. "I moved back home with my parents. They were getting ready to celebrate their twenty-fifth wedding anniversary and we were having a big party. Your father remembered me talking about the event, and at the time, how badly I wanted to go home to celebrate with them." Dabbing at her eyes, Catherine went on. "He showed up at the party dressed in his service uniform." She smiled. "He looked so handsome."

Teagan couldn't help but smile too. "And what did you do when he showed up?"

"I wanted to be mad, I really did, but he walked up to my parents and wished them both a happy anniversary, then he went over and greeted my grandparents."

Her smile grew. "Then he came over and asked me to dance."

"Aww…"

"I had missed him so much, I couldn't deny it. And he told me he wasn't re-upping. When his term was up, he was leaving the army. It was everything I'd ever wanted. I immediately began planning our lives again. I went back with him to our place in Virginia—that's where we were living at the time—and he began looking at civilian jobs. He still had another year in the service, but I knew I could handle one more year."

"So what changed?"

Catherine waved her off. "He wasn't happy, and I could see it. He was willing to make the sacrifice for me, but he had been climbing the ranks in the army—really making a name for himself. How could I take that away from him?"

"Yeah, but then you ended up being the one making the sacrifice," Teagan stated. "How was that fair?"

"Turns out it wasn't really a sacrifice. It was a lot about me being immature and acting a bit like a spoiled brat."

"Somehow I doubt that, Mom. You've never been like that."

"Trust me, I was back then. But I realized that a life with your father was better than a life without him. Even a military life."

"That's a wonderful story, and when I look at you and Dad, I can see how in love you are. But I don't see how this relates to me and Logan."

"Teagan, you would have resented Logan's military career and he would have quit it for you."

"And? I don't see what's wrong with that. It happens all the time. Not everyone who enlists stays in for life."

"No, they don't, but without you, Logan would have. That boy had military blood in his veins and every time you talked about him leaving, we could see it. We could see how conflicted he was. But he was an honorable man and he would have put your happiness first. That's not a good foundation for any relationship, especially a marriage."

"You're wrong, Mom. Logan would have told me. He would have mentioned that he didn't want to leave the army. You're just…you just think you saw something because it's what you lived," Teagan argued.

"Sweetheart, ask your father. He and Logan used to talk. A lot."

"I don't know why we're talking about this now," she grumbled. "It's all a moot point. We'll never know if Logan and I would have lasted or if he would have stayed in the army. Why bring it up?"

"Because I'm watching you make the same mistake again. Only this time, I think you're going to lose the great love of your life."

Her eyes widened. "Sorry, what?"

Nodding, Catherine said, "Teagan, you're my daughter and I love you, and I can say with great certainty that I have never seen you as happy as you were whenever you and Bobby were together."

"Mom—"

"Hear me out." She paused. "I know how disappointed you were with our lifestyle. Besides the moves, there was a lot of uncertainty. A lot of time where we were scared and at home praying for your dad's safe return. And I remember being there when we got the call about Logan."

Tears immediately stung Teagan's eyes and she wanted to curse them. She was so tired of crying, so tired of reliving the pain and the loss. When was it ever going to end?

"I think because of that loss, you're afraid. You had no control over so many aspects of your life that you're overcompensating now and trying to control everything. To the exclusion of really having a life."

"I have a life!" she cried. "I have an amazing son, I'm getting ready to start a new job, we just moved across the country... I'd say that's living!"

"There's a difference between living and having a life, Teagan. And for a little while there, you looked like you finally had both, and it made me so happy. It made me feel like it was okay for your father and I to step back a little."

"What do you mean?"

"We've stayed close to you because we wanted to be there if you needed us. And when you met Bobby, it seemed like you were finally moving on and ready to, you know, need us a little less."

"Wait—are you saying that I'm needy?"

"Oh, gracious, no!" Catherine said with a small laugh. "We felt like we should be there for you because...well, we felt partly responsible for you being where you were. If we had moved, if your father had left the army... I know we wouldn't have Lucas right now, but you also never would have had to go through all that you did."

The lump in her throat grew as she realized just how

much her parents loved her. The fact that they somehow blamed themselves for her heartache was something she never would have considered.

"Maybe you don't want to hear this but we really liked Bobby. He was good for you and good for Lucas. Seeing you happy was all we ever wanted."

Tears fell in earnest now.

"I wish you'd let yourself be happy," her mother whispered as she let Teagan cry.

"I feel bad saying this, but…I survived losing Logan. It was hard, but I survived." She looked up at her mother in despair. "I wouldn't survive losing Bobby. And that terrifies me to the point of paralyzing me."

"But you've already lost him, sweetheart. Don't you see that?"

She shook her head. "It's not the same. I can detach myself. I can pretend what we had wasn't real. That it wasn't the best thing to ever happen to me." Bowing her head, she cried. Her heart broke fully in two at her admission. "I can't just stand there and wait for him to be taken from me. It's too much to ask."

Then she was done talking and so was Catherine. Instead, they clung to one another and cried.

"This is the worst idea ever," Bobby murmured Tuesday morning as he stared into his cup of coffee.

"A little early to be talking to yourself, isn't it?"

Looking up, Bobby saw Quinn standing next to the table. Quinn had called on Sunday and asked to meet for breakfast and—because he was a glutton for punishment—Bobby had agreed. Sitting down in the booth, Quinn flagged the waitress over and ordered his own cup of coffee.

"You look like hell, Hannigan," he said when they were alone. "What gives?"

Bobby looked at him like he was crazy.

Rolling his eyes, Quinn said, "Look, I get it. Things didn't really go your way. But the Bobby Hannigan I knew would never walk around looking like…well, like this." The look on his face was pure disdain and yeah, Bobby deserved it. He hadn't shaved in over a week and the clothes he had on were seriously wrinkled.

"Was there a point to this?" he asked with annoyance. "You asked me to meet with you, you wouldn't tell me why, and I agreed. So? Just get to the point so I can go."

Leaning back in his seat, Bobby stared at Quinn until he started to squirm.

"Do you remember when Anna and I started dating?"

"Quinn…" he said with exasperation.

The smug bastard just sat there and grinned until Bobby had no choice but to sit back and listen. "You were so certain I was going to break her heart. And for a time, I did." He paused. "And when I hit rock bottom, when I'd lost everything and you could have just swooped in there to gloat, you didn't."

"And?"

"And I never thanked you for that."

"That's why we're here at seven in the damn morning? So you could say thanks for something that happened years ago?"

He shrugged. "Do you remember the Fourth of July parade?" Quinn asked instead.

Bobby nodded.

"Teagan asked me to say something nice about you."

Teagan had never told him the specifics of what the two of them had talked about, just that she had put Quinn in his place.

With a mirthless laugh, Bobby asked, "How long did it take you to think of something?"

"Not as long as you'd think."

This was getting them nowhere and all Bobby wanted to do was go home and crawl back in bed. "Color me surprised," he muttered, reaching for his coffee.

"Yeah, well, here's the thing," Quinn began. "You totally made a liar out of me and I can't have that."

"Excuse me?"

"Yup. I told Teagan you were one of the bravest people I know. You've totally proved me wrong, and now you need to fix that."

It was way too early in the morning for this kind of conversation. Picking up his coffee, Bobby drank it all down, burning his throat a little in the process. He slammed his cup back down and waved the waitress over to order a second cup.

"You're insane, dude, you know that, right?"

Quinn shrugged.

"What is it you want from me, Quinn? It's early and I—"

"And you've got nothing else to do, so don't even," Quinn argued. "I just drove an hour to meet you when I could still be home with my family."

"I drove an hour too, and need I remind you, this was your idea?"

He grinned. "Oh yeah. Right." He sat silently for a minute. Leaning forward on the table, he went on.

"Look, Teagan's one of the strongest people I know, and right now, she's a mess. And you? You're one of the bravest people I know and you're hiding from everyone and everything. None of this is good and it has to stop."

"She asked for time, Quinn. This isn't on me, it's on her."

"Don't pass blame," he said with disgust. "You're better than that."

"Stop, I'm blushing," Bobby replied flatly.

"Yeah, yeah, make jokes. But I'm here to tell you that you need to man up and quit being a coward."

Straightening in his spot, Bobby had to fight the urge to reach across the table and grab Quinn by the throat. "I am not a coward," he snarled.

"Wouldn't know it from where I'm sitting."

"You have no idea," Bobby argued. "You have no idea what I'm dealing with, so don't you dare sit there and pass judgment on me."

"Too late. I already am."

"We're done," Bobby snapped, sliding out of the booth.

"Do you want to lose her?" Quinn demanded.

And just like that, Bobby stopped and sighed. "I already did," he said solemnly. "She's scared and there isn't anything I can do about that. She knew what I did for a living when we met. And the thing is, I get it. I understand why she feels the way she does, and I would never pressure her to spend her life with me just because that's what I want."

Quinn stared at him hard for a long moment. "Do you love her?"

Swallowing, Bobby nodded. "She's it for me. I know

we weren't together for very long, but every day we were? Those were the best days of my life."

They sat in silence for a few minutes and Bobby slowly slid back into the booth. "Dude, you know me. I'm overly logical in my approach to life, and at times I'm one of the most cynical people on the planet. But the day I met her and Lucas, all I wanted to do was rescue them."

"You didn't even know them."

"I know. I fell for the kid just as much as I fell for his mom." He stared down at his hands. "So what does that tell you?"

"It tells me that you're a moron for not fighting for her."

Shaking his head, he said, "This isn't something I can fight. Teagan needs to feel safe and secure. And as weird as it sounds, considering the police motto is to protect and serve, they're not the same thing. She needs something I don't know how to give."

"How about by starting with not giving up? Damn, Bobby, she's used to people leaving. Hell, she's used to being the one forced to leave. Be the one who stays. Be the one person who shows her she means so much that you won't go."

It wasn't quite so easy. He'd spent more than a week trying to figure out how to convince her to give them another chance, and was still coming up empty-handed. "I don't know how to do that."

Then his brother-in-law—the one who lived to annoy the shit out of him—was back. Sitting back and crossing his arms over his chest, Quinn grinned confidently. "Would you like to know how?"

For a minute, he couldn't think of a snarky comeback.

He was too stunned. "Aren't you the same guy who's been doing his best all summer to convince Teagan that she shouldn't go out with me?"

"Yup."

"Then why? Why are you doing this? Are you setting me up to do something stupid that will guarantee I'll never have another chance with her?"

"As fun as that would be, no. That's not what I'm doing."

Could he possibly be telling the truth?

"Does Anna know you're here?"

Quinn shook his head. "No one knows I'm here. To be honest, I wasn't even sure you'd show up."

"I contemplated staying in bed this morning."

Resting his arms on the table, Quinn looked pleased. "Trust me, you'll be glad you didn't." He paused. "Are you in?"

"I don't know. I don't see how you could possibly know how to fix things when no one else seems to."

"Oh, everyone else knows as well. You just haven't bothered to answer your calls or texts, so how would you know?"

"What?" Bobby cried.

Quinn's smile grew and Bobby couldn't help but laugh and throw up his hands in defeat. "Fine. But I must really be desperate if I'm willing to take any advice from you."

Chapter 10

"I THINK THAT'S EVERYTHING," TEAGAN SAID QUIETLY, looking over her supply list one last time. School started in three days and she was already exhausted. At least her personal shopping and supply list was done, but her son's was the one she was working on now. It was hard to believe a kindergartner needed this much stuff.

Tossing the bags in the trunk, she climbed into the car and sat down with a loud sigh. Her parents were babysitting Lucas so she could get everything done more efficiently, but she was definitely dragging now.

"Coffee. I need coffee."

There wasn't a drive-thru Starbucks in town, but what was one more stop when the reward was caffeine? It took ten minutes to get across town and find a place to park, but the thought of that first sip of vanilla latte spurred her on.

As usual, the line was long, so she pulled out her phone and checked her messages while she waited. When it was her turn, she smiled, ordered, paid, and was practically bouncing on her toes in anticipation. Two minutes later, her name was called. She thanked the barista, turned, and froze. Standing in the line was Bobby.

And his ex-partner, Bree.

Fabulous.

Just as Teagan was going to turn away and try to sneak by unnoticed, Bree called her name. Forcing a smile on her face, she faced them. "Oh, hey…"

Bobby didn't say a word. His hands were stuck in his front pockets and all he did was offer a small smile and a nod.

Bastard.

"Great minds, huh?" Bree said, smiling.

In other circumstances, maybe Teagan would like this woman, but right now? Not so much. "I needed a shot of caffeine to finish back-to-school shopping," she said, her face almost hurting from the fake smile.

"It seems to get earlier and earlier each year," Bree said. "But I'm sure it's a little exciting too. You're starting a new position at the elementary school, right?"

Did it bother her how this woman seemed to know things about her?

Hell yes.

Nodding, Teagan said, "Yes. I'm the new guidance counselor."

"That's awesome! And your son's just starting kindergarten, right?"

With a swift and annoyed glance at Bobby, she replied, "Yes." Then, before she had to make any more small talk, she pulled her phone out of her purse. "I really need to get going. I have about a dozen more stops to make. It was nice to see you again, Bree." And with one last glance at Bobby she walked out the door, her heart beating wildly the entire time.

Her hand was shaking as she took out her keys and tried to unlock the car door.

"Teagan!"

She didn't even bother to turn around. She'd know Bobby's voice anywhere.

"Hey," he said a little breathlessly.

Door unlocked, she opened it and tossed her purse onto the front seat before looking at him.

"How are you?" he asked.

Seriously? Now he wanted to talk? It would have been easy to make a snarky comment, but she didn't believe in being petty.

No matter how much she wanted to be.

"Fine. And you?"

When he didn't answer right away, she didn't know what to do. Her eyes greedily drank in the sight of him. He looked tired and sad, and everything in her ached to reach out and caress his face.

Instead, she moved back until she was practically in her car. She wanted to ask why he had followed her out here, why he hadn't called her, and what he was doing with Bree, but again, she didn't.

"Like I said in there, I really need to go," she said lamely. Looking over his shoulder, she spotted Bree standing beside the door to the coffee shop. "And it looks like Bree's waiting for you. You shouldn't keep her waiting."

He didn't move. Hell, he barely seemed to breathe.

Why? Why here? Why now? she wanted to demand of the universe. Why did she have to fall in love with someone she couldn't have? And why did she have to watch him moving on so quickly?

Bobby reached out and touched her hand. It was a simple caress, yet she felt it to her very soul. Her gaze held his and time stood still. Whispering her name, he moved a little bit closer, and she was so ready to meet him halfway. But out of the corner of her eye, she could still see Bree.

Clearing her throat, Teagan moved and made herself get behind the wheel of the car. "I…I need to go. Bye." Thankfully, he stepped aside so she could close the door. But he didn't move any farther, and he didn't walk away.

Carefully, she pulled out of the parking spot and looked at him one last time before turning her gaze forward and driving away.

The last thing she wanted to do was more school shopping. All she wanted was to go home, crawl into bed, and cry. How was she supposed to stay downtown and run the risk of seeing him again? Her vision was blurred and driving was dangerous. She was a block from the beach, so she decided to pull into one of the public lots and take a few minutes to calm down.

It was after four in the afternoon and the beach crowd was thinning out. Rather than sit in the car, Teagan got out with her coffee and decided to walk in the sand for a little while to clear her head.

She slid her sandals into her purse. The sand between her toes felt glorious. Instantly, the tension started to leave her body.

Why was this breakup hitting her so hard? She'd broken up with people before, and while she knew it would hurt, wasn't she too old to still be feeling this devastated?

"Okay, think about your breakups," she murmured to herself as she walked along.

It took less than thirty seconds for reality to hit and she slowly sank to the sand.

This was the first time she'd been in a relationship that had ended without anyone leaving.

A shaky breath came out and her heart was racing again. When she was a teenager and broke up with someone, it was usually because one of them was moving away. Then with Logan…

"Oh God," she said, her voice trembling.

Bobby Hannigan was the first person she'd ever broken up with who really meant something to her. And he was the first person she'd have to keep seeing afterward—possibly forever.

But more than that, he was the first person she had really, truly loved.

Her mother had been right. As guilty as it made her feel, Logan was a first love, but not a forever love.

Bobby… Bobby was her forever love.

How could she take that risk? How could she possibly live every day knowing he was purposely putting himself in harm's way? Could she really live like that? Could she honestly make her son live like that?

But.

Wasn't life about taking risks? Wasn't love about taking risks? How many people had told her how she wasn't really living right now—how her fear was keeping her from having a full life? Her stomach clenched at the thought of staying on this path.

Now that she had known what it felt like to love somebody, how could she possibly live without him?

He's moved on. It's too late.

Oh, right. That.

All she had wanted was time to think, and she'd taken too long. In her mind it hadn't been that long, but clearly in his mind it was. And he'd gone back to his old ways. The pain of knowing that, coupled with seeing the two of them together, made her want to wretch.

Around her people were laughing and smiling and playing, while she sat in the sand and tried to convince herself not to cry.

It was no use.

Tears fell in earnest and she didn't care about the strange looks she was getting, didn't care if people thought she was crazy. Right now, this was what she needed to do.

Time passed, she knew that, but it wasn't until her cell phone rang that she realized the sun was setting. Looking at her phone confirmed just how late it was getting.

"Hello," she said, her voice weak.

"Teagan? Where are you, sweetheart? We thought you'd be back for dinner."

"Hey, Mom," she said and forced herself out of her fog. "Sorry. I lost track of time."

"Are you all right? You sound funny."

"Yeah, um…no. I'm not all right."

"Where are you? Do you need me to come and get you?"

The thought of driving was nearly overwhelming, but sitting in the sand waiting for her mother to arrive wasn't appealing either. "Would it be okay for Lucas to sleep with you tonight? I think… I think I just need to be alone tonight."

"Of course he can stay over, but I'm worried about you. You don't sound like you should be alone."

"I'll be fine, Mom. I swear."

"Teagan, honey, talk to me."

She swallowed hard and willed herself not to cry again. This time it worked. "I ran into Bobby today."

"Oh?" her mother asked, sounding hopeful.

"He was out with another woman."

"Oh." All hope gone. "Oh, sweetie, I'm so sorry. No wonder you sound like this."

"It's going to be okay," she said and really wished she believed it. "This is what I wanted, right? I said I couldn't live with the fear of losing him to his job and now—now I don't have to worry about it. I'm free to just...to move on with my life."

She cursed under her breath, the tears starting again. "Tell Lucas I'll call him later, okay?"

"I really wish you'd let me come and get you."

She shook her head even though her mother couldn't see it. "I'm okay. I'm sitting out on the beach over by the Islander resort and I'll head home in a little bit. Maybe I'll grab some Chinese food on the way home."

Sighing, Catherine said, "If you change your mind and need a ride, call me. Or go inside the resort and relax until you're ready to drive."

"Thanks, Mom." When she hung up, Teagan looked out at the ocean and sighed. Behind her was a really nice hotel where she could possibly get a room, order room service, and hide out for the night.

For easily twenty minutes, she sat weighing the pros and cons of being responsible. Room service and no driving were such a strong draw. When was the last time she had indulged in a little pampering for herself? And that didn't include going to get a haircut. Something frivolous and seemingly unnecessary.

Never. The answer was never.

Unfortunately, she was ridiculously practical and couldn't justify spending the money on a room when her house was only five miles away and empty.

"Damn practicality."

Her coffee was cold, her stomach was growling, and the sky was getting dark. It was time. Just as she was about to stand, someone sat beside her. She was about to turn and comment about personal space and how there was forty miles of beach they could sit on when she realized who it was.

"Bobby." His name was out before she could stop it. He gave her a small smile. "What are you doing here?" She immediately began looking around for Bree. With the way her luck was going, Bree would be with him.

"You took off like a bat out of hell earlier," he said, and man, had she missed the sound of his voice. "I went looking for you, but—"

"How did you know I was here?"

She'd kill her mother when she saw her tomorrow.

Shrugging, he said, "I saw your car when I was driving around."

It was possible, she thought. Not probable, but possible. Maybe her mother's life would be spared.

"Why were you looking for me?" She hated that she even wanted to know.

Instead of answering, Bobby looked out at the water, his arms draped over his bent knees. After a few minutes, he turned to her. "I've been waiting for almost two weeks, Teagan. I know you said you needed to think, but I didn't think it meant we were never going to speak again."

Shame filled her, because he was right. She'd been avoiding him—them—and for what? It clearly hadn't helped her make any decisions.

"I know," she said quietly. "I thought it would make things easier."

"How?"

"If we didn't talk, then I wouldn't be swayed, and could make a logical decision about…about our future."

"Shouldn't I get a say?" he asked. "This isn't just about you."

Nodding, she said, "There's Lucas to consider, too."

"I know, believe me," he said, his voice calm and soothing. She just wanted to lean into him and finally have a little peace after struggling and trying to be brave for so damn long. "I know Lucas is a major factor in everything we decide, but we need to figure some things out about ourselves first."

That was spot on and all she could do was nod.

"Tell me what you want from me," he said, his voice so low she could barely hear it over the waves.

Unable to look directly at him, she stared out at the water. "Right now? I don't want to talk about jobs and safety," she said, letting out a shaky sigh. "I've been in my own head too much lately and I just…I don't want to go there right now."

Bobby's shoulders sagged and he hung his head, and she realized how what she'd said could have been taken. Plus, she really hadn't answered his question.

"I want to go somewhere that we can shut out the world for a little while and just—be together," she said boldly.

Slowly, he turned his head and looked at her, his

expression sad. "Teagan, we can't avoid talking about this forever. And I don't think it's a good idea."

"Is it because of Bree?"

"What?" he cried, sitting up straighter. "Where did that even come from?"

His reaction seemed a little strong, but Teagan figured it was because she was being brutally honest and pointing out the elephant in the room. Or on the beach, as it were.

"I'm a terrible person, right?" she said, annoyed with herself. Here she was propositioning him, knowing he was involved—no doubt casually, per his old MO—and being rather bold about it.

"What are you talking about? You're not making any sense!" He rubbed his temples even as he shook his head.

"Look, I get it. You…you already went back to the way things used to be. And while I'm not thrilled you were able to just jump back into casual dating thing so fast, I understand—"

She never got to finish.

Bobby closed the distance between the two of them and covered her lips with his. It didn't matter that she wasn't expecting it, she was greedy for the taste of him, the feel of him. Her hands instantly raked up into his hair and before she knew it, her back was in the sand and half of his body was covering hers. One of his large hands anchored in her hair and gripped it hard, causing her to flinch, but not enough to make her break the kiss.

The kiss was wild, untamed, and it felt completely decadent to be out here in the middle of the sand. Like they didn't care if the whole world watched because they were both that desperate for one another.

Was it wrong to be completely relieved that it wasn't all one-sided?

Bobby shifted and broke the kiss, but his lips traveled along her cheek. He gently bit her ear lobe before resting his head against hers. "Dammit, Teagan," he said breathlessly.

She needed a minute to catch her own breath and didn't want to move. This was perfect. It didn't matter who saw them or how long they stayed here, just as long as he was there beside her.

Or maybe…

"You know, The Islander is right behind us," she said, practically purring with the need to get closer to him. "In a matter of minutes, we could be—"

He pushed away from her and sat up. "Is that really what you want? What we've been reduced to?"

Leaning up on her elbows, she looked at him with confusion. "What do you mean?"

"It's okay for us to have sex but we can't talk about our relationship, do I have that right?"

When he said it, it sounded like a bad thing. In her head, however, it sounded just about perfect.

Oh God, what is happening to me? Who am I?

"That's not what I was suggesting."

"It's exactly what you were suggesting," he corrected. Growling with frustration, he jumped up and paced a few feet away before turning around and glaring at her. "What is going on with you? I get that you're freaked out about me going back to work. But what we have has never been just about sex, so I don't get why that's all you're looking for right now!"

"It's not!" she yelled, coming to her feet.

"That's not what it just sounded like!"

Pinching the bridge of her nose, she silently counted to ten to try to gather her thoughts.

None of them made sense.

Dropping her hands to her side, she said, "I should go. Just forget what I said and…I'll see you around."

She made it all of three steps before Bobby grasped her upper arm and spun her around. "No. No more running, no more walking away. You need to decide right here, right now, Teagan. Are we through or not?"

"Bobby…"

"I'm serious. Are we going to talk and move forward, or are we done? I can't keep living in limbo. Every other part of my life is like that and there's nothing I can do about it. But this? This I can. I need an answer from you."

Her heart thundered in her chest. If she said yes, they were through, she would be devastated for a very long time. But if she said no, that they were good, she'd have to live with the fear of him going back to active duty on the force and worry about his safety forever.

And that would be devastating in and of itself.

"I…I don't know what—" She stopped and stared down at the sand for a moment before looking at him. "You have no idea what you're asking of me."

"That's where you're wrong," he said, his voice thick with emotion. "I'm asking you to talk to me. I'm asking you to trust me. To trust in us." He moved in closer. "I would never hurt you, Teagan, and I wish I could give you all the guarantees that you need. But I can't. No one can. Don't you think that I'm terrified you'll break my heart?"

Her eyes went a little wide at his question.

"You scare the hell out of me," he added softly. "Everything I feel for you is terrifying. And just when I think we're okay, I go and do something to upset you."

"It's not like that…"

"I've never done this before. I've never been in love before. I don't know if I was afraid to put the effort into a relationship before or what, but with you, I wanted to. I wanted to do whatever it took to be with you. And it's not easy because I know you're scared, and there isn't a damn thing I can do to change that. But I'm willing to try."

"You—you're in love?" she asked shakily.

He laughed softly, resting his forehead against hers. "Yeah, Teagan. I'm in love with you." He let out a long breath. "Do you want to know what scares me the most?"

She couldn't speak, she simply nodded.

"The fact that you don't need me nearly as much as I need you." He raised his eyes and met hers. "I've said it before and I'll say it again—you're one of the strongest people I've ever known. And I know if you tell me right now that we're really done, you'd go on and be okay. You'd be able to move forward and go on with your life. You even told me that once." He paused again. "But me? I'd be gutted. Because you give me hope. You brought laughter and joy and all that goes with it into my life. If you're gone, then I have nothing."

His name was a mere whisper on her lips as she moved to wrap her arms around him. No one had ever said anything like that to her before. No one had ever made her feel so important, so vital.

It chipped away at the last of her resistance. The last of her doubts.

Reaching up, she cupped his cheek in her hand.

"You know what we're doing, right?" he asked softly, and when she looked at him curiously, he explained. "We're talking. This, Teagan. This is one of the things I love most about us."

Tears burned her eyes. "I do too."

And then he smiled, that sexy, heart-melting smile that always made her weak.

"You know," she began shyly, "there's a beautiful resort right behind us and the parking lot doesn't look too full. Maybe we can see if there's a room—"

He silenced her with a finger over her lips. "No. I'm not looking to jump into bed with you. I don't care if we just sit and share some pizza while we talk about the weather. I like what we're doing right now." Sighing, he nuzzled her cheek. "The physical part of our relationship is amazing, but I like the intimacy of a conversation with you."

How could she possibly say no to that?

"That has always been one of my favorites," she admitted.

"How about pizza on your couch?" he suggested.

"Actually, I was thinking Chinese," she said with a slow grin.

"I can make that work." Placing a kiss on the tip of her nose, he said, "Let's go. I'll meet you at your place in thirty minutes."

Then, hand in hand, they walked back to the parking lot and parted ways with nothing more than a soft kiss on the lips.

And Teagan felt just as giddy as if they were heading into the resort.

In some ways, this felt like a first date.

In others, a test.

But as Bobby sat back and listened to Teagan talk about all her fears about her son starting kindergarten, he realized he'd take this. No matter what it was.

"It's not like we spend all day every day together. I mean, up until we moved here, I was either going to school or working, so I know I'm being a little bit crazy," she was saying, "but it's not about missing out on time together. It's the fact that he's growing up."

"That's what they're supposed to do," he said lightly, because he could see her tearing up. "Your job is to love him, guide him, and set a good example, and you've done that." Reaching out, he squeezed her hand. "He's a great kid, Teagan, and you're both going to be fine."

"I don't know. Maybe. Everyone tells me I'm being overly dramatic because I'm going to be working in his school and I can see him anytime I want, but again, not the point."

"So you're saying you're *not* going to walk down the hall and peek in the classroom several times a day?" he teased, and was relieved when she blushed and smiled.

"I didn't say that. Not exactly."

"And what about you," he said, reaching for his can of soda. "Are you ready for your new job?"

"I am," she replied confidently. "This is the position I've always wanted, and honestly, I'm anxious to get started. I've been to the school a lot over the past week to set up my office and get organized, and all I'm waiting for is the first day of school so I can officially begin."

Nodding, he asked, "So what exactly does an elementary school guidance counselor do in an average day?"

"Believe it or not, it's like a combination of teaching and psychology. I'm oversimplifying, but I've been trained in child development, learning strategies, self-management, and social skills. I need to be able to work with a diverse range of students."

"Wow—that's very impressive!"

She blushed and took a sip of her own drink. "Plus I work with the faculty in organizing community programs—sort of like when the fire department comes in to teach fire safety, or when the police department comes in to talk about stranger danger and the antidrug programs. I get to wear many hats in this position and I'm just too excited to get started!"

He laughed softly, excited for her. She was so obviously passionate about this new job.

"Listen, I know you don't want to talk about anything too serious, but I'd really like to see Lucas before he starts school Monday. Just to wish him luck," he added quickly for clarification. "I can understand that you're probably worried about me coming around if we haven't figured out where we are or what it is that we're doing, but…" He looked at her pleadingly. "It would really mean a lot to me if I could just stop by and wish him luck."

Leaning back against the sofa, Teagan smiled at him. "I think he would like that a lot. How about tomorrow after lunch? He's with my parents tonight. I'm going to pick him up after breakfast and finish our school shopping, but we should be back here around two."

"Uh…tomorrow I can't," he said slowly, evasively.

If anything, he looked everywhere but directly at her. "How about Sunday?" Reaching for the container of dumplings, he popped one in his mouth.

"Oh, um…okay," she said, equally slowly. "Sunday we're busy all day, and I want to get him home and to bed early since we'll need to be up and on the go early Monday."

Damn.

"Maybe you can call him on Sunday night," she offered, and he knew she was trying to sound optimistic. "We should be home by five, so any time after that should work."

He nodded but couldn't help feeling disappointed. If it were any other day or any other reason, he'd cancel his plans, but not this time. He knew her well enough to know she was curious about his plans but wouldn't ask him, and telling her ran the risk of ruining what they were doing right now. Yet he hated keeping it from her.

"That would be great," he said after a minute. "Thanks."

Things got quiet to the point of being awkward. They finished eating in silence, and for the life of him, Bobby had no idea what to say to turn things around.

Clearly, Teagan didn't have that same problem.

"So you never answered my question about Bree," she said boldly, her expression neutral. "Are you involved with her again?"

After he finished choking on his soda and remembered how to breathe, he held a hand to his chest and looked at her. "Geez, Teagan, what the hell?"

She shrugged. "Like I said, you never answered me.

Is that why you can't come by tomorrow? You have plans with Bree?"

"First of all, I'm not involved with Bree," he stated, more than a little annoyed that she thought so little of him. "*You* are the one I'm involved with, and only you. Do you understand that?"

She didn't look fully convinced.

"I ran into Bree earlier and we went to grab some coffee. End of story. I wouldn't be here with you right now if that were the case." Then he sat up a little straighter. "And you know what? I thought we were beyond all this. That you'd been able to let go of the image everyone seemed to have of me. More than that, I thought you believed in me."

He knew the instant shame hit her. And he didn't feel bad about it, because when he did finally explain it to her, it would all be worth it.

"I'm sorry. You're right. I just…" Sighing, Teagan looked up at him. "I got jealous."

It was maybe the hottest thing she'd ever said to him. Ever.

"There is nothing for you to be jealous about," he said gruffly. "There's only one woman I want, and that's you."

"Really?" she asked shyly.

"Yeah. Really." Reaching over, he gently tugged her closer to him and was rewarded when she straddled his lap. All he could do was look at her face—that beautiful face that meant everything to him. "Hey," he whispered softly.

"Hey, yourself."

His hands rested on her hips before slowly moving around to cup her bottom. Teagan let out a soft little moan and moved against him ever so slightly. "What are you thinking right now?"

She focused on him as she started to move in a much more suggestive way. "I'm thinking how much I missed you. And how I would like it very much if maybe we didn't talk for a little while."

One brow arched at her words. "You mean you want me to leave and not speak to me for another week or two?"

With a knowing smile, Teagan shook her head.

"Then what did you mean?" he asked, leaning in close and trailing kisses along her jaw.

With her head falling back, she was panting a little. "I was thinking...maybe—oh, that's a good spot—maybe we could take this inside and...and..."

He gently bit her neck and pulled her close when she gasped his name. "It's just the two of us here," he reminded her. "We could stay right here in this very spot and...not talk."

And for a minute, he thought he had her convinced. But she surprised him. Lifting her head, she gave him a sexy smile and said, "But I was hoping to sprawl out on the bed and let you undress me. Slowly."

Before he could blink, Bobby was standing with her in his arms and striding for her bedroom. Sprawling Teagan out on the bed and undressing her was one of his favorite things to do.

Gently, he put her down on the mattress and groaned as she squirmed to get more comfortable. When he placed a knee on the bed and went to reach for her, he was surprised to notice that his hand was trembling. He had sworn to himself during the drive over that they wouldn't do this. There were too many things they really needed to discuss. But there was no way he could stop now. No way he would deny her—them—this.

She was already barefoot and his hand trailed slowly from her slim ankle up her leg. Teagan had on khaki shorts that allowed him to caress a whole lot of smooth skin. She purred as his hand moved farther and farther up. He gently tickled her thigh before reaching for the waistband. Her hand settled over his.

"I want you to know," she said breathlessly, "I wasn't prepared for this."

It was a weird thing to say, but he took it to mean that maybe she hadn't put fresh sheets on the bed or something. Leaning down, he kissed her. "It's okay," he said.

With the shorts unbuttoned, he pulled down the zipper and then gently began to tug the fabric over her hips. Once they were off and he had tossed them aside, he studied her and grinned widely.

"I wish I had thought to change," she said, smiling shyly.

Running his hand up her leg again, he said, "You know how much I love you in white cotton."

"I thought you loved me in those lacy thongs I bought?"

He laughed. "Sweetheart, I love you in anything and everything." He paused and marveled at how soft she was all over. "Which reminds me, I still owe you about a half dozen of those."

"It's okay. I know you're good for them." Next thing he knew, Teagan was pulling her shirt up and over her head, tossing it aside like he had done with her shorts. "One of us is severely overdressed here."

Straightening, he quickly undressed, adding his shirt and shorts to the growing pile of clothes on the floor. They both sighed in unison as he settled between her thighs. "You feel so good," he murmured, kissing her throat, her shoulder, the swell of her breast. "And you taste even better."

"Mmm…is that right?"

He nodded because he couldn't speak. His lips didn't want to leave her skin. She was so warm and soft and… still overdressed. Using his teeth, Bobby moved first one bra strap and then the other from her shoulders, then nudged the cups aside.

Glorious.

Teagan's back arched. She reached behind her and unhooked the garment before throwing it over his head. When she lay back, she smiled victoriously at him. "Isn't that much better?"

For a moment, he was speechless. She was perfection. There wasn't an inch of her he didn't love, didn't crave. It was impossible to touch her everywhere at once, no matter how badly he wanted to.

"You're so sexy," he said, kissing one breast and teasing her nipple with his tongue. "So beautiful," he whispered, kissing the other one.

"Bobby?" she moaned, her back arching again to get closer to him.

"Hmm?"

"No more talking," she panted.

And that was fine with him. For the moment, his mouth had other plans.

Sunlight was just beginning to streak through the blinds when Teagan felt Bobby trailing kisses along her shoulder. She was exhausted, had maybe slept a total of two hours, but the night had been worth it.

"Mmm... Good morning," she said huskily, rolling over to face him. He looked super sexy with his hair mussed up and stubble on his jaw, and her hands twitched at the thought of touching him. She got as far as his shoulder when he stopped her.

"I hate to do this, but...I need to get going."

Her heart sank. They'd never finished discussing what his plans were for today, other than the fact that they weren't with Bree. And her curiosity was going to get the better of her. "Can't you postpone it? Or be just a little late?"

Smiling, he placed a soft kiss on the tip of her nose. "I wish I could, but I can't." He wrapped an arm around her waist and pulled her close. "Had I planned better, I would have made sure there was something here to make you breakfast in bed before I left."

"As wonderful as that would have been," she said, staring at his chest, "it would be better if you were here enjoying it with me." Then she held her breath and waited to see if he would offer her some sort of explanation as to where he was going and why he couldn't stay.

"Teagan," he said, rolling onto his back. He flung one arm up over his head and the other rested on his stomach. It was an extremely sexy pose and she wanted to curse herself for even noticing that right now.

"I'm sorry if I'm prying," she said carefully, "but you have to realize why I'm curious."

His expression was...bleak.

She didn't take that as a good sign.

"Last night you said you didn't want to talk about work or anything like that so—"

"You're going back to work?" she asked as panic began to rise. Sitting up, she looked at him. "I didn't know you got your clearance."

He nodded solemnly. "Today's my first day back."

Her heart sank and for the life of her, she had no idea what to do or say to him in that moment.

Bobby sat up beside her and took one of her hands in his. "It's going to be all right, I promise you."

But she was already shaking her head. "You can't know that." Her voice was no more than a hoarse whisper. "You can't guarantee that nothing is going to happen to you out there." Her vision was blurred with unshed tears. "I know you have to do this, but you have to understand why I'm scared, Bobby."

He looked down at their hands. "I need you to trust me." Then he looked up. "Have a little faith in me."

She nodded, she knew she nodded, even though her heart was screaming no.

Cupping her face, he kissed her—long and deep and so full of emotion that she never wanted it to end. Breathless, he lifted his head. "I love you."

"I love you too, Bobby, but—"

He instantly silenced her with a finger over her lips. "No *but*s, Teagan." He kissed her again before climbing from the bed. He looked magnificent as he stretched, and she slowly eased back against the pillows and watched him dress.

It was on the tip of her tongue to ask him not to go. To stay with her, to consider other career options. This was something she excelled in—helping people achieve success. True, her forte was more in the school-age children sector, but she could totally make it work here!

Think, Teagan! Think!

Once he was dressed, he looked down at her with a small smile. "It's all going to be okay. This is going to be a good thing. Trust me."

Her mouth wouldn't work even if she wanted it to, so all she could do was nod.

Bobby kissed her one last time. "I've got to go back to my parents' place to shower and change, and then… it's going to be a full day. Can I call you tonight?"

Again, she nodded.

His shoulders sagged. "Say something. Please. I can't leave and focus on everything I need to do today if I know you're this upset."

"What do you want me to say, Bobby?" she asked after taking a minute to collect her thoughts. And oddly, that was all she could come up with.

"Wish me luck!" he said with a mirthless laugh. "Or at least say something when I ask if I can call you! I mean, come on. I thought we were moving forward with this."

"Why would you think that?" she asked, finally finding her voice. "We just barely touched on the topic and the last I heard, you weren't going back to work. I thought we had more time to—to figure this out!"

"Figure what out?" he snapped. "This is my job, Teagan! That was never going to change!" He seemed to realize he was shouting and turned away with a muttered curse. After a minute, he faced her again. "I wanted to talk to you about this last night, but it was the one topic you said was off-limits. What was I supposed to do?"

He had a point. "I know, I know. I'm just…" She looked up at him helplessly. "I need time to get a grip."

Bobby was already shaking his head. "Not if it means you're going to completely cut me out of your life while you think. Absolutely not."

"I won't. It won't be like that again. I promise."

He stared at her long and hard before giving a curt nod. "Okay then." Glancing at her bedside clock, he cursed again. "I really need to go. It won't look good if I'm late on my first day back." With one last quick kiss, he was out the door.

Teagan waited until she heard the front door close before letting out a shaky breath.

This was so not the way she'd imagined starting her day. After an incredible night, she'd had visions of breakfast in bed followed by another round of love-making before she went to pick up Lucas. Even though she'd already known Bobby wouldn't be with her for that part, she had still figured a satisfying morning would energize her for the rest of the day.

"Man, was I wrong," she murmured.

Kicking the blankets off, she walked into the bathroom and opted to go right into the shower. It was ridiculously early—too early to go out and do anything—but the thought of staying in bed alone wasn't appealing either.

Once she was showered, she pulled on her robe and walked to the kitchen to make some coffee. The remnants of last night's takeout were still all over the living room, so she cleaned it up while her coffee brewed. It was a mindless task that did little to keep her from thinking about Bobby and what he was doing.

Was he back to full active duty?

Then what was he doing here if he was going back to the force in Myrtle Beach?

"It's way too early in the morning for this." Wiping off the coffee table, she finished tidying up before taking a mug down for her coffee. The clock read seven fifteen, not much earlier than when she normally started her day, but she felt as though she'd already done about a dozen tasks.

Most of them mental.

Unfortunately, Bobby was right. She did need to have faith. Just because he was going back to work didn't mean something bad would happen. When had she gotten so pessimistic? It was completely unlike her in almost every other aspect of her life, but this had struck a chord in her that she couldn't shake. And sitting in her kitchen obsessing about it wasn't going to help either.

Taking her coffee with her, she did her hair and makeup before getting dressed. By eight o'clock, she was walking out the door to finish her shopping. Logically, it was just going to be easier to run all her errands without her son along.

So she shopped, crossing things off her list, getting the best deals—and by eleven, Teagan felt like she had run a marathon. When she arrived home and put everything away, she looked around, feeling like now she could finally relax. Lucas's book bag was all packed for Monday, her own satchel was packed with her own supplies. Laundry was done, the house was clean, and she was happy to say she'd gotten it all done.

Then the phone rang.

"You're being stupid," she chided herself. Her heart

kicked hard in her chest as if preparing for bad news. Grabbing her phone, she saw her mother's face on the screen and let out a breath of relief. "Hey, Mom!"

"How are you doing today? Any better?"

Sitting on the sofa, she told her mother about running into Bobby—leaving out their overnight activities—and how things had gone this morning. "Did you know he was cleared to go back to work? Did Mary say anything to you?"

"She might have mentioned it, but I can't really remember."

That was odd. Since Teagan and Bobby had started dating, her mother had been almost rabid in her attempts to get as much information on their relationship as possible. And after their emotional girls' night, she knew her mother was just as anxious for news on what Bobby had decided to do as Teagan was. So what was up with her vague response?

"Really? I would have thought you and Mary would have talked about that at great length, considering how close the two of you have gotten."

"Believe it or not, Teagan, we do enjoy talking about things other than our children," Catherine said defensively.

Yeah, something was definitely up.

"Okay, okay…sheesh." She sighed. "So I was up early this morning and finished all my shopping. Want me to pick up some lunch for all of us on my way over?"

"That sounds wonderful! Lucas was asking about fried chicken." She laughed. "I swear, our boy is a foodie. I don't know where he gets it from."

"A foodie? Really? This is the same child who would

only eat peanut butter and jelly for lunch for almost a year."

"Oh, I had forgotten about that. Hmm… Either way, he's been talking about chicken. I told him maybe there'd be some grilled chicken tomorrow at Quinn and Anna's, but he insisted he wanted it fried."

"No worries. I'll head up to the grocery store. I know the kind he prefers. I'll pick up some salads too, and something for dessert. Anything else I should get?"

"No, I think we're good here. I have plenty of drinks, so just text me when you're on your way."

"Sounds like a plan," Teagan said before hanging up. There wasn't any reason for her to sit around and wait, so she grabbed her purse and left.

At the supermarket, she grabbed two buckets of chicken because the pieces looked small and she knew her father would eat half of it on his own if given the chance. Along with that, she grabbed some potato salad and a fruit salad. As she passed the bakery, she picked up a box of oatmeal-raisin cookies and a plate of brownies. Her stomach was growling as she paid for her order and by the time she was standing outside again, she was tempted to eat a cookie to hold her over.

She was standing on the sidewalk waiting to cross to her car when she noticed a trio of policemen walking into the pizza place at the other end of the shopping center. Her eyes followed them for a minute, then narrowed.

Bobby.

For a moment, she was too stunned to move. If he was back on the local force, why wouldn't he say that? Why was he being so secretive?

Shaking her head to clear it, Teagan made her way

to her car. The entire drive to her parents' house, she was thinking about Bobby. If he was back on the force here, willing to move back, it would mean he really was serious about them. But why keep it from her? She hated not knowing what was going on, and at the exact same time hated how needy she was feeling!

By the time she walked into her parents' house, she was a little calmer but still desperate for some answers. Rather than make a scene, she put a smile on her face and greeted her son with a massive hug.

"Hey, buddy! I missed you last night! Did you have fun?"

Nodding wildly, he said, "Uh-huh! We watched movies and played Go Fish and Meema made us Rice Krispie treats!"

Smiling at her mother, Teagan commented, "Rice Krispie treats? You haven't made those in years!"

Catherine laughed and shrugged. "We saw a commercial for them yesterday and they were on my mind. I went to the store and got the ingredients while the two of them played cards. And they were delicious, by the way. Just like I remembered."

"Any left?" Teagan asked, suddenly craving the sweet treat.

"When I went to bed there was half a plateful left, but when I got up—"

"They were small!" her father said as he walked into the kitchen. He kissed his daughter on the cheek. "I was watching the eleven o'clock news and didn't realize just how many of them I'd eaten."

Rolling her eyes, she said, "Somehow I think you had at least a general idea."

He grinned. "Maybe." Then, walking over to the dining room table, he said, "Ooo, chicken! Nice!"

Over lunch they all listened as Lucas talked about how excited he was to start school. At one point, her mother made knowing eye contact with her and Teagan knew right then and there that she'd figured out that Teagan wasn't quite in the moment with the rest of them. She nodded back, a signal that they'd talk after they were all done eating.

Thirty minutes later, they sent James and Lucas out to kick the soccer ball around.

"Spill it," Catherine said. "At this rate, your father's going to sleep for a week. Lucas has been running him ragged for the last twenty-four hours. Either that or he'll demand more treats."

Unable to help herself, Teagan laughed and told her mother what she saw. "I don't get it. Why is he being so secretive? Why wouldn't he just tell me? Knowing that he's working here rather than Myrtle Beach? Well, it kind of helps."

"Really?"

She nodded. "This is small-town living at its finest, Mom. Not that there isn't crime here, but it's just not on the same scale as a bigger city."

Catherine nodded. "Makes sense."

"Which brings me back to the original question— why?"

"You'll have to ask him that. Does he know that you'd feel better with him moving back here and working?"

She looked away uncomfortably. "We, um…we never really talked about it."

"Oh, Teagan. Honestly. Why wouldn't you have that discussion?"

Jumping up from her chair, she began to pace. "This all happened so fast! And you know what, it wasn't supposed to happen. I wasn't supposed to move here, meet someone, and fall in love! That wasn't in the plan at all!"

"Teagan—"

"No, it's true! And then when it all started to hit me that he was eventually going to go back to work—I freaked! I wasn't only scared about his job, but I was scared about how I felt. All I asked for was a little time, and then everything changed!"

"Other than the possibility that he's come back here to work, what's changed?"

"Everything!" she cried. "I miss him when he's not here, I think about him all the damn time. I need him! And you know me, Mom. I don't want to need anyone. I've done just fine on my own and…well, except for you and Dad, everything's been on me."

With a sad smile, Catherine walked over and hugged her. "You have been so strong and so brave for so long. I'm sure it's scary to think about letting go a little and letting someone else in." Pulling back, she looked at Teagan. "When you find the right person—the one who's going to be there beside you to share everything, including your fears—it's a wonderful thing. Don't cheat yourself out of what could be the greatest love of your life because you're scared. Talk to Bobby. Tell him what you saw and let him explain."

Nodding, Teagan hugged her. "Thanks, Mom." After a minute, she pulled back and smiled. Off in the distance she could hear her son yelling happily about scoring a goal on his old Pops. Laughing, she made her way over to the back door. "I think I'll go out there and give Dad a bit of a break."

"I'm sure he's fine."

Waving her off, she said, "Maybe. But it's a beautiful day, the sun is shining, and my son is happy. I should be out there taking it all in." She was out the door and in the yard a moment later, calling out for someone to kick the ball to her.

Inside, Catherine reached for her phone and quickly dialed Mary Hannigan's number. "I think we have a code red situation."

Chapter 11

"Bobby! What are you doing here?"

Smiling shyly at his sister, he said, "My niece is start-ing kindergarten tomorrow. I had to be here for that." He'd been practicing that line for days and he thought it sounded perfect, but when Anna's face started to crumble, he was certain he'd done something wrong.

"Are you just the sweetest man ever?" she said, her voice wobbly as her eyes filled with tears. Before Bobby could react, she threw herself at him and hugged him hard. "Thank you."

Wow. This was…way more emotional than he thought it would be. When she finally stepped back, she motioned for him to come into the house. Kaitlyn and Brian immediately ran over and lunged at him.

"Hey, you guys," he said, hugging them both.

"Kaitlyn! Where did you…?"

Bobby looked up to see Lucas running into the room.

"Bobby!" he cried and joined in on the group hug. Bobby's heart squeezed hard in his chest.

Did he hug Lucas a little harder? Maybe. Looking over at his sister, he said, "I guess I should have called first, huh?"

"Never," she said adamantly. "We're having a bit of a back-to-school celebration today. Teagan's here, but so are Aidan and Zoe. Plus Mom and Dad, Ian and Martha, and James and Catherine, so…"

"So…?"

"So it's too late to sneak back out. The kids will rat you out," she teased and then looked down at said kids. "Why don't you guys go and see if it's pool time yet?"

Bobby almost fell over as all three kids immediately released him and ran off. "Looks like I'm no competition for swimming, huh?"

"You never were," she replied with a grin, patting him on the back. "Come on, we just finished lunch but there's plenty of food left."

It would have been so easy to turn and walk out the door, to make some kind of excuse and leave, but…no. They were done playing the avoidance game. Yesterday had been long and exhausting, and by the time he had finished, it was too late to call her.

So he'd texted an apology and got back a one-word response.

It was worse than the nod from yesterday.

What he found ironic—particularly at this moment— was how she hadn't mentioned she was going to be at his sister's house today. All she'd said was that she had plans. If she had been sincere about seeing him and letting him see Lucas, why not just ask him to join them today for this—what did Anna call it?—back-to-school celebration?

It didn't matter. He was here now, he'd see her and talk to her, and not do anything to ruin the kids' party. So if he had to wait one more day to tell her about his job, so be it. Maybe it was a little petty on his part, but he was determined not to tell her about it yet. He wanted to surprise her. He'd worked it all out in his head, and if he could just get through this afternoon without blurting it out, it was going to be awesome.

It was going to secure their future.

She was his. He'd known it from the very start. He could understand her fear, but they were going to work through it.

He'd make sure of that.

"Bobby?" Anna was standing by the sliding glass doors watching him. "You coming?"

Nodding, he headed that way. He was almost to the door when Quinn walked in, got right in front of him and, slamming a hand hard on Bobby's chest, stopped him.

"We'll be out in a minute," Quinn said over his shoulder, but then his attention was right back on his brother-in-law. He gave a hard shove and Bobby stumbled back a couple of feet. "You. Me. In my office. Now."

It was pointless to argue and really, the last thing he wanted to do was cause a scene. With a sigh of resignation, Bobby walked toward the home office Quinn had right off of the garage.

As soon as they were in the room, Quinn slammed the door shut and said, "Dude, what the hell are you doing?"

"I thought I was coming to see Kaitlyn and wish her luck on her first day of school. Didn't think it was a crime," Bobby said defensively. "And besides, you told me to be here!"

"Yeah, well..." He looked over his shoulder as if checking to make sure the door was still closed. "I needed to make this look believable."

"Oh my gosh, enough. What's going on? I came here like you asked me to, and I was all set to go out there and talk to Teagan. Why am I in here talking to you instead?"

"Because she's not outside, she's upstairs in the guest

room changing into a bathing suit. I figured you might want to talk to her without an audience."

Right then and there, he could have hugged his brother-in-law. Who would have thought his one-time nemesis would be his biggest ally in getting his girl back?

"So she's alone upstairs?"

Quinn nodded. "In the room you usually stay in." When Bobby reached for the door, Quinn stopped him. "Can I offer you one piece of advice?"

"Sure."

"Speak this time. I heard you were fairly mute at the coffee shop on Friday."

"Wait, how did you hear about that?"

He shrugged. "Bree brings her car into my shop all the time. She came in yesterday for a tune-up and mentioned how the two of you ran into Teagan."

"Shit."

"Yeah. Use your words, Hannigan. God knows you never shut up when you're trying to prove something to me."

"That's different. And anyway—"

"No," Quinn quickly interrupted, "there's more."

Bobby huffed with annoyance. "Today, Quinn. It doesn't take someone that long to change into a bathing suit."

"Okay, look. She saw you yesterday."

"Who saw what?" No one knew about him spending the night at Teagan's, so he was a little confused. What was Quinn talking about?

"Yeah, she saw you going into the pizza place with a couple of other cops." He smacked Bobby in the shoulder. "You were supposed to lay low! We discussed this!"

Unfortunately, Quinn was right.

Dammit.

"What were the odds of her being up there at the same time?" he cried.

"It wasn't just to make sure *she* didn't see you, you idiot, but anyone who knows you. Now she's freaked out because you didn't tell her you were working here and she's probably second-guessing wanting to get back with you because you're a liar!"

"Hey!" Bobby demanded. "That's enough." Then he paused. "Wait—did she say that? Is that what she told Anna? Because I need to know this before I go up there and make an idiot out of myself."

"You're already making an idiot out of yourself."

Both of them turned and saw Anna standing in the doorway. "I swear, the two of you are the loudest couple of morons ever." She glared at Bobby. "You? Go upstairs and talk to her. And you?" she said to Quinn. "Get back outside and play lifeguard while the kids swim. They're waiting for you."

Neither argued as they both practically ran from the room.

Bobby took the stairs two at time and was just about to knock on the door when Teagan opened it and gasped.

"Bobby? What are you doing here?"

Talk about déjà vu.

"I, uh… I came to wish Kaitlyn good luck on her first day of school." He paused because the sight of her in a bright-blue bikini had him practically swallowing his own tongue. His eyes devoured her and when he met her gaze, he gave her a lopsided grin. "Sorry. You look amazing."

"Thanks." But she didn't seem flattered.

Or happy to see him.

"Can I talk to you for a minute? Alone?"

With little more than a nod, she turned and walked back into the bedroom. Bobby followed and closed the door. "I wish you had told me you'd be here today. I would have come over sooner and had lunch with everyone."

She shrugged. "I didn't think it was a big deal. I figured your parents or Anna would have mentioned it to you."

He hung his head and sighed before looking up at her. "Okay, I get it. You're angry with me."

"No, I'm not," she said, but he didn't believe it for a minute.

"Teagan, you're upset because I didn't tell you about work. I didn't mean for that to happen, okay? Can we just be honest here and admit that you're mad?"

Her gaze held his, but her expression was completely neutral. "Fine. I was upset."

"And now?"

Another shrug. "I get why you did it. I don't like being kept in the dark, but…I understand that you were trying to respect my wishes by not bringing up work Friday night."

He immediately relaxed and moved in close to her, carefully placing his hands on her waist. "I really wish I could have been here earlier—especially when you came up here and changed into this." His fingers played with the Lycra on her hips.

"It's your sister's suit," she said with a slight smirk.

"Aaand you just ruined it," he said, laughing. With a quick kiss on her lips, he stepped back. "So are we good?"

"We're good, Bobby. I think we still need to talk, but

not today. Today's about the kids getting to celebrate their last day of summer vacation. Can we promise to make time maybe next weekend to sit down and do that?"

He hated the thought of waiting that long, but for now he'd go for it. "We'll see if we can get a baby-sitter Saturday night. Or maybe we can have a family dinner—just the three of us—and talk after Lucas goes to bed."

Her smile was slow and beautiful. "I like the sound of that. Thank you."

With one more kiss, he reluctantly led her from the room, down the stairs, and out to the yard to join their families.

"Aren't you going to swim?" she asked when they stepped outside.

"I guess I could borrow a suit from Quinn." He shuddered dramatically. "Or maybe I'll just sit with everyone and have something to eat."

"Spoilsport. I was kind of hoping to spend a little time in the water with you." She inched closer. "We could go over in the corner of the deep end, I could wrap my legs around you while you helped me stay afloat."

Just the thought of it was making him hard.

"But…you should go eat," she said lightly. "I'll just swim by myself." And with that, she walked toward the water with a sassy sway of her hips and gracefully dove in.

"Quinn!" he called. "I need to borrow a suit!"

—∿∿—

The rest of the day was spent relaxing more than Bobby had in a long time. The focus was on the kids, no one was asking about his job, and that was more than okay with him. Quinn lit up the grill one more time for an early dinner, and by six thirty everyone began packing up and heading home. Bobby wished Aidan and Zoe's kids good luck on their first day back to school, and hugged Kaitlyn extra hard because he couldn't believe she was old enough to be starting kindergarten.

"Uncle Bobby!" she cried playfully. "You're squishing me!"

"Yeah, well…maybe I'm trying to squish you so you'll stay small forever," he teased.

She giggled uproariously as she squirmed to get out of his arms. "I can't stay small forever! I have to grow up!" Then she settled down and eyed him curiously.

"What? What are you looking at?"

"I think you're going to need to work on Bailey," she said.

"Bailey? Why?"

"Because she's already small. Maybe squish her a little and she'll stay like that longer!" And with a wave, she skipped away.

Straightening, he caught his sister's eyes and smiled. "You've got a great kid there, Anna."

Walking over and wrapping her arms around his waist, she said, "Yeah, I do."

He kissed her on the head. "You okay with this? With her starting school?"

She nodded. "I am. I think it's going to create a whole new level of chaos around here, even though I'll have a few hours with one fewer kid underfoot. But she's excited about it and so are we." Pausing, she looked up at him. "What about you?"

"What about me?"

"When are we going to be talking about your kids going to school?"

That one statement made his heart kick hard in his chest. It was something he'd been thinking about more and more in the last year or two, more so since meeting Teagan. In his mind, he already did have a kid starting school.

Lucas.

Not that he was going to voice that out loud to anyone. It was his own private thought.

When he didn't say anything, Anna sighed and took a step away. "How did things go with Teagan? I'm guessing pretty good, since you were all over her in the pool. If you hadn't already been in the water, we'd all have turned the hose on you."

That made him grin. Yeah, it had been pretty sexy—albeit G-rated—fun, and he wished he could have gone home with her and continued it.

"We agreed to wait and talk about this next weekend. This really wasn't the place to do it. Not with everyone down here and it being a party for the kids."

"Next weekend? But—what about tomorrow?"

"She doesn't know about that yet." He stopped and thought about it. "Actually, I'm not even sure we were having the same conversation earlier. I mean, she knows I'm working, and according to your husband, Teagan saw me yesterday in uniform while I was at lunch. But it was a fairly vague and generic conversation. We didn't talk about the specifics of my job or anything like that. I kept waiting for her to ask, but she didn't."

Smiling, Anna said, "Good. Hopefully you'll surprise

her and she'll be happy. She deserves it more than anyone I know, and I'm glad you're the one who can make that happen."

"That's what I'm hoping for." Raking a hand though his hair, he let out a small laugh. "Did you ever think you'd see the day?"

"The day when my big, bad, skirt-chasing brother would be looking to settle down? No." Then she laughed. "And the thought of that happening with one of Quinn's relatives? Definitely not!"

He couldn't help but laugh at that one. "I think he gave me more of a hard time just because of all the years I did it to him. Not that the two were even remotely similar." He paused. "My rage toward him was totally justifiable. His toward me? Not even a little bit."

"Oh, no," she said, walking toward the kitchen. "I'm not weighing in on that debate. You're both overprotective of the people you love. End of story."

He followed her. "Yeah, but…he deserved me being hard on him because he was such an ass for so long! There was no reason for him to continually try and warn Teagan away from me."

"Says you."

"C'mon, Anna," he whispered conspiratorially. "Admit it. No one's here to hear us. Admit I was right and Quinn was wrong. You know you want to."

"Wrong!" They both turned when Quinn walked into the kitchen holding Bailey. "She's not going to admit that, because my wife isn't a liar," he said confidently, walking over and placing one arm around Anna. "Big words from a guy who I helped out today."

"Helped out?" Bobby asked with amusement. "You

told me to come over, yelled at me, and then sent me to have a conversation I ended up not being able to have until next week!"

"Or maybe tomorrow," Anna corrected.

"Or maybe tomorrow," Bobby repeated. "Either way, it doesn't matter. After tomorrow, I'm going to have my girl back."

"And you're going to live happily ever after? Is that what you're saying?"

Quinn snorted. "Anna, c'mon. We're guys. We don't say things like that."

Grinning, Bobby leaned in. "Speak for yourself." He looked at his sister. "And Anna, that's exactly what I'm praying for."

———

"Okay, be good." Teagan kissed Lucas on the cheek. "Be sweet." She kissed his other cheek. "And remember to listen to your teacher." She kissed him on the top of the head. "And remember that if you need anything, I'll be right up by the front office, okay?"

Lucas smiled and nodded. "It's going to be okay, Mom. We got this." With a thumbs-up, he turned and walked into his classroom.

His teacher, Ms. Preece, smiled. "First days are always harder on the parents."

Teagan placed her hand over her heart and nodded. "Apparently." Rather than stand there staring after her son, she made her way back to the front office where she was needed. Well, maybe not needed, but the office staff were supposed to stand at the entrance to greet all the parents and students, so that's where she should be.

By the time the school day officially started, her cheeks hurt from smiling and she was in desperate need of a cup of coffee. Teagan's first month at school would largely be spent on organizing programs and events for the upcoming year. It normally took the teachers several weeks of evaluation to find out if any of their students were in need of her services. Glancing at her schedule, she saw she had a meeting later this morning with the new school resource officer. Sighing, she leaned back in her chair. The title normally belonged to a police officer who was responsible for safety and crime prevention in schools.

She hated thinking of needing one at the elementary school level.

Either way, their appointment was scheduled for eleven o'clock. The office would have the program binder with the information on the officer's level of involvement with the school and the kind of programs they'd previously run.

"No time like the present," she murmured. If there was anything she didn't quite understand, she could always ask Bobby about it. He knew the local officers, obviously, so maybe she could get pointers on things she could do to ensure a smooth working relationship with him. Or her. She really wished she had a name written down.

Standing, Teagan went into the main office area to the receptionist's desk. "Hey, Gloria! I have an eleven o'clock with the school resource officer, but there's no name on the appointment. Do you have it somewhere?"

"Sorry, Teagan. Last I heard, the position wasn't

officially filled, so they're probably sending an interim officer."

"Oh. Okay. Thanks." Heading back to her office, she was mildly annoyed by the lack of information. She preferred having some advance notice of who she'd be dealing with.

Sitting back down, she opened the binder and began reading, jotting down notes and questions as she went. Before she knew it, it was almost eleven. She got up and stretched, then made a quick run to the ladies' room to freshen up before her appointment.

Five minutes later, she was walking back into the office when she spotted a uniformed officer talking to Principal Martin. His back was to her, but she'd recognize that fine butt anywhere.

And suddenly she had a whole new appreciation for his uniform.

Casually, she walked over and smiled when both men turned to her. "Ah, Ms. Shaughnessy," Principal Martin began. "I believe you already know Officer Hannigan."

She could feel herself blushing. "Yes, I do," she said with a smile.

"Then I'll leave you two to talk," he said with a smile of his own before walking away.

"What are you doing here?" she asked quietly. "Are you here to check on Lucas?"

Bobby grinned and gently grasped her elbow. "Which one is your office?"

Pointing down the short hallway, she said, "Second on the left." Teagan let him guide her, feeling a little giddy at the thought of being alone with him in her office. Once they were inside, she closed the door and faced him. "Seriously, what are you doing here? It's my first official day of work, I can't be caught playing around with my boyfriend on school property." She paused and gave him a very thorough look. "No matter how good he looks in his uniform."

He gazed at her curiously. "Teagan, I don't think you understand—"

"And I do have an appointment in, like, five minutes, so…"

She watched as he stood a little taller and took on a more professional stance. Then he held out his hand for her to shake. "Teagan Shaughnessy, I'm Officer Robert Hannigan, your school resource officer. We have an eleven o'clock appointment, I believe."

Her jaw hit the floor.

"Um…excuse me?" Blindly, she reached behind her for the desk—or anything to help hold her up—because she was sure she was going to fall. What was going on? Was this a joke?

He stepped forward and led her to the chair and helped her sit. Once she was situated, Bobby walked around and sat in one of the chairs facing her. "As I said, I'm your official school resource officer. I understand we're both new to our positions, and I'd be very interested in talking with you about plans to keep all your students and faculty safe and up-to-date on all school safety programs."

It took her a full minute to find her voice. "I…I don't understand. When did you accept this position?"

He let out a breath as he sat completely at attention. It was a side of him she'd never seen, and she wasn't sure if she was more impressed or turned-on.

"After I failed to get my medical clearance several weeks ago, I began to realize I had a choice to make. I could stay at home and be bitter, or I could be thankful I still had a career I believed in. Even if I couldn't do my job in the same capacity as I had for years."

She nodded and waited to see if there was more.

"I had several reasons for moving to Myrtle Beach when I did. I was tired of being a small-town cop, tired of everyone knowing my business, and I thought moving to a big city would be the answer to it all. But it never really was. I love this town, I love the people in it, but...I thought that if I moved back, people would see me as a failure."

"I'm sure that's not true, Bobby."

"It may very well not be, but in my mind, that's the way it was." He paused. "I sat in my condo for several days just... I was in a daze. I didn't return calls or texts and everyone was starting to freak out. That's when I realized I wasn't the only one hurting. I was hurting the people who cared about me."

All she wanted to do was get up and hold him, but he obviously had more to say.

"Believe it or not, it was your cousin who really kicked my ass into gear."

"Which one?" she asked with a small laugh.

"The one you'd least expect."

Her eyes went wide. "Quinn?"

Nodding, he explained. "He called me and pretty much snapped me out of my pity party. Seems like he's quietly had my back for a while now—at least since the shooting. He'd been talking to my former captain, along with a few of my other former colleagues, and once I pulled my head out of my ass, there was a position waiting for me. All I had to do was ask for it."

"Wow."

"I know. I want to punch him and hug him at the same time," he said with a lopsided grin and then instantly went back into professional mode. "This is where I'm meant to be, Teagan. Back in my hometown, back with this police force, and here with you and Lucas."

Her heart soared at his words.

"I can't promise there won't be any risks, or that this position will be permanent. There may come a time when I'm cleared for active duty and will want to go back to it. I need to know you're okay with that."

For the first time in weeks—maybe ever—Teagan was confident in her answer. "Bobby Hannigan, I'm in this with you. Risks and all. I think we're good for each other and can balance one another out." She swallowed hard. "I have every faith in you—in us—that we'll be more than okay. We're going to be great."

The look of relief on his face was absolutely perfect, she thought.

Clearing his throat, he leaned a little closer to the desk. "I kind of wish we weren't in the middle of your office. I'd like nothing more than to kiss you right now."

Unable to help herself, she giggled. "I'd really like that too."

"Please tell me I won't have to wait until Saturday," he begged.

Boldly, she stood and walked around her desk until she was standing right in front of him. "You know, this is the first time I'm really seeing you in uniform. Up close, anyway."

His smile grew. "And what do you think?"

"I think there's a spot behind the door where no one can see in, and I'd really like for us to check if that's true."

Without waiting, Teagan went and put her back against the wall, breathless. When he stood up, he was magnificent. Slowly, he walked over until they were touching everywhere. "This is the first time I'm seeing you in a skirt and heels," he said. "It's sexy as hell."

"Oh yeah?"

He nodded. "Yeah." Then he captured her lips with his and devoured her. She was expecting a slow build, but once again, he surprised her. It was wild and needy and she wanted to climb him like a tree right there in her office. She figured he was on the same page since she could feel his erection nudging her stomach, until he abruptly broke the kiss. "Every time," he growled against her throat. "This is what being near you does to me every time."

"It's the same for me," she whispered. "I kind of hate how there isn't anything we can...do about it." Reluctantly, they moved apart and returned to their seats.

And then, somehow, they managed to focus for the next hour on their plan of action for the school year. When they were done, Bobby stood and smiled at her. "Thank you for your time, Ms. Shaughnessy."

"The pleasure was all mine."

"I wish," he whispered before looking at the clock. "What time do you get lunch?"

"I don't have a set lunch break, but I'm sure I can go now." She grabbed her purse. "What did you have in mind?"

Laughing, he replied, "That's a loaded question,

sweetheart. I'd love nothing more than to take you back to your place for a little while and continue what we started up against that wall."

She moaned at the thought of it.

"But we have to be responsible adults," he said with a sigh. "So how about a quick burger at the pub?"

"That sounds absolutely perfect." They walked out together, and she let Gloria know where she was going and when she'd be back. They were walking through the main hallway when she turned to him. "Don't make fun, but…I just want to run down the hall and peek in at Lucas. Would you mind?"

He shook his head. "Only if you promise not to make fun because I'm going with you. I'm curious as hell about how he's doing."

Hand in hand, they made their way to Lucas's classroom and stood there grinning from ear to ear when they spotted him listening intently to the story his teacher was reading.

"That's our boy," Bobby said.

And Teagan couldn't help but agree.

$\sim$

"I feel guilty."

"For what?"

"For being this happy."

Bobby held her close and kissed the top of her head. "Don't be. You deserve to be happy."

"So do you, you know. It's nice to see you smiling so much."

"The credit goes to you on that one. You're the reason I'm feeling this good. And not only because of what we just did." He winked at her comically and she pinched him. "Hey!"

It was Saturday night, Lucas was with his grandparents and Bobby and Teagan were wrapped around one another in her bed. As much as she loved these moments together, she hated how they had to be so carefully scheduled in order to have some time alone.

"What are you doing tomorrow?" he asked.

"Nothing much. Some laundry, food shopping, the usual. How come?"

"Well, I'm just about ready to lose my mind living with my parents. It's time for me to find a place of my own."

"Oh." Why was she disappointed at the thought of that?

Maybe because she had hoped the next place he looked for would be a home of their own.

"Do you have any places in mind?"

He shook his head. "Anna referred me to a former colleague of hers. I don't know if you knew this, but my sister used to work in real estate."

"Wow. I did not know that."

"True story. Anyway, we've got a couple of places lined up to go look at and I was hoping you'd come along with me. For a little moral support and a second opinion. What do you think?"

"Sure. Sure. That sounds great. What time were you thinking? I'm going to have to see if my folks can keep Lucas with them. He'd be a handful to bring along."

He nodded. "I'm supposed to meet him around one tomorrow and hopefully we'll be done by three. Will that work?"

"I'll make sure of it," she said, kissing his chest. They lay in companionable silence for a few minutes before her stomach growled, making her chuckle. "Sorry."

He laughed with her. "No need to apologize. Skipping the takeout and going straight for the bed was entirely my fault. I couldn't wait to get you naked."

"And I believe I was completely onboard for that, but now? Now I need food."

Bobby rolled away and off the bed. "Then by all means, let's eat."

For the next hour, they ate reheated Chinese and talked about their respective first weeks on the job. They saw one another daily at the school, but neither had much time to sit alone and talk. What Teagan noticed more than anything was how much Bobby seemed to enjoy working with the kids. He was genuinely excited about starting some of the safety programs with them.

It struck her then just how much she loved seeing this side of him. When they'd first met, she'd appreciated how great he was with Lucas, but never realized how much it was part of who he was. If they had met under different circumstances, she probably never would have pegged him as a man who was good with kids in general, not just his own nieces and nephews. Back on Monday, when he had claimed Lucas as theirs, she knew in her heart that she couldn't wait to have more kids with him.

Something she wasn't sure she was ready to bring up yet.

"You're kind of quiet," he said, his voice going soft. "You okay?"

Nodding, she said, "I'm fine. Just…thinking."

"About?"

Ugh, way to not bring it up, Teagan.

"You're just really good with kids," she said, smiling. "I'm listening to you talk about your week and whenever you talk about the kids, you…you smile more. And I think that's awesome."

He looked a little embarrassed.

Reaching out, she rested her hand on his forearm. "It's true. I haven't been around a lot of guys who are as comfortable with children as you are. I always knew my dad was good with them and obviously Uncle Ian. When I moved here and reconnected with my cousins, it was very eye-opening to me to see all these dads being so hands-on. But I thought it was just because they were the dads. Then I look at you and I'm…well, I feel even luckier."

His eyes lit up. "Yeah?"

She nodded. "Yeah. Because you're someone my son looks up to. You're an amazing role model for him, and it just makes me love you even more."

He pushed his plate aside and gently tugged her into his lap and kissed her. It wasn't one of their ravenous kisses—no devouring this time. But it was sweet and thorough nonetheless. When he lifted his head, his gaze was serious.

"That means the world to me, hearing you say that. But it's not only Lucas I want to be a role model for."

"Of course not," she said, settling in on his lap. "You have Kaitlyn and Brian and Bailey, plus the entire student body at school."

But he was shaking his head. "Don't get me wrong,

those are all great but—" He let out a long breath. "Someday, I'd like to be a role model to other kids. Our kids. Yours and mine."

Her heart felt like it stopped, and then kicked hard. How did he do that? How did he always know what she wanted—what she *needed*—and how to put her mind at ease? Hugging him close, she sighed. "I really like the sound of that."

He held her for a long time. "Soon, Teagan. I want that for us soon."

"Me too," she whispered. "Me too."

For a minute, all she could do was stare.

Bobby was walking up the driveway with Jerry, his real estate agent.

A driveway that led to a house.

A large house.

"Teagan? You coming?" Bobby called from the front porch, and all she could do was nod mutely.

This wasn't an apartment. It wasn't even a condo. This was a house. And that wasn't what she'd been expecting at all. Clearly, he could see she was hesitant— and confused. She heard him say "excuse me" to Jerry before coming back to her.

"What's going on?" he asked, smiling and completely at ease.

"I thought we were going to look at condos or apartments. I had no idea you were looking for something quite so…" She motioned toward the house.

Looking over his shoulder, Bobby chuckled. "It's a nice-looking house, don't you think?"

"Absolutely. I just wasn't prepared for something so…"

"You can say the word, Teagan," he teased.

"It's big, Bobby. This house is way too big for one person."

He shrugged and took one of her hands in his. "Come on. Let's see what the inside is like."

For a half hour they toured the house. It had a full wrap-around porch on the outside that included a swing. Inside, they found a large, first floor master bedroom that would easily fit three of her bedrooms at home. There was a massive en suite with a soaker tub, a large walk-in shower, and a double vanity.

She could imagine never leaving this space.

Attached to the master bedroom was a screened-in porch with a hot tub, and Bobby spent a long time listing its merits.

The rest of the house was just as spectacular. There was a large family room with cathedral ceilings and a fireplace, and the kitchen looked like something out of a design magazine with all top-of-the-line appliances. On top of that, there was a formal dining room, an upstairs with three bedrooms and two bathrooms, a large laundry room, and a detached garage with a bonus room over it.

"So what do you two think?" Jerry asked. "It's a great house and it sits on a half acre. There's lake access, plus the community boasts a pool, clubhouse, and tennis courts."

By that point, Teagan was fairly certain this place was too good to be true. Everything was just too… perfect. The only thing she hadn't heard Jerry mention was the price. Although, she was sure he and Bobby would have discussed it before coming here—not that it was any of her business. But she couldn't help being curious.

"Would you mind if Teagan and I talked about it for a few minutes?" Bobby asked.

"Not a problem. Take your time." With a smile and nod, Jerry walked out the front door, quietly closing it behind him.

"So? What do you think? It's pretty amazing, right?"

Nodding, she said, "Amazing is too mild of a word."

"But…?"

"But," she said, letting out a breath, "it's a lot of space for just you. Like I said, I thought you were going to look at condos or apartments. Maybe a cottage, or a bungalow like my place. But this?" She motioned to the space around them. "This is more space than you could possibly need just for yourself."

He studied her for a long moment. They were standing in the family room and he took her hand and led her to the french doors that opened onto the back deck. He pulled the doors open and looked out at the property.

"I know the community has a pool, but it would be kind of nice to have one here in the yard. You know, like Quinn and Anna's."

"Sure," she said, picturing a pool there.

Wrapping an arm around her waist, Bobby pulled her a little closer. "And that corner over there? I think it's perfect for a jungle gym." Then he grinned. "One that's twice the size of the one Quinn built."

She laughed. "It's not a competition."

"You're wrong," he murmured close to her ear. "Everything's a competition."

"Bobby…" But she was still laughing.

"And on the other side of the yard, I'm thinking of a batting cage. Someplace where a boy can learn to hit a ball and not worry about breaking any windows or hitting anyone in the face."

"That's pretty specific. I mean, what are the odds of—"

And then it hit her.

Eyes wide, she stared up at him. "Are you…were you thinking…"

His answer was to get down on one knee with her hand in his. "I'm not saying it has to be *this* house, but I want whatever we find to be ours. Yours, mine, and Lucas's. You're my family. My heart. My home. And I want nothing more than to start a life with the two of you and build on it."

"Oh my gosh," she whispered, unable to believe this was happening.

"I've waited a long time for you, Teagan Shaughnessy. I've been wandering through life, searching for something. I had no idea what I was looking for until the day I met you. And now that I have you, I don't want to ever let you go. Hell, I barely want to wait. I feel like everything in my life has led to this moment. All I can think about is how much I want you to be my wife and have Lucas as my son. If you'll have me."

He pulled a ring from his pocket and held it up to her. She gasped, too stunned to speak.

"I know this is soon, and I know you're going to need time to think about all of this, and I want you to know I'll wait. I may be grumpy sometimes, but I'll wait. I'd wait forever for you." He paused and looked at her with so much love that she felt her knees go weak. "Will you marry me?"

Sinking down onto the carpet with him, she nodded. "Yes. Yes, Bobby Hannigan, I will. I love you so much and you made me believe in so many things again. Things I never thought I'd have. You're everything to me too, and Lucas and I would love to be a family with you."

Bobby slid the ring on her finger before cupping her face and kissing her. And he kissed her for a very long time. When they finally broke apart, she hugged him tight.

"Come on," he said softly, "Jerry's waiting in the car. There's only one other house for us to look at today. The third one sold already."

"Wow, that stinks."

"It's the way it goes around here. Coastal towns always have a high demand for real estate. That's why I wanted to start looking now. With school back in session, the demand goes down a little, but a lot of inventory has already sold. I'm hoping we'll find something we both love and make it happen quick so I can get out of Mom and Dad's place." He shuddered dramatically. "Although the free laundry service my mom provides is kind of a perk."

She swatted him playfully as they came to their feet. With a sigh, she looked around the room. She could already see it furnished, knew the perfect spot for a Christmas tree, imagined nights sitting in front of the fire. "What's wrong with this place?" she asked, afraid to meet his gaze.

"Nothing. Nothing at all. I just thought we were supposed to look at more than one," he said with a laugh.

"Normally, I'd agree."

"But...?"

She shrugged. "But this place is kind of perfect."

His smile was the biggest and brightest she'd ever seen. "I was hoping you'd think so, because I really love it too! I'm ready to make an offer."

"Bobby, do you even know the price? Something like this must cost a small fortune!"

Pulling her in close, he kissed her soundly. "I've been living the thrifty bachelor life for a long time. I make good money on the force and learned to invest when I was young. Trust me, I'm well aware of the price and already know what I'm offering." Another kiss. "And besides. You, Lucas, and our future are more than worth it."

Epilogue

Six Months Later

"GOOD MORNING, MRS. HANNIGAN."

Teagan hummed softly as she slowly opened her eyes and stretched. "I really like the sound of that." Smiling, she placed a kiss on his chest.

"What's on the agenda for today?"

"Hmm, let's see. There was talk of a lazy morning in bed…"

"Check."

"A whole lot of touching and kissing…"

"Check and check," he murmured against her skin, kissing her shoulder while touching her breast.

"Breakfast," she said. "I definitely remember breakfast being mentioned."

"Hmm…doesn't ring a bell."

"Room service. We said breakfast from room service so we didn't have to leave the room."

"Okay, now I remember." His mouth was on the move and it didn't take long for Bobby to roll her onto her back so he had better access. When he moved down her body and stopped over her belly, he looked up at her and grinned. "Still can't believe it."

She knew exactly what he meant. "Nothing like finding out we're pregnant on our wedding day, huh?"

"I didn't think I could be any happier than I was

seeing you walk up the aisle toward me, but when you told me that news? It felt like my heart was about ready to burst."

Raking a hand through his hair, she smiled. "It seems like we don't waste time in any way, shape, or form. From the moment we met, it was all full steam ahead."

He shrugged. "What's the point in waiting when you know exactly what you want?" Dropping a loving kiss on her stomach, he moved back up her body and kissed her soundly on the lips. "And now I realize breakfast should be first on our list of things to do today." Reaching for the bedside phone, he called in an order that was for way more than two people.

"Bobby, I'm eating for two, not twenty," she teased.

"I'm refueling too, you know. It takes a lot of muscle and energy to keep my wife satisfied on her honeymoon."

Blushing, she playfully pushed him away. "Stop it. It does not."

But he was grinning and nodding even as she said it.

"Okay, fine. Whatever," she said, kicking the sheets off and rising from the bed. "Is it wrong that I want to go out and explore the resort a little?"

Bobby came up behind her and wrapped his arms around her waist. "I kind of wish we had known about the baby before we planned this trip."

"How come?"

"Sweetheart, we're in the heart of wine country. Hugh told us all about the vineyards we should tour and which wines to taste and now…?" His hand gently patted her belly. "You're not allowed to do any of that."

"We can still do the tours. You can taste them and tell me all about them."

"It won't be nearly as fun."

"Somehow, I think you'll survive," she said soothingly.

"Can I ask you something?"

"Yes, it's totally weird that we're standing naked in the middle of the bedroom, and yes, I really have to pee."

Chuckling, he released her and swatted her bottom as she walked away. When she came back out, she had on her robe and smiled when she saw he had slipped on a pair of shorts.

"Sorry," she said, sitting on the corner of the bed. "I'm sure you really did have a question."

Nodding, he sat down beside her. "Two, actually."

"O-kay…"

"When should we tell Lucas about the baby? I want him to feel one hundred percent involved and I want him to be excited about being a big brother."

Could she love this man more?

"I'd like to wait until we go for our first ultrasound, if that's okay. We already have confirmation from the doctor that I'm pregnant but…I don't know, being able to show him a picture could be kind of fun."

He nodded again. "Okay, good. Good." He paused and stared down at the floor.

"You're looking pretty serious there, Hannigan."

"There's something I've been wanting to talk to you about for a while now, and I wasn't sure how to bring it up."

"All right. Mildly freaking me out right now, but just say it."

"I want to adopt Lucas. I want him to have my last name."

Her eyes went wide. "Really?"

"I know it's an awkward request, and I'm not trying to take anything away from Logan, but—"

She took his hand and squeezed. "Believe me, in a perfect world, Lucas would have known his father. But that's never going to happen. He knows who Logan was, and we talk about him a lot. But you? You're the one who's going to raise him. I think it would be amazing for you to adopt him." She sniffed as she blinked back tears. "Actually, I think he's going to love that."

Cupping her cheek, he eased her back onto the bed. "No crying," he said softly, caressing her skin. "There's no crying on honeymoons."

"These are good tears," she said as more tears fell. "The best kind. I love you."

"I love you too," he said seriously, resting his forehead against hers. "Thank you for rescuing me."

She looked at him curiously. "Rescuing you?"

He nodded. "When I first met you, I felt like I was the one helping you."

"Well, you kind of rescued Lucas that day, so—"

"No. It was more than that. I looked at you and I thought that what I needed was to take care of you—the both of you. But it turns out it was the other way around. You rescued me from an empty life and a bleak future."

"Bobby…"

"Now look at me! I've got a great job, I own a beautiful home, I'm married to the woman of my dreams, and I'm about to be the father of two! All in a year's time!"

She smiled. "I think it's safe to say we rescued each other. And I'm so glad we did."

"Yeah," he said softly. "Me too."

Return *to* You

Available now from Sourcebooks Casablanca

Chapter 1

"I DON'T UNDERSTAND. I THOUGHT THIS WAS A DONE DEAL. There wasn't enough interest or funds to make it happen, so I just thought we were through," Selena Ainsley said over the phone.

"So did all of us," Jen continued, "but it seems like someone has stepped forward and is providing the funds to cover the cost of the entire reunion. All we need now is a person who is able to pull together an event of this magnitude on short notice. You know, the kind of woman who is super organized, great with delegating and numbers, and who maybe, perhaps, does this for a living. Sound familiar?"

"You can't be serious," Selena said with more humor than disbelief.

"As a heart attack."

"Jen, as much as I would love to help out, there is no way that I can get away for the length of time it would take to put together something like this reunion. You need to find someone local who can handle all the particulars. It's too much to manage from six hundred miles away." She could have added that Jen should probably look for someone who actually wanted the job and the chance to go to the reunion, because that certainly wasn't her.

"Oh, please," Jen said with a snort of mock derision. "You know as well as I do that you can delegate a lot of the particulars. We have a venue, and you can speak to the catering staff anytime you need to, even from six hundred miles away. I'm sure with all of your connections you can organize the invitations and activities and whatever else is needed for this reunion. C'mon, say yes."

Selena was torn. Ordinarily, this was the type of job she loved: big venue, short notice, and a bit of challenge. The problem wasn't the job, per se; it was the location. It had been years since she had gone back to the small Long Island town where she had grown up, and just the thought of returning there now made Selena break out in a cold sweat.

If it were anybody else calling, she would have had no problem telling them no. But this was Jen. Her best friend. Her confidante. Her conscience.

Dammit.

"Don't do this to me, Jen," she began.

"Do what? Offer you a fabulous challenge? I know you thrive on this sort of thing. Everything is essentially paid for; the donor wrote us a huge check. It's a no-brainer. Basically, all you have to do is talk to a few people and show up. You can do this kind of thing in your sleep."

"Then I'm sure you or someone else can handle it. Seriously, I don't have that kind of time—"

"Okay, look," Jen interrupted. "I think I've been more than understanding. You moved away and never came back, and I never pushed you to. I come and visit you, and I love seeing you, but I'm beginning to feel like this friendship is a bit one-sided."

"That's not fair—"

"Not finished!" Jen snapped and instantly felt bad about her tone. "I'm not saying you weren't within your rights; however, it's been like…forever. Enough is enough. The thought of our ten-year reunion without you is just not even within my realm of comprehension. You were student body president, Selena. Everyone will expect to see you there. And on top of that, I'm your best friend and…well, to be honest with you, things haven't been going so great for me lately, and I could really use a little time with you." Jen knew it was hitting below the belt using her private issues to flush Selena out, but desperate times called for desperate measures.

"What's going on?" Selena asked, concern lacing her voice.

"Remember that guy I told you about? Todd?"

"Vaguely."

Jen would have felt annoyed at her friend's lack of memory, but Todd had been nothing but a blip on the radar. "Well, he's kind of been stalking me. It's starting to freak me out."

"What? Oh my gosh! Jen! Are you okay? Have you gone to the police?"

"I have, and basically there isn't a whole lot they can do because he's not threatening me or anything like that. It's just harassment."

"Like what?"

"He calls a *lot*. I run into him everywhere. Honestly, it's kind of creepy."

"What does he say when you answer the phone or see him?"

"Basically, he's pleasant."

"And…" Selena prompted.

"Until I say that I don't want to see him again; then he tends to get a little mean."

"But he hasn't threatened you?"

"No," Jen said with a sigh. "Like I said, I went to the cops and filed a report, but unless he threatens me, there's nothing they can do. Their hands are tied and so are mine."

"Have you thought about changing your phone number?"

"About a dozen times a day."

"Then why haven't you?"

"Because I keep thinking he'll stop and just go away. I hate having to disrupt my life because this loser can't take no for an answer."

"Jen, you have to do something. If he continues to have access to you, then he wins."

"I'm finally at a place where I feel like my life is going well: I own my own little house, my job is good…

If I could just get rid of this creep, life would be perfect. Plus, it wouldn't hurt if my best friend would come to our ten-year reunion that we planned together."

Selena laughed. "Cheap shot, Jen."

"I'm not above begging."

"I just don't think—"

"Then don't think," Jen said quickly.

"But what if—?"

"You won't."

"How can you be sure, Jen?"

It was times like this that Jen hated the physical distance between them because all she wanted to do was to wrap her arms around her best friend and hug her. "Selena, you are a grown woman. You own a successful business, and you never turn away from a challenge. Except this one. It's time to own it and face it."

Selena's gut clenched. "What if people, you know, bring it up?"

"So what! It happened, Selena, and all of the denial in the world isn't going to change it. I'm not trying to trivialize it, but there it is. And believe it or not, everyone has moved on with their lives. I'm sure the topic of you and James Montgomery isn't something everyone we know is dying to talk about. People have gotten married, had kids, gotten great jobs, and some have crazy stalkers in their lives… It's not all about you, you know." The last was said with a smirk that Selena could detect even over the phone.

It was hard to say which emotion was the stronger one at the moment. Hearing James's name out loud for the first time in years knocked all of the breath out of her and left her shaking, but Jen's teasing tone helped lighten the mood almost immediately. Perhaps she was the only one who remembered or even thought about her past relationship with James. Clearly he hadn't, since he'd never bothered to look her up. Maybe it was time to put some old ghosts to rest and go back to her childhood home and see her friends.

"*If* I say yes," she began, but Jen's whoop of delight stopped her and had her laughing. When they finally calmed down, Selena continued, "If I say yes, then I'll need you to email all of the information to me right away so I can get started. What kind of time frame are we looking at?"

"Eight weeks," Jen answered and prayed that she wasn't cutting things too short.

Selena did a mental check of her calendar and all that would have to be accomplished in order for her to pull this off. "It's going to be tight, Jen, but if you promise to help me and get a committee together quickly, I think we can have one heck of a ten-year reunion."

"I've already got the committee lined up and the email is drafted. I was just waiting for you to say yes."

"Mighty confident, weren't you?"

"Hopeful. And yes, there is a difference."

"Only you could talk me into this, Jen. You know that, right?"

"That's what I was counting on," she said and let out her first relaxed breath of the entire conversation. "So when do you think you'll actually come up here?"

That is a good question, Selena thought to herself. "I should be able to do the bulk of it all from here, but I'll come up a couple of days beforehand, to make sure everything's in place."

"A couple of days? *A couple of days?*" Jen cried. "I pour my heart out to you about everything that I'm going through, and you can't even spare me a little extra time? That's just cold."

Selena pinched the bridge of her nose and counted to ten to wait out her friend's audition for most dramatic phone conversation. Finally, she relented. "Fine. I'll block out two weeks of time to come up there. A week before and a week after. How's that?"

"Is there any way I can convince you to stay longer?" Jen asked.

"No."

"Fine," she said with a sigh. "Two weeks, but I would prefer that it be more time before the reunion."

"Why?"

"Because that means you'll get here sooner. You have no idea how much it means to me that you're finally coming home, Selena."

She wasn't going home, Selena reminded herself; she was just going back to a place she used to live to visit a friend. Her home was in North Carolina now. She wanted to remind Jen of that fact, but the emotion in her friend's voice was enough for Selena to avoid trying to back out again. "I really am sorry I've stayed away so long, Jen. I never realized I was hurting you."

"I understand why you have, but I miss you."

"Well, by the end of those two weeks, you are going to be sick of me. I'm staying with you, right?"

"As if I'd let you stay any place else! I will do my best to make my guest room a place you'll never want to leave!"

"Ease up there, Sparky," Selena said with a laugh.

"I have a business that needs me and employees who depend on me here in North Carolina. I'm giving you two weeks, but then it's back home for me."

"Fine, fine, fine," Jen said dismissively, "be that way. All I'm saying is that maybe it won't take another reunion to make you come back again."

"One trip at a time, Jen. One trip at a time."

By the time they hung up, the knot in Selena's stomach was finally starting to ease. The reunion itself wasn't going to be a problem; she could organize one of those in her sleep. The problem was going to be facing the memories she had been doing her best to forget. The old adage "time heals all wounds" clearly didn't apply to her. She'd go for Jen's sake, but it was going to take every fiber of her being to get through it without having some sort of nervous breakdown. It didn't seem to matter how together her life had become; there were just some things that had the ability to knock you on your butt and make you doubt yourself. Returning to Long Island was one of them.

Ten years ago, her life had been turned upside down by forces beyond her control, and she had spent a large part of that time letting other people dictate her life. Not anymore. Selena had broken free of a lot of the negative forces in her life, but just because she had taken that step didn't necessarily mean she was over the pain. She doubted she would ever fully be over that part; it was something she had learned to live with.

Jen was right. It was time to face her demons and prove to herself, if no one else, that she could go back to the place of her greatest failure and walk away with her heart still intact. She wasn't looking forward to it.

If it weren't for the reunion, she wouldn't ever make the pilgrimage back to her old neighborhood. Her life was fine without having to go back there. And while Selena knew that Jen really did need her right now, she was certain that with a little persuasion, she could have convinced Jen to take a holiday on the Carolina coast with her. Sure, she would have fussed for a while about the reunion, but with the whole stalker issue on the table, Selena had a feeling Jen would have seen the reason in getting out of town for a while.

"Too late now," she mumbled as she pulled up her calendar and began making notes. "I am a grown woman. I am in control of my own life. I don't have to answer to anybody but me."

It was a good mantra to have.

If only she truly believed it.

James Montgomery was a leader, not a follower. He liked being in control of his own life without having to answer to anyone. True, his career in law enforcement had him answering to many people, but it was different from having to answer to his own family and dealing with their expectations of him. At this point in his career, he was well established, and the only pressure he felt was from himself. He wanted to be better, stronger, and more in control of himself personally.

Maybe someday it would be enough.

Maybe someday he'd be able to look in the mirror and know that the man he was, was good enough for... well, anything.

It had been a long time since he'd openly admitted

to himself that he still struggled with a sense of inadequacy, and if it hadn't been for today's events, he wouldn't be admitting to it now. Staring at the door to the station, James leaned back in his desk chair and nearly growled with frustration. Jennifer Lawson had left only minutes ago, and yet, instead of feeling like he was sitting in the present, her visit had taken him back to the past.

Ten years to be exact.

To say it was a shock to see her would be the understatement of the century. For too many years, James had distanced himself from just about everything and everyone he had ever known. It was necessary in order for him to become the man he wanted to be—needed to be. And yet, one hour of time had brought everything back as if it were yesterday

"I'm looking for James Montgomery," she said when she walked into the station, and it had been a coincidence that he was walking by right then or he might have had someone take a message or help her instead. Jen's eyes had lit with recognition as soon as she'd seen him, and one look at her and James had suddenly felt like that boy he had been way back then—not good enough. He actually caught himself looking around as if suspecting his coworkers were looking at him in the exact same way, that by Jen being there, they were going to know his secrets and demand he turn in his badge or something. Odd how old insecurities can rear their ugly heads at the most inopportune times.

"It's good to see you, Jen," he said, doing his best to sound impersonal yet professional, but her grin had always been infectious.

"You too," she said and then anxiously looked around. "As much as I wish this was a social call, I really do need to talk to you about a possible criminal matter."

Her statement piqued his curiosity, not that he thought Jen would stop by after all these years on a social call. James escorted her to his desk, sat back, and listened to her tell her story about her ex-boyfriend and the recent harassment. Unfortunately, the guy hadn't broken any laws and so there wasn't anything James could do but offer his sympathy and tell her to keep a journal of the behavior. While he knew it was of little comfort or help to her, there simply wasn't a damn thing he could do.

He hated the look that came across her face: defeat. There had been a time in his life when he'd known that feeling all too well. Most days he was over it, but every once in a while—like now—it was easy for it to creep back up on him.

"I'm really sorry, Jen. I wish there was more I could do. I'll run a check on this guy and see if anything turns up."

Once they had covered that, Jen had visibly relaxed in her chair and smiled. "I still can't believe it's you," she said easily. "I mean, I knew I was going to find you here; I still keep in touch with your cousin Kent. He was the one who suggested I come and talk to you. I guess I hoped there was something that could be done even though all of my online research told me there probably wasn't."

"I'll start a file about it, and I'll check in with you to keep up to date on what's going on and if this guy's pattern of behavior changes or gets more aggressive."

"Thank you." She paused and then considered her next words. "So, how have you been? It's been a really long time. How long have you been a cop? Where are you living now?" She must have thought she was throwing him too many questions and blushed. "Sorry. I'm just really glad to see you. But really, how are you?"

How was he supposed to sum up his life since they'd last seen each other? Was he supposed to tell her about all the ways he'd been to hell and back? That he'd been working his ass off to prove to the world—or at least to one person in particular—that he was good enough and that he'd made something of himself? Probably not. Rather than go on a rant, James decided to keep it simple. "I'm good," he said. "I've been a cop for the last eight years. Actually, I'm a detective now."

She nodded. "Do you enjoy it? I mean, not that it's a fun job or anything, or maybe it is. You never know." She stopped her rambling again and smiled. "It suits you. You look good. Happy."

James shrugged. *Happy?* He wasn't sure he'd go that far, but he wouldn't argue with the fact that being on the force had him feeling somewhat satisfied. "How about you? What are you doing with yourself?"

"I am an elementary school teacher now, third grade. I love it."

Even if she hadn't added those last words, her face and smile said it all. Jennifer Lawson had changed very little: her blond hair was a little shorter, her clothes more conservative, but she had an aura about her that bristled with energy and enthusiasm. Years ago, she had always greeted everyone with a smile and had been nothing but kind to him. It hit James then how much he had missed her friendship. Her smile. Her optimism.

"That's great, Jen. I bet your kids love you." He could

easily picture her in a room full of eight-year-olds— laughing and smiling and doing projects with them. She had often talked about her desire to teach even when she was still in school, and James was proud of her for following through on her dream.

"Oh, I'm not so sure about that," she said. "They like me fine when it's recess or we're doing art projects, but once it's test time, then I'm the meanest teacher on the planet."

James smiled at her. "I remember feeling that way myself back in the day. Teachers were great just as long as they weren't handing out a test."

"I'm teaching at the same elementary school I went to, and it's kind of weird walking those halls as an adult. When we were students, everything looked so big, and now I walk around and feel like a giant."

"You couldn't pay me to go back to school," he said, his tone a little more serious than he intended. "I couldn't wait to get out. I give you credit for doing what you do, Jen. Not many people want to do it. Once the diploma's in your hand, you just want to take it and run and never look back."

She shrugged. "I always enjoyed school…and not only for social reasons, although I guess that was a definite perk. I know it makes me sound a bit nerdy, but I enjoyed the friendly competition between me and my classmates and the sense of accomplishment I felt when I got good grades." She heard herself and almost cringed. "Wow, that definitely made me sound nerdy, didn't it?"

James chuckled before agreeing with her. "It's okay. Nerdy works on you. So, what challenges are you finding in the third graders?"

"Other than behavioral stuff, nothing too exciting. We have a curriculum we have to follow, so I don't get to be as creative in the classroom as I'd like, but it's fine. Right now I have a bigger challenge at hand. I'm actually planning our ten-year reunion. Gosh, can you believe we've been out of school for so long?"

"Well..." James began.

"Oh, right. Sorry."

James had dropped out of high school at sixteen, so all this talk about reunions and whatnot was lost on him. Still, he could see that it was something Jen was excited about, so he figured he'd grin and bear it and hear her out. "No big deal. So, what are you planning?"

Jen ran through a list of details, including the venue, the theme, the response from classmates, activities for the weekend, and even the menu.

"That seems like an awful lot of work. I hope you have a big committee helping you."

Jen nodded. "We have about two dozen people pulling it all together. It's amazing how many people are stepping up and volunteering their time and services to help out. A lot of the graduates stayed in the area and have businesses of their own, so we have someone volunteering printing services for the invitations, another person donating balloons, flowers, and decorations, and even have someone offering the use of the bowling alley for a get-together. It's going to be such a great weekend, but there's so much to do to make it all happen."

"It certainly sounds like it," he said with a chuckle. "So what are you, chairman?"

That made her laugh. "I am great at following

instructions and delegating, but I'm not organized enough to pull off something like this. It's just too huge."

"Oh, come on," he said playfully. "You have to be organized, being a teacher and coordinating lesson plans and all that, plus you teach a roomful of eight-year-olds. You can't tell me you're not organized. It's not possible."

"Well, it's true I'm organized in my classroom, but that's different from putting together an event of this size. With my students, I have a curriculum and lesson plans. I can mix things up a little bit with them, but for the most part, the organization is done for me. With the reunion, it's so much more, and there's no formal plan to follow. Luckily, we have a chairman…or chairwoman, and I'm perfectly okay with following orders. It makes me happier, and I'm sure the graduating class as a whole will appreciate it just as much."

"As long as you have fun with it, how bad can it be, right?" he asked.

They sat in silence for a moment while James wrestled with the question that had been on the tip of his tongue since Jen had walked in the door. Knowing he would never have peace unless he asked, he took a calming breath, willed his heart rate to slow down, and did his best to sound casual. "So, you must be excited to be getting together with everyone. Is your old crowd going to be there?"

Jen wanted to smirk but did her best to keep her expression neutral. She was surprised it had taken this long to get to the subject. "Well, Kent is coming, and I think Tom, Russ, Chris, and Kerry are going to be there too." She paused for dramatic effect. "Selena wasn't going to come, but I talked her into being our chair-woman so now she has to. I spoke to…"

James knew Jen was still speaking, but all he could hear was a loud buzzing in his head. His heart pounded, and he was pretty sure he was starting to sweat. She was coming home. Finally.

She'd be close enough to see.

Close enough to talk to in person.

Close enough to touch.

"Well, anyway," Jen said as she stood, "thanks for taking the time to see me. I'll do like you said and start keeping a journal of any time Todd calls or I see him. I'm hoping that he'll just get bored and move on, but you never know. I would've thought he'd get bored by now. Clearly he has nothing better to do with his time. It's pretty sad actually." She smiled. "Anyway, it was really good to see you again, James, and I hope it isn't another ten years before we see each other again." Before he knew it, she had her arms around him and was hugging him and placing a quick kiss on his cheek. The whole thing took him by surprise and the next thing he knew, she was waving and walking away.

By the time Jen left, James was sure he'd come off without sounding too much like a babbling idiot, and if he could remember correctly, he was sure he had said he might stop in on some of the reunion activities…just to see the old crowd, of course.

Right.

If Jen suspected anything different, she had kept it to herself. James looked at his calendar and saw that he had about six weeks to prepare himself and to come up with some kind of excuse to put himself in Selena's path that wouldn't seem like he was trying to be there. He had no idea what that would entail or what he was going to do once he saw her again. It had been a long time, and although not a day had gone by when he hadn't thought about her, he had no idea about the woman she had become. Would she be happy to see him? Would she even be coming to this thing alone? That thought made his fists clench. He may not have any claim on Selena anymore, but that didn't mean he'd be happy to see her walking around town with another man.

She was his.

It didn't matter how much time had gone by since they'd last seen one another; James would always consider Selena to be his. He just couldn't decide if that was a good thing or a bad thing. Either way, he had six weeks to figure out what he was going to do about it.

Part of his job in law enforcement was having confidence and not shying away from a challenge or a dangerous situation—even at the risk of his own life.

And there was nothing more dangerous to James Montgomery than coming face-to-face with the woman who had essentially destroyed his whole life.

About the Author

Samantha Chase is a *New York Times* and *USA Today* bestseller of contemporary romance that's hotter than sweet, sweeter than hot. She released her debut novel in 2011 and currently has more than fifty titles under her belt! When she's not working on a new story, she spends her time reading romances, playing way too many games of Scrabble or Solitaire on Facebook, wearing a tiara while playing with her sassy pug, Maylene… oh, and spending time with her husband of twenty-five years and their two sons in North Carolina.

RESCUE ME

In this fresh, poignant series about rescue animals,
every heart has a forever home

By Debbie Burns, award-winning debut author

A New Leash on Love

When Craig Williams arrived at the local
no-kill animal shelter for help, he didn't
expect a fiery young woman to blaze into
his life. But the more time he spends with
Megan, the more he realizes it's not just
animals she's adept at saving...

Sit, Stay, Love

For devoted no-kill shelter worker Kelsey
Sutton, rehabing a group of rescue dogs
is a welcome challenge. Working with a
sexy ex-military dog handler who needs
some TLC himself? That's a whole
different story...

My Forever Home

There's no denying Tess Grasso has a way
with animals, but when she helps Mason
Redding give a free-spirited stray a second
chance, this husky might teach them a few
things about faith, love, and forgiveness.